MASTER WILLIAM AND THE FINMAN

Editor: Richard Williams
Cover and Book Design: Jeff Hewitt

First printing, 2019
ISBN: 9781948717137 (Paperback)

Rolling Olive Press
www.RollingOlivePress.com
Franktown, Va, 23354

XenophonPress@gmail.com

MASTER WILLIAM AND THE FINMAN

BY ROBERT P. ARTHUR

Rolling Olive Press

2019

TABLE OF CONTENTS

THE ROOKERY

Chapter One

I never learned to read or write so well until I retired from the sweat of the doldrums and the sweep of the trades.

Until that moment of sweet withdrawal, when I lay my head down with no worrisome thought of the a-borning day, I plied the bloody lanes of Hornigold from Madagascar to the river Thames, where once swung in chain the black, tarred carcass of Captain William Kidd.

And during all the bloody roving and rogering with the sons of Bedlam, and through the wild, spirited times with more fun-loving masters, I have learned what? Well, mate, among such revelations as pirates generally do not bury treasure but spend it and the blessed secret of counting to oneself when dancing a jig, I have learned that God's domain does not extend to the sea.

So carve me a pulpit, boys, in the shape of a bow, and place a bowsprit on it. From the bow railing, extend a net to catch shells, the trumpets of the sea, that I may be heard rightly and loudly in proclamation when I implore ye to worship God in thy nightshirts and in thy counting houses, while harvesting thy grains and walking the land. But, should ye in any way encounter the sea, no matter if it be by a child's skiff or galleon massive as a cloud floating over flat water as far as the eye can see, then abandon thy faith in the protection of the Lord as if it were the bauble of a child.

Leave thy sacred articles home for safekeeping. Put thy Bible in the closet, thy crucifix in a drawer. For the moment thy first toe crosses the wrack between land and sea, ye are in the kingdom of the devil, and all that shall protect ye shall be the bribes of gold in thy pockets and thy willingness to do his transgress.

In support of this, I offer that no man long remains holy upon the sea but straightway upon removing himself from the sight of the hedgerow and stink of the sty, he begins putting shadowed moons between himself and the laws of God.

It is also clear that the waves themselves curse the name of mercy with their arrogant spittle and do not respond to prayer or the throwing over of crosses or even Jonahs themselves (though the Bible says *yea*.) Thirdly, as is whispered among seamen the world around, the sea buries no man but captures each dead man's soul as wind to drive the sail.

Always further from God does the sailor move, though he is a Christian man, such as I, and that is the truth of it.

My name is William Claddah, and I was born on the Orkney Islands north of Scotland in a year I do not recall, in the middle of the golden age of piracy.

I was suckled by the sea as much as by my Ma, whose milk tasted of salt, whose hair was wild with wind though no wind blew, and who sang to me in her rocking chair with the voice of a selkie, or so I thought as I grew, for much I thought of such things.

Superstition hung about the Orkney archipelago as a heavy yoke from Ayenaby and Hoy Sound to the Ring o' Brodgar. All seventy or more sea-drenched islands were black as night almost all day in winter and the islands' ancient burial mounds of ruins and standing stones were circled round by howling waters.

How we hunkered down in the magical mystery of it all, in our battered cottages and in the taverns of the town of Hoy, and listened to the talk of the old sailor men smoking by the chimney. Outside, the mist would lie over the sea as thick as a pudding, or a storm would lash out without warning, sending cannon fire of thunder and lighting into our barns to sizzle our cattle.

What was the cause of it all? Why, the devil, mate, or a thousand other things in the Devil's sway. The mermaid, lad. The Kraken. The Stronsay Beast. The sea itself, with its evil mind and wayward soul that whip up riptides, whirlpools, flood waters, skerries, stacks, and caves, a magical realm of ice more forbidding than a landscape of tombs.

The voices would be low in the Hoy Sea Trow tavern, with the dark winter bluster upon us.

"Further than Hoy... the mermaids whisper," sang George Mackay Brown, "through ivory shells...a-babble with vowels."

Then I, a lad of six sent to the Sea Trow for my Da's bucket of beer, would pull down my cap and duck my head that I not be sent from the place while the stories were told.

"There was a wrecked ship yesterday at Kirkwaa," said Jon Haraldsson. "We salvaged well, for which we thank God, but there was not a seaman to be found."

"Some taken by mermaids likely," said a voice near my hiding place in shadow.

"Likely so," said Jon. "Was ten year ago Johnny Croy of Sanday came home after a year of living with the merfolk. Them who don't believe so may sail to Sanday and find out the truth of my claim. Was a mermaid who charmed him and loved him, then let him go, they say, and the proof of it is the comb of her head he carries in his pocket to this day."

"It's true," said Rever Sinclair, himself well known for wide adventuring on the Pentland Salty.

"Now if it had been a seal woman and not a mermaid," said Jon, "there'd been less of a chance of Johnny Croy ever returning to an Orkney shore. The seal people hate us for slaughtering the seal, for bashing them in their heads and skinning them alive, likely as not."

"Lower thy voice, Jon."

The voice grew low, like the moan of wind in the throat of a chimney.

"My lads, we have done a great wrong, for I see in the back of the room the young Claddah boy, listening."

Every eye turned toward me, and I could feel my face redden. I was a stammering, blushing boy and rose quickly to my feet, dashing for the door, spilling beer on my trousers.

Once outside, I slammed into the wet northwest wind blowing in from the arctic. There was no star glimmering. Just below the sea's yammering, I could hear its tentacles beating inland behind me, slithering up the main, so ran to our cottage that flickered with light where it sat on a high bank of the cove.

I ran all the way, my feet knowing better than my eyes the location of each rock or pit in the roughened road. Halfway home, I was caught in a squall blowing in from Stromness that drenched my clothes and filled my Da's bucket. The beer was drowned but he would be too sodden to detect it by this hour, so, it was only with relief that I escaped on this occasion from the dark and the sea.

There was no immediate need for the beer, for Da was asleep, and my Ma never drank, nor did she often look up from her knitting or help me with my clothes.

The winter had gathered us up in its arms and put us together in that single room. The cattle were locked safely in the barn. Lamps were lit on a table and a wide windowsill, as if for a beacon, and the sky closed round, pitch black and threatening. It was three o'clock in the afternoon, and the long evening stretched out before us.

My mother spoke of her delight—the *nuggle*, sometimes called the *nix* or the *water horse.*

"Ah, William, such a beautiful thing," she said, "a gorgeous little horse with a wheel in its rump and a tail to conceal it. But just try to ride the water devil, lad, for that is what it is, and straightway it makes for the water and gives ye a dunk."

"I have seen a nuggle, Mother!" I lied.

"And likely been dunked by one too," she said, a curious light in her eyes, for, deep down, she sided with supernatural things.

"Aye, Mother," I said.

"Then, I suppose, after the dunking, ye saw the nuggle disappear into the water in a tiny blue flame."

"Aye, I did."

At this my mother said something in a language I did not know, possibly Gaelic or Norwegian, and got out her knitting. As she knitted, she sang songs in a language unknown to me and doubtless to any entirely human creature. My mother's voice had the low notes of the selkie in it. As she sat and sang by the fire, me on the hearth, my Da on his corn-shuck cot in drunken repose, I heard beneath her words the unmistakable grief of the seal people.

More, I heard the call of the sea from the far north beyond Shetland and Westray and North East beyond North Ronaldsay.

"Oh, ye'll be a sailor man right enough," my mother said, "but not in Thule Skerrie."

How those words frightened me, for they had meaning that may not at first seem apparent, but played upon my fancy!

It is true enough that at eight years old I thought my mother to be a seal.

What is more, every man jack on the island of Hoy, with the exception of my drunken Da and his brothers, thought my mother to be a seal, as did their wives and daughters and my mother herself, the truth be told.

What I knew of the matter in its infancy, I learned in strictest confidence, time and time again from friend and foe, from playmate and relative.

On a dark day, one year before the day I was born, my father arrived at the harbor of Hoy to sail for herring with the fishing fleet. Then, suddenly, during the singing of a rowdy shanty on the family curragh, he put an ear to the wind, sniffed once, and leaped ashore.

"Well, lads," he said. "I'll not be sailing with ye today."

"William!" my uncles cried, for well they guessed how matters stood. And when they saw my Da run to uncover his seal skin boat with the tiny sail, they shouted for him to return, growing frantic, and then hauled together on the warp to return to the pier until the windlass gave and flew into the sea.

Then, despairing and calling out to their brother, they drifted, helpless, themselves curiously becalmed as Da set sail into the mist, bound for the ice flows of Thule Sherrie without looking once behind him.

That night lay funereal over the length of Hoy Sound and in the quieted belly of the Sea Trow tavern. Men talked in hushed tones of sea-going ghaists, and all the women wept, for in those salad days, Da was a robust youth and beloved by most. I was yet to be born, but well I can imagine them naming the culprit—the lascivious mermaid who enchants a man to act as her lover as long as his beauty lasts.

"It is a daughter of Lillith who has him in thrall!" one of the village women might have cried out. "Was the first wife of Adam not thrown into the sea for refusing to lie under him? And does this same Lillith not come to men in their dreams and have congress with them or call them to sea and take them into her?"

At this, there would be groans from the women, and the men would shake their heads, imagining the breasts of a woman and the womb of a fish.

Still, these considerations were less dreadful than the probable truth—that the dreadful Orkneys had finally driven my father mad and there was no chance at all he'd be heard from more.

The seventh day after he had cast off broke a bright, balmy day, the kind of day inhabitants of Hoy might have talked about for months, even if the fishermen on the pier had not spotted my Da's sail closing fast in the grip of a favorable wind. A young woman was with him, wrapped in fur.

Da explained he had found her adrift in a sealskin boat, much like his own, a tale believed by no one.

Then, I was told, the young woman, who would later cast me bawling onto the waters of the world, cried each day for a year and stood hours on the bank of our cove looking north over the sea, and when he slept, she relentlessly searched the fields and the town for the seal skin that he cut from her that would allow her to be a seal again.

Not even my birth could ease her anguish. Suckle me and play with me, clean me and sing to me as she might, even hold me close to her and fill my face with kisses, still, often, her eyes ran with tears and I could feel her sobs against my heart when she held me in her arms.

Thus passed my infancy, in loving bondage to a woman who was habitually disconsolate, even more so than the typical resident of Hoy, many of whom would have left the Orkneys and lived as Scotsmen had the Scots not so often been slaves of the British and subject to skinning.

So time passed slowly, as it ever did in the Orkneys. Hardy seamen grew brittle; others drowned in nets and washed up on the islands bloated and blue as the roaming whales, and many hands were torn by the hooks or feet crushed by iron. My own Da, hale as a youth, wore a white slash on his cheek and began coughing blood.

As for me, I toddled about my Ma and held onto her skirts, mewing when we parted for only an instant. So sure I was that if I let her go, she would instantly be scurrying about the rocky coast of Hoy looking for her skin, and then, upon finding it, would be gone.

By my fifth year of life, the long nights of winter grew unbearable. Like her, I could sense the seal people calling from the ice caves of Thule Skerrie and so became acutely aware of her increasing agitation. First, there would be a sigh from her rocking chair, then a stirring of embers in the fire, then harsh words for my Da, who had taken to strong drink to force back the blood in his lungs. Then, came entreaties and accusations.

"I never skinned thee, woman!" my father would say, though there were times at the Sea Trow he admitted to one and all that he remembered nothing of the trip in the seal skin boat that brought him a wife, "nor have I hidden thy skin."

"Liar," she would cry. "Liar!"

Then, like as not, she would leap for his throat, curses on her lips, and he would roll away, no longer the brawny boy but quick with fear and coughing fresh blood on his shirt.

He would leap to his feet and run through the door, straight to the cemetery, where she would not go.

What haunts she feared I cannot guess. Even today it seems unnatural that she feared those lifeless bones but not the sea.

Nevertheless, with my father safe in the society of the dead, pottery flew against the walls of our shack, shattering to pieces in my father's stead.

"William!" she would cry, blind with tears and rage, stumbling about the darkened house, herself like a spirit returned from the grave. "Where is my skin? Where is my skin?"

At such times, she was as mad as a bloody seal barking across an ice flow before plunging into the sea.

"It is thy father who has hidden it from me!" she would rave, shaking me by the shoulders until my uncles came crashing into the house to pull her off me, shouting and slapping at her arms to bring her to her senses, then bidding her sleep. Sometimes, they would feed her, then sing to her and tell her what they thought to be lies.

"There are no selkie folk," said my Uncle Sinclair. "It is just that the seal's head bobbing above the waves looks human, and the seals' eyes have an uncannily human look."

"So, it is then," my Ma said. "Ye can let me go now. I've cleared my head of such notions."

Whereupon my Uncle Sinclair would sigh, then order Ma tied to her bed for days, if need be, with only me there for much of the time, a small boy, to feed her hot soup and wash the soft ropes of her long blond hair.

I was ten years old when I acquired a knife of my own, and that a short knife with a handle of white stone, given to me by Jock Stewart, a sailor who fled the British from Inverness.

"Ye must tuck it into ye sock," he said, as the two of us sat upon a summer bench and gazed off idly into the crystal clear waters of the Scapa Flow, where slept a thousand wrecked ships and innumerable lost souls. "The blade is only three inches long, according to the law, but sharp enough, if ye take my meaning."

With the sharpened sgian duhb in its place in my sock and the leather band holding it in place beneath my trousers, I felt struttin' proud, a man of my own.

I had handled fish knives before and used flailing knives in the skinning of seals, for by ten I had begun sailing out for a living with my Da and his brothers. But never before had I handled a blade whose first purpose was not for hunting or fishing or cutting bait.

"I know thy thought," said Jock. "Ye wonder if ye are a man of Orkney or a man of Scotland. Well, I tell ye, lad. It does not matter what ye consider thyself to be. The British consider ye to be a man of Scotland and a slave to them."

By this time, several of the villagers who had not sailed out that day gathered by the bench to listen to Jock Stewart talk.

He was what the fishermen of Hoy called a "provocateur" and would every now and then sail over from Inverness to inflame us.

"And if ye want to be a Catholic man, ye may not be a Catholic man," he said to angry murmurs, "unless ye want a British soldier breaking down thy door in the dead of night."

"Ye have the right of it, Jock," said a voice behind me.

"But there is a more basic truth even than that," said Jock, "for all over the British Isles and Europe as well, if a poor man takes an apple fallen from a tree to stave off hunger, he may swing from a thick branch for it, or he may be whipped by a laird at the latter's discretion or lose his life or freedom by rash judgment or false accusation. It is this concept of kings, my lads, the notions of princes, and the stench of nobility that is the great evil of the world."

"Ye might say to thyself, lads, 'Why, what will the King of England want with the Island of Hoy?' and feel secure that he may never take it as his own, for sure he feels he owns it, but that is not the question, lads. The question is: 'what do ye want with the island of Hoy, and why have ye never been able to show it thy back?'"

"Is it not an ancient graveyard of burial mounds, tombs, and standing stones raised above freezing waters on a limestone rock? Do ye love the runes and cairns and the sky like a shroud? Not even the Vikings stayed here nor the Norwegians but only the Picts and now ye have been doomed here, them by war, ye by a Protestant on the throne of England."

To this last business I could scarce react, for until that moment I had not known that the standing stones and ruins of Hoy were artifacts of the Picts from years before or that the sunken ships in the Scapa Flow included those of the Vikings and Norwegians. So there I was at ten years old, sitting by Jock Stewart, connected in a new way to the world of men by a sgian dubh in my sock and by Jock's words to the world at large.

"Mates, look at thy hands!" Jock Stewart shouted, and every man jack one of them gathered on the pier, about twenty by then, looked at his hands as if he expected to see his future writ large in blood upon them.

"Those are deep lines made by netting, ratlines, and chain," said Jock. "Would ye have thy sons wear such webs of injury to their graves? See thy knuckles, how swollen, like knobs? Do they bend? I think not. I think ye straighten thy fingers by pressing them on some hard surface and how they ache when sleep is needed and thy sore legs are kicking out from beneath thy miserable blankets in thy freezing stone cottages.

"How many of ye have lungs filled with blood because the cold mist at sea is inhaled and cuts like a knife?"

At this, Jock spat on the pier and everyone could see that he had spat up blood.

All fell silent, for my father had just walked from the Sea Trow and it was clear he had heard Jock's words and seen the spitting of blood.

"And what would ye have us do about all this?" my father charged. "The British have defeated the Scots and it is too late for a call to arms."

I was surprised by his calmness, for Jock was an imposing figure of almost six feet and great piles of muscle in spite of his sickness; what is more, he carried not only a pistol in his belt but a huge Scottish sword, the claymore, slung over his back.

"I ask ye again, Jock Stewart. What would ye have us do, now that ye have lost the war?"

Stewart eyed my father warily, and I noticed then that none of the Hoy men seemed as surprised as I, nor did Stewart seem surprised.

"I did not intend to offend ye, William," said Jock, and I shook my head to clear it. My father, though he may have been nearly six feet tall himself at one time, had by then shrunken four or five inches, and his shoulders had collapsed, taking his chest with them. What's more, his hands shook, and his knees shook, and surely that glint of steel in his eyes came from the sunlight reflecting from the sea, not from the fierceness of his character.

Till then, I had been blind to the virtues of my Da, so taken I was with his weakness in dealing with Ma.

"William, consider. What if thy son here, this fine boy, stays here on this island? By the age of thirty, he'll either be dead or maimed by the sea or have the appearance of an old man, as ye do now. Listen, all. If this boy lives, there'll be darkness and pain for him every day of his life at the end of the world."

Voices rose in protest, but my father raised a hand.

"There is much in what ye say," admitted my father, "but continue. Ye have not yet answered my question. What would ye have us do about anything?"

"Well, surely," said Jock, "I would not have ye flee to Italy or Spain or Germany, for in all those places the nobility reigns and there is no way to escape the ulcerous eye and empty pot. If one is born the son of a dweller in mud, a dweller in mud one must be. If one is born poor, one must serve the landlord or die by cannon fire in the King's navy."

"We are free men here," said my Da.

"But ye are not free to leave."

"Then what would ye have us do?" insisted my Da.

Pressed, Jock paused, and Long Weldon Planck appeared suddenly and sauntered over to the bench, planting a long leg beside Jock. He spoke in a loud, reedy voice, the men cheering and waving their woolen hats.

Long Weldon had once been a pirate for a single voyage, as he claimed, with the bloodiest pirate that ever lived, the famous Captain Robert Culliver, and was so sickened by Culliver's love of murder that he escaped with four other hands in a longboat to the west coast of Africa.

"I shall have my say," said Long Weldon, with an eye smeared in blood threatening Jock, my father, and anyone else who might act against his inclination to speak.

"As my friend, Bellamy the buccaneer, once informed me, I am a free prince and have as much right to make war on the whole world as he who commands a thousand ships of sail."

"Aye!" shouted Jock. "So ye are."

"Lads," said Long Weldon, his unruly hair flowing over his shoulders, "ye will find no faith of mine pinned to parson, pimp, or fool who bids a master flail him or suffers himself to be ruled by laws devised to fill another's treasury."

"Nor do we, Sir," said my Da angrily.

"What the rich may take in court, I take by the black strength of my heart," shouted Long Weldon, "so my conscience tells me."

"And by this morality ye would scuttle the fishing craft of my family and set my brothers and their children as well as my son to starve," said my Da, his face turning red, the crowd behind him taking his part with supportive cries.

"Nay, William Claddah, I would not take thy fishing ship," said Long Weldon. "I would take the King's brigantine instead and settle upon ye and thy family a portion of the gold, and if I am hung for such a crime, once into the winds of hell, I'll shriek the names of my many children."

The crowd quieted instantly, changing their thoughts of Long Weldon from day to night, and back again. My Da looked at Jock Stewart, as if he expected help. Well he knew that Jock was the scourge of all piracy, having hailed from the Minch, where pirates were heinous complements to the terrors of that sea, but Jock looked away, saying nothing.

"If called upon by the king to hang the man who burned the king's ship," said Long Weldon, "would ye be quick to bring the rope? Would ye do the king's murder?"

My Da fell in what appeared to be a deep gloom, but which I soon knew to be deep thought. "Nay, for I hold the king to be a great criminal," said my father, "but, by and by, now I know that ye, Long Weldon, and ye, Jock Stewart, do not visit us here on Hoy on the same day by coincidence—so nicely do thy arguments fit. Now, admit it, lads. There has been collusion, has there not?"

Long Weldon sputtered, then laughed, as if the notion were absurd, but none of the men believed his deriding of my father's notion more than they believed in the notion itself. There was a chorus of coaxing and questions until Long Weldon took his foot from the bench and sat himself down, signaling he had nothing more to say.

Then Jock rose from the bench and fired his pistol into the air to be heard.

"Gentlemen, ye are correct," he said. "Long Weldon and I are together in this matter."

"And what is the reason for thy visit?" said my Da.

"Ah, William," said Jock. "That is a mystery."

"Hang thy mystery," cried Thomas Clinton, one-eared and smelling of fish blood and urine of his own that trickled all night and day down his legs.

"A mystery," shouted Jock Stewart, "and damn my soul if I shall tell it."

"Have ye discovered a way for the fishermen of Hoy to take the British crown?" said my Da.

"There are men of the highlands who are still free men," said Jock Stewart, "and Thomas Jones has been pardoned by the crown and granted a commission as a privateer."

To my puzzlement, at the mention of the name, Thomas Jones, every man on the pier, except for Jock, fell into stunned silence, and a few removed their caps, as if they had arrived at the door of a kirk.

I shall not forget that moment. Suddenly, the sea-going drunks were sobered, the crippled could swim, and it seemed to my enlivened imagination that far over the Scapa Flow a great black ship with three masts under full sail emerged like a dark ghost from a mist newly fallen over the stacks of Kirkwaa.

Yet, I had never heard the name before meaningfully uttered, and it was a common name, after all. Still, from that day hence, I never thought of the name without playing with it on my tongue and investing it with magical properties.

"I do not know the meaning of anything ye have said," said Mathew Campbell, our blacksmith and worker in iron.

"Nor do I," said Cobb, the fisherman and farmer.

"And I understand nothing either," said my Da, "but my friends and I would appreciate less confusion at our place of business. Would we not, lads?"

"That we would," said someone. I could not see whom, for Da was leading me into the shelter of the Sea Trow Tavern.

"The mystery will soon be no mystery," shouted Jock Stewart to our backs. "And ye will have us to thank then."

"That ye will," said Long Weldon, with a great reedy laugh. "The mystery shall deliver ye. It shall make ye free."

"Do not turn around," said my Da, holding my hand tight. "Say nothing to them more."

"What do they want, Da?" I asked.

"I don't know," said my Da, "I'll put my mind to it. As for ye, have no more conversations with them. Accept nothing from them."

At those words, my heart broke in half, but I said nothing about the sgian duhb, though it seemed to burn me under my sock.

That night I could not sleep, so soon rose from my cot and walked the high limestone cliffs of Hoy, which in mild weather was a fine occupation, a quiet one too, for there are times when the sea settles down from its carving of blow-holes, arches, and inlets and the principle noise is that of the thousands of nesting wings of Hoy's sea birds, which fill the mind with comfort, even if one is ten years old and carrying in his sock a forbidden knife.

I settled in my favorite spot, on a high cliff across a small stretch of sea from a pillar of sandstone hundreds of feet high called the "Old Man of Hoy," because some have thought at some time that the pillar resembles the face of a man.

Ye might well ask, "Well, mate, how is it the pillar stands against the sea when it is obvious that all else around it has been washed away?"

Now, at ten years old, I did not know that the Old Man of Hoy had survived centuries of thrashing waves because it stood on a solidified flow of black volcanic lava; rather, I found destiny in its aspect. I believed for an hour it had stood for ages to speak to me.

Further, I believed that the events of the day had been chosen by the universe to bring me to the Old Man that I might pose to him the most important question of my life.

How would I stand when all else about me was washed away?

My Ma thought herself to be a seal, my Da was dying. The winds of Thule Skerrie carried the winter pogonip to scrape the shingles of the world, and there stood I, head bowed before the knacker's whim, my nails slimmed with the herring's scale, my sheep's shirt as if on fire with blood. Then, in the roar of the waves, I found a cry, the cry perhaps of my own innocent soul, and strength came to me that I had never felt before, all of which kept my knife warm and humming at my calf.

There I prayed, as I never had at church, facing the Old Man as if he were a god of the Picts or Vikings from long ago, and then, at last, after hours had passed, and a cold wind had brought a pipe of mist down the Scapa Flow, I raised my eyes and straight before me saw myself as a brawny lad standing on the bowsprit of a brigantine, itself running the sea under black sail, a *bone in its teeth*, which was a way of saying that the sea rolled frothy and white under the speeding bow.

"Why, I will be a sailorman," I said to myself, and by that I did not mean a keeper of hooks, a puller of nets, or a hunter of whale, but I meant that I would taste of the depth of the battered blue sky and chase the tall ships around the Cape of Horn.

Chapter Two

Since that evening with the Old Man of Hoy, I counted a day lost if it were not spent in learning the craft of the sea. Previous to it, when fishing with my uncles and Da, it was always I who was slow to get a hand out or to move my sluggish feet, which were likely as not to slip on the deck, but after that night, both my hands and feet were transformed and I became the most nimble of fishermen and handler of rigging and gear. So quick was I to run up the sail or crank the windlass or untangle the lines that after the day's work was over Uncle Sinclair would light up his pipe before the hearth at the Sea Trow Tavern and praise my dexterity and lively eye before my Da and Uncle Mangus.

More importantly, my uncles and Da, discovering my intelligence, began to find delight in teaching me what they knew.

Uncle Mangus it was who taught me not to fear the phosphorous wake but rather to study it for signs of changing weather.

"Someday, we'll understand it," he'd say. Then, in the dark he would teach me how far off the pods of whales were by the pitch of their sorrowful singing and the latitude and longitude of the nearest skerrie by only the bark of the seal. For though Mangus had sailed little but the waters of the Orkney Isles and the mighty Scapa Flow, he was a student of the sea and knew some wondrous things.

"See there, where the color of the sea changes," Mangus said, pointing to a bit of sea of a slightly deeper blue. "There runs a current below the surface that will turn our craft toward the bergs, but hold the tiller strong and we'll go through all right."

Always, I did as he said and learned throughout my eleventh year, even as my Da's health held and my Ma's passions grew stormier. Now and then, I would test my strength gained at sea against other village lads on the moors and usually ended up limping home at night covered with blood. Of lads my age, I ranked no better than fifth of seven, having been severely and repeatedly thrashed by the Campbell boys and James Acey and knocked once into Sunday by Harley Pruhs.

No matter. Not one of them had learned the art of mastering ice storms and fogs as thoroughly as I, for I had noted, marked, drawn, and studied the shapes of the Orkney Islands from diverse directions and needed only the smallest break in a storm or fog bank to mark my position. So, too, could I identify Orkney craft by their outlines, horns, and bells, and guess the lanes they traveled and, by the pitch of their noise, gage their bearings and speeds.

Some islands (those with pigs, most of all), I could find by nose.

But it was Uncle Sinclair who surpassed all understanding. No cloud to him was a cloud, but was instead a "thunderhead," a "mare's tail," or in mass a "mackerel" sky. "If clouds look as if scratched by a hen," he would say, "prepare to reef thy top sail." And by these old saws he would live each day, adjusting each to each with a consummate artistry. It was true he thought a green Christmas meant a fat cemetery, and oil skin jackets on clouds meant rain, or a high hill mist and evaporating clouds meant no rain, or a "sun setting clear as a bell" meant "it's going to blow sure as hell," but he also knew that any of these signs could be contradicted by another—that a rainbow (good), and a red wind (foul), or a moon ring (snow), or a moon in the clouds (tempest) could cancel out one another. All signs could be scoffed off by a full moon strong enough to resist any weather.

Still, in matters of the sea, I was becoming his inheritor. When the stars drew too near, I would tug at his sleeve and say, "Uncle, a storm."

"Right ye are, William," he would say, "but do not rely too much on any one thing."

I understood him right enough. Thereafter, I would note not only the stars too close, but also the oily sea and an easterly glint, the weight of the wind by the sound it would make and the size of the swells. Then, noting there was no full moon to scuff the matter off I would tug on his sleeve with greater confidence.

"Storm," I would say.

"William, once ye have noted all ye have noted in an instant, with no need for thought, ye will be a true man of the sea."

Had he said such a thing to me months before, how disappointed I would have been! But, then, I was not yet twelve.

Once, in the middle of the day, our sailing curragh lurched, throwing Uncle Sinclair to his knees and causing his head to strike the pitching gunwale. There he lay, unconscious, the catch flopping all about him, the herring run still too strong to let us quit for the day. So, we bundled him up in wet woolens to keep him from the frosty cold and fished on until the setting sun sank and we had daylight enough left to put into Westray Island, where we carried his dozing form to the Crusty Lion.

"We have already let our proper accommodations," said the tavern keeper, a hog of a man with a ring in his ear. "But ye and thy scoundrels may sleep in the kitchen if ye are toting thy purses."

So, to the steaming kitchen we went with Uncle Sinclair and laid him out on a warped table by the blackened hearth.

"Shall we sing to him of cherry pippins and punch?" said my Da, but we were too exhausted with the day's labors to take much notice of Da's weary jibes, or even of Uncle Sinclair's ghastly snoring. While Uncle Mangus and Da dozed in crooked chairs, the ugly cook put a squealing old teakettle on the fire. From the tavern's great room came sudden whiskied shouts and drunken thumps from the Orkney Islands' most evil looking crews of fishermen and thieves.

Uncle Sinclair woke, in great revulsion and anger.

"Are ye without wits!" he cried to his brothers. "Why did ye bring us here to Westray Island with the snow so near upon us so we'll be stranded here and probably robbed?"

Uncle Magnus and Da looked at Uncle Sinclair and then to one another. The cook, a Westray man of suspicious features, glanced up from the iron stove and out toward the windows of the kitchen, which were tightly shuttered against the evil blasts of an artic wind not troubling itself to slow down as it reached Westray Island.

There was no snow visible, nor yet the sound of snow.

Uncle Sinclair rubbed the great bump raised upon his head. "Well, dast!" he said. "The snow's already falling and a fine price we'll pay for it too."

With that, the suspicious cook, grown inquisitive, opened the back door a crack and then slammed it shut again as a great flurry of snow kicked up by the devil's boot soared over the kitchen and came down with a melting cackle over the blazing hot stove.

"Damn me!" said my Da. "How did ye know?"

"Well, didn't ye hear that teakettle sing," said Uncle Sinclair, sitting up angrily and throwing away the rag Uncle Magnus had placed on his head.

"Maybe, aye, I did," said my Da, "but thought nothing of it until now."

"Or that blue flame that burns on the coal fire, both of which signify weather coming?" shouted Uncle Sinclair. "And did ye not notice, Mangus, the sputtering of the fire, which it pleases the old folks to call 'treading' snow?"

"Aye, maybe I did," said Uncle Mangus. "And maybe just now as ye point it out, but how did ye know we were on Westray Island, rather than another, for I heard no boat whistle or horn to help ye name this sodden tump?"

"Why it's the smell of the swordfish that's in the tavern today, lad, carried by the boots and rough jackets, for who would go out long-lining on a day such as this but a fisherman from Westray?"

At this, my Da and Mangus roared with laughter, for as long as they had fished upon the sea they had never heard of a man who could tell a particular fish by smell.

"Don't laugh, my mates, for its perfectly true that a man who has in him a genius for the sea has such a gift, and I am such a man."

The laughter continued, even the cook joining in, Uncle Sinclair becoming ever more a creature of anger rather than the loving brother to my Da and Uncle Mangus, who were occupied with stripping off their woolens and hanging them on the backs of chairs to dry by the stove. Myself, I was not so quick to take off my clothing, howsoever desirable it might seem, for something hung in the air I did not like and great bursts of laughter continued to issue from the great room like claps of thunder.

"So, ye do not believe in the seamanship possible from an Orkney Islands' man, my brothers." said Uncle Sinclair. "How strange, since ye have heard a thousand stories. Nay, more!"

"Myths, Sinclair."

"Nay, real deeds."

"Do not give thy mind to stories," said Da.

"They are not stories, brothers," said Uncle Sinclair. "And I mean to prove it, not by just my own skills. I declare young William is just such an Orkney Island man we've been discussing and I'll wager ye each ten pence that William can identify a majority of the fish that our good cook here can provide from his ice chest."

"S'death, what a bet!" said the cook. "It cannot be done!"

The cook was an evil looking fellow, with eyes that looked always in opposite directions and bald slabs of scalp as if he had lost chunks of hair to the bite of frost. Still, he went about the business of pulling wrapped packets of fish from the chest, where they had been sitting on blocks of ice.

"Shall I remove the cloth wrappings," said he, "and should the young gentleman be blindfolded?"

"No need of that," said Uncle Sinclair, rubbing the nasty welt the gunwale had left on his head. "Young William can smell through the wrappings. What? Is four all ye have?"

"Aye, four!" said the cook. "There has been much fish eating here tonight."

"Very well, then," said Uncle Sinclair, jumping down from the table. "Put them up here."

The cook then found himself pleased to put the four packets of nearly frozen fish on the groaning board and Da and my uncles gathered round. Never in all my days, up to the stroke of that hour, had I felt myself to be such a fool. I knew full well I could identify no fish on earth by smell, cooked or uncooked, iced or not. The smell of fish, in fact, I had never thought to include in my studies, or ever imagined there would be the slightest use for, and would have, at that very moment, protested there were none, except that my Uncle Sinclair minutes before had proven there was.

"I can not do this," I said.

"Do it," said my Da,

He and Uncle Mangus were half naked by this time and were becoming quite intolerant about being left standing about in the half warm kitchen.

My Da cuffed me in the back of my head. Even Uncle Mangus pushed me forward. Then, seeing my reluctance, Uncle Sinclair let loose with such a bellow of rage I stumbled forward and bent toward the first packet of fish.

"If I say ye can do a thing, then ye can do it, by God!" said Uncle Sinclair. "When ye are grown ye may have thy own contrary opinions, but not before."

At first there was no smell and my eyes began to well with tears. Then, coming from the cold, there raised an almost intolerable oily scent I could in no way associate with human food but only with a ground-up fertilizer spread on the fields.

This is menhaden," I said.

When the cook opened the packet there was much back slapping and hoisting of tankards of ale, for I was clearly right, the cook admitting the fish was only in the ice chest to keep it fresh for the cat.

The next one was easy. I suppose anyone could have done it, even after Uncle Mangus and Da swore they would have been stumped by the piece of swordfish. I was able to identify it not because I could pick a swordfish from an ocean of fish, but because I could smell a little of the aroma that Uncle Mangus had smelled wafting from the boots of jackets of the great room of the Crusty Lion.

Uncle Sinclair then laughed at Uncle Mangus and Da, though still his head hurt him. He took a clean cloth, dipped it in hot water on the stove, and sponged his wound, even as he taunted. Perhaps the next victory would relieve the throbbing at his temples.

The third was the easiest of the identifications. The lump of fish was a piece of herring, which I must have known the aroma of all along without knowing I knew it. During my childhood on Hoy, many a herring had been flopped on my plate. The mystery then, to me, became not that I was able to identify it so readily but that Uncle Mangus and Da had to open the package to see if I was correct.

"Do ye see, William?" said Uncle Sinclair, his headache considerably better. "There is evidence of thy gift."

"But here is the fourth packet," said the cook, with a peculiar slyness. "And I venture to say young William will not be able to sniff out its contents though we wait here for an answer a hundred days or more. Nor will ye Sinclair Claddah be able to help him. Nor will there be a man of the Orkneys so talented as to be able to identify this fish, though I reveal freely it comes from the North Coast of Shetland and leapt there into a skiff."

"Let the boy smell of the fish," said Uncle Sinclair, impatient to lie down again.

For the fourth time, I bent over a packet, and this time there was no lack of odor that rose to my nostrils, but rather a powerful sweet stench quite beyond my experience mixed with the smell of sea bass. I paused, thinking overlong, nothing making sense, until the cook and my uncles became impatient, after which, in my view, everything in the kitchen grew indistinct and disappeared into shadow. Finally, I was alone with the aroma of the fish, and, at last, I knew.

"This is one part herring," I said, "and one part man."

How my uncles bellowed in outrage and how white the ruddy cook became, backing up against the stove so that he blistered himself and shrieked like a whistle. I swam down and away, burying myself in a corner of the room, as in soft mud, and saw from my hiding place that my uncles were focused more on each other and the cook than me.

The cook crossed himself and muttered "Hail Mary." then he walked swaying to the table as if he would fall and revealed the fish, the cold, stiff cloth, dramatically unfolding. We all gathered round, and by the light of the whale oil in a lantern we saw a sight never to be forgotten by the Claddahs.

The fish's body was clearly the body of a herring, down to its tail, through its back, gullet, neck, and fins. But where its fish head should be there was a thick, freakish mantle like a hump and within that mantle what appeared to be a man's eyes, nose, and mouth.

"The man who brought it in was the fisherman, McGrady, of the Shetland Islands," whispered the cook. "He called it the 'Bishop Fish' and swore it leapt into his skiff and quoted scripture until it died."

"I believe it," said Mangus, who was a great supporter of super-natural beings, except selkies, and that omission because of Ma. "And doesn't young William's smelling it as human even without seeing it weigh heavily toward that conclusion?"

"Aye, it does," said the cook, eyes brightening. "I must tell the others."

With that, he bounded from the kitchen before he could be stopped, yelling out the news of my feat in the great room of the Crusty Lion.

"This is unfortunate," cried Uncle Sinclair. "Gentlemen, draw thy knives!"

Uncle Sinclair then forgot the pain in his head and ran for the heavy kitchen door, which he securely bolted, then ran for the outer door and bolted it as well, even as Da and Uncle Mangus were securing the shutters. No sooner than they were bolted, there came a banging on the kitchen door from the nine or ten fishermen who had been drinking by the fire.

"Open the door!" someone shouted.

"I think ye do not come peacefully," said Uncle Sinclair.

"We only wish to share information with ye about the Bishop Fish," said the voice.

"I think that is a lie," said Uncle Sinclair.

"We can break down this door!" said the voice.

"I have never seen a sturdier door than this one," said my uncle. "Probably designed to keep the tavern keeper's goods from his roguish customers."

"The kitchen shutters outside are not so strong!"

"But they are strong," said Uncle Sinclair. "To break into them ye will have to endure the wind and the snow. Then, if ye, half frozen, succeed in breaking in, we await ye with knives."

"Send out the Finman," said the voice, growing impatient.

"There is no Finman here!" shouted my Da. "There is only my son!"

"We know he is young," said the voice. "But at one time or another even Finmen must be young."

"If he were a Finman, we would not hesitate in giving him to ye because ye could offer him no danger," said Uncle Sinclair. "But he is no Finman, and we will not give him over."

"If he is no Finman, how did he know the Bishop Fish by smell?"

To that, neither Da nor either of my uncles had easy answers. So, my uncles dressed quickly and we all settled down to wait out the superstitious fishermen of Westray, who had long disgraced the Orkneys and would now rapidly become even more besotted. Between the kitchen, which functioned as a repository for kegs of rum, and the great room of the tavern, there was a tiny stoutly framed window large enough only to pass through tankards of drink.

This window was manned unceasingly by my uncles, who were free with passing out great draughts of the innkeeper's rum. Over the rising volume of snores as the fishermen dropped off to sleep one by one, we could hear the hoggish man weeping.

"They're almost all asleep," said my Da, "and they've left no guard."

"Of course they haven't," said Uncle Mangus. "They know we can't sail away in this snow. They can round us up at leisure in the morning and burn young William here for being a Finman and the rest of us too for being with him."

"Well, then," said Uncle Sinclair. "We'll sail away."

"Which cannot be done!"

"Aye!" said my uncle, cheerfully. "And we'll let the boy do it, for otherwise he'll never have had the experience of captaining his own craft."

"Well," said Uncle Mangus. "Sinclair, I have underrated ye as a man for the entirety of my life."

"As have I," uttered my Da, with an amazement that made his eye grow wide and his jaw hang slack.

"What justice for all his work and study," said Uncle Mangus. "It would be far better if we were all to live, but that not being a possibility, what more joy can be snatched from the moment than this?"

My Da's eyes were welling up with tears.

"What pride I have in ye, my son." He held me to his chest so I could feel his body heave. "To face these sheets of snow and sea, this death that awaits us, with thy brave hand on the tiller...ye have grown into manhood at eleven years old."

I could hardly speak. It was as if I had never been loved until now. When Da let me go, I hugged my uncle Sinclair and tried to put on a steely look. Da put a fish knife under my belt, even as I resisted the urge to inform him of the sgian dubh lashed to my shin. We all went to the shutters, unbolted them, and looked out. From the back of the tavern we could mark the swirling masses of white that ran through the low hills of Westray Island, and how the stars and moon had all gone to bed, pulling up their blankets of snow so no one could find them.

"There's no one waiting out here," said my Da.

Uncle Sinclair quietly slipped the bolt of the door and seconds later we were bent against the wind and drifting snow, trudging knee deep toward the front of the tavern and the disappearing fishing craft at the pier. Even on the pier, with the sea lapping under it, the snow was three feet deep, so we fell to our knees, felt for the gunwale of our curragh, made bridges of our bodies and then forward rolled into our sailing craft, which had become a bucket of snow.

There we labored mightily for an hour or more clearing out the snow as it turned to ice and beating away icicles from stays and shrouds. The mooring lines we cut, for their knots had stiffened. But the halyard and sail were frozen to the mast and had to be freed, a task which promised to lacerate our bodies and further from harbor might have thrown us into the sea. So, we climbed with care, and fairly up the mast we pulled with all our strength the frozen assemblage until the sail hung loose from the mast but stiff in the wind like a parson's collar.

"And thy orders, young William," said my Da, smiling beside me, even as my uncles were sitting lost in the dark and snow in front of me.

"We'll go south toward Scotland," I said, "for it's well I know that's where we're pointed, and I know well enough we'll never succeed in coming about."

"Aye, aye, Captain," three voices rang out.

Then my Da left me at the tiller and groped his way in the blasting snow to the mast where he and my uncles passed a flagon and began a ditty about a roving lad who swears he'll "no longer go a-roving with his fair maid." At first, I thought the song high spirited, just the thing to begin our voyage, but then, when we moved not from the pier but rather just slammed against it, I though the song too rough and rowdy.

I'll go no more a-roving with ye, fair maid.

Things, thought I, were becoming perverse. The boat was grinding to pieces instead of sailing forward and suddenly it was clear that the young rover was accusing his fair maid of having the pox.

I was fairly shocked by the combination of circumstances. I had seen drunkenness before from Pa, a bit of bawdiness from Uncle Mangus, and certain heedlessness from Uncle Sinclair, but never before had I seen all three behaviors so active in all three men at once. I prepared to shout out my objections.

Then a lurch threw us from the pier. We heeled to port and almost blew down, all of us grabbing onto rigging for life itself. Thrashing up and down, we blew southeast, beating into the snow at the urging of my tiller with no need for more sail than provided. So powerfully was the snow slung toward the weather shore, it drove our starboard planking, reefed sail, and mast, and we moved, squeezed like all mortal things between wind and keel.

There was no question of living, but of whether the mouth of the harbor could be found before we went under. The wind lashed at my face. Spray became particles of ice as it flew over the gunwales and drove my uncles and Da to the bottom of the curragh.

The sea rose to meet us, sometimes fore and aft at once, always starboard, for in those close quarters of the harbor, if I tried to turn away from the wind, I heard at once the sound of a reef striking wood.

We might have found our end blinded by snow cast up on some harbor wreck or shoal, or breached by a shout from shore of an unseen breaker from the Stygian dark. Equally likely, we might have died ignominiously of cold, and our good craft and frozen corpses blown about until the Westray fisherman came to harvest them when the sun rose.

I rather hoped we would make it to open sea and there die gloriously in steepled waves.

"Ye are doing very well, young William!" rang out my Da's voice along with other words of encouragement from Uncles Sinclair and Mangus as they passed the bottle. Still, I found no cheer in their uplifting mood, for well I knew their bodies to be wrapped freezing around one another as they laughed; not even a man of Hoy could wear woolens enough to weather such an icy blow.

In minutes, as I judged, we would all be dead, my kin in their cups singing their rowdy songs.

Then a miracle struck, one that has left me a Catholic man, if only in name, for the duration of my life. Our curragh righted itself. The wind driving the snow eastward into our starboard bow ceased of a sudden, and the waves quieted down as if old Poseidon had been paid his weight in Aztec gold and had lost all interest in storming about.

"What is it?" shouted Da.

"Don't know!" yelled Uncle Mangus.

"Look around ye," I almost screamed in my excitement, and we all looked both fore and aft. Not fifteen yards distant in either direction, the snow streamed as before, almost parallel to the water.

Uncle Sinclair's voice came booming out of the darkness, loud enough to be heard over the crashing of the waves, soft enough to be understood as controlled.

"Something has blocked off the snow and the wind," he said. "We are in the lee of a whale as large as an island, or in lee of an island itself that has arisen in the harbor. It could also be an iceberg newly arrived from Greenland, or a ship that is much larger than ours. Those being the possibilities, which is it, Captain?"

I quickly thought the matter over and came to a conclusion.

"Why, Uncle," I shouted. "We are in the lee of a ship much larger that ours. I would also add that we are parallel to its stern and are about to scrape it, and my guess is that it could be as long as ninety feet and thirty feet high."

"A remarkable deduction," young William, shouted Uncle Sinclair. "So what is thy order?"

In another instant, Da and Uncle Mangus were joyfully shouting from the forecastle for my command, as if freezing to death or drowning in the combers of an unknowable sea's relentless hammering had tossed them into a jocular mood.

"Very well, the order!" I thought, looking up at the blackness where I guessed a ship must have been hiding. "Here's an order for ye all. Board her!" I cried.

How far beyond my power it is to describe that first pure act of piracy. Many a man, I suppose, would say something mitigating like, "I did it to save the lives of my Da, uncles, and myself!" to justify his crime. And I myself might say, "Ah, yes, that was a part of it!" and cite the simple fact that I was too shaken with cold to spend another voluntary minute on our craft. But were I to go only so far, the substance of my comments would total a lie.

For nothing in my life, before or since, has given me such a taste of soul uplifting joy. Even as I climbed with bitter hands up the frozen hooked line hurled by Uncle Mangus up the black wall of that unknown vessel, my heart sang out. Great beams of warmth flooded my whole being. So, little cared I what lay ahead, what renewed wind or sweeping snow or worse. In my elation, even battle with whatever seamen were left guarding the boat was acceptable. Nay! Rather hoped for, far above friendliness!

The ship was mine.

Climbing over the gunwale, I was again buffeted by snow but was now without thought of it. I walked rapidly to the far side of the vessel then back, counting steps, then to the forecastle and aft to quarterdeck and bowsprit, then back to the hatch amidships. In the dark, I lay the rope ladder I knew would be there. Hailing below, I ordered my kin to tie our craft to the vessel and ascend.

In the captain's cabin we rummaged at length until finding flint and an oil lamp.

What pleasure it was, all the more so because the cabin and craft had been taken by courage and stealth, by fishermen of Hoy.

In the rosy glow of the lamp, we lit the captain's stove and soon were warm as fellows at a hearth and stoked with the captain's best brandy, much finer than rum.

"Who shall explore the ship?" said Uncle Sinclair. "It appears to have been abandoned by its night watch during the storm, which seems to me almost certainly true and infinitely reasonable, but perhaps it would be well if we made certain."

"I order myself to do it!" I cried.

My kin looked upon me as if I was demented but readily gave way. They were hardy, strong fishermen of Hoy, except for my Da, who coughed blood even on days most balmy, but at present my kin were rather torn and bloodied and still frozen where yet the brandy had not touched. Besides, they were drunk, whereas I was sober and strong and already warmer, lit by triumph and interest. That morning, I had been the youngest fisherman of a tiny sailing boat on the Scapa Flow, but under the night's black sheathing of evening stars had taken my first prize and become the captain of a tall ship capable of sailing around the world.

I lit a second lantern of my own, slipped on my heavy clothing, and left the cabin shielding the lantern from the snow with my body. After a moment on the quarterdeck, which was deserted, I feared the lantern would be put out and hurried to the hatch amidships, where I climbed down into the shadows of the hold. Just aft of where I stood, there was the noise of many feet, and I wheeled around, my lamplight catching the eyes of dozens of rats fleeing back further toward the bulkhead in the stern.

There by the bulkhead were scattered rags of all sorts, as if the seamen who sailed the ship did not know that rats are born from rags. My stomach turned over, and I turned toward that portion of the hold closest to the bow, where many open and empty wooden containers lay waiting to be filled.

Search as I did, from one container to the other, I found no clue as to the tall ship's business, which caused my young brain a revelry. Perhaps the vessels' business had been left by providence for me to determine.

Having left the hold, I entered the forecastle and there found rows and rows of hammocks for members of the crew, and elsewhere aboard the ship I found ample provisions and a well-stocked galley. Still, nowhere aboard did I find a living thing but rats and no item to shed light on the ship's identity or calling.

"There are no records in this cabin of any kind," said my Da, when I again reached the cabin covered with snow.

"Anyone aboard?" asked Mangus.

"No one!" I said.

If the crew had gone ashore, would we not have seen foreigners at the Crusty Lion?" said my Da.

"There are now several taverns on Westray Island, not just the Crusty Lion," said my Uncle Sinclair.

"Let's don't worry about it then," I said. "But rather about escaping."

"What manner of boat is this one?" said Sinclair, who, for all his expertise with small craft, had never before so much as seen a vessel as large as the one currently shielding us from the storm.

"This is a 'snow,'" I said, aware of the irony of its name. "It's a square-rigged, two-masted vessel with a sail aft."

My Da looked at me closely, a bit of shock in his eyes. "It's a ship with guns, Da," I said, "not of the grandest, but used for pirating or used as ship of war."

"And how do ye know so much of a warship?" said my Da, the matters of the evening beginning to shake his patience.

"I've heard Long Weldon talk of the cut of such a ship, Da! It's sturdy enough to be our deliverance. We'll cut away the anchor since we haven't the men to lift it and trust the snow and wind to drive us to sea. We'll attempt no maneuver but ride before the storm, which this ship can safely do, but our curragh cannot. When the storm blows out, we'll abandon it for our boat and sail for Hoy. What say ye?"

"I say we'll be hung for piracy!"

"And I as well." said Uncle Mangus.

"Aye," said Uncle Sinclair. "We'll likely be tarred and hung."

"At some later date," said my Da.

"Why, certainly at some later date," said Uncle Sinclair. "Nothing is ever done promptly."

"And some things never at all," said my Da.

"Ah, sad but true," said Uncle Mangus. "In this day and age, some things that should be are never done at all.

Having decided to steal the ship and live by virtue of our cleverness and audacity, we became a merry crew. Would Da and my uncles have become pirates in less pressing circumstances? Certainly not! So much were they creatures of the kirk, though they never attended. But were they aggrieved to be of the brotherhood by their accursed luck? If so, why did they laugh and push?

Even before their bellies were quite filled with fine drink and their clothes half dried, we were all dressed in our woolens and scrambling on deck to again be half buried by still falling snow. The first piece of business was easy enough. We secured our tiny curragh to the stern of the vessel with a second and third line.

Our original plans having slightly changed, the anchor cable presented some difficulty. Neither had we muscle enough to retrieve it by the capstan nor the wish to do so. We had decided to create the impression the ship had broken from her cable because of the storm, not slashed by thieves who should be tracked down and hung.

"Impossible," said my Da.

"Quite impossible." said my Uncle Mangus. "Let's just slice it, lads. Perhaps the owners will never figure out it was us took her in the first place."

"And who do ye think they'll accuse?" said my Uncle Sinclair. "They'll accuse the Westray Island fishermen of stealing their ship. Then, the Westray men will say. 'Oh no! It was those men from Hoy, who took thy ship to ride out the storm and left it to founder and then sailed home in the curragh they probably had tied behind it.'"

"I don't know," said my Da, scratching his head. "Do ye think the Westray men have the brain workings to say all that?"

"Maybe one among them does," said Uncle Sinclair. "And him we must fear."

"Then what should we do?" said Uncle Mangus.

"Fray the line apart," said Uncle Sinclair. "In the galley, there's likely a grinding wheel for sharpening knives.

An hour later, the four of us crouched at the capstan and tried to inspect the massive bitter, but an academic pursuit of such irrelevance to the moment proved foolhardy. No sooner had we escaped our mooring than we discovered how little a tall ship with a large forecastle and no anchor wished to remain headed into the wind.

Its bow swung so violently toward Scotland we grabbed for the gunwales and screamed with involuntary joy even as the snowy wind swept over us and the icy sea climbed aboard. Then, quick upon our screams came fear, first of heeling over, then of splintering on some inky shoal of the harbor, then of a knock-down at the harbor's mouth when the cross winds of Westray and Hoy caught us stern and starboard.

Then, finally, we were free, running with the wind on skeleton masts, away from the harbor with no stitch of sail, snow and darkness all about us, and the ship on an even keel with danger behind us.

I hove her to by tying off the whip-staff.

"There," I said, "we're headed southeast. Even if the winds blow us too far, we'll end up harmlessly in the open sea."

"Pray, Lads," said Uncle Sinclair, "that the owners of this ship are smart enough to recover it, but dumb enough to attribute its breaking away to the storm."

"And pray they are dumb enough to believe the rats have been getting at the captain's brandy," said Da.

The four of us, then, shared a sinking feeling. Still, there was nothing to be done about it, so we all trudged and slipped our way back to the captain's cabin to have another glass or two and maybe a good warm sleep while waiting out the storm.

I awoke in the middle of the night, not because I was not tired but because I was like a boy given a precious gift and could not sleep for the excitement. My Da had left a single lit lantern swinging over the table. It threw shadows first against one side of the cabin and then the other. "Such elegance," I thought.

The bulkheads were of a dark, rich mahogany of almost six foot of height and over much of their surface contained carvings of god and goddesses and clusters of grapes and grape leaves. One panel, however, seemed of more importance than the rest, not only because it was situated directly behind the captain's ornate desk but also because its two figures were half again as large as those in the other panels. Both wore laurel crowns.

They were the Roman Emperor, Maximus, and his Welsh wife, as I guess, the subjects of a thousand stories told in every part of the British Isles.

I drank it all in—the panels, the desk, the charts stored in a wooden barrel, the stuffed bookcase, the leather cases of curious instruments, and carved captain's trunk, the hammock upon which I slowly swung, eyes wide open. No place I had ever been inside had ever been so polished, so cozy, so modern, or orderly, with everything shiny and tucked in its place. Nevertheless, after half an hour or so of admiring glances and warm fantasies of never leaving the place, my truer love of the upper deck presented itself, snow or not, and I again dressed and walked the ship to the quarterdeck.

The storm continued but not so virulently as before, so I found more than a measure of joy in planting myself behind the whip-staff and in my mind setting sail for Jamaica. The clouds of snow in each mast became great billowing masts of sail, every shadowy mound of indeterminate mass aboard the ship yet another seaman anxious to execute my will. All about me, these figments of my dreaming burst into shanties and hauled down on hawsers or else raced up ratlines and shrouds to yardarms and crosstrees where distant ripples of wind were spotted leaving whitecaps on the water.

At long last, the snow lessened momentarily and the howling of the wind dropped off to a low moan. Gazing over the dark sea, I took myself of a sudden to be dreaming, for it seemed there was something off in the weather, yet there could not be. No small boat could be negotiating such jagged waves in such a blinding snow, but yet it seemed to be.

"Wake up," I cried to my uncles and my Da, knowing full well that it was impossible they should hear me. Perhaps I cried out to myself. Then, I braced on the quarterdeck, looking northward from the stern into the fury of the storm. Behind the ship there formed a long funnel that reached through both wave and falling snow, and through the funnel there glided improbably a sealskin boat in a greenish light. It had no sail.

Fists of snow drummed at my chest and I stumbled backward toward the naked mizzenmast. Both ends of the black boat were pointed upward like the horn of a bull. But more remarkable, the sea-going craft did not seem ten feet long from one end to the other yet passed through the tossing waves like an arrow through the air.

Worse still, paddling the tiny boat was a dark long-faced creature wrapped all in dark fur, eyes aglitter. With effortless motion, he powered his craft within yards of our ship and gazed about, as if looking for something or someone. Then, he turned his small boat and scurried away, only to appear again a few minutes later.

"Do not look at him," said my Uncle Sinclair, his right hand suddenly on my shoulder, his left hand slipping his own crucifix around my neck.

Again I shouted to wake myself, the crucifix drawn to my lips by my quickened fingers.

"Do as I say!" said my uncle, his voice steady as the wind.

At last, I was struck by a fresh blast of snow and succeeded in turning from the sight of the strange dark man paddling away,

"Find me a line!" said Uncle Sinclair. "Quickly, young William!"

I ran about the slippery, snow-covered deck, terrified, yet my lungs on fire, until at last I used the sgian dubh to cut a piece of hawser from the mizzen mast.

"Give it to me quickly, lad!" shouted Uncle Sinclair, who had found a plank some five feet long.

He lashed the two planks together to form a rude cross and then lashed the cross to the stern of the ship. That done, he cautioned silence, and we waited on the quarterdeck and kept a wary watch over the sea.

A half-hour passed before the strange boat came again, and this time it came with less boldness. It barely peeked at us before it turned tail and was off again into the darkness. My Uncle Sinclair breathed a heavy sigh of relief, as did I, for something about the paddler's leaving made it clear he would not soon come again.

"The snowing is done," said Uncle Sinclair, "and all the signs say there'll be clear weather and fair wind in the morning. We'll abandon this ship and sail for Hoy at the breaking of the light."

"Will we be safe then?" I said.

"Aye, in the sun," said my Uncle Sinclair. "What a dark and gloomy race of sorcerers they are!"

"Who are, Uncle?"

"Why, Finmen, of course!" said Uncle Sinclair.

"Finmen, Uncle?"

"Aye," said my uncle, "I have said Finmen. Have I not?"

Chapter Three

Da hunkered down with me in the Dwarfe Stane, his voice filled with shadow, the wind only faintly whistling in the cracks, the new moon filtering in, making soft lines of light. Though my limbs had returned to our curragh and the fast land of Hoy for three weeks now, my Da knew my brain to be stirring still with the tall ship's sail.

"Do not despise the traditions of Hoy," said my Da, "or ye may lose a hand or a foot."

"And how would I do that, Da?" I said.

"Thy mother would have ye believe in the nix, the little horse with the wheel tucked between his hind legs and hidden by his tail."

"Aye! She would."

"Aye," said my Da, "but there is no such thing as the nix. It is a child's fancy. There is, however, a big brother to the nix and ye know its name."

"Aye," I said, "but I have not believed in it. It is called the kelpie."

"Aye, the kelpie," said my father with a curious intensity. I could not see his face. A cloud must have passed before the face of the moon because all inside the Dwarfie Stane was black. "Do not forget the kelpie because it is the most beguiling little horse. Few can resist it. On a spring morning, with the skylark and a blue sky above, a little stream beyond and a water wheel, who would not be drawn to such a pure white creature?"

"Yet, if ye touch it, thy hand will stick to it and ye will be lost, for the kelpie will rush to the sea and his magic will hold ye until ye are drowned...unless..."

My Da paused and I waited in the darkness for the revelation.

"Unless what, Da?"

"Unless ye can cut off thy hand with that little knife ye wear in thy sock," said my Da.

I reached into my sock and removed my sgian dubh, took it by its blade and extended the handle into the dark. For a moment, the knife was gone and its absence was heavy in my hand.

Then, to my surprise, I felt its warm handle nudge again into my palm.

"Ye have earned the knife," said my father, coughing.

No doubt blood was flowing into his hands.

"I'm sorry I did not tell ye about it!"

"Here's another weapon ye'll need," said Da, ignoring my comment and handing me a much longer knife. "Wear it at thy belt."

"Aye, father," I said, much puzzled.

"And here is another weapon, also." said my father.

Reaching out for the weapon, I gave a little cry of surprise. What my fingers touched in the dark was no blade or handle of a knife, but rather the barrel of a pistol.

"Take the pistol and put it under thy belt," said my father, "but also under thy blouse that no one might see it. Now take this horn of powder and this bag of shot that the pistol might do ye some good."

So shocked was I by my father's words and deeds that my delight gave way to incredulity and I could hardly speak.

"Why is it ye are giving me a pistol and a knife, Da?" I asked. "I have often heard ye say that a pistol is never needed by a fisherman and a knife with a blade like this one only when a lad reaches sixteen and goes off to war. And I am only twelve."

Da reached out, took hold of my shoulders, and pulled me toward him. In the pitch darkness, I could feel wetness at his cheeks and imagine tears, just as I imagined the wetness at his blouse to be blood from his mouth. I took to bawling then. Only rarely before had I been in the embrace of my Da and was giving myself over to it—all in the knowledge he would be in the earth soon and I would have him no more.

"I have seen ye fight with the other village boys," said my Da, "and ye often get thrashed. From this moment forward ye must never be thrashed again. Ye must train with the pistol, the cutlass, the knife, and the marlinespike, and with whatever weapon falls to thy hand. Ye shall not be a fisherman of Hoy, and likely no fisherman at all."

"What?" I said. "Not be a fisherman of Hoy?"

"It seems not," said my Da. "The British King has declared bloody war on the French, and soon the British will be fighting both the French and Spain. If ye stay on Hoy the time will come soon when ye'll be pressed into service. If so, thy life will come to nothing and ye'll find a watery grave before the worms find me in mine."

"Where shall I go, Da?" I said, not fully understanding my Da's fear of the navy.

"From one of these Orkney islands to the other," said my Da. "To Iceland if ye must, or even St. Kilda, or Shetland, or the Island of Skye. Ye must be wary and sail away from any place the British arrive, and if any man attempts to hold ye, ye must kill that man."

"For how long, Da?"

"For as long as the British are sending out to press seamen for their wars."

"Why not just chance a term of duty and then go my way?"

"Because the British do not honor terms of duty," said my Da. "They also feed ye so poorly ye'll die of the scurvy or whip ye so severely ye'll die of thy wounds, or die of thirst while the officers have plenty. They'll also keelhaul ye for forgetting to salute, or maim ye for life to keep ye from wanting to go ashore, or chain ye below in port to keep ye from escaping. Then, when ye are wounded in battle, they'll deny ye the knife and let the green take thy heart.

"Worse, yet, for the living that are married. Should a miracle save a mate who is married, the mate will reach homeport to find his family starved to death in the street and the navy forgetting to pay him. What waves Britannia rules, lad, have been bought by the blood of its poor. "

"Perhaps they won't come, Da," I said.

"They'll come," Da said. "At the first sight of a strange sail, my brothers and I will help ye launch a curragh we've provisioned and stashed on a shelf of the cove near the Old Man of Hoy. From there ye can sail to thy cousin in Sanday, and from there to North Ronaldsay, then to Stromness and Kirkwaa. Then ye head to Rousay and from there again to North Ronaldsay cairn."

I felt a touch of a sea fairy go up and down my spine—a delicious thing to savor. How I lusted, of a sudden, for a ship of twenty guns or more to come rounding into the wind and down into Hoy harbor. Then I fancied I might shove out to sea in the black curragh and hoist sail for Sanday, keeping to the shoally water that could mean doom for a beamy three-masted craft riding low from its weight in guns and iron.

I longed too to feel the icy salt spray on my face, the wintry sun sitting lightly on my nose as gulls screamed overhead.

"I am also concerned over the matter of us having pirated a ship," said Da, the moon overhead so reaching a chink in the ancient roof of the Dwarfie Stane that a pale light fell upon his face. The endless sound of the Scapa Flow rising and falling against the rocks of Hoy seemed the rumble of a curious battery of guns. Again, I was thrilled to feel the fairies' touch. The mist rolling in from the coming tide painted my naked skin with a thin film of salt. "How are we to know what ship it was? It could be a British ship in search of recruits, so think Mangus and Sinclair."

"Aye, it could," I conceded. "So, I will practice with the weapons ye have given me."

"Ye will," he said. "Ye will practice under the eyes of my brothers and me for several hours daily before we put out to sea. Sinclair is an excellent man in wrestling and striking with his fist, Mangus with the marlinespike and knife, and I was once the best shot with a pistol on Hoy. More's to the point, lad, we'll teach ye to kill and never to hesitate, for thy life depends upon it."

"I've crushed the life from many a seal," I said.

"A beginning," said my Da. "But what if an armed seaman of sixteen or seventeen stops and calls out to ye on High Hill as to how to find his way to port. What will ye do?"

"I will proceed most carefully, looking for suspicious moves." I said.

"Ye will not," said my Da. "Ye'll proceed toward him casually in a jovial fashion and pull thy pistol from thy tunic and blow a hole in his chest. Then, ye will proceed to the curragh and launch her from the shelf."

"But, if he is innocent!"

"Is not the seal innocent?"

"But the seal is not human."

"There are times I prefer the company of the seal."

"But the human may be Christian."

"Then God will look after his interest in heaven," said Da, "but the man who calls to ye will not be innocent. If he were, he would be circumspect, not armed and strolling about Hoy in a time of war."

My exultation of a moment before gave way to my curiosity about how and when my father had acquired such knowledge. I recalled my astonishment at the respect Long Weldon and Jock Stewart, the Scottish provocateur, had accorded him, as well as the many times I had questioned him about his past and the pasts of Uncle Mangus and Uncle Sinclair without receiving an answer. Perhaps, in the Dwarfie Stane, in this chamber of tombs with the ashes of lost kings still floating in the moonlight, my Da would at last speak up and make all things clear.

"Da," I said. "Will ye tell me the adventures of ye and my uncles before ye were married?"

Da laughed then, blood, no doubt flowing all over him. So much had I seen him lose on so many occasions I knew beyond doubt the body provides an endless supply. And that nobody might ever again bleed to death if a way be devised to pump blood into veins as rapidly as it flows out.

"Aye, I will," said Da. "I'll clear up all mysteries, for ye must steer under a new moon now, and what I have to say may be of some help. If not, so be it. But if it goes unsaid, it can help no man.

"My brothers and I once terrorized the Island of Hoy with drunken violence and whoring. Who could stand against us? We good-naturedly thrashed young and old alike, married all the whores and let no one else touch them, and closed down the kirk. Our drunken bouts were legends. We began in the afternoon by tossing the other Hoy drunks of the Sea Trow out in the street. And we continued all night until in the morning the citizens gathered at the door to carry us home."

"In our spare time we beat one another senseless on the pier. We brought down gulls with our shot and fought one another with knives to first blood until we became so proficient with defending strokes and dodges that blood seldom flowed.

"Then, one day Sinclair conceived of a raid on the continent of Asia that left our neighbors both hysterical with laughter and hopeful they would be rid of us forever.

"According to Sinclair, the three of us would sail on a provisioned curragh to South Ronaldsay, loot a village there, and then hit a Scottish town in the North Sea. After succeeding in these first attacks, we would rob the Dutch as night raiders and make for the Baltic. In the Baltic, we would pillage our way to the exotic Black Sea.

"'Sinclair,' I said. 'How will we do all that without being hunted down and hung?'

"'Why, it will be blamed on the Vikings!'

"'Sinclair,' Mangus said, 'the world has not been pillaged by Vikings for centuries.'

"'Which will make the story an irresistible thing to believe,' Sinclair said.

"To that, all agreed. So we recruited a crew of ten additional men and set out to save us all from lives as fishermen of Hoy. So, young William, that is how we became proficient in the arts of fighting and why we are respected for those arts even now, though we have changed our ways forever. That is how we obtained our experience."

"By piracy?"

"Aye, lad. For a short time, we were pirates. Then we were again for a short time when we stole that vessel."

"Did ye not want to keep on after ye first set sail in the curragh?"

"Nay, lad. Of the thirteen of us, only nine returned.

"But they were men. They made their choice."

"Nay. Those that go to sea are rarely men. Not one of us was over sixteen."

"And did ye come back with gold?"

"Some gold, some silver. Most of all, with goods…silks and furs, perfumes, oil for lamps, carpets. It made the four of us the leading citizens of Hoy, with farms and businesses, as well as the fishing. But, lad, I caught first the flux and then this wasting sickness and drank my treasure away in fighting the blood."

I lapsed into silence, and so did Da.

The ghaists of those four dead boys seemed to flit about the Dwarfie Stane.

"I would give all I made to have just one of those boys back again," he said with such sadness I turned the conversation away from his thoughts.

"Da, ye have said ye do not remember how ye took Ma into thy boat when ye captured her? Is that true, Da? And what of her skin?"

Da laughed a bit coldly. "I believe thy Ma to have been put to sea in a sealskin skiff from a little island south of Rousay. On that bleak rock, the weathered old people believe that the call of the seal people may take a human soul and make a selkie of it, and this new-made selkie must be sent to the sea. I imagine thy Ma to be such a sacrifice, but inflamed in the mind so she imagines she is what she fears. She was placed in a fur coat so she would lie down in the boat, which was of seal skin, which calmed her, then sent to her death in the waves."

My fists clenched and heat rose to my cheeks.

"Your anger is not fair to the weathered ones," said Da. "The hunters of Rousay are frightened of madness, which they don't understand, and the selkie, which they think they do."

"Go on, Da!" I said.

"When I took her into my arms, she was a young woman, sleeping, probably dreaming the life of a seal swimming at sea. To save her I stripped her, gentled her, tied her up in my curragh, tossed her coat to the waves, sank her death boat, and brought to Hoy to marry. I've never had more than a bitter day or two for it. She's been a fine wife, her only fault being that she occasionally keeps us awake all night screeching away for her skin."

"And why have ye never told the truth about her to anyone?"

"Because I am guilty of kidnapping and forcible marriage, lad," Da said. "Have ye no feeling for the law?"

"Why should I? I'm twelve, and my Da was a pirate!" I said, for I knew full well when he was sporting with me.

"Hush, lad!" he whispered. "Do ye not hear it?"

"Hear what?" I heard nothing but the breeze curling in among the stone and the constant lapping of the sea.

"The step of thy Ma!" said Da. "She won't come in here because she is afraid of the dead. She has come to listen to us talk—in hopes I'll disclose to ye where I've hidden her seal skin."

"What then shall we say?" I whispered. I could hear my Ma creeping close up to the hallway of the great Dwarfie Stane and saw the tiny shadow of her crouched form cross the threshold by moonlight. Sobs broke from her throat.

"I don't know what to say," said my Da. "If I tell ye loudly there never was a skin, will the truth cure her madness, or make it worse?"

"I don't know, Da." I said. "What if we say nothing about the skin at all?"

"Then we lose an opportunity," said Da.

"Do ye trust in God?" I asked.

"I trust him to mind his own affairs."

"I would like a mother who is well," I said at last, as quietly as I could.

"And I would like a wife who is well for the time I have left," my Da said, in a voice even more quiet than mine. "And I would like her to follow my casket to the kirk."

"Well then," I said, as loudly as I could, without seeming to be screaming. "Da, I am a man now. I demand to know what ye have done with the seal skin ye peeled from my mother's body."

"Alas, my son," my Da said loudly. "The whole truth is I never skinned thy Ma. She was wearing a gnawed old fur coat the old people of her island had convinced her was a seal skin to get her into the boat. This coat I ripped from her body to see her naked, then flung it in the sea. I brought her home to marry, but could never convince her she wasn't a seal."

For a moment after my Da's wooden speech there was a moment of silence. Then, my Ma let loose with such a wail of indescribable sorrow that tears sprang to my eyes and Da and I raced to the door of the Dwarfie Stane. Already, she was gone, as if the night had swallowed her. No matter how we strained our eyes, we could make out no particle of her form as she fled from us over the rolling plain.

But hear her we did, for there was no end to the wailing, the heart-breaking, soul shattering cry brought forth from her fragile chest by the two that loved her the most.

For days after I did as Da suggested, and Uncles Mangus and Sinclair endorsed. The fishing was delayed for two hours after first light, the time spent with the three former pirates coaching me in the survival arts. Da had me shooting at chunks of wood, first fixed, then thrown, for the better part of each morning until my trigger finger grew bloody and my arm hung heavy with soreness.

Then Uncle Mangus would provide instruction in the hurling of the knife, insisting each week upon deeper penetration and greater accuracy and in the matter of hand-to-hand fighting demanded seemingly infinite repetitions of stab patterns and slashes coupled with feints and evasions. A half-hour with Uncle Mangus, especially when he hauled out the marlinespike, left me breathless and silently praying Uncle Sinclair would lack the energy for grappling and fisticuffs.

"This is the most important part of thy training," he would say. "Ye are not naturally a lad of strength or agility. It is here ye must make the greatest improvement."

I sadly agreed. At the age of twelve, I was cursed by arms and legs that refused to take on the lumps of muscle of a man, just as my face refused the slightest suggestion of hair.

"There is a likely connection between thy lack of hair and thy lack of muscle," said Uncle Sinclair. "Such seems the will of the Almighty. Still, ye are not so strong as many of the lads of the village who have as little hair as I see upon thy face. I have some thoughts about it, if ye would like to hear."

"Aye, I would, Uncle," I said, Da and Uncle Mangus gathering round. "It seems the stronger lads of the village are the lazier lads who do not work everyday, but spend many a day at restorative rest. I therefore suggest that ye pilot our boat every other day and do not handle the nets."

"What say ye, Da?" I said.

"I'll put my mind on it!" he said.

"And I suggest ye double or triple the quantity of meat ye eat with vegetables and fruits, for I have observed the strong are great eaters of meat. We can afford such expenditures."

"I have observed the same," said Uncle Mangus, "It is the poor who live on grains and vegetables alone and are therefore weak."

"And lastly," Uncle Sinclair continued, "I suggest two measures of securing good health that are necessary for any young lad who would be fit and strong. First, he must vow never to drink water unless he boils it himself or there is a goodly bit of rum or other alcoholic drink mixed with it to make it pure. Second, he must swear never to visit anyone who call himself a doctor of physic, for that is the way of chronic sickness and death, lad, as well as a lightening of the purse."

"These things I swear, Uncle," I said, for I had no disagreement with any of them.

Then my Da came round on all the proposals and the three of us took them up as principles and practices. Within a month I felt vigorous and cheerful, could shoot birds from the sky or kill small animals with a thrown knife, and occasionally caught Uncle Sinclair napping with a hook to the jaw.

"So where are the muscles for my arms, Da?" I inquired, "or the whiskers for my chin?"

"May the Lord bring them to ye," said my Da. "I am doing what I can!"

In the course of my life, how often I have heard there is some revelation or event reckoned by authority as incident upon a boy becoming a man. Yet, I confess if I were to judge the matter I would find no single prompt. Rather, any number of events moved me from the stature of boy to man. Still, there is no forgetting that windy night of the October chill when I arose from my sacking pushed near the fire, and after dressing in heavy clothes was forcibly drawn outside, my knees quaking even as I closed the door behind me.

The moon was yellow and sickly, with both horns down and shedding rain. A single dark cloud passed over its shoulder. Then, such a presentment of black birds flew from the cloud's mass and along the silver crescent to the further horn that I stamped three times to drive the devil from me and, shuddering, looked out over the sea.

There was no lack of light, for the storm was of yet far off. The stars were still shining on the roaring, white-capped waves.

On normal occasions, I would not have felt my blood turn as cold as the Baltic Sea, for we fisherman of the Orkneys have both Scottish and, as I had recently learned, Nordic blood. Usually, we love a good tussle with lighting and a phosphorous sea, and I myself had been known to enjoy the sight of St. Elmo's fire wrapping itself around the spire of the village kirk.

How may I better describe this particular night than as *fatal to the blood?* Those words came to me exactly, though I did not know what they meant.

For some time, I stood in terror, not knowing what to make of my fear or which way to walk. One moment, it seemed I should move to the sea, but then, no. It seemed then I should climb the high hill toward the Dwarfie Stane or walk to the village, then to the Old Man of Hoy. I picked up a foot to move, the evil presentment still upon me but could not move. Each way seemed equally compelling, each equally wrong.

My desperation grew. In five minutes, I was wringing my hands and cursing myself for a fool.

At long length, I decided to go home.

Imagine my terror then. I had thought the decision to return home would put down the rising fear in my breast, but the first step toward that ridge where our stone croft huddled in shadowy darkness brought me a compulsion to run. I quickened my steps, resolving not to give way to irrational fears, but giving way all the same, step by step. Soon, I was racing full speed, shouting for my Ma and Da, tears in both eyes.

By the time I reached our home, my Da was outside the door in his nightshirt, a candle in his hand.

"What is it, young William?" he said. "Have ye seen the Hag O' the Dribble?"

I felt foolish before him, sheepish as a child. Still, the fear was upon me, and I could not speak.

"Back to bed, then," he said. "But, first where is thy mother, and why is it that ye did not come back together?"

The question alarmed me into speech.

"Da," I said, "I haven't been with my Ma, nor have I seen her. I went out alone, because it seemed to me something was wrong."

Da said nothing. He had lowered the candle so I could not see his face but I could imagine all the color flushed from him, so reached out for his free hand. It felt preternaturally cold, as if bathed in icy water. He returned into the croft and came out with a second lit lantern for me. We set out at a run for the homes of Uncles Mangus and Sinclair.

At one or both of those places I expected to be invited inside, calmed down by less excitable minds, given drink, food, and fruitful council. Instead, both Uncle Mangus and Uncle Sinclair greeted our news with great roars of alarm, awoke everyone in their households and sent them running to neighbors and even to the Sea Trow in the village.

Within an hour, bands of lanterns were bobbing over the plains and glens of Hoy, up and down the high hill, throughout the Dwarfie Stane, along the rocky coast and the village docks. How the men cursed in the dark, and then fell silent when they saw me. The women wept, throwing their arms around me. Every piece of old clothing abandoned upon the ground was examined, for there were many who thought my mother at last had found her seal skin and abandoned her human clothing before swimming away.

"I wish that were so," I heard my Uncle Sinclair say, thinking me out of hearing. "That is a far better ending than what I imagine."

Three days searching brought us nothing, not a scrap of Ma's clothing or a print of her foot. I had gone home early to light a fire, exhausted with the searching. Night was coming on when I heard the door open behind me and my Da and uncles come solemnly in. As the kindling burst into flame and I rolled the first log on, I felt their eyes on my back, and, still crouched, turned toward them.

"Sit here at table with us, son," said Da, his look quite serious.

"Ye have found her?" I said.

"We have not," he said, motioning me to sit.

I sat down, words dying on my lip, my Da and two uncles all looking at me strangely.

"What if she were partly a seal," said my Da. "Would that not make ye also partly a seal?"

A little quiver ran through me.

"So I have often thought, Da," I said, at last, "but I tell ye honestly, I have never had an impulse like a seal's, or at least that I could identify as such."

"Thy gift for navigation?" said Uncle Mangus.

"Thy ability to identify fish by smell?" said my Da.

"Thy keenness of sight and sharpness of reflexes!" said Uncle Sinclair. "Who's better with a sword or a pistol?"

"Do ye think…?" I said.

"Nay," said my Da, "I don't. But I'm willing to give the idea a thought and so are my brothers."

"Aye, we are," said Uncles Mangus and Sinclair at once, but then added Uncle Sinclair. "It is nonsense, of course."

"Aye, nonsense," said Da, "but there have been times, young William, when ye have looked off toward the sea and gone blank-eyed and heard nothing human for minutes at a time, then woken suddenly and shouted out a truth."

"When Sean Campbell stole the captain's boots," said Mangus, "ye woke from a fever in thy nightshirt and shouted out, 'Aha, Sean Campbell, so ye've hidden the captain's boots in thy curragh in Thule Skerrie.' Then, later, they were found stashed in Campbell's gear."

"But, I don't know how I knew!"

"Ye may have been told by the seals," said Uncle Sinclair, "though I don't believe it."

"Listen again to the seals," said my Da.

"I do not know that I have been talked to by seals," I said.

"Dream on thy mother, then," said my Da.

That night in my dreams I heard the seal voices of Thule Skerrie and saw my Ma's naked crab-picked body a foot below the surface of the Scapa Flow where the waves had pounded her tiny form into a limestone crevice.

In my Da's curragh I broke out a little of the sail and went alone in steep waves to retrieve her. Having pulled her aboard, I wrapped her in a fur blanket as Da watched from a cliff of the cove. I sailed her back so he could take her in his arms and cover her once again with kisses.

"So, was she a seal after all?" I asked.

"I don't know," said Da. "It doesn't matter. She was my wife."

"It doesn't matter to me either, Da," I said. "But the seals knew her."

"Aye, they did, son," said my Da. "The seals did know her."

My mother's swollen body was carefully removed to our sorrowing cottage. There for three days, it was laid out in white linen on the rough kitchen table. Both women and men in covered heads and dark shawls attended it with prayers and fearful keening, as if it might cast the gold coins from its cold eyelids and arise again to join the quick. But my bluish Ma was no victim of coma and spell that simulated death but of madness and death itself and from neither can any being wake—be damned those who say otherwise and line their purses by the selling of false hope.

On our chipped crockery, there were rye bread and fish and goat's cheese laid out daily with the bottles of wine on the mantle. Well I ate and drank when I was not busy being consoled or sleeping or crying. Finally, it was seen on the third day what everyone had known from the first. My Ma's sea- battered chest no longer pumped air. Then, the black priest came round with a heavy cross about his neck to talk to my struck Da about making sure her body and soul stayed to rest.

A shudder passed though me and, as I guess, through my Da. As much as we did not want to practice the Orkney custom of binding the dead, it had to be done. We also knew we had played our parts in the past when it had come to the binding of the dead relatives of others and were bound to cooperate with our neighbors now, not draw our weapons as both of us wished.

With solemn mien, we took a pallet bearing my Ma's corpse to the cemetery behind the kirk where late summer birds sang in the branches of the gathered trees, which all morning long had been collecting themselves and rustling in their dark, mournful robes. Every citizen of Hoy, from the wealthiest farmer to the most wretched inhabitant of the village was in attendance. Not just out of respect and fear for my family, but also to see what happened when a seal was given a Christian burial.

"Damned blokes!" said Da. "Look at them!"

"Aye," said Uncle Mangus. "We shall not forget this day."

"Hush, lads," said Uncle Sinclair. "Perhaps she will rise up and run for the sea. If so, I'll happily gun down any who pursue her."

I felt tears come to my eyes, whether for Ma or because of the revelation that my dead mother, on the day of her binding, was to be treated as a curiosity, I do not know. But there was an edge of anger to my feeling. I was sensible of the two knives on my person, the pistol inside my blouse quite hidden.

After the priest performed his unintelligible service over the body then spoke perfunctorily, the binding began.

First, the priest raised high the cross and withdrew my mother's name.

"No longer is there a Mary Claddah in reference to this woman," he intoned. "For now this woman's name is 'She Who Came from the Sea.'"

"Aye, amen!"

"And she has no place here, but only in heaven."

"Aye, amen!"

"And what is her name?"

"She Who Came From the Sea!"

"And where does she belong?"

"With her Father in heaven."

"And what is her name?"

"She Who Came From the Sea!"

That done, the priest moved to Ma's body and with three men of the congregation lifted it carefully into a wooden coffin. There, my Ma's toes were spread wide, and kernels of corn were placed between each. Then kernels of corn were placed between each finger and barleycorn was scattered over her chest and then over the bottom of the coffin. Then came the staking.

Previous to her being carried to the churchyard, carpenters had installed a fitting at the coffin's bottom and worked a hole through Ma's chest. Now through her body they inserted a pole they screwed into the fitting. Then, they drove a crosspiece into the top of the hole with such expertise that no one of the faithful doubted my Ma would remain in her coffin forever.

"We come back tonight," said Uncle Sinclair to my father, who was livid with rage. "To dig her up and let her go."

Chapter Four

The miller's boy stood stuttering behind his counter, filling my bag with flour as an old woman of the village kept up her patter.

"Now young William," she said, wiping fishy hands on her heavy woolen dress and then opening the drawstrings of her purse, "ye can do no better than give it wide berth."

"Aye, young William," said the miller's boy. "There is …evil… evil…in…in…."

"Evil in the Sea Trow Tavern," said Elizabeth McArthur, pursing her lips as if she tasted something sour. "Greater evil than the usual drunken lot of fisherman and thieves and whores that inhabit it."

"We speak…of….uh…uh…." said the miller's boy, in such excitement that he overfilled my bag and flour poured across the wooden floor.

"Who knows of what we speak," said Elizabeth, her eyes growing wide, her voice grown so enormous the miller, white haired and red nosed, poked his head into the front of the shop.

"What goes on here?" he barked.

"There is a man," said Elizabeth, oblivious to the miller, who rushed in to clean up the flour.

"What kind of man?" I asked.

"Why, a dark man with black eyes and a long face and a black coat. He sits all day in the back of the tavern, ordering nothing, saying nothing."

"Why isn't he asked to leave?"

"Everyone is afraid to him."

"Then he is armed."

"Nay, just of better than average height, but very dark. He looks at no one, and frightens everyone. First, the children stopped going to the Sea Trow. Then the farmers, then the fisherman, then the whores. Now only thieves and scoundrels go, and, even so, in much reduced numbers. No one dares light a fire."

"Thank ye for telling me."

Straightaway, I went to find my father, whom I was certain knew much of this matter and had deliberately kept silent about it in my presence. He had not yet returned home from helping Sean McAllister mend his great stone fence so I walked the high hill and found him at last lunching on bread and cold fish by McAllister's waterwheel.

"Da," I said angrily. "A Finman is spending his days at the Sea Trow and keeping the village in terror and ye told me nothing about it."

"And why should I tell ye about it, William?" said Da. "Any day now, he'll climb in his boat and paddle away."

"He shall not, Da," I said. "It is clear he has come to threaten me in particular."

"And why should ye believe so?" said Da.

"A conviction of the blood!" I blurted out heatedly, my shoulders shaking.

"William," said my Da, "regardless of what ye might think, ye are not to go into the Sea Trow, or even the village. Instead, spend the days here in the fields practicing with thy weapons. A rumor has reached us that the British will move their navy into the Scapa Flow and there rendezvous with the Dutch. There's no time for wild speculations about ancient creatures of the sea."

That night, when Da was off to visit Uncle Mangus and discuss the most vital questions of our fishing business, I practiced throwing my knife by candlelight, imagining the stout log by the fireplace to be the Finman's bulk. And all the next day, with uncles Mangus and Sinclair and Da continuing to instruct me, I imagined whatever target they proposed to be the Finman's gullet, and was, therefore, inspired to my best work.

By this time in my training with the pistol, I had learned to stand correctly, to breathe correctly, to let the world stand still, then squeeze, never jerk, as well as to load, clean, reload, and draw pistols by the brace from my sashes with no loss of motion. Also, I had learned to fire without first thinking of firing and to aim without being conscious of aiming.

In addition, I had found such learning applied to other aspects of my training and had begun to use the same cold approach and execution with knife, fist, and marlinespike. One would think, I might have been led by my training to caution as well as to confidence. Still, such conquering of emotion in my breast during mock combat with my uncles and Da did nothing to quiet the senseless hatred that raged in me for the black-clad Finman seated in a back corner of the Sea Trow.

"Everyone is afraid to come in!" wailed the Sea Trow owner to anyone who would listen.

"Why, he wears all black!" men would say in my hearing.

"Aye," they would say, "and carries the winds of the world in that seal skin bag hung around his neck by a golden cord."

"What is he doing here?" asked many, shaking their heads.

"He neither eats, nor drinks," observed others. "Then for what does he wait?"

To hear such cowardice from the mouths of my neighbors made me burn with anger and shame.

"Then we should attack the Finman!" I shouted to a group of fisherman, who had been complaining. But they fell silent and slipped away.

One evening filled with an icy wind, I thought I heard Ma's lonely voice blowing in from the northern sky and remembered Uncle Mangus' angry declaration that we would dig her body up and let her go. Envisioning the deed already done without my knowing, I rose from my sleep and raced outside into the storm that lashed at the cliffs of the cove. There, in pouring rain, in my soaked nightshirt, I heard my mother's selkie form howling the lament of the seal from the Shetland Islands to the Pentland Salty.

And damn my soul if there were not a note of the Finman in her voice. I looked to the village and saw a light still burning in the Sea Trow Tavern, but saw an unnatural darkness hover about it too, as if she were using her voice to throw bowls of blackness over the Finman's light.

The days that followed, for me, were days of resentment and obsession. Each moment that passed found me furious the citizens of Hoy were prevented by this loathsome specter from freely entering the Sea Trow. No claim made for the Finman's powers could be made without incurring the wrath of my twelve year-old brain. The notion that a Finman could control the wind, I found most laughable. That he could paddle to Greenland with a single stroke, I deemed to be beyond contempt. The notion that he could blow the unwary to another century, I judged most ludicrous, and that he could perform any of the lesser enchantments— such as disrupt good fishing or conjure a storm— I thought to be the fancies of children.

So, one wintry day, after the fishing had been done and Da had fallen asleep after a heavy dinner of mackerel and bread, I secured my knives and pistol about my person and covered the cutlery and pistol with a heavy dark cloak. Then, closing the door quietly so as not to wake him, and, bristling with the usual outrage, I took a stroll to the village to have a glass of ale at the Sea Trow Tavern.

"Where ye going, young William?" said a seaman I had never seen before, standing idly dockside before the tavern.

"Do ye know me?"

"Aye," said the seaman, whose eyelid drooped to his cheek, "for the Finman has described ye and bid me bring ye inside to consult about a matter."

No statement could have chilled me more, yet I made a great show of nonchalance. "Does he have business with me, then?"

"I have said that he does," said the seaman. "He is waiting inside where it is warm and drinks are to be had for the asking."

Judging from the sounds of voice and laughter, the tavern was at least half full, hardly what I had suspected. Often had I heard of how even the drunks of Hoy had given up their sanctuary to the strange Finman who had commandeered the place. I felt a jot of fear. Aye, I confess it, even more than a jot. It ran through me in such great icy rivers that my heart, in reaction, pumped up gouts of great hot blood. Then such a flash of anger exploded across my brain it was all I could do to refrain from drawing the pistol from my cloak.

"Will ye go to him?" said the seaman, "Or shall I report that ye will not?"

Without a word, I moved past, careful that my shoulder should bump his as I clattered toward the door.

Upon entering, I discovered at once the temperature was not as warm as was promised but rather cold as the Minch thrashing with snow. No fire blazed on the frigid stones of the hearth. The whole of the atmosphere was misty, sharp with jagged particles of ice. This mist the seamen breathed, quiet at their tables, their heads covered with woolen caps, their rough coats pulled tight at their necks. Not a few coughed silently, muffling the noise with gloved hands.

No glass of wine or beer sat upon a single table, nor was there in the whole place a morsel to eat.

At first I saw no Finman, nor anyone of his like. But then the air cleared and there at a bare table at the end of the room sat the long-faced dark man I had seen that night from the quarterdeck of the pirated ship. His face was unmistakable, in silhouette like the nicked cutting edge of a serrated knife. When he turned toward me there was the same black flashing of the eyes I had seen in the waves of the whitening sea.

His business with me, I did not know. What I remember are his flashing eyes, his clothing black as the Scapa Flow at night, and my consuming hatred. Spreading wide my cloak, I drew my dagger, charged across the room and leapt full upon him, slashing and screaming out my rage until at last he seemed to disappear from under me, and I lost all knowledge of what the world was about.

When I awoke, there was no Finman at the Sea Trow, only the usual cheery fire, the drunkards, and my uncles and Da. Not a few of whom were pounding me on the back and hailing me the liberator of Hoy in that the Finman had mysteriously fled.

"And who saved me, I wonder," I said, for in all of my assaulting of the Finman I recalled not one strike that had seemed substantial.

"Why this man, here," said my Da, bringing a man forward. "When we ran in to assist ye, we found the captain here already in the act of reviving ye."

The man presented by my Da with such proud ceremony was dressed in the uniform of a major in the Welsh military, which I thought to be unusual for a man surrounded by seamen. At the first sight of him, I took in my breath. Even when put on a chair and given a glass of ale I could hardly draw away my eyes, so perfectly was his white uniform cut and so blue his eyes. When he spoke, it was with an unusual softness, and though he was barely thirty, every man bent to listen.

"Young William," Da said, "ye now have the acquaintance of Captain Major Thomas Jones, formerly of the Welsh Navy."

We sat up late that night in my father's croft, our table filled with shadows from the fire, wine from the vintner, and slices of bread and goat cheese. Ranged about in our crude chairs while I sunk wordlessly into my cot were my uncles and Da with Captain Thomas Jones, Mr. Pryor and Mr. Starr, and provocateur, Jock Stewart."Ah, well. He fought the dark man exceedingly well," said the captain. "Nay, I did not intercede to save thy son, but to save the dark man. Then, curiously, of a sudden he was gone. Oh, a Finman, ye say? Well, I don't know that I credit those old stories. May we speak of my needs and how they might coincide with those of young William?"

"Ye are a man with a ship, Sir," Da said. "If ye were any man but Thomas Jones, my brothers, Mangus and Sinclair, and I would be setting thy dead body out to sea in a flaming curragh at this moment, Sir."

"As well ye should be!" said the captain, "but I am Thomas Jones and here is the long and short of it. The British have issued me a letter of Marque as a privateer either hoping I'll destroy French and Spanish shipping for them or that they'll be able to concoct a case against me as a pirate. Perhaps they hope both. But it scarcely matters, since it's a certainty that the French, as a result of all this, wish my ship ten thousand leagues under, and the Dutch, who sail with the French, would love to ingratiate their allies."

"So ye are surrounded," said Da.

"Surrounded, aye!" said Captain Jones. "By the French, the Dutch, and our allies, the British. In particular, we are blocked to the west."

"Worse, yet," said Uncle Sinclair, "ye are surrounded in these seventy islands and confused waterways of the Orkneys, where no charts have been made, no shoal is expected, no channel clear, no wind less than fluky, no sea less than treacherous."

"A mixed blessing," said Captain Jones. "To have a superior navigator in the Orkneys would swing the advantage our way. Then we could spring free by various stratagems."

"Mangus or Sinclair could serve superbly," said Da, blowing blood into his handkerchief.

An awkward silence. Jock Stewart got up, went over to my Da and whispered in his ear for some few moments. I saw Da's eyes widen in protest, but after a moment they quieted down a bit. He nodded a little and Jock Steward went back to sit again in the rocking chair by the fire.

Da spoke up. "Jock has explained to me that the *Bleeding Gull* was fleeing French and Dutch ships and having lost them in the Orkneys would do well to secure its advantage by finding an excellent navigator on Hoy. However, he adds that Captain Jones will not be able to soon put such a man ashore. Nor can the Captain Jones guarantee his return in the next few years. Therefore, he cannot take a family man aboard."

"Whom do ye wish then?" said Sinclair, to Captain Jones.

The captain remained silent.

"The boy!" said Jock Stewart.

A confused murmur of protest, broke out, as did appeals to my Da, who lifted a hand, not wanting to hear out all arguments.

"Mr. Pryor," said Da, "Jock told me that ye have been drawing up suggested articles of agreement between Captain Jones and me. I would like to hear them, please."

"Certainly," said Mr. Pryor. "Article One: On the death of William Claddah, Captain Thomas Jones agrees to take on the full responsibly of parentage of one William Claddah, Jr. From this day forth, Captain Thomas Jones shall provide ample room, board, clothing, education, and sundries as befits a gentleman of the realm to William Claddah, Jr., son of William Claddah, to whom he shall function as godfather on the sea."

"For his part, William Claddah, Jr. will submit to his godfather's training as man of the sea, scholar, privateer, and pirate."

"Aye, then," said my Da, refusing any further argument.

Chapter Five

The deck of Captain Jones' *Bleeding Gull* was in no way similar to the deck of the ship I had stolen abroad some months before on the snowy night in Westray Island harbor. The deck of this one, as large as the other by the measure of my strides, was nevertheless, in the light of day, seemingly diminished in size, no doubt by a recent outfitting of forty guns, twenty on either side, and huge racks of cannon iron at each gunner's station, as well as by a bustling crew of well over a hundred shouting and sweating men as they tugged and swore at bags of provisions and gear.

I had intended to make for some conspicuous part of the ship to establish a position from which to wave to my uncles and Da, but before I had made ten feet aft the heel of my shoe stuck tight to a tarred seam of the heated deck.

"Ow!" I cried, then sprawled, red faced, forward into the shoulder of Andrew Stewart, the gunner's mate, who cursed me for a dunce, then went about his business.

"Send word from the Americas," shouted my Da, who pretended not to see. I gathered up my sea bag, which I had dropped, and made for the hatch as if that had been my intended destination from the start. After a few bumps and bruises with able seamen, I descended with the intention of depositing my sea bag and then climbing again onto the deck. Then, came a second shock, with others following in close order. I had expected a well-lit hold, but it was dim with only one swaying lantern. Then, too, I had expected to be able to walk about, but found I could not, for the ceiling was no more than five foot in height and I could move only in a crouch and even so knocked my forehead on a beam every few feet.

How then had I been able to walk about the hold of perhaps the same ship on that snowy, remembered, night? After a few seconds thought, I concluded that I had previously been forced by the fierce rocking of the boat to go about it in a crouch and had therefore been unaware of the closeness of the ceiling.

Now, it was terrifying, and I felt a moment's panic. Then, no sooner than I found my wits restored, I clattered into all manner of water casks and barrels of provisions and gear, from great sails to capstan bars to kegs of rum and ale, and then heard a low moan. Nay. Then, I heard low moans, a multiplicity of them.

My little knife in hand, I pushed further into the hold, where hung at least seventy hammocks in the faint light, perhaps fifteen of them swaying, each with two heads, one above the other, each dangling four legs. I heard a woman's cries, then another's, then the laughter of a man and a woman; and, finally, the voice of a woman.

"Come into the back here, young gentleman," said the voice, with a high giggle. "We'll make a man of ye, I believe."

"Hush, Maggie," I said, putting my sea bag under the hammock closest at hand. "Haven't I known ye from the time I was born?"

"Oh, it's William!" said she to the bunch of laughing girls, none of whom had been known to stay away from the Sea Trow long. "And he should tell me 'hush,' when it's me who's fifteen and it's he who's only twelve years-old."

"Another word, Maggie, or any of the rest of ye, and I'll have ye put from the ship by the captain himself, who has no love of whores."

At this remark, the seamen, still pleasuring themselves and their whores in their hammocks, let loose great peals of laughter that paused for satiric comments bandied about in the dark, then started again and continued until my eyes watered over and my ears burned with rage.

"And if Captain Jones wishes to throw whores from his ship," said a seaman, at last, "what man of his crew will vote for his side?"

"Perhaps, I will," said a sailor man in a girly voice, "for this wanton whore has taken up my horn too tightly in the dark."

At these words, there was a new cascade of laughter, and, in truth, I might have laughed as well had I uttered such words instead of him. As it were, so great was my humiliation that I called the man out to face me.

"Pig face shite!" I barked out, my unworthy oath disgracing my Da, my Da's Da, and his Da before him, and setting off not only a fresh storm of laughter but two lanterns that lit the forecastle simultaneously.

"Fight, fight, fight, chanted the men," and it seemed to me then that I could be experiencing the shortest nautical career in all of human history.

"Nay. Certainly not," I thought to myself. "Surely, at some time, somewhere, someone must have died on a gangplank before reaching a boat."

"Dispatch him quickly, Thomas Peacock," someone yelled, "that we might return to our swiving."

Thomas Peacock stood grinning in the forecastle, so short in stature that he needed not crouch to avoid striking his head on the ceiling beams but with arms and legs so massive they seemed hewn of the *Bleeding Gull's* bulkheads. In keeping with the fashion of the day, he wore no underclothes, but rather wrapped his shirttails fore and aft around his private parts, thus giving off a ripe whiff before pulling up his trousers.

I swooned under the attack.

I staggered backward, momentarily certain of defeat, but then regained clarity.

Peacock charged like a bull and knocked me to the deck, whereupon I immediately flipped him over and climbed aboard his massive chest.

"Get off me!" he yelled, kicking at the deck and wildly flailing his arms. "Get off me, I said!"

In an effort to stay atop his bucking body, I gave him a little rap on the head with my pistol's barrel.

"Schizzlewit bastard!" roared Peacock. "What's that all about?"

"Now, lad!" said a tall seaman, leaning down and talking to me softly. "There's no reason to go knocking Thomas Peacock on the head."

"But he's twice my size!" I protested, now sitting on the massive Peacock's chest.

"But, lad," said the seaman, "he's a drunken man. And even if he weren't, he's the worse wrestler on the ship. Everyone thrashes him. Now ye just ride on top of him there for a bit like the rest of us do and then he'll fall asleep like a kitten he will, and ye'll be free to go."

"Maybe I'll just let him go now!" I said, surprised at finding so bulky a seaman as Peacock lacking sufficient art as a brawler to force a lad of my size from his chest.

"Nay, lad, no. That would be a mistake. He'll just bull rush ye again, and sometimes the tide turns with him on those foolish bull rushes."

Fifteen minutes later there was no one left in the forecastle but Peacock, myself, and three of the Hoy girls, including Maggie, all of whom were still lit by lantern light.

Peacock's thrashing was only sporadic, but still I hesitated to let him up. The girls crouched down beside us, as if they had never seen one man astride another.

"Young William," Maggie said, in a voice so serious I could scarcely credit that it came from her, "how is it that ye have never asked to swive with me?"

"Well, I don't know, Maggie," I said. "I have never given it thought."

"Do ye not find me attractive, William? Have ye never noticed the fullness of my breasts and the shapeliness of my legs and buttocks?

"Aye, Maggie, I have noticed," I said, giving Peacock another little knock on the head, "but I have thought myself too young for such things and have lacked money for it as well."

"I think ye may let Peacock up now," said another of the girls. "He seems to have fainted."

Looking down, I saw that Thomas Peacock was, in fact, either unconscious from combat or having fainted, a slight smile teasing his lips.

"Is it that ye look down upon my family, young William," said Maggie, "ye, whose Da is a drunkard and whose Ma was a seal?"

"Aye, she was a seal," I said to the girls, whose eyes grew wide, "and I am a seal as well."

I rose from the body of Peacock and stood up into a crouch high enough to allow my head to touch the ceiling of the forecastle.

Maggie was trembling in the faint light, and the other girls were trembling beside her.

"Are ye saying that ye Ma was a seal as rumored?" Maggie said, at last, and I noticed the other girls backing up from me slightly in spite of the fascination that gleamed from their eyes.

"And do ye say that ye are a seal as well?" said one of the others, Mary, I believe it was, for the voice that came to me from the dark came from the direction of Mary though it sounded nothing like Mary's voice.

"And do ye make love like a seal then," said the third girl, with a medical interest.

"Aye," I said. "I do make love like a seal and must have ample icy water in which to curl and dive."

"O God!" cried the girls all at once, and then I was saved from further exercises of my wit by the boson's whistle.

I clambered past them, though they reached out to restrain me and made it up the hatch, not worrying they would follow directly on my heels, for none of them were more than half clothed. Reaching the deck, I was delighted to see that the gangplank was still attached to the pier and my Da and my uncles were still waving their hats at Captain Jones and the crew.

Mr. Courtney spied me dawdling at the rail and in danger of being trampled by the men making their way off the *Bleeding Gull,* so ordered me to the quarterdeck where I would be under the direct supervision of Captain Jones. There, the waiting was not long. A favorable wind had blown up in the harbor and those who were going ashore were hastened ashore, including Maggie and the other whores who were escorted from the ship to great applause.

Seaman raced up the ratlines and riggings and threw their bodies across the yardarms. Mates manned the halyards, the warps were released, and rowed skiffs positioned us into the wind, and then we were gone, the sea kicking up just below the bowsprit, the square sails billowing one by one as the men in the yardarms dropped them.

I waved to my Da and uncles as long as I could see them, my eyes all misty with the bracing windy weather lit by such a gorgeous sun. If ever it occurred to me then that I would never see them more, I do not remember so terrible a moment, but I do remember reflecting on how I would likely not see them on the morrow, and the thought was a knife.

"Put thy sorrows aside, lad," said Captain Jones, "his spyglass held toward the channel between South Ronaldsay and Kirkwaa through which we would reach the vast expanse of the Scapa Flow. "If we do not have trouble today, we shall likely have it tomorrow."

"Aye, Sir." I said.

"And ye must remember," he said, "that ye are of surpassing importance to us."

"I hope to serve ye, Sir," I said and meant it, fiercely.

"Young William," he said, "it is not often that a young man of thy age finds himself with such a heavy responsibility as ye have here. I am aware, Sir, that in many ways it is utterly unfair to ye, as well as is the risk. But I can only say to ye now, that in exchange for ye efforts in our behalf I will grant ye whatever is prudent and is in my power to grant. Is that understood?"

"Aye, Sir," I said.

"Good!" he said. "Now tell me. If ye saw a galleon headed at us when we reach the Scapa Flow and coming from the southwest or north-east from the Baltic, how might we escape him?"

"Only by running toward him until we are west beyond South Roundsay, then turning north," I said. "There is a shallow along the west coast of Kirkwaa that we may rub over but will catch him. Otherwise, we would be caught, unless he were a long way off."

"Bless the child!" said Captain Jones. "And may we be caught in these seas by a ship larger than our own, if that ship were a long way off."

"Nay, Sir," I said, "not if we are willing to sail the Orkneys and the Icelandic or Irish Sea or around the Isle of Skye, and then back again if that way be blocked. May I ask our destination, Sir?"

"Our first port of call, Sir?"

"Aye, Sir."

"Wales."

"Wales?"

"Where piracy begins in the coal dust of the mines, young William!"

"Well, Sir," I said, "I repeat, if the ship is now a long way off, we can not be caught. However, if the destination is Wales, there is no plan that can be made in advance through these islands. Plans would have to be made according to the wind and the tides and the skills of those who pursue us, Sir."

"Thank ye, William."

The captain then turned his attention to the meeting of his officers, mustering at the foremast, the wind and water swaying us blandly under an untroubled sky, rainbow leeward, as we sailed, wind in our hair.

"So we sail willy-nilly," said Second-in-Command, Mr. James Morris, fretting at a rail, his long thin fingers tapping the sea-salted wood. "Our training has prepared us to execute plans, but we have no plans. This being the case, how will we proceed? And to what end?

"We'll adjust as we go and end where we must," said Mr. Pryor.

Mr. Morris frowned. " This morn we rose to a blood-red sky. Didn't we see it!"

"Why, man, we are privateers!" said Mr. Pryor, a thick, burly man not much taller than I who must have not used his razor in days, for he was dark with stubble. "We are no longer a part of the Welsh Navy, for there is no Welsh Navy, the British having sunk it. What can we do now but to accept the King's invitation to bloody the French and Spanish?"

"It's a simple business," said Captain Jones, ignoring the chatter, pulling me aside to the bow and speaking quietly to me, as if he were now my kindly teacher, so handsome in the sunlight. "For now, the British are relieved of the fret that we'll put their ships under, for they know we fight their enemies. In exchange, we receive respite from the British and the right to plunder the French and the Spanish."

"And what intelligence do the British share with us?" cut in Mr. Morris, taking a step from the rail. "What do they care if we go off blind and are killed? Do ye think as privateers we endear ourselves to the British?"

"We have no delusions," said former officer, Mr. Musgrave, a man with little chin, but a fine manly voice, "Neither do the British. Do ye think the British are under the impression we will share our spoils with them, or love them eventually? How do ye think of it, Mr. Starr?"

"I do not think of it," said Mr. Starr, flatly, "Thinking of this matter is a ludicrous activity, like cursing the hangman before being hung. I side with the captain and fight for my country. When we're strong enough to again fight the British, we'll again fight the British!"

"And be happier for it," said executive officer, John Courtney.

As I would later observe, dark of hair and eye, Mr. Courtney was a great one for doing all the proper things. Most pirate ships or ships of privateers showed no pride of ownership but were ragged, filthy ships from hawser hole to stern. Though perfectly maintained in relation to firearms and sailing, for no pirate or privateer could tolerate the notion of losing a prize because of a clogged swivel gun or a slipped stopper hitch, they were stinking hulks in matters of simple cleanliness, unless pure luck directed tempest winds and rain to cleanse them.

Mr. Courtney, though, was a privateer of another sort, whom I could fathom ready enough early on. Each time a seaman, now released in part from the discipline of the Welsh Navy, either scraped a boot or spat upon the deck or tossed the refuse from his plate where he might, Mr. Courtney suffered a pained look upon his visage and looked away, his shoulders hunched and trembling with spasms of discomfort and despair.

So too was the kindly and always just Second-in-Command, Mr. Morris, who was also subject to dark moods, as well as to momentary feelings of loss. As I understood it from the seamen of formerly lower rank, Mr. Morris had always been a great one for making the men regularly wash and change their socks, but now, in the new era, he had to hold his tongue and, consequently, underwent the fevers of the damned.

"And I, too, side with the captain," said Mr. Morris. "I speak loyally as a true man urging caution."

"And that he does, mates," said Captain Jones, taking up a spyglass that he trained on the eastern sea and employing a firm, but patient tone, "but I do remind Mr. Morris that we have before this functioned very well without receiving intelligence from the Welsh Navy. I speak of those forays we have previously made to the Spanish Caribbean for the glory of Wales. In those past campaigns, we were buttressed only by our common cause with pirates."

"Aye, Captain, but this is a new matter," said Mr. Morris. "Our safety is compromised as never before. There is no longer a Welsh Navy, only us Welsh men in this mediocre ship. Also, the English might turn on us at any moment it suits them. Beyond that, thy friend Captain Henry Morgan may love ye because he thinks of ye as a fellow Welshman and son, but Henry has always loved gold more than any breathing thing. Lastly, my captain, will the pirates of New Providence still love ye when ye arrives not just to kill Spaniards, but to act as a competitor?"

"Well spoken and thought out," said Captain Jones, his spyglass still trained on the channel to the Scapa Flow. "Ye make a hold full of excellent points, not one in error. But I ask ye in all sincerity, what are our options?"

"None for me, Sir," said Mr. Musgrave. "As a former junior officer of the Welsh Navy, I'm certain to be pressed by the Royal Navy the moment I leave this ship."

"My father tells me strange men have already come calling at my house," said Mr. Starr."

"I do what Dandy does," said Bulldog Mr. Pryor, putting a protective arm on Mr. Starr's slight shoulder.

"Alright," said Mr. Morris.

"Do ye wish to stay on, Mr. Morris?" said Captain Jones. "No man is a prisoner on this ship, and if ye say that ye'll be happier put ashore, we'll do it for ye. No man here will but drink a toast to ye in friendship, for ye have been a just and caring officer, as well as a brave man."

"That is true!" said Mr. Courtney.

"Well, I don't know," said Mr. Morris, "I love ye lads, but I am getting older and I have grandchildren… and the Royal Navy will pass me by. Still I must think on it. I must think on it. I can help ye, I know it!"

The moment was a poignant one. I sensed and suddenly feared that someone would speak up and tell the older man that he was not so keenly needed. To preempt the question, I blurted another.

"Captain Jones, after the English defeated the Welsh, why did they allow ye to keep this ship?"

There were several minutes of silence, no one daring to say a word. The captain kept his eye to the spyglass but I could hear a grinding of his teeth.

"After the war I was exiled to a miserable estate in an ugly, poverty stricken part of Ireland, where I lived in a place no larger than a pig sty."

So saying, the captain put down his glass and turned toward us all.

"There I might be living still or be dead by now, but my railing away against William and Mary put them in fear of their lives, as did the exploits of the Spanish at sea. Therefore, they decided in their wisdom to give me this ship, that the Spanish and I might annihilate one another.

"Then ye hate the Spanish?" I asked, speaking out of turn…to my embarrassment… as if I had somehow grown older. The sea then kicked up a mighty swell and ruffle under us, as if it were impatient that we rush down the route turning silver that was forming in my mind.

Thus I knew from that point that the great seas of the earth were my heart's destination, despite their trickery and violence to breath and bone.

"Only the Spanish of our time," said the captain. "I have no dislike of the Spanish people of other times."

"Will ye educate me of these matters?"

"Aye, young William, but I have to think of other things now."

There seemed a thickening of the air, for it was going on three o'clock in the afternoon and the sun would be setting soon. We finally reached the channel above South Ronaldsay, a critical juncture. Once into the channel there was no wind to turn back and we were committed to reaching the Scapa Flow, even if the entire Spanish navy was awaiting us with its ships of war. Luckily, we reached the open sea without incident. From over my shoulder the sun threw a radiant blush like the flowing raw yoke of a broken egg on the lightly tossing waves of the Scapa Flow.

"There are two sails," I said to the captain, pointing to the southeast where they were scarcely peeking over the far horizon. The captain hastened to train his glass onto the sails, and then handed the glass to me.

"What say ye?" he said. "These are more thy waters than mine."

"Dutch ships," I said. "A Dutch hoy and a bilander, but then a third ship behind the first two, possibly a French ship, from the look of the rigging."

"Then it's run we must, lad," said the captain. "How brilliant I seem to myself now for inviting ye aboard."

"Aye, Captain," I said. "The night is coming on. It would be wise to douse all light and bypass Kirkwaa to the northwest and then run all the way northwest past Stronsay before morning. Then, we should hide northeast of Stronsay during the day. This fleet behind us will likely sail northeast of Kirkwaa and tuck in there so as not to lose us in the coves. Then, they'll find so little wind and the going so dangerous they'll have to sail back to the Scapa Flow to find us again. By then, we'll be half way to Westray."

"And if they split up?" said Captain Jones.

"There are treacherous, unmarked shoals and many a ghost just off Sanday Island," I said, "just north of Stronsay, the Island of the Beast. There are also the two deadly channels of the Orkneys, one off Sanday, where the merfolk live, and the other nearby between Rousay and Mainland. Also, among these places, are islands which move, and islands of seal people, and islands from which no one returns. There are places from Stromsay to Rousay to Kirkwaa where the common Dutch seaman may not be persuaded to go."

"I see," said Captain Jones.

Then he gave the order. The great square masts shifted. The helmsman moved the rudder. A hundred throats gave out with a roar, and dozens of blood roses sprang from men on the yardarms beating their hands bloody to let out more sail.

The next morning out blew up breezy and bright with the sun bright in a hot, clear sky.

We were anchored fast just north of Stronsay, not to set sail until our watchers on the Cape of Stronsay reported our pursuers either trapped in irons north of Kirkwaa or headed out again to the Scapa Flow or attempting to split up and sail around Stronsay from both sides at once.

"It seems they want to do some waiting," said Mr. Morris, with a laugh.

"A characteristic of the Dutch," said Mr. Musgrave, "to drink all night, and then fight at their convenience."

After seeing to the appointing of Captain Jones' quarters as a part of my dual function as navigator and cabin boy, I descended again to the hold. There, I made my morning ablution below the bowsprit while balanced above the sea on the pissdale, which in those days was nothing more than an extended board with a hole cut in it. Mightily did I struggle to tidy up my arse, but found I could not without risking a plunge into the sea, so made do with the chance cleansing afforded by the spray kicked up by the *Bleeding Gull's* bow. Set about such a task, I was customarily given to great thought, but this morning I was pestered by the men behind me, all of whom were issuing dire threats should I not make haste.

"May the bitches who spawned ye drag ye off to hell!" I cried.

Instantly, I had cause to regret my remark, for a hand sporting fingers as large as sausages was around my throat and squeezing, pulling me backward, and a sgian duhb was instantly in hand and sawing away at the giant's thumb.

"Little Bastard," growled Isiah Corn, still half asleep and depositing me with no particular ceremony back in the hold, whereupon he shook his head a couple of times and crawled out on the pissdale. There, he did his business half consciously, looking off blankly at the sea.

I waited for a while to see what trouble he would cause me next, but then grew bored and wandered off toward the quarterdeck. I knew that Captain Jones would be there at the whipstaff before he and I and a second shift of men took our turns for breakfast.

And find him there I did, dressed as a gentlemen of the Welsh Navy, in fine hat and white wig, double breasted blue tunic, white trousers and hip boots. He was as elegant a creature as roamed the seven seas, his handsome face of soapstone only half-visible, for he had a spyglass to an eye, and its shadow cloaked his features.

When he lowered the glass, Captain Jones spotted me at once, and, bidding me forward with a wave of his hand, suggested to the helmsman that I be allowed to take the whipstaff, for in those early days of going to sea in tall ships there were not yet many wheels with spokes, but still the necessity of moving a rudder and the need of acquiring the skill to do it.

I grabbed the whipstaff and at once felt the staggering weight of the ship as it swept through the ocean, but managed to hold the *Bleeding Gull* on course.

"This is the *whipstaff,* whose name the world's seamen have chosen to give the male organ," said Captain Jones. "It is nothing more than a giant pole on a pivot with its bottom end connected to a rudder that turns the ship."

"Aye, Captain," I said, out of respect, for well I knew what a *whipstaff* did, without instruction. There were other things that bothered me more.

After some few minutes, Captain Jones spoke directly to the matter.

"There is word about the ship that ye begrudged thy mates their last few private minutes with their wives before we left the Island of Hoy.

"But, Sir," I said, "not one of them was legally married to the other."

"So, I grant ye," said Captain Jones, "but does not the clergy of England operate in cooperation with the king?"

"I have heard said so," I said.

"Then should we, as free men, ask leave of the king's representatives to marry or should we behave as free men and take what wives we will?"

"We should take what wives we will, Sir," I said slowly, having given the matter thought for the first time. "But what say ye to the notion that the men sweating with their wives in the hammocks should have been helping the other men working on deck."

"Well, perhaps the crew will decrease their earnings," said Jones. "It is none of my business."

Such information knocked my cap around, and I found myself red faced and sputtering. "But…" I cried.

"No time for talk now," said Jones. "There is our breakfast bell."

In the galley we sat at long table with the second shift of seamen, many of them still red-eyed and smelling of rum, even as cook brought us coffee and bowls of bread mixed with sliced onions and radishes. There rang out a constant chorus of shouts, even taunts, and then, the heavy pounding of boots.

Then, to my concern, in stalked the huge but sleepy Isiah Corn, who groggily pulled up a chair at the table just opposite Captain Jones and myself. I fought the impulse to duck my head and avoid the gaze I was sure Corn would let fall upon me, but nevertheless soon caught myself looking into the excellent breakfast that the cook had set before us.

"We never ate so well when we were in the Welsh Navy!" cried out Corn, apparently according me the attention a man accords his neighbor's buttons.

"Aye!" said Captain Jones.

Of all the dozens of men in the galley, he alone took the trouble to eat his victuals with his thumb and a knife, which I took to be the mark of a perfect privateer gentleman. The rest ate as I did, shoveling the food in rapidly with two stuffed hands and then wiping our hands on our trousers. It was an established truth among all adventurers of the sea that all matters, including grease and vegetable, should be rubbed into one's clothes at every opportunity—a preparation for the day when a stiffen jacket or pair of trousers would be needed to deflect a sword's blade.

"Corn," said Jones. "What has happened to thy thumb?"

I grew quiet as a rat in a barrel.

Corn paused in his eating and bent his huge neck so that he could stare with black eyes at the bloody slash of his bread loaf of a finger. No ready answer sprang to his lips. First, he stared at the bleeding finger from every angle, examining it, turning it about in the faint light until he had a close view of one end, then the other, and was able to gauge its drip as it deposited blood on his shirt. Then, the curious seaman tasted of the blood, holding a spot of it on his gangway of a tongue as if testing it for salinity.

"I do not know how I've been so injured," he said, finally. "Perhaps I've been injured in battle."

At this remark, all of the mates at the table laughed, for bonuses were paid to all privateers seriously injured in battle.

"Corn," said Captain Jones. "It is doubtful ye have sustained that injury in battle. We have not engaged in a battle in a good long while. Even if the injury were sustained in a battle, which it was not, it is doubtful the crew would vote ye a bonus for so slight an injury."

"Aye, Captain," said Corn, in deep complaint, "but how may we be injured severely enough to earn a decent bonus when ye win so often from strategy and from such distance? Why, there are times when a man may wish to ship out with the Dutch, for Dutch commanders have the spirit of the fray and love to turn their lads loose in lovely hand-to-hand against the enemy. There is a wealth of good in all of that, Captain Jones, I say."

Having spoken his piece, Corn shoveled the rest of his bowl of food into his mouth and chewed most moodily.

Captain Jones' face then underwent a transformation, as if a light had fallen upon it. He stood nimbly at the table and wiped his mouth and hands with a greasy cloth, as a hurried gentleman might. Then, bidding me follow him at once, he strode immediately from the streaming galley, up the hatch, and onto the sunny quarterdeck where for the second time that breezy morning he assembled his officers.

"They'll come over Stronsay at first dark, over land carrying long-boats," said the captain, "and board us at night. We'll be overwhelmed."

"Aye, the Dutch," said Mr. Morris. "Of course, they will. But I imagine we'll turn it on them."

"Mr. Starr and Valley," said the captain, please inform the gunners that we will be under attack from the shoreline at first dark and that they are to light the waters so that our sharpshooters will be able to pick off Dutchmen and Frenchmen in their longboats."

"Mr. Morris, at my command, set sail to the northwest of Stronsay, then southwest past Skara, then northwest past Westray, then southwest past Mainland before turning south."

"But, Sir," interrupted Mr. Morris.

"I know none of those places are charted, Mr. Morris," said the captain. "That is why young William is with us."

"In the dark, Sir?"

"Aye, Sir!"

"By what sense, Sir?"

"Well, sir. I understand that almost any of his senses will do. I am assured, for instance, that he can navigate by the sense of smell."

"By smell, Sir?"

"He can smell types of crops, livestock, fish!"

"Fish, Sir!"

Mr. Morris turned to face me, his visage, once kindly, now drawn up in anger, yet no further word escaped from his lips. Only at that moment did I realize that Captain Jones had not only already divined me to be the great thief of his ship at the Isle of Westray but had come seeking me as a member of his crew precisely because of it.

I turned away to hide the whiteness of my cheeks.

Later, Captain Jones brought Mr. Morris and me together on the quarterdeck.

"Young William, for the rest of tonight ye are not to be found more than three foot from Mr. Morris' side. Thy mission is to follow the escape route ye have already outlined to me, but make adjustments if ye have to. Mr. Morris, thy mission is to translate young William's strategy directly into naval commands and to keep me alerted of exigencies. Is that clear?"

"Aye, Sir!" I said.

"Sir," started Mr. Morris.

"Mr. Morris?" asked the captain.

"Sir?"

"Can ye get us through the Orkneys at night?"

"Nay, Sir."

"William?"

"Sir?"

"Have ye sailed the Orkneys at night without instruments?"

"Aye, Sir."

"The discussion ends here, Sirs. At thy posts."

Just as night fell, there was a preternatural silence, not only of birds but also of wind and sea, as if all of the Orkneys and even the Scapa Flow and Northern Sea awaited the splash of the first longboat keel in water or the first cutting stroke of an oar out toward the *Bleeding Gull*. At a signal from Captain Jones, Mr. Musgrave, taking care to keep his head concealed, pumped a slow love song on a concertina as if to lighten the heart of anyone rowing toward the *Bleeding Gull* with cutlasses and pistols.

Minutes were allowed to pass. All hands on deck or in gun ports or in masts with rifles waited and listened. A second order was given. Simultaneously, the gun ports opened. The sky was rocked by impossible thunder and night and day flashed on and off. Longboats raced the choppy sea from Stronstay to within thirty yards of the ship, but many of the dutchmen caught inside them, including those closest to us, seemed to panic at the first sounds of the cannons.

"Fire!" screamed Curtis Payne from his position behind a bulwark, and our riflemen made tubs of blood of the closest longboats to us. The attackers screamed. Splotches of blood ran down their faces and chests and backs and longboats reared up like horses. Other longboats behind the first to go down buckled or capsized or fought to turn back.

I stood on deck, enthralled, unable to take cover. Then, a second volley rained bloodshed and death among the attackers and rifle fire from shore and the more distance longboats pinged through the *Bleeding Gull's* rigging and plunking its hull.

"Cast off," ordered Captain Jones.

It was easily done. The anchor line was fixed to a crude slab of stone that could be slashed away without loss of time. The sails were already loosened and were therefore only dropped. The course was already chosen. In only a moment, the *Bleeding Gull* was sailing seemingly inland at an impossible speed in the absolute dark and then, after only a few minutes, it was gone.

It remains, beyond doubt, one of the most mystifying escapes by in all of Orkney history, but not, perhaps, so mystifying to us.

From the beginning, we, or I, had known that we could negotiate the channel moving southwest down Stronstay and had known with a certainty that our pursuers could not. It was always just a matter of getting them stuck in it or a bit behind us before we started down it that was the concern. As it were, they attacked us to the northeast of the channel with the crews of the two Dutch ships in longboats, doing us the favor of disposing of the ships themselves; then they obliged us further by running their French ship aground trying to follow the channel west of Stronstay.

"Ye may turn to port here, Mr. Morris," I said. "The southern channel begins here."

"And how would ye know that?"

"Do ye see the light of the high hill, sir?" I explained. "That is where the Widow Lambert does her reading. Now, we must move quickly two hundred yards to the outer edge of the channel to avoid any ship that may have gone aground in an attempt to reach us earlier."

"Is there such a ship?"

"Aye!"

"How are ye able to say so?"

"I'm not permitted to say, sir."

"Then, ye Orkney people do have a code?"

"I have not said so, sir."

In the pale moonlight, we could just make out the silhouette of a large twenty-gun French sloop caught bow first in the mud, its bowsprit pointed to us like an insect's long beck and its backside wagging harmlessly in the rear.

"Poor thing," said Mr. Morris. "Should be put out of its misery."

"I agree, sir," I said, taking cognizance that the captain and Mr. Starr had come again to the quarterdeck, followed by Mr. Pryor and Mr.Courtney.

"Gentlemen," said Captain Jones. "Here is the case, in short. We are on the run and have no time to fiddle with this craft or its crew. On the other hand, Mr. Courtney here tells me we need its munitions and supplies. On another hand, we are not willing to lose life over any of these matters. Any suggestions?"

Mr. Starr raised a hand.

"Aye, Mr. Starr."

"Let the Frenchman handle it."

"Aye," said Mr. Morris. "Only a Frenchman can understand a Frenchman."

"Aye," said Mr. Pryor. "Bring out Monsieur Tozier."

A few moments later, the grotesquely proportioned Tozier had bumped his head on a spar and was doffing a gentleman's top hat.

"More rouge, more rouge!" he cried. If Tozier had been able to stand up straight, it might have been said that there were no men of almost equal height aboard the *Bleeding Gull.* As it were, his backbone collapsed upon itself and ran like a switchback road in several places, giving him the appearance of one in need of being stretched out on a board and flattened. Nevertheless, half man, half beast, he strutted the deck with an arrogant aplomb, holding high a bright lantern as we drew ever closer to the wallowing sloop.

"And a cheery hello to ye Frenchie lads from a countryman," shouted Tozier, not minding that his lantern made him a fair target for any Frenchman sharpshooter perched on the dark ship's forecastle. "I am Monsieur Dickie Tozier, whose snake, ye may judge, is long enough, to serve as a warp between us."

Most of us laughed a little at that in our places of hiding, but Mr. Morris scowled, and we quieted down, trying to take the matter as a serious business. There followed a number of paragraphs in French from Tozier, and then, stunningly, a laugh from the French ship, followed by a comment and then a flood of laughter.

"Tozier told them his snake sometimes wakes him up at night and takes him for a walk. The Frenchman then yelled that the story is probably true because the queen sometimes says she dreams of being entered by a worm. That's when they all laughed."

"Aye," laughed Tozier, staring off into the inky night and no longer bothering to speak French. "Ye lads are as quick of wit as ye were when I was pleasured to serve on thy sloop."

To this last comment, there was no reply, save the lapping of small waves against the *Bleeding Gull's* hull.

"The time for meaningful negotiation approaches," shouted Tozier, "but first, Snake wishes to say a special fond hello to my good friends, Andre and Pierre Lafitte. Now on to other..."

Tozier's speech was interrupted by the sound of feet running the deck of the French sloop and two splashes in the water, one quickly following the other. In the moonlight, we could see two swimmers headed directly for our ship. Pulling them aboard, we found them cooperative but sputtering with anger.

After some moments, Tozier returned to his original task with as upright a posture as he could manage. "We have consulted the fugitives," he intoned, "and have found, in short, difficulties in allowing thy craft to continue to exist."

A scream of rage came across the waterway, presumably from the French captain.

Tozier was heartless.

"We will need the oak chest in the hold. Please do not attempt to lighten it. We will also need the four barrels of powder aboard. Ye may keep the shot. Please send five flintlocks. Thank ye. Ten cutlasses. Please send the three kegs of port and the remaining keg of dinner wine. Nothing else of thy larder will be required. If the captain were to include the contents of his safe the gesture would be looked upon with great favor."

"If all of the above can be accomplished by the use of small boats within the next hour, no action will be taken against thy craft or crew and we will bid ye adieu."

While awaiting the French captain's response, Mr. Starr quickly signed Andre and Pierre Lafitte on as crewmen of the *Bleeding Gull* and I caught a glimpse of an amused Captain Jones smiling in the dark.

"Captain," I said, "will the French comply?"

"They will," said Jones.

"Why are ye so certain?"

"Because Tozier has discovered the French captain's secret and with one word more could cause the captain's loss of career and crew," said Captain Jones.

"Oh," I said, feeling less clever than I had previously thought I was. Not far away, the Frenchmen were loading their goods into their small boats for delivery to our larger one. An hour later, our sails were filling and we were leaving the French sloop stuck in the mud somewhere in the black night behind us.

"Captain," said Andre, "I congratulate ye on thy generosity."

"But I have shown none," the captain said.

"Ye have let our ship go," Andre said.

"Only an illusion," said the captain.

"But when the tide is high, the ship will be able to break free and will be on its way again."

"The tide is already high," said the captain.

When we had quite passed Eday to the West but not quite Stronstay to the East, we caught a quick slip of northwest wind and then beat up the short coast of South Eday. There, we rode with the wind's icy touch swirling amidships and battering at the hatches until at last we passed the coast of North Eday. Finally, we sat in irons to the northwest of the Isle of Westray.

Soon daylight came on with the barking of the seals. It was fine to be alive. Gazing upon Westray, an island I never much fancied, I never-theless was thrilled to watch the cold sea pounding upon the rocks and thought how fine it looked-- my whole country. Captain Jones and the officers alike, as well as the cultivated of the crew, moved toward the bulwark of our craft almost without thinking and gazed all about them with such wonderment that an ocean of pride swelled the hold of my mind.

"These are my lands," I wished to cry out. "My seas!"

But, of course, I held my tongue.

There, at a place I thought as a lad to be the top of the world, we caught a small breeze at last.

"And what now are our prospects, William?" said Captain Jones, ambling over to my side.

Mr. Morris looked much chagrined.

"They are excellent, sir," I said. "The French ship is no doubt locked forever in the channel, and the two Dutch ships would now seem to be seriously undermanned."

"Damn thy estimates of casualties," shouted Mr. Morris. "Can those two ships get at us?"

"If they left one ship behind and brought the bilander," I said, feeling suddenly the bashful lad again rather than the hero of the moment. "They could sail around the Island of Sanday to the east and then brave the strait between Sanday and North Ronaldsay. If they did that, they could perhaps catch sight of our sails before we disappeared again through the strait between Westray Island and Papa Westray."

"Then we could be caught!" said Mr. Morris angrily. He took a spyglass from Mr. Starr and stalked to the stern rail of the quarterdeck, where he focused the glass on the strait between North Ronaldsay and Sanday."

"It is not likely the Dutch captain even knows the existence of that strait," I said. "Even so, it would be hours before he could get there, maybe most of a day. By then, we'll be out to Sule Skerry and striking out for the Irish Sea."

Mr. Morris seethed at the rail, and the captain found just enough wind coming over the rocky back of Westray to move at two to three knots toward Papa Westray that sat atop the western Orkneys like an ancient cap of stone. How magnificent it became in that milky morning light with the cold wavesj rising in roaring peaks about it, but it was ghastly too! There, at the end of the earth, it sprouted ancient houses of rock over much of its surface, yet showed no sign of ever having fed, comforted, or clothed any race of men.

"And what in the name of God are they?" said Captain Jones.

"Why, they are the homes of the old ones," I said, not liking to say the words aloud. "Some say those houses are thousands of years old and their owners knew the deepest secrets of the world. That is why those stones have never fallen."

"They were men and women, like us all," said Captain Jones. "And the stones have not fallen because they built those houses well."

"May those ghaists protect us!" said Mr. Morris.

"Beyond those ghaists," I said, "the Dutch will never see our sails more."

Chapter Six

Forty miles west in the shelter of the islet of Sule Skerry we woke in anchorage in the morning to the barking of the seal. How delicious the North Atlantic on so fine a fall day, with the cold water but moderate, the mist thick like a custard but golden and not shivery with ice, and not far away the blue back islet itself so rich with puffin and the gray seal sprawled across the rocks! I felt tears come to my eyes as I rushed to the quarterdeck and watched the day break over the islet, not heeding the bell for breakfast, but rather dreaming of my old Ma, in spite of myself. After a while, the captain returned from breakfast and stood beside me at the quarterdeck rail and silently watched as a mother with disapproving eyes and a nasty bark chased her pups across a sea-washed shingle.

"Are ye a man, then," said the captain, "who believes in the myths of the sea?"

"Are ye asking if I believe in the seal folk?" I asked.

"I am," said Captain Jones. "I have heard that ye men of the Orkneys believe in the seal folk."

"Some do," I said. "I would not be one of those men."

"I see," said Captain Jones. "I am glad to hear that ye do not. I don't think it wise for a man of the sea to be shackled with strange fears and shadows that may cloud his judgment. If I am to be thy mentor, I must insist ye put aside any of those Orkney beliefs ye may have been raised with."

I was startled by the captain's remarks. I had understood from the first that he would teach me his craft, but in my ignorance I had assumed I would learn from him by watching, not by being actively taught.

"I renounce them all," I said at once.

"Very well!" said the captain. "We can begin perhaps today. But tell me first, how do we sail to Wales from here?"

"Go southwest to there to Stack Skerry," I said, pointing the way with my finger, "and then further southwest to Cape Wrath, then continue southwest on a line to the Minch, bear around on the Little Minch and out to the Atlantic, then curl in again to the Irish Sea."

"Aye, yes," the captain said. "That's enough. I know the way from there."

"Aye, sir!"

"William," said Captain Jones, "ye have served us well as a guide through the maze of the Orkneys and it would be churlish of me to withhold my admiration, but before I give of it unreservedly let me learn more."

"I am at thy service, Sir."

"Quite so," said the captain, "and I am gratified by it. But, in the course of our travels, I have not observed ye taking a fix on any star."

"I have heard of such a thing," I said, "and understand the principle. But, aye, I have not done."

"And I noted too that the winds of these islands might twist or corkscrew or turn in any direction from Sanday to Westray to Hoy or Eday."

"Aye, they might," I said.

"In short," said the captain, "there is no consistency."

"Nay, none."

"Then how, may I ask, do ye fix our position," said the captain, "for we have sailed by night and no land forms we've passed have been distinct enough for ye to recognize them in the dark."

I shrugged my shoulders, not knowing how to answer.

"And how do ye know that direction which is north or south or east or west," Captain Jones asked, "for I know full well that no such deduction can be made from an observation of the tides?"

"Well, because that way is Iceland," I said, pointing to the West, "and from that I deduct that the other way is east, and that way is north, and that way is south."

"Nay, William," said Thomas Jones, "that doesn't answer it. Let me put it another way. How do ye know that that is the way to Iceland?"

"Why, because it is!" I burst out with a laugh, and it took a few moments for the captain to convince me he was not joking and a few moments more to see that my answer had only mystery to it.

"Why, I don't know," I said, as puzzled as he. "Iceland has always just seemed that way, but now that ye've made me look at it, I see, like ye, that there is no sense in it just seeming that way. Just, it does just seem that way."

"Not to me, it doesn't!" said Captain Jones. "From the look of it to me, that direction could be any direction, unless I could fix on the North Star, or....or..."

"Or what, sir?" I said.

"William," he said, "I would like to conduct an experiment with ye, but before I do, I must ask ye to agree never to share the experience with anyone else. This is a very important matter, and I wouldn't ask ye, but… well, ye seem so unusually intelligent and bound by loyalty, I think…"

"I will be very glad to serve, Sir, and will say nothing to anyone."

"Very well, then!" said Captain Jones. "Let's get to it then."

Captain Jones clapped his hands in some excitement and then called to Mr. Morris, who immediately reported.

"Mr. Morris," said the captain, "I expect the clouds to the northwest are bringing flurries of snow. Set sail at once to round the edge of Stack Skerry at its western shore. By then, I'll return."

"And if the Dutch ships…?" said Mr. Morris.

"There'll be no Dutch ships," said the captain, beckoning to me with a wave of his hand. Then, I followed him from the quarterdeck, down the short flight of stairs, and into his cabin. In the cabin, the captain sat at his desk and momentarily studied what looked to be charts and then rose from his chair and having taken a key from his waistcoat, opened a drawer of the heavy mahogany secretary that was bolted to a bulkhead. He retrieved the drawer and placed it on his desk. Then, with a little flourish of his sleeve, as if to enact a small ceremony, he withdrew from the drawer an oblong bronze plaque and placed it on his desk. Inset off center was a circular disc covered with glass, and surrounding the disc and extending across the surface of the plaque were numerous markings— flowers, dashes, letters T, G, L, S, O, L, P and M, tiny stars, and curious moons or suns.

"Look here, William," he said. "What is it that ye imagine ye see?"

Under the glass, a trembling blue iron needle appeared to be floating in air."I see a needle." I said. "Its tip points to a fleur-de-lys and its opposite end points toward a rose."

"And what do ye suppose the flowers represent?" said the captain.

"I don't know!" I said.

"I'll give ye a clue," the captain said. Then he revolved the whole apparatus so that for an instant the needle appeared to be headed where the fleur-de-lys had been but then quickly flipped back to its former position and found the rose there instead.

"Now what do ye make of that?" said Captain Jones, rising from his desk again to pour himself a brandy.

"Nothing yet!" I said, in anguish.

"Put thy best mind to it!" he said, and with that he finished his glass and left the cabin to make his rounds. He did not come back for an hour and a half.

"Has understanding at last come upon ye?" he said upon his return.

"Aye," I said. "It is a magical device."

"Magical?"

"Aye!" I said. "That is why ye must hide it from the crew. Otherwise, ye might be taken for a sorcerer."

"There's something in what ye say," said the captain. "In this day, captains do hide such instruments from their superstitious crews, not just to avoid charges of sorcery or witchcraft but also to make their crews in awe of their navigational skills and themselves indispensable. Otherwise, many of them would be taking a long swim home."

Captain Jones laughed and poured himself a brandy, and then, thinking about it, poured me a brandy as well. I took it up at once. So delicious it was on my tongue that I closed my eyes to savor it.

"But come now," the captain pressed. "What do ye make of the instrument itself? In what way is it magical?"

"Why, the point of needle always points north," said I.

"Good lad," said the captain, enthusiastically. "What else?"

"If the arrow pointing North is lined up with the fleur-de-lys, then one can quickly see that these stars and moons and suns on the plaque indicate various other directions and that this rose indicates South."

"Aye," said the captain.

"And these letters on the plaque indicate the directions of the winds," I said, "though I do not know what the letters themselves signify."

Aye!" said the captain. "I will explain the letters later. And these dashes?"

"I don't know," I said, "but if each were numbered, a captain would be able to shout up to the helmsman how far to adjust the whipstaff to reach his destination."

"Astonishing," murmured the captain, "I am delighted by thy observations, except in one particular."

The captain bid me move away from the desk and relax in a stuffed chair of the cabin. He pulled up a second chair and sat across from me, only a few feet away. He lit a cigar and offered me one, but I refused it. He took a sip of his brandy, a puff of his cigar, pulled a pistol with shiny gold plate from his boot and handed it to me, grip first. I gratefully accepted and slipped the pistol into my boot. Smoke curled in the space between us. We sipped at the brandy.

"Thy notion that the compass is magical is in error," he said at last. "That it works may mean that there is an enormous mass of iron or lodestone near the earth's northern pole that attracts some other metals that become susceptible--by what circumstance I have no idea. Such a metal is on the tip of the arrow of the compass. Therefore, the arrow points nearly north and one can determine the direction of actual north by mathematical deduction."

For a moment, I was stunned by such knowledge. An instant later, I burned to know how some pieces of metal become susceptible.

"I am in sympathy with thy wonder and await discoveries," said the captain.

Finally restored to the quarterdeck with warm coats bearing the marking of the Welsh navy wrapped about us, we hunched against the sharp flakes of snow beating against our backs and settled in the speedy but seemingly motionless track of a great ship. The day darkened about us and we heard from every direction the crashing of the sea and the blowing of the whale.

On occasion, a seabird swooped low to discover us, shrieked his displeasure, and was gone, off to the Hebrides or lonely St. Kilda.

Mr. Starr took his turn as officer at the whipstaff, Mr. Musgrave beside him. Mr. Pryor had use of the spyglass and searched the horizon for sight of Cape Wrath, the most northwestern point of Scotland. Mr. Morris strode the deck below us, shouting to the seamen. Captain Jones, as if to flatter me further on this most magnificent day, approached my post at the stern rail.

"Lad," he said. "Here's yet another chance to show thy gift. Can ye point a finger at where we will find Cape Wrath before Mr. Pryor finds it?"

"It will be there," I said, pointing my finger to the southwest, "but before we reach it, care must be taken to avoid Craeghatir, which will be there." Again, I pointed my finger.

"Craeghatir!" said the captain, "I have heard of it, but my memory fails me. Can ye refresh me?"

"Sir," I said. "Craeghatir is a place of evil, a lonely rock off the stormy Cape Wrath. Those that venture there leave their bones behind them, sir, for there are hidden places and a monolith and a berserker possessed of the spirit of a wolf."

"Or so they say in Orkney," corrected the captain.

"Or so they say," I said, catching myself, for, truly, I did not believe the story. "But, sir, there is such a rock!"

"Land ahoy!" cried the crewman in the crow's nest and Mr. Pryor simultaneously, Mr. Pryor having spotted the storm lashed Cape Wrath and the crewman having spotted the cliffs of Craeghatir.

"Make for the starboard side of Cape Wrath and into the Minch," ordered Captain Jones. "What madman on this earth would try to catch us or trap us in there?"

Mr. Morris, who had returned to the quarterdeck, conveyed the order to the men and then turned toward the captain.

"Thy reliance on Henry Morgan could be the death of us!" said Mr. Morris, "What difference does it makes that he calls himself a 'privateer' now?"

Captain Jones stared at him, for the moment, speechless. Then, electing to say nothing, turned his back on the older man, whose brows were becoming white with snow, and spoke instead to me.

"So, ye are correct again, young William. What I think ye have, most of all, is an almost uncanny sense of latitude. I can't account for it."

A suspicion then struck me that he perhaps he could.

"I don't know the word," I said.

"Nay! I don't suppose ye do. But we'll continue working together, and in the course of thy studies I'll make these things clear to ye. Now, let's sail, Sir. Let's sail."

"Aye, sir!" I said. Then I kept away and enjoyed myself.

For me, Cape Wrath was the end of the world I knew. I had never in all my sailing been south of it, and seldom closer to it than a few miles off. Its great cliffs were battered by a savage, splashy sea of icy waves like mountains and windy blasts from the arctic. Also imposing were the ghaist ships that ringed around it, for hundreds since the time of the Vikings had been picked up by the winds and hurled at the cape to the bottom of the sea.

Captain Jones be damned. It was no Orkney myth that armies of men had lost their lives there. Once drawn close to the rigors of the Cape and the hellish racket of mad sea birds—the puffins, the razorbills, the fulmars, the kittiwakes, and guillemonts— the mates of *The Bleeding Gull* themselves grew white as ghaists and heard the ancient voices.

"Back to thy posts," screamed Mr. Morris, and it became necessary for all of the officers to draw their weapons.

"Ye shall be among the dead instanter if ye do not!" shouted Mr. Pryor, his pistol aimed first at Lewis and then at Boots, our tallest seamen with the exception of Tozier, who took shelter in the hold.

At Mr. Morris' direction, I took control of the whipstaff, yet it did little good. Without hands to man the braces, the sails luffed and the ship made such little headway we rolled sickeningly. Their broad backs resting against the capstan, where they sat smoking at their leisure, the lords of our boarding parties, Lemuel Valley and Curtis Payne, laughed at their fellows and laughed doubly loud when a beam sea spit over a bulwark and put out their pipes.

Captain Jones finally stepped forward and signaled for his officers to put down their pistols.

"I apologize, lads," he shouted, so that he could be heard over the sound of the wind and waves and new falling snow. "We have been officers in the Welsh Navy too long and have made the mistake that we still have authority over ye, our mates. Please forgive our impertinence!"

There was a murmur among the seamen.

"In our new status as privateer, of course," said the captain, "it is quite clear that all of us are equal and that no man serves at any position without the approval of a majority of the others."

"Aye, aye!" shouted a chorus of voices.

"Very well then," said the captain. "The choice belongs to ye. What shall we do?"

There was a minute of silence, each man looking at the other for an answer.

"What have we to do?" shouted the cook, finally.

"Well," said the captain. "We may continue with unmanned sails and either be capsized, or live to wreck on the stacks of Cape Wrath."

"Nay, Captain!" shouted the crew.

"Or we may come about and tack into the teeth of the storm and possibly run into the Dutch ships!"

"Not to my liking!" said the cook.

"Or we may sail to the starboard of Cape Wrath and duck into the mouth of the Minch, where we may hope to find safe harbor for the night in a small bay off the town of Lochinver."

"That seems desirable!" shouted Curtis Payne from the stern of the ship.

"But we will have to face the ghaists!" shouted Lemuel Valley.

"Better to face a ghaist than be a ghaist!" Payne responded with authority.

"Aye!" was bellowed from every direction.

"Shall we vote?" shouted the captain.

"Aye!"

Through the light mist, we swept past the cape without incident, save the spotting of an eider drake and two ducks riding the surge. Tucked into the Minch, we were safe in harbor just after dark, our anchor flukes taking their first icy bites since the Northern Ocean.

The day had all in all been an easy one, so after we had all dinned in a lordly fashion on salted beef, radishes, and English beer, Captain Jones ordered me to his cabin to receive what he termed the "first of my nightly bits of instruction." With some trepidation, then, I knocked upon his door. I had never been to a school as such, and was quite at a loss as to how to behave.

It was with some relief, therefore, that I discovered that I was not to be the only student present or Captain Jones, sitting at his desk, the only teacher. Mr. Morris was sitting beside Captain Jones' desk in a cozy leather chair, and the other cabin boys, as well as seaman Thomas Boots, were there, as nervous as I, all bolt-upright in the straight-backed wooden chairs brought in from the galley.

Mr. Morris began the instruction by naming all the oceans of the world and discussing their probable locations. Then, he put his knowledge of them together with his knowledge of the seas, whose locations caused brief and minor disagreement between himself and Captain Jones. Then the two of them informed us of the continents and of the areas of the earth where there might still be continents unknown.

We listened in some disbelief, I fear, especially to news of ice caps in a southern ocean and yet other oceans on the other sides of Cape Horn and the Cape of Good Hope, which we had, hitherto, heard much of but had considered sailor talk of the taverns.

"It is time to throw off thy provincialism, mates," instructed Captain Jones. "There is more to the world than the Northern Ocean. Land masses drift apart, islands surface like whales from the bottom of the sea, die in fire and sink, waves covering all. Is there anyone who doubts it?"

Not a hand rose in response, yet I felt a certain skepticism about me. Captain Jones spoke on to reveal much never before imagined by me, of how the winds blew and currents ran predominately from North America to England and France and Spain and then from Spain blew and ran back across the ocean to the Caribbean. So, too, he explained, there was an equator in the middle of the earth so close to the sun that the weather was always burning hot, and that there were latitudes called the "horse" latitudes so hot and dry that horses were often driven from the ships to conserve water.

Cabin boy Billy Goode raised his hand. "And I have heard," he said, "that there are places of no wind."

"Aye," said Mr. Morris. "There is a band around the earth, near the equator, that is a place of no wind. It is called the *doldrums*. A ship such as ours may languish in the doldrums for days."

"And Finmen?" asked Boots. "Are there Finfolk in the Minch, as I have been told?"

A hush settled over the room. It occurred to me that Boots was new to the crew and had not had the opportunity to witness Captain Jones' sourness at the most passing reference to the sea's more darkly surfacing creatures. I feared a storm. As Boots waited for an answer in perfect open-faced innocence, Captain Jones' lips tightened into a straight line. At last, he spoke.

"Boots," said the captain. "When I have heard men profess of Finmen, I have heard of kinds. The first I have heard of is akin to a man, but with fins cleverly folded behind him like a cloak. The second is a furred thing of little design given to paddling in small craft in storms and jerking fishing lines from lads who go sharking without crosses. Of what kind of Finman do ye speak?"

Boots lowered his eyes and looked at the floor.

"I take it, then," he said, "that there are no such things as Finfolk. I thank ye for the counsel, Captain Jones, and shall turn my curiosity toward more useful things."

The captain nodded, and, after drilling us on the material presented during the course of the evening, sent us off to our hammocks.

The next day, the Minch blessed us with little wind and unseasonably sunny weather, and Captain Jones, not to be outdone, declared, if not a day of actual holiday, at least a day of no real chores. It was rather to be a day of lying about and furthering our transition from a ship of the Welsh Navy to full-fledged privateer.

That day, all day, I was drunk with the sea and the spectacle it provided. Not poetry, nor wine, but rather with the sea all buttery and delicious in the morning in its first brush with sun and all the sun-dappled display that followed in the afternoon. I stood on the quarterdeck or roamed about the ship from bowsprit to stern, all drenched with the glory of the Minch and the Outer Hebrides riding the blue sky in the distance.

For the sheer blessed fun of it, we ran flag after flag up the mast and cheered them all: the Dutch, the French, the Spanish, and others we would soon fly aloft to fool our prey. Then we ran our Jolly Rogers too, the blacks with their various arrays of skulls and bones and the French *Jolie Rouge*, as red as blood, that promised no quarter.

When the latter flew aloft and spread wide in a trickle of wind there was a great, high-spirited roar from the men below. Then, the mates, on Mr. Morris' order, dragged forth crates of clothing and trinkets from the hold that had been taken from North Sea pirates when the *Bleeding Gull* sailed as part of the Welsh Navy.

When the crates were broken open, the men let out another "hurrah," so ludicrous were the garments within, especially as they gleamed in the sunlight as spread about the deck.

"Ye shall strip off ye clothing of the Welsh Navy and put each article folded in a crate," shouted Mr. Morris. "Only then may ye put on this outlandish garb!"

Soon, tattoos of lions and kraken appeared on muscles and backs and calves and huge belt buckles gleamed over silk and billowing pantaloons.

Seaman Tozier pranced about, offering his ring to kiss, laughter attending him. Captain Jones ordered kegs of beer brought on deck, and the singing began.

For my own wear, I found a pair of corded Welsh trousers and a Malucca blouse.

"Take these, lad." Mr. Pryor held out three sashes he had been quick enough to snatch for my sake. "Crossed sashes for thy shirt and one for thy waist!"

"Do I need so many?" I asked.

"What sort of man will ye become?" said Mr. Pryor.

"I don't know!" I laughed.

"Take three then!" he said. "Come with me, lad."

I had a liking for Mr. Pryor, though all I knew of him was that he had a strapping back and the head of the beast, so thick in back that it seemed as wide as my chest, his neck as thick as his head.

Mr. Musgrave, on the stair at the quarterdeck, was patiently issuing cutlery from a crate to a line of waiting men.

"Make way, mates," growled Mr. Pryor and the line gave way. "Carry but one sword, William, a second being cumbersome, but at least three other blades—in thy belt, thy boot, and strapped to thy thigh."

"And now for the knives," said Mr. Pryor, and both he and Mr. Musgrave tested and issued me three knives without asking me if I already had knives of my own.

Mr. Pryor laughed quietly.

"Always assume a pirate to be armed," he said, "unless he is stripped naked, his arse examined, and there be no stick of wood within five hundred yards!"

"Aye," I said.

Some mates blackened their faces, teeth and eyes, and greased their clothing, so best to turn a blade.

"See here, that man, Johns Dea," said Captain Jones to me, toward evening, as we prowled the deck.

Following the direction the captain was pointing, I spied Johns Dea spread out drunk in the bit of clear space directly before the capstan.

"Aye," I said. "It's Johns Dea, who does no work, but lies about drunk all day in the sun, letting others do for him."

"Aye," said Captain Jones. "Yet I have no authority to discipline a man on a privateer. Such a matter is the business of the crew."

"Then why will the crew not do its business?"

"Because he's a marksman, lad, and as brave as a fool. Did he not dress on Hoy as he is dressed here now? Nor dress in London with the same saucy cheek? Of that, I may assure ye."

The captain's words meant nothing to me but mystery.

"Lad, I speak of sumptuary laws that reign over Europe. A man without property can be imprisoned for the putting on of fine wigs or fur collars or silks or jewelry. Those pantaloons and sashes and rings could be his tipping point. And that tight waistcoat with gold buttons, lad, could get him hung, tarred and strung up at the mouth of the Thames as a warning both to mariners and to peasants not to improve their lot."

"And was his lot so painful before he set to sea?"

"Aye, lad! Most of this crew hails from Scotland and Wales, two countries that were bullied into poverty by the British and then suffered the loss of their young men to the press gangs of the Royal Navy."

"Aye," I said, "I have heard ye speak harshly of the English many times."

"Aye," said the captain. "In the Western world there are two nations that may fairly be called 'evil.' One is Great Britain, for what it does to its own. The other is Spain, for what it does to those who are neither Catholic nor Spanish."

"Thank ye for the answer. May I ask ye one question more of good and evil, and this a selfish question?"

"I know thy question, young William," laughed Captain Jones. "Ye want to know if ye are to be evil or good, or better yet, ye wish to know thy place in the world. Is that not so?"

"Aye, Captain."

"Why, ye are to be both good and evil, Master William," said Captain Jones. "I knew it the moment I knew who it was that first stole my boat. Thy destiny is to be a pirate captain and ply the waters of the world for a hundred years and fifty years."

That night, in my hammock, I stared into the dark; bidding it to speak such words to me that I would pass quietly into sleep, but long did I hear only the creaking of the masts and the snoring of my mates. Then, at last, when I dreamed, it was not of glory, but rather of a long black cloud rolling into the Minch over the Outer Hebrides and a second storm creeping northward over the Isle of Skye.

Suddenly, the darkness was upon us, and a thunderous convulsion of water threw hammocks from their hooks. The *Bleeding Gull* writhed in harbor, and we woke to deafness, falling one upon the other, lanterns breaking into flames. In an instant there was screaming and shoving, men beating out fires with their blankets. Hatches opened and then slammed shut again when seawater rushed in.

Then, in complete blackness, we rolled from side to side, first dipping a yardarm to starboard, then a yardarm to port, all helpless as lambs, not one of us sure he were awake but rather suspecting he were caught in a nightmare.

"Do nothing, men," shouted a voice. "Do nothing, just hold tight. There's nothing to be done."

The night thundered all about us, doubtless filled with lightning as well, but we saw no light, only trusted that we were well anchored, battened down, and sound enough to last.

Prayers went up all about me, prayers to God, and to the devils, and an older seaman took up praying to all the gods he knew, just as a precaution, though he said to all there were none he believed in.

By and by, it was over, the Minch having redeemed itself for the beautiful day it had given us the day before. Peeking from the hatch, we discovered not only a suddenly calm sea but also the sun coming up in a light mist of some elegance, like lace, and we poured on deck.

There was no damage, a tribute to our luck. The masts were sound, the sails intact. Hatch covers, both fore and aft, had proven water tight, and no long boat, nor coiled line, nor small piece of gear had slipped from its place. It was as if the storm had playfully picked us up and, like a caring child with his toy, put us down again.

Mr. Morris and Mr. Pryor strode happily about on the quarterdeck, apparently appreciative of our good luck, when, suddenly, Mr. Starr lifted his right hand from the scroll work at the stern rail and pointed to a point west, not five hundred yards from where we lay in anchorage.

Others saw him point as well as I and let out a roar. I raced to the quarterdeck, hoping to get a turn at one of the brass spyglasses that were being passed about.

Two tall-masted ships lay wrecked in the Minch, neither to arise, prayers or no. One lay broken in half at amidships with both ends flooded, masts broken free, and its great sails washed over with small breakers. The second was aflame from deck to mizzenmast, its sails blown into rags, its waterline a foot from the tops of its bulwarks and its ongoing slow drop to the bottom of the Minch apparently straight down.

"What flags do ye make out, Mr. Pryor?" asked the captain.

Mr. Pryor studied the matter intently though his spyglass, then handed it to the captain.

"Both flags appear to be Dutch," the captain said.

Billy Goode, the cabin boy, appeared suddenly on the deck with Mr. Starr's and Mr. Morris' spyglass. Then, all three men trained their glasses on the two ships.

"Many bodies in the water," shouted the lookout from the crow's nest, and the men crowded the waist rail and shouted up that burnt bodies were drifting up against the *Bleeding Gull's* hull.

"Young William," said the captain, handing me his glass. "Look for thyself."

I focused on the wreckage of the two ships, their hulls and masts and sails now in ruin and also the heaps of debris floating on the Minch. Then I spotted the bodies. I refocused and saw them clearly, most floating face down and already bloated in the morning light as the tide brought them to us by the dozens in a ghastly invasion of the dead.

Putting down the spyglass, I sensed the captain beside me.

"There are those who would think that a miracle has saved us," said the captain.

"I do not," I said.

"That's a good lad," said the captain, "Who would guess that the Dutch would be so foolish as to come for us here?"

"I guessed none of it!" I said.

"What were ye thinking of it last night in thy hammock?"

"I thought nothing," I said.

"Aye," said the captain, with a sweeping arm indicating the wreckage of the two Dutch ships and the two crews of drowned seaman. "And after, when ye slept, did ye see black sails."

"Nay, sir," I said, "I dreamt nothing."

"Nothing?"

"Nay, sir."

Looking upward toward the left, I saw the captain's blond hair disappear into the blinding sun's light.

We made due haste, nostrils pinched and faces drawn. We fished the face-down Dutchmen from the drink with marlinspike and grappling hook and said the holy words we prayed would bind them down.

"There'll be none of these for Davey Jones or Fiddler's Green," said Mr. Morris, "For the Dutchman has always been a good Christian man."

We burned the gathered bodies on the beach, then hoisted yard and good mates high to sail billowing out before a following sea. At the dinner bell, some stayed aloft or in the waist; others ate their fill and lost their rations before they slept. Our labor done, Thomas Boots's long fingers wiped sweat on his shredded trousers and he and I stretched out on deck, our heads propped up on coils of line.

"If there be one true God, it was a Finman murdered the Dutch," whispered Boots at last, the syllables of his words easing in as if in the dress of an echo from far away.

"Nonsense," said a mate, Temper Blount, close at hand, lying down as if to sleep, his head at rest on a holy stone used to scrape the deck. "I have seen no little boat in our wake or heard anyone speak of such."

"No matter," said Boots, his eyes grown grave,

"A Finman is under no rush to announce his whereabouts. Seeing the high surge of a wave upon him, he has a trick of sinking his boat until it passes over."

These words of his for some time hung over us, and we were silent.

"Aye, I know it," said Blount, at last. He was an Irish man with thick black brows and ruddy cheeks, the color of apples, "but that is only to avoid being turned over."

"Or to escape from view," Boots said, turning his head toward us and gazing level..

"To escape from view," said Blount, sucking on a pipe that as he lay lifted its bowl to the skysail overhead, "What would be the point of sinking his boat, no matter if it be of sealskin and sure to be bobbing up.

He might choose to give three warts with his little oar and be to the shore of Iceland?"

"Three warts?" I said.

"Strokes," said Boots, "And those for show, for it's sure he drives his boat by other powers."

"Three warts," said Blount, ashes failing to his chest, "To cross an ocean?"

"Aye," said Boots, his eyes sharp upon me. "It's all the same. Sink or flee. A Finman is not likely seen."

"If it's a Finman ye wish to see," said Blount, "Ye must sail back the way we came, for some say near Stronsay of the Orkneys is Hildaland, where sea one day met sky. From there, they say, they came."

Again, there came a silence, as if the very waves had ceased to rise and the blessed sun was on the verge of winking out.

"Aye, through a bank of clouds at the end of time," said Boots, "And ever afterward, as summer home, Hildaland floats as an island a few feet above the sea or under, appearing to one mortal man, now and then, but not the other."

"As they say," said Blount, rising from where he lay on deck to throw a shadow from hatch to scuppers, "but there is sometimes seen a Finman riding in black silence here upon these coasts, beyond Cape Wrath and out to Stronsay and Westray Island. Some have spied him nigh to shore and ventured out to sea, only to find him fled, mysteriously."

"Can he not be a Finn from Finland?" I asked.

"Nay, Master William," said Boots, leaning forward, his voice again grown hushed. No mortal man could travel so far in a little boat as Finland to Orkneys, though that boat is made of sealskin or leather. He's a fisherman fishing in storm-thrust sea with his little line, but yet is daunted by Christian cross and sprole, which is a singular device that dangles two hooks. And where he fishes no fish may bite or wind may turn without his leave."

That night, in my dreams, it was no storm that brought the Dutch ships to grief. As if through a dark sea, I saw the Finman climb the anchor chains to the knights heads of both and there open his bag of winds. Then, I saw, wide-awake, the winds go rushing out.

"Stifle thy cries," said Boots, having run to my hammock to clap a rough hand over my mouth, "Would ye have thy mates rouse ye out and pitch ye over the Bleeding Gull's side."

In vain, I tried to shake my head.

"I heard the Captain walk the deck last night," said Boots, keeping one hand over my mouth, and with the other hanging a lantern on a ceiling hook.

"How may ye have heard him during such a storm?" I asked him with my eyes.

"I did I tell ye," said Boots, his tall, frail frame shaking in lantern light, his long fingers of his free hand gripping the web of my thumb. "The Captain saw the Finman, mark my words. There's nothing of storms and sea that our captain doesn't know."

As if as a second thought, Boot removed his hand from my mouth.

"How may he have seen a little boat at night, in driving rain, with great waves crashing all about?"

The light from the candle in Boot's hand made a little bower of wood of the compartment in which my hammock swayed.

"Have ye noticed a sinister cast to the look of seaman Platt who prefers to stay below on sunny days and also hangs a sealskin bag the size of a fist from a chord that dangles from his neck?"

"Aye, I have, but have thought nothing of it."

"What if he were a Finman?" said Boots, his features grim, the candle's light falling away before it reached his eyes.

"Platt!" I whispered.

"Aye," said Boots, "It's the lust for silver that pulls a Finman from the sea to walk the earth in the form of a man. Often, it's said, in Aberdeen, to beware the Finman when taking on a crew. He'll dress the part of common seaman to earn a wage in coin that he will never spend, but collect like pretty shells."

"Will ye not tell ye stories in hell!" yelled a groggy voice from the forecastle compartment just abeam, "I was dreaming of morning cream for the table until ye woke me up with chattering."

"Did ye not just learn from the Captain," shouted another voice, "That such as a seal is what a fool calls a Finman."

"If he wishes to deceive us, Platt should not wear the bag, or look so sullen," shouted yet a third voice, a mild one, from a hammock aft in the dark forecastle, where mates hung like sway carcasses in a butcher's shop. It is only the captain he deceives, my dears."

"Aye," cried one. "Nay," cried another. Then cursing broke out and flared up until all was quiet again and Boots and I, still awake, he crouched beside my hammock, were all that remained unsleeping in the wide Minch's motion.

"It may be that he cannot change his look or mood and dare not do without his bag of winds," whispered Boots, more ominously than before. "It's said in Aberdeen that a Finman might earn his silver without incident; or, if crossed by Captain or any mate, will loose the bag so his winds might blow the ship to splinters or so far away it's seen no more."

"So ye believe this Finman, Platt, called his little boat to him through the storm, and left this ship at night and attacked the Dutch?"

"Aye," said Boots, "And I believe one thing more. The Captain saw him."

Throughout the next few days, Mr. Morris and Captain Jones taught lessons in navigation by day on the treacherous seas of their home, which roared between Scotland, England, Ireland, and the Outer Hebrides. By night, we harbored snugly, there being no alternative in such a maze of shallows and rocky islets beset by unpredictable storms.

I thought of the Minch as the wildest place in the world, the Isle of Skye the loneliest, especially when visited by wind and unsettled weather. Crossing the Sea of the Hebrides after a night of heavy rain, we sailed a thick soupy mist that never lifted until we had achieved the narrow Little Minch and then harbored, as we thought, near Gighay.

In a noisy sound there, we were kept awake all night by sheep on nearby ledges and seabirds, as well as midges and flies. Then, ashore, on the next evening, mates in long boats trapped lobsters on the Isle of Muck and others shot black rabbits in the Trenish Isles. For a time then, all seemed a holiday. There was laughter on the ship from morning to night.

Then, finally, we found our sails starched with wind as we entered the North Channel on our way to the Irish Sea.

"That is the Isle of Man." The captain pointed out the famous Island. "Beyond the Isle of Man to the west lies Liverpool, England. To the southwest of our position lies Cardigan, Wales, where we will meet Captain Henry Morgan, unless the English stop us."

We were to find, soon, there was no wind or high sea or ship that sailed upon the sea that was destined to stop us. We sailed the Irish Sea unmolested and slipped unseen into Cardigan Bay off the coast of Wales, a body of water known the worldwide as a witch's pool of piracy. There, from the rugged, rocky coast of Wales, wandered a steady stream of short, swarthy men past the ruins of ancient castles and brutal lure of coal mines to listen to the strange urgings of the sea.

There were crews to join and new ships to hijack. To the men aboard the *Bleeding Gull*, Henry Morgan was the greatest pirate in the world, a worthy successor to the legendary Welshman, Sir Francis Drake, and also a mentor of Captain Jones, and some years later an inspiration to the Great Pyrate Bartholomew Roberts. No amount of deference paid him could be thought excessive, yet fear was a part of it.

On first spotting his ship among other pirate vessels in Cardigan Bay, the men ceased speaking his name aloud. Rather, they used it in whispers. Mr. Musgrave, hailing Captain Morgan's ship when we had drawn close, seemed in such poor voice that Mr. Pryor was forced to take over the job for him. By the time the hailing was done, our whole crew was mustered out and each man was making every effort not to fidget in his place while awaiting the appearance of Captain Morgan.

By the time of Morgan's appearance upon his quarterdeck, so great was my expectation of the famous Captain of Piracy that no man or creature may have satisfied it lest he be eight foot tall and in possession of a mighty tail. Therefore, I felt a momentary sinking of enthusiasm when he at last stepped out, human, upon the boards and tar. This sinking, I repeat, was momentary. For no sooner had the captain taken a step and extended an arm toward our Captain Jones, then did the entirety of our crew raise such a din of salute that no more mighty a welcome could ever have been extended by so few to any king of the earth.

From topsail to yardarm to stern and bowsprit, the *Bleeding Gull* shook with tribute. Captain Jones himself, on the quarterdeck, gave a long and formal salute of a captain of the Welsh Navy, even as the Jolly Roger was run up the mast and the cannons fired in salute.

Henry Morgan, himself, was a manner of pirate I had not yet imagined, one as far from the common lot, at least in appearance, as Captain Jones himself. I had come to understand through conversation and observation, as limited as it might be, that pirates in general were despising of the upper classes and loved to dress in mockery of them, but Morgan appeared to dress not in mockery of the upper classes, but in their imitation.

He was, in fact, a perfectly refined gentleman, to all appearance, with faultless powdered wig, waistcoat and breeches, long stockings, and buckled shoes. One assumed he had a pistol about his person, but saw from a distance only lacy sleeve, handkerchiefs and a gentleman's sword.

Captain Morgan climbed into his long boat, which was outfitted with pillows for his posterior, and was swiftly rowed by eight of his most gruesome cutthroats to the *Bleeding Gull*.

"Henry, my friend," said Captain Jones, throwing his arms around Captain Morgan.

"It's good to see ye, countryman," said Captain Morgan, tears in his eyes.

Then coldness blew over me and I backed up a step. What man on earth with no crown upon his head or kirk at his back had caused more deaths than this one?

After more enthusiastic talk, Captain Jones and Captain Morgan retired to Captain Jones' cabin for the rest of the morning. For the most part they drank and conferred but now and then called in one of their crew to provide information. At one o'clock, I found my presence required and reported on quaking limbs.

There, I was introduced at once to Henry Morgan, who looked up at me with black eyes lit with a flicker of interest.

"How many times now have ye seen the Finman?" said Captain Morgan.

Quite surprised at the question, I hesitated to answer.

"Answer him truthfully," said Captain Jones. "Include the first time."

"Twice," I said.

"On what occasions?" asked Captain Morgan.

"I saw him first after stealing Captain Jones' ship. The second time I saw him, I knifed him with my little knife in a tavern on the Isle of Hoy in the Orkneys."

"And ye lived both times?" Captain Morgan retorted, looking at Captain Jones.

"Aye, sir!"

"It is the Finman who is dead, then!"

"Nay, sir."

"Then, grievously injured, I assume."

"I don't know, sir." I said, "He vanished."

"I've heard." Morgan smiled. "Tell me, lad. Did he remove himself to another place, Greenland perhaps, or another time, perhaps the time of the Dragon?"

"Do you mean Francis Drake, Sir?"

"Let me see thy knife," said Captain Morgan, "I would like to determine its maker and the year of its birth."

Reluctantly, I drew my sgian dubh from my sock and put it in Morgan's hands. He turned it over and over, his black eyes flashing.

"Fret not, young lad. This little knife of yours will be fit for fighting Finmen by and by."

At last, he spoke to Captain Jones.

"What do ye think?" he asked.

"It would seem to me that I should educate him as one of my own," said Jones.

"This lad will be a killer," Morgan replied.

"And what fault do ye find with that?"

"None at all!"

"Then I shall do it with thy blessing," answered Jones, "holding ye responsible if it does not end well?"

"See that thy Mr. Starr watches his back," Morgan laughed. "It would not do to have thy project ended early."

"Aye, the same thought have I," said Jones. "Young William, ye are henceforth to regard Mr. Starr as thy shadow. Further, tonight ye will dine with me and my officers, as well as Captain Morgan and members of his crew. Dress is formal, as a pirate."

"Aye, sir," I said, and gratefully left the room.

The dinner over, the two gentlemen privateers settled back with their sherry and for the education of those assembled began a general discussion of their battle craft. Each played primarily for my edification, it seemed, but also with an eye to the seamen and officers ranged about the captain's table, which had been stripped of all but maps of the Bay of Biscay and tiny carved ships.

"First, let it be said," said Morgan, the dandy, smelling of his fine kerchief and tucking it under a sleeve, "that in all military matters, in particular those at sea, there courses a current of luck, an undeniable vein of it…like a river in the sea."

"Expressed quite well," said Captain Jones. "There is always the chance typhoon, the false cape, the leviathan rising from the depths to crack thy hull."

"Bringing death to all," said Henry Morgan. "Yet, should we cry about it all, my lads, or should we persist?"

"Persist, I say!" said Captain Jones, and I thought him at that moment, in lamplight, the most curious and pleasing of creatures, for no slight flaw hung about him. No girlish look rode his face, yet his eyes were cloudless, and the stubble of his chin, light, as was the whole aspect of his being,

Captain Jones, however, in spite of the white Welsh uniform he persisted in wearing, was no pure white stone, rather sported a touch of a Welshman's color, as did Morgan, who had the look of raw earth in spite of costly powders. Still, there was a look of marble about Captain Jones, a look of hardness to his hands.

"Is courage all that matters, lads?" queried Captain Jones. "Think on it. Did the British last defeat the Welsh by virtue of their courage alone?"

"Nay!" cried one and all.

"Nay, it is!" said Captain Morgan, rising to his feet and approaching a table, "The head is also needed. One should mass superior force at the enemy's weakest point and there initiate a disciplined strike."

Morgan lined up a row of tiny Spanish ships on the map of the Bay of Biscay and pointed out an obvious weak point in the line. Then, he directed the mass of his ships toward that point.

"Most importantly," said Morgan, looking over the men, "If ye are a commander of a privateer or pirate fleet, ye should have a hangman aboard each of thy ships. If a captain does not strike where and when, as ordered, he must be hung at once, before others take his lead."

A bit of laughter erupted in the room, and then died at once as Morgan continued. "Know nothing personal of thy men," he said. "Do not drink with them, congratulate them, whore with them, or say 'Good morning.' Do not remonstrate with them or converse with them unnecessarily or give orders directly. In regard to the men, send for the paymaster or the hangmen."

At these remarks, there were nervous coughs about the room and the sound of shuffling feet.

"Now here's an excellent principle of battle," said Morgan, again discussing tactics as if he had never deviated from the subject. "If thy weight of metal is superior to that of the pinks or other victims of thy craft, attack at once and do so unrelentingly"

"Have no illusions about thyself," said Captain Jones.

"Aye, overestimation of one's own prowess will kill ye!" said Captain Morgan.

"Aye, it will," said Captain Jones.

"The late Admiral Welbourne comes to mind," said Captain Morgan, fluttering a scented handkerchief. "He was approached and politely informed that the course he had plotted would lead his whole fleet to the rocks of the Baltic Sea, and what did he do, lads? Why, he called the young navigator who had warned him a 'mutineer' and hanged him. Then, no sooner than the young man stopped kicking at the end of the rope, the fleet went aground and two thousand seamen lost their lives."

"Such is the danger of hubris," said Captain Jones. "What a captain doesn't know he must learn from another."

Captain Morgan laughed, red in the face, choking on his wine.

"And then one must shoot the man who teaches ye better," said Morgan, "unless the men make him captain."

Everyone laughed at that and drinks flowed round, but then Captain Jones soberly called me forward. I rose to my feet, my legs trembling. Never could have I imagined as a lad that I would rise to such greatness as to be recognized by the great Welsh patriots Thomas Jones and Captain Henry Morgan.

My head fairly swam.

"This young man, William Claddah, has within his brain the architecture of the globe, not because he imbibed unwillingly of dry lessons at schools, but because he, throughout his life, has listened to the wave and the shell. I tell ye lads, he knows the way north by the counsel of his blood, not the sign of the stars. Without his counsel, we would not have escaped the Dutch who prowled for us with the French in the Scapa Flow?"

"Hear, hear!" cried every man present, even Captain Morgan, then lifted glasses high, drank the wine off straight, and threw their glasses to the floor.

"Now let us return to these matters at hand," said Captain Morgan, easing back in his chair as if he were Aristotle, whom I learned of later.

The lessons continued, but for some few moments my head had swollen far too large for listening. Only with time and effort was I able to refocus on the captain's words, no matter their value.

"When vastly superior to an opponent, disregard safety and rush in at once and seize him!" said Morgan, closing both his fists tightly. "The danger is that he will escape ye, not that ye'll lose some rigging. Rigging can be repaired."

"And men!" someone shouted.

"They can be replaced," Morgan shouted backed.

Morgan rose from his seat and lined up ten ships on the table. Explaining his maneuvers to a wide-eyed audience, he showed his ships concentrating fire on the middle ship in a convoy until damaged rigging caused erratic movements that disrupted the whole line.

There was enthusiastic applause, Captain Morgan reveling in it with a mock bow. Then, to my astonished eyes, a hardtack biscuit sailed through the heated air of the cabin and plunked the captain on the forehead.

"Why, no man alive would dare such an outrage upon my person…" he growled, concentrating his menace on Stubbs, who sat to his left, "other than my good friend, the whore-mongering Thomas Jones!"

With that, Captain Morgan grabbed two hands full of hard tack biscuits being held in a basket by the steward and fired them off at Captain Jones, who ducked beneath the table at Captain Morgan's right. Soon, both men were screaming at one another on either side of the upturned table, both firing off biscuits when they could and ducking when they had to.

"Villain!" shouted Morgan.

"Scoundrel!" returned Jones.

In another instant, the men were chasing one another about the table and flinging epithets.

The rest of us froze in place, white as ghosts, uncertain as to whether to sell our lives in the captain's quarters or run hide in the forecastle until the Devil had tired of his joke.

"Ye are a Welsh pig bastard!" said Captain Morgan.

"And ye a Welsh bastard pig!" said Captain Jones.

"And didn't I diddle thy sister, Nancy, in Plymouth?" said Captain Morgan. "And didn't she say I diddled her better than ye?"

"What's that ye say?" said Captain Jones. "Ye have taken to diddling those creatures that can converse? That'll be good for ye. But I have no sister named Nancy. Perhaps ye mean Sister Nancy. It was perhaps a holy sister ye diddled."

"I hope to heaven that one of the sisters I've diddled is holy," said Morgan, "and not all bound for hell like all of thy sisters, but let's return to the subject, lad."

"Gladly will I return to the subject." said Captain Jones. Then pausing for a moment, he looked soberly about the cabin, from one set of eyes to the other, until the last of the laughter died away. "If I might interject: all of this knowledge passed on to you tonight is for no purpose other than the exercise of thy wit. It must be remembered that we are privateers now and, as such, primarily commerce pirates for the British crown, not military men conceiving of future attacks on the Royal Navy."

At this remark, attended with no hint of a smile, there was a burst of laughter and a smattering of applause.

"Ah," said Morgan. "It is music to the ears, lads, especially the clashing of the steel. And should ye anticipate a great loss of blood upon the boarded vessel, it is well to have powder monkeys throwing buckets of sand upon the deck, the better to insure solid footing."

"That is one I have never practiced," admitted Captain Jones, "but I have on sunny days had my lads attack the enemy with mirrors dangling from their necks so as to blind the opposition."

"Have ye now?" said Captain Morgan. "Then ye must know that often I have fooled pirate and navy ship alike by switching to full sail and then making a move that could have been more sensibly done under battle sails."

"Aye, there is wisdom in that," said Captain Jones. "But surely, Captain Morgan, there must have been a time when ye were but mortal man and as such made a mistake that taught ye plenty, for sure it is that even the great among us learn by making mistakes."

Captain Morgan was then silent for an unconscionable long time, considering the matter, leaning back in his stuffed chair and lighting a cigar and then softly puffing smoke toward the cabin's ceiling as if there he sought a rare and distant recollection.

"Such occurred when I was a young man and found myself in owner-ship of my first fleet," he said. "By failing to keep in line formation when superiority was in doubt, I allowed half a fleet of East Indiamen to escape me off the coast of Africa. It was a mistake I am never to repeat."

Each man in the room shook his head at the wisdom. There was a lull.

"Are there further rules ye may give us?" said Mr. Musgrave after a while.

"Quite so," said Captain Morgan, puffing again on his cigar and sipping on his sherry. "Lads, I must speak of a captain's constant attention to the weather gauge."

"I beg thy pardon, Captain?" said one of Morgan's rowdies. "Will you explain to us what the weather gauge is?"

"A weather gauge is said to be kept when one is between the wind and the enemy," said Captain Morgan, much annoyed by the apparent ignorance of his crewman. His face reddened moment by moment, until, at last, it appeared that blood had risen to his skin, though his voice remained steady, "Used properly, the weather gauge places one on the initiative, regardless of many other factors. It allows the ship possessing it to choose the angle, time, and distance of attack."

"Ah," said Jones. "How right ye are, Captain. What could be of more importance?"

Morgan grew thoughtful, withdrew the cigar from his mouth, and placed it in a seashell before him. A wistful look came into his eyes and he put a well-manicured fingernail against his powdered chin.

"I have always found it helpful to travel with a hangman," he said. "Orders must be obeyed or all is lost. I do not recommend flogging, for it breeds resentment, and the whipped man lives on, perhaps to exact vengeance."

At these words the room lapsed again into quiet, but Captain Morgan seemed not to notice.

"My friend Captain Jones and I disagree on this point," said Captain Morgan, speaking in a matter-of-fact manner and pointing to Mr. Musgrave. "For instance, this officer earlier asked a question I took to be impertinent. I said nothing because he is not my officer. If he were mine I would call the hangman upon returning to my ship."

All eyes went to Mr. Musgrave, who turned whiter than a sail.

"Another case in point involves one of my own in these quarters," said Morgan, "a seaman who has this evening embarrassed me with his ignorance. The man, I assure ye, will be disciplined later tonight at the end of a rope."

"Nay, Captain, no," said the sturdy fellow, who had not known what a weather gauge was. "I was but playing the fool that ye might expand upon the matter."

"Now that will be a hard one to believe, Muckle," said Morgan. "I am surprised that ye have the wits to think of such a lie."

"Haven't I served ye well, Captain?" the man put forward, tears in his eyes as he fell to his knees.

"Aye, Muckle," Morgan said, "but are ye now suggesting that Henry Morgan must justify his behavior to ye?"

"Captain, ye barmy," spoke up Jones at once. "Ye are correct in every particular of thy business, of course, as all men know, but will ye be granting me a favor if I ask it?"

"Concerning this fool? Ye wish to intercede?"

"Aye," said Captain Jones. "I am presently in need of a great fool, and this man Muckle appears to be perfect for the task I have in mind."

"Done!" said Captain Morgan. "He belongs to ye."

Then Morgan spoke to us all from his stuffed chair with his soft fingers intertwined and carefully placed over his puffy little belly. In the lantern light, and dressed in his fine silks and embroidered waistcoat, there was the suggestion of a mandarin about him—though this in retrospect, since, at the time, I had never seen a mandarin or heard tell of one.

"I suggest a serious man have no more than one friend," said Captain Morgan, "and that that friend be a countryman and, if possible, a relation. If not a relation by blood, then by mentorship. Such a relationship I have with Thomas Jones.

"I am further of the belief that such a relationship be of such strength that the serious man should allow the other to hit him in the face with a hardtack biscuit. But one man only. All others who try it must be sent to the hangman."

With that, Captain Morgan rose to his feet.

"So, gentlemen," he said, "it is time to retire for the evening. Good luck to all as we hunt together from the Bay of Biscay to the Caribbean. Only know that if ye run afoul of Henry Morgan, ye shall meet the devil while ye are kicking in air."

A moment later, he was gone, with all of his crew, save Muckle, following behind him.

That night as I lay in my hammock's swaying ease half awake I hear such singing as bid me hold my breath in the forecastle's dark. From where did the singing come; the deck? hold? empty vastness of my head? Even today, I do not know if the voice belonged to Boots or a joking Mr. Starr, or Tozier.

> *Eynhallow fair,*
> *Eynhallow Free*
> *Eynhallow stands in the middle of the sea*
> *With a roaring roost on either side*
> *Eynhallow stands in the middle of the tide*

A children's song, lilting, seeming to come from far away. I refused to call out; instead, resolved to accept my fate, though haunted, as I thought. In another moment, I saw a long, thin creature darkened from head to toe sitting on a ledge of a small island's shingled beach. He sang no song, but was silent as a sepulcher; oblivious to the two great cords of roaring water that rushed around the island's either side.

Of a sudden, the creature reached into a wave that threw itself splashing against a hidden ledge, and with a deft movement extracted a fish. The two then talked, until, at last, the Finman stroked its head and threw it back into the sea.

I cried out for my mates and struggled to be fully awake, but no sound issued from my lips, no light broke through the shroud thrown over my head.

"Ye had no dream," said Temper Blount, "Thy spirit was briefly taken."

"Aye," said Boots, "To Hether Blether."

"Aye," said Temper Blount, "I do not doubt it. It was a Finman Master William saw. What other creature may use a fish as a messenger."

"None other," said Boots, "I ask ye, Master William. Was the Finman similar in appearance to seaman Platt."

"I don't know," I said, "I have seen Platt so rarely. He stays bellows or off from others."

"As a Finman would," said Blount.

We were working in the sweaty hold with Billy Goode and several seaman more, no one with a liking for seaman Platt, who had shunned them all, typically preferring standing at the rail and looking out over the ocean to exchanging oaths.

"What is Hether Blether?" I asked, rolling up my sleeves and wiping my finger through my dirty hair.

"A place of Finmen like Hildaland, but an island unlike Hildaland in that it remains," said Boots, his voice lowered, the men paused in their work. "It's an island of sea-mists and thick fog-banks, a vanishing place. Some say it sinks and rises. Seamen coming upon it become lost in its magical clouds of ice must row straight for it with steel in their hands and then place a foot on its shore for its spell to be broken.

"Beware the Finman. Always beware the Finman," Blount said, murmurs of agreement running about the hold like so many small animals.

"Aye," said Billy Goode, who seldom spoke at all, then spoke a flood. "The Finman is inclined to follow a ship into port and then, at night, slip off the ship's anchor stone...."

"Aye," said Temper Blount, " And then release the winds from his pouch and blow up a storm as well, so that the ship will never more be seen whole. Worse, the Finman may hold a vessel in port so as to later cost a fisherman his life. At sea, he may yank away a rower's oar. Ye must cut a cross in thy sinkers, lads, and draw a cross with tar or chalk on thy ships or boats."

Then up spoke a mariner with one seeing eye, the other made of glass, "Here's a tale with truth hanging all about it," he said, "Not long ago on Sanday, a ferryman hauled a dark man and a cow, not suspecting a Finman, even when the stranger paid him double the usual fare and took up the full grown cow in his arms.

"At each island passed the dark stranger called out, 'Keep to the East!' and each time the ferryman asked wither they were bound, the stranger said, 'A close tongue keeps a safe head.'

"At long last a black fell over the boat and all things were, for the moment, still. Then, the fog thinned and cleared and a strange sun rose in the evening sun over a enchanted dark land lush with sweet music, as if mermaids in the shallows were calling out for human husbands."

"More likely Finwomen," said Boots, cutting in, "For its sure that Finwomen are beautiful as young women, but grow daily into hideousness if they settle for husbands of their own kind."

"That's the truth of it," said the mariner with one good eye. "It was at the sound of the unearthly voices that the ferryman knew his passenger was a Finman, and his heart, from fear, almost stopped. He accepted the blindfold the Finman tied around his eyes and when the Finwomen learned he was married he endured their screeches.

"A close tongue keeps a safe head," the Finman warned again, stepping off the boat and onto the island, leaving a bag of copper coins."

"No Finman can endure parting with silver," said Temper Blount."

"Right ye are," said the mariner, "Then the Finman spun the boat withershins against the course of the sun, pulled away the ferryman's blindfold, and sent the ferryman on his way, without looking back."

"No wonder of it," said Boots."

"Aye," said the mariner, removing the glass eye from its socket and wiping it clean with a handkerchief. "Then the Ferryman saw the Finman a year later in a tavern in Sanday and said to him, 'I am blithe to see ye,' taking a long draught from a cog of ale.

"'Did ye see me?' said the Finman grimly, "Then, ye'll never have to say ye see me more.'

After those words, mates, the Finman pulled a box of powder from his coat and blew some at the Ferryman's eyes. Luckily, the ferryman turned his head in time and lost but one eye, not both, and before he could cry out the Finman was gone from the door."

"Ah, curse the devil and all his brood," said Temper Blount.

"And ye were the ferryman, as I suppose," said Boots, catching the mariner's reddened eye as it inward moved.

The mariner turned toward the three of us and crooked a finger. "Say nothing of what a wight does what of Finmen when the sea is listening. It will send its spiraling shells themselves to tell Finmen of it."

Chapter Seven

Off the coast of France, we charmed the fickle breezes. To achieve our pleasure, we tweaked the sheets and worked the braces. Once past the doldrums, we ran for the looming coast of Portugal, keeping watchful eyes for vessels and distant frothy caps marking pathways of wind.

The top men, their watches ending, climbed down from the ratlines, a crowd of chattering magpies anxious to preen for battle. The new watch climbed up. In bare feet, mates scurried upward on windward ratlines, then bracing their feet against monkey lines and draping their bodies over the swaying yardarms, they sang at their struggles with the disobedient sails as seamen on the deck manned the braces.

We jolly sailor boys up, up aloft, and the landlubbers lying down below, below, below.

At midday meal, I found an empty seat beside the large-armed Payne. He said prayers with shoulders hunched, his massive jaw set, and shaved white head bent low. He of all the seamen seemed the least enthralled with being in hailing distance of the Iberian Peninsula with its shipping and its promised gold. Having finished his prayers, he heaved a thick sigh and stared straight away at a heaving bulkhead.

"Are ye not wearing ye earrings today, Payne?" I said. "Or can ye see well enough without them?"

"Nay, young William," said he. "To see well enough to shoot, I need my earrings on, like any other man. But I suspect I'll have plenty of time to put them on after sighting a sail."

Payne was quite an important man aboard our ship. Though official rank had become less a formal thing since the Bleeding Gull had become a privateer in relation to the English but a pirate craft in the hearts of many, he was a second sergeant to Sergeant Lemuel Valley and would be but a step behind Sergeant Valley when the boarding party leaped the Spanish gunwale.

"And are ye not happy to be aboard this day?" I persisted.

"Aye, happy enough," he said. "For what is life but a blister and death a bother? Long has it been true, since the Garden, and no man sails far without want of water, I say. So, what if we catch the richest galleon ever sailed for the Main? What shall riches buy us?"

"Well, ease," I answered.

"Which we shall have soon enough when we're dead, when all debt is canceled."

"And women," I ventured.

"All of whom would as soon have one of us as another, depending on fortune. And who can blame them? There is a sameness to us. Ask any whore!"

"And wine!"

"Which turns the color of the natural stomach."

"And food?"

"Which both nourishes and kills."

"Aye," I said, "but thy outlook is too gloomy for me. How may men follow ye when ye lead a boarding party into the fury of shot and blade?"

"Look here, young man," began Payne, a look of lecture in his face. "I may be a privateer now, because of ill luck, but I am no less a learned man. I will sum up my view of the universal principal by use of a simple metaphor. Do ye understand my language?"

"Aye, I do," I said, telling something of the truth.

"It is well known that a sea captain by the use of the astrolabe may fix on the North Star and deduce the ship's latitude. Is that not true?"

"Aye," I said. "He measures what appears to be the star's distance to the earth."

"And it is also true that there is no comparably easy way to deduce a ship's longitude, so our commonly used method involves guesswork and can often yield results that are wildly wrong."

"We call it 'dead reckoning,'" I said. "And yes, it can often be wrong."

"So wrong that a reasonable captain setting out for the Cape of Good Hope may end up in the mid South Atlantic with half his crew dead and his water all gone."

"Aye, yes," I said, seeing where he was going.

"That is how the universe has presented itself to me," sighed Payne, "as one without a Western Star. Do you understand my meaning, lad?"

"I do," I said. "Ye are saying that we don't know where we are or what we are doing, and even if we succeed in our plans, our success may well end up destroying us or have no meaning."

"Precisely put," said Payne. "So, if ye'll excuse me, lad, I'll not be taking up too much space in this latest whirligig of exultation."

The jeering men gathered around the quarter deck laughing and shouting, "Lemuel, Lemuel, Lemuel, Lemuel!" and I struggled forward to slip between the far larger bodies of my mates but was each time thrown back.

"Damn ye blighters to hell!" I shouted, pounding on the back of Davies, who did not bother to turn away and pound me back. A great cheer went up, and so I leaped with the utmost desperation to catch the barest glimpse of what had inspired it.

"Easy now, little man!" called Boots, who stood coolly at the outer rim of our company because only he of all our company could match George Lewis and Long Weldon in height and therefore could observe the festivities without much troubling himself. So saying, Boots kindly picked me up and put me on his shoulders, a vantage point from which I found the view most splendid. A circle of crouched seaman formed a crude boxing ring in the waist of the ship.

"Lemuel Valley has challenged the Finman, Platt, to fight," said Boots, his words nearly lost in the laughter and taunts of mates laying down their bets.

"Platt has proven a Finman then?"

"Aye! though a Finman may sometimes swim about with a seal's skull upon his shoulders."

 A familiar fear punched my stomach and gave me a winded voice.

"How do ye know?

"Such is the suspicion of the ship," said Boots, "It's said he wears a bag of winds beneath his shirt. Look, there's Valley now."

Along the rim of the crowd, the gunner chiefs Vann, Peacock, Robb, and Fenwick all held their torches high, sufficiently lighting the black night so that Lemuel Valley's strut around the ring brought forth loud exclamations of appreciation.

"Lemuel Valley has an eye for the way of it," said Boots, "Divination of spirits is said to be his gift. Who am I to doubt it?"

"Ye have the makings of a rational man," I said, as I had heard Captain Jones say to others.

Boots laughed at my effrontery, his shoulders shaking, and I shook with them.

Valley was a snub-nosed, high-spirited man of comic brutality, one moment a demon, the next a posing, mincing clown with wit. He pranced about the circle in his Welsh leather leggings wrapped with cord, and when he removed his tunic, his muscles rippled down his back and arms like living creatures beneath the skin.

"I have dreamed of Platt, swimming below the water's surface, jerking fishing lines from human hands, his cloak spreading out like a monstrous fin," said Boots. "It's said he spoken of things he's seen of a hundred years ago."

In a dark part of my brain, I imagined Lemuel Valley laid out limp upon the deck and seaman Platt dissolving into a salty mist.

Valley was led by Mr. Starr and Mr. Pryor, neither taking notice of the raucous obscenities of the crowd. The senior officer present, Mr. Starr, took over the proceedings and announced that Platt would be allowed only five minutes to warm up and then the bout would proceed until he and Mr. Prior determined a winner.

"There will be no killing, maiming, crippling, blinding, gouging, gelding, or any other unchristian act toward a participant or member of the brotherhood in the audience," announced Mr. Starr, "on pain of marooning or other severe penalty."

Then all eyes watched Platt. Whatever amount of admiration there was for Valley's physical prowess, it was as nothing in comparison to the awe of Platt that spread from forecastle to quarterdeck when the seaman later peeled off his shirt in the lantern light and threw quick punches of the jaws of night. He had fast, long arms and a great barrel chest upon which sat a stovepipe of a neck and a very handsome dark head.

With a shake of his head at Mr. Prior, he declined to remove the leather pouch that hung from a chord around his neck.

Almost immediately, there was a flurry of new bets, and I understood at once there flowed a great quantity of fresh coin for Platt. Valley understood it too; I was looking at his eyes when I saw the understanding come over him. Then, he gave out a sudden laugh as if he had just been told the finest joke in the world.

That night I crept to Valley's bunk to see if he was awake, for I wished to talk to him and could not wait until the morning, such was my wonder. At his side I paused, he in his swaying hammock. Old seamen such as he had eyes tattooed on their eyelids, either to hide when they slept or to see while they slept. I feared waking him.

"What do ye want, lad?" he said.

"I've never seen the like of what you did."

"Platt was no Finman, lad," said Valley, "Through I thought so upon a time. He had only dried flowers in a bag to thwart a plague. Useless as fodder, needed only by a goat, after all"

"I want ye to show me how ye did what ye did to him," I whispered.

"I'm going to call ye William. I think I'm going to call ye William," he repeated.

"I'll give ye gold when I get it," I bargained.

"Aye, ye will. It's all in the elbow and the hip and the way ye move thy feet."

"And I can learn to do it?"

"Aye, William, for gold."

Chapter Eight

From the captain, at night, I learned not only the trade winds of the world and the peculiarities of longitudes, tides, and the hidden seas but also the dangers of the Bay of Biscay, cursed by Caribbean-bound sailors of the British Isles and the French coast alike.

"And not just for bad weather!" said the captain. "The bay's western boundary runs from the peninsula of Brittany to the Iberian. There's a shelf between this bay that stretches out from France, and its shallow water in a gale breaks in short, steep waves."

"In that case, may the ship escape the shelf by running off westward?" I replied instantly.

"Have ye not been listening?" barked Captain Jones, with agitation. "What have I taught ye about gales at this longitude in the Northern Ocean?"

My cheeks burned with embarrassment. "Aye!" I said. "Ye have said clearly enough that gales blow up from the west and make of Europe a lee shore."

"Aye," said the captain. "And what would be the consequence of that?"

"Why," I said, chastened. "A square-rigged ship such as ours would find no sea room. We would have to stand and fight. The wind would ever drive us closer to the French coast and though we worked our way westward as much as we could, if the gale continued long enough, we would run out of water and be swept against the coast."

"Aye. Square riggers, be they barks, brigs, or brigantines, are often trapped on lee shores. Therefore, we must do anything to escape one. Master William, remember this. It is not the ocean that kills ships, lad. It is the shore."

After his pronouncement, the captain lapsed into a reflective silence that I honored by saying nothing. Lantern light fell upon his desk in the quiet.

After a while, he spoke again.

"There is something else I choose to say to ye." He looked at me closely. "According to my observation, a company that owns ships may expect to lose better than half of them in ten years time as well as all hands aboard. Second, I do not think it typical for a privateer or a sailor in the navy to stay alive more than two years at sea, an ordinary whale man or merchant seaman not more than five or six."

"Aye, but I expect to beat those odds."

"Aye," agreed the captain. "Ye will beat those odds. I can guarantee it. I have not brought ye so far for any small purpose. Remember that, too, when things do not seem to be going well."

There was no day now that I did not have my mortality under discussion in my mind. Both my lethal studies with Valley and words with Captain Jones brought about such effect, but greater still were the influence of the Finman's boat and retreating seas in the *Bleeding Gull's* wake.

Always in the path of the dying sun or silver trail of the risen moon I could spy through an extended glass the shadow of the Finman's tiny Serries carrach being paddled or sailed over distant waves and storm tossed peaks or gently rounding the seas salty curls.

"Is he there?"

"Aye," I would say, "He is always there. At least his boat is!"

From such observation, we were not long in deducting that the darkened creature had perhaps followed us from Hoy itself, or Sule Skerry, or even the mist shrouded harbor of a vanished isle. The mere thought of it drove me to fury.

"No creature of the sea could I abhor more!"

"Hush, lad," said Boots, "Do not let the sea hear ye speak of ye heart. For the sea doesn't love ye, and like as not would give one of its own the upper hand."

We flew the Jolly Roger, not to frighten the Castilian gulls that winged out to greet us for scraps, but rather to lift our own spirits, as the captain said, "In superstitious hope of capturing a prize."

By midmorning, the men, sixty strong, were arrayed like dazzling parrots in their reds and greens and golds as they stood on the yardarms to loose the sail as their mates clung to the rigging and the deck crew hauled on the halyards. And all about the ship there was the cheerfulness of puffy clouds and the infectious singing.

The gunner's mate went about his business, supervising the racking of iron at the twenty guns. Those specialists amongst us who were the best with pistol, knife, and sword did no sailing when a fight was near. Instead, they spent their time sharpening blades or cleaning and charging pistols.

The sun was directly overhead and we were moving heeled over at twelve knots and in five-foot seas when at last we heard distant fire in the Strait of Gibraltar. Then, before an hour had passed, the lookout spied four ships, two of tall sail and two others which appeared to be allied with each other, all bearing our way unmindful of us.

Many men immediately let a loud cheer rise to the billowing clouds and rushed to the railing or up the rigging to cling to the mast and yardarms. Yet, some did not. These sullen few, who sat quietly in thought or simply continued their preparations, I thought the worse of because I was a fool. So, I emulated the most clamorous of the crew until I spied Captain Jones and his officers talking on the quarterdeck in perfect composure.

"The lead ship is an ancient galleon!" shouted the lookout, which set the mates off in yet another burst of hysterical enthusiasm in which any number of them began grunting loudly and imitating chimpanzees. "And it is being chased by two corsairs!"

At this news all celebration ceased, for not a man jack among the crew could conceive how we might take an old Spanish galleon that was already earmarked as a prize by Latin-rig corsairs.

"Damn the Moslem pirates," said a mate in my hearing. "We should help the Spanish ship sink the Arab ones, then take a creaking galleon for a prize."

I raced up the quarterdeck stair and took up a position at the fantail, where several officers were searching the strait with their glasses and Captain Jones awaited further cries from the lookout above.

"Gentlemen," said the captain. "I'll wager that this is the situation. I believe the galleon to be in full flight from the corsairs and the other ship behind her, and I believe our good friend, Henry Morgan, is chasing the corsairs. What say ye lads? Will ye take the bet? Who else but Morgan would dare such a thing?"

Captain Jones waited for no comment but rather moved instantly to the bulwark and stared over the rocking ocean whose white caps were beating into froth. He ordered a change of course that would take *The Bleeding Gull* far to larboard of the approaching galleon.

"Roll up the Spanish colors," he ordered, and they were quickly raised to the topmast.

"The second, third, and fourth ships fly the Jolly Roger!" cried the lookout. "There are puffs of smoke from small-arms fire. The galleon has lost sail and may be damaged."

"Scandalous, William," said Captain Jones, giving me a look. "Four pirate ships in these waters at one time and only one honest vessel."

"How will we manage?" I asked.

"Oh, we'll not give Captain Morgan all three, lads," said the captain to those assembled. The wind is such that we may pass the galleon's larboard side, an advantage for us because the galleon is heeled over leeward to a degree that its guns may not fire into our rigging or sails.

"Aye, sir!" I said. "But why will it not maneuver away from that position?"

"Because it is damaged," said Captain Jones, "and because it hopes we're Spanish."

"Aye, sir!" said a young officer. "Then, we may sink her."

"Sink her! Nay, sir! Take her!" cried Captain Jones. "We'll pluck that clumsy lady from a century past to be our ship of forty guns, high castles fore and aft, one of the most picturesque on the Spanish Main. When we are within cannon range, we'll put not a single shot in her planks but rather bring down just her lofty masts and sail, for they can be easily fixed."

So saying, Jones shouted orders to Valley and Payne, and the boatswain's shrill pipe brought a contingent of seamen down from the yardarms and other capricious perches to their duties as boarders. Other mates took up their muskets and headed up the rigging. There was the rough padding of bare feet from quarterdeck to bowsprit, loud oaths and cries for battle from all, and the trumpeter's blast making music with the groans of hawsers and creaking blocks.

Soon, the galleon's sails and gilt beak head were visible, and the gunner chief, having received last minute instructions from Captain Jones, plunged down the companionway to the gun deck to man his post.

"Ye men, there! Run aft and wave thy caps to thy countrymen, the Spanish, so they might know that we come to their aid!" said Captain Jones. Then I, with several other cabin boys, ran aft to wave madly at the Spanish and were not unmoved by the sight of the fabled galleon as we approached it.

Having reached the first gun port, I quickly felt myself in a madhouse of cheering lunatics, not seamen pirates preparing for a second broadside. The powder man was stinking Thomas Davies, barely recognizable in the powder of his craft, and first and second captains, the Prichard Brothers of Cornwall, looked parodies of demons as they laughed and slapped the backs of their spongers and loaders.

How congested a place it was! Power monkeys ran about in the blazing heat. The gunpowder's smell mixed with the scent of blazing flesh. I felt nauseous in the darkness, almost collided with the cannon ball rack, and at last sat down upon the heaving deck to watch the dizzying sea roar past the gun port.

"And what will be the medicine this pass?" said Cain Prichard, eyeing me with ill humor.

"Ye are to use chain shot," I said.

"Chain shot!"

"Aye."

He did not speak at first. Chain shot was little more than crude round shot linked by lengths of chain. Fashioned to slash through rigging and sails of a ship, it stripped a ship above decks and killed and bloodied crew.

"Then the captain means to snuggle us close to the galleon's guns," said Prichard, "For I'll wager the wag of my arse we'll not find the galleon heeled over sweet and with guns in the water on this first bloody pass, and we'll needs be close to use chain shot."

"Aye, sir," I answered.

"Then we can expect heavy damage to the bowels of our ship," said Prichard.

"It would seem so," I said, "and little to theirs. For what purpose, if I may ask?"

"Leave the lad alone," said Davies. "Haven't ye understood well enough that the captain wants to exchange this ship for that one?"

"Aye," said one of the spongers, nodding.

"Ye won't be so quick to nod when that galleon blows a ball into our gun port from ten feet away," snapped Prichard, "and us tossing chain shot up into the galleon's sails."

I broke in then to inform them that not every cannon of our line was firing chain shot.

"Some are firing case shot," I said.

"Case shot!" Prichard spat. "And will that do structural damage?"

"And grape shot…" I began.

Prichard's ear-splitting laugh rushed me from the chamber with my ears burning and profanity streaming from my lips. Here I was, as I thought, in a self-pitying fashion, almost thirteen years old and in the midst of my first real naval action, only to find the day ruined by a hairy old bastard of twenty with no real appreciation of strategy.

"Ahoy, Captain," cried the lookout. "The Spaniard has changed course for the south."

"Aye, she has," muttered Jones, "for her captain's no fool. He has marked us a pirate. Now, there's a mystery, Mr. Morris. Strike the Spanish colors and run up the Jolly Roger. Better, sir, run up the Jolie Rouge."

"Sir?" puzzled Mr. Morris.

"The red pirate flag!" shouted Jones. "We're threatening no quarter."

"Sir! I object!"

"A bluff!" said the captain. "We'll later offer them a chance to surrender."

"There'll be no surrender," said Mr. Morris. "These seas will soon be red with blood."

The captain's lips tightened and he motioned for me to join him again at the bulwark.

"Let this be a lesson to ye, young William," he said. "The captain of the galleon in some way signaled this ship to learn if it were truly a Spanish vessel, but not being aware of the signal, we missed it entirely. What was it? The flashing of a mirror? The positioning of a sail or some clever dipping of a yardarm? What have ye learned, lad?"

"Perhaps to avoid flying colors of the country whose ship I am trying to fool," I said. "It might have been better to fly the colors of a neutral country."

"Aye," said Jones. "That might be so."

In another moment, there was a great shout. In pursuit of the galleon, Mr. Morris had ordered a change of course that had brought *The Bleeding Gull* full into the wind and its great sails at once filled with violent air. The ship lunged forward, a bone in its teeth, and within another minute every man on deck could see that in regard to speed the heavily laden and already damaged galleon would be no match for the lighter *Bleeding Gull.*

On board *The Bleeding Gull,* the mood grew festive. Relieved from sail mending, hull caulking, and holystoning, the men shouted in their sweaty shirts with high spirits and pleasure. Mr. Starr and Mr. Pryor shouted out at them to fill the water casks, to bring forth the barrels of sand, and to ready their weapons.

I was all eyes, ears, and nose.

For quite some time, the general elation continued; but then, at a different crest of wave and splash of sea for each man, the timbre of each individual voice subtly changed, some not for the stronger or more resolute.

In some there were notes of caution or reflection or an instant of weakness. When we had drawn close enough to see the gleaming helmets of the Spanish soldiers on deck and the galleon's heavy cannons, there were many crewmen who whitened and held their stomachs or crossed themselves.

At this, the leader of the boarding party designated to attack from the stern, Valley, sat laughing. Payne, his back against the bulwark in the waist of the ship, sat cleaning his pistols, taking note of nothing, neither wind nor sun, nor powder monkey vomiting into the sea. I watched from the quarterdeck, restrained by Captain Jones from running errands.

My heart beat so fiercely it seemed it would knock me down.

"Observe everything," said Captain Jones, "Having first observed the way of things; second, ye are to shoot someone!"

"What?"

"First, observe. Second, shoot!"

We were less than a mile from the galleon.

My blood turned as icy as the wind off Hoy and I held my breath, almost forgetting to let it out.

The top men in rigging ceased to chatter, their muskets shining. In the belly of the ship, the surgeon was making his instruments ready. The boarders hunched all together behind the bulwarks with their grappling hooks and blunderbusses, each man jack of them in an outsized body of livid scars. Those who had once been pressed into service howled with the greatest fever.

"Like as not, this galleon will have chests of gold aboard!" shouted Porter.

"Aye, it will!" said Whitman, whose right eye had been lost to mutilation by the Royal Navy as a punishment for attempting to escape ashore. "What Hildago sails with less than a fortune?"

"Why, this one, lad!" laughed Valley. "For don't we all know that ye are a Jonah, Whitman, and not even a Spanish galleon loaded for fifty Hildagos will contain a treasure if ye are aboard."

"May ye swive ye grandmother in hell!" shouted Whitman, crouched behind the bulwark, a pistol in each hand.

"No hard feelings, mate!" Valley chuckled, not bothering to reach for his pistol, but standing and laughing with great windy joy as the wind that drove the sail caught his hair and the ship heeled slightly further to larboard. "I like a Jonah myself. We'll know ye to throw over in case of a storm, lad."

For a moment I expected gunplay between Valley and Whitman, but apparently no one else did. Payne ignored the whole affair, and, still leaning back against the gunwale, closed his eyes, as if trying to catch a nap as we tried to catch the galleon.

"Lads," Valley announced, "false expectations are a cruel thing, and I shall not suffer thy entertaining them. This galleon is a treasure ship but it is outward bound, not inward bound. It sails to the Caribbean, not back from it. Therefore, it contains no treasure."

There was a general groaning among the boarding parties.

"We pursue the galleon to take her," said Valley. "We wish to sail the old and plodding beast in mysterious channels."

"Aye," muttered a seaman, "It's true that Captain's Jones' most inexplicable actions bring the greatest returns."

"Aye, it is!" said another

At these words, all the men perked up again and issued forth mighty shouts as if the prospect of a deck running with blood were equal to the prospect of a chest piled high with gold.

At last we were upon the fantail of the galleon, then veering away, salt spray raining upon us, the creaking ship heeling and banging into the waves, the grapeshot shredding the galleon's sails and sending its yardarms spinning about its mast. From our rigging, Johns Dea and his sharpshooters sent a storm of deadly shot to the deck of the galleon, and in an instant all was noise and smoke and we veered again, this time to the side of the galleon itself.

Suddenly, *The Bleeding Gull* exploded beneath us with such force that I was knocked from my feet.

Rising, I was thrown down again by a second explosion and looked up to see our gunner crews streaming from *The Bleeding Gull*'s hatches.

Our guns below deck had ceased firing, and all deck guns on the sinking *Bleeding Gull* were being directed to the galleon's deck, remaining rigging, and sails. I climbed again to the quarterdeck and contributed random pistol shots while crewmen crouched behind the boarding parties threw grenades of powder, shot, glass, sulfur and rotten fish into the galleon.

The stench was overwhelming.

Again, from pointblank range, the *Bleeding Gull's* lower decks were rocked by cannon fire, and the great ship shuddered as if in death throes.

Captain Jones came up beside me.

"She's a dead ship," I said.

"Aye, she is," said the captain, "but we've lost none of the crew. Yet, look at the galleon."

The hull of the galleon was undamaged, as the captain had planned, yet she was bald of sail, rigging, and yardarm. There were no snipers in sight, nor did her armored soldiers seem capable of great resistance. Many lay trapped or crushed by rigging and sail; others lay in their blood, mutilated by grape or bundle shot.

"Grappling hooks!" ordered Valley and Payne, almost simultaneously, and hooks immediately flew out from *The Bleeding Gull* and caught the gunwale of the galleon.

Just as quickly, Spanish soldiers in their flashing helmets rose at the gunwale with axes and chopped the lines of the hooks, some paying with their lives as cutlasses slashed or blunderbusses blew open their skulls.

"Hooks!" cried Valley, and again, out came the axes, then the cutlasses, then the blunderbusses with their loads of pellets, scrap iron, nails, and spikes. I watched, in surprise, to see a Spaniard's face impaled by coins.

"Hooks!" cried Payne, and immediately upon throwing the hook, a line of our boarders stood up with their swivel guns, flintlocks, and muskets.

When the Spaniards emerged to again cut the lines, there was such a roar of fire that I could not imagine there would be a soldier left among the Spanish yet willing to handle an axe; and so there was not.

A signal from Johns Dea in the rigging told all that there was no able opposition left upon the deck of the galleon.

"Doubtless, the living have fled below deck," remarked Captain Jones, who stood on the quarterdeck, thinking the matter over rather than giving the impatient Valley the signal to board. "But perhaps not."

"Begging thy leave, Captain," called out Valley. "We've sat on our hands for an eternity now. It would be a cruel thing to keep us waiting longer."

"It would not surprise me if ye were to have thy head split with clubs or cutlasses were ye to climb over the gunwale now."

"But, Captain," Valley begged. "What are we to do? Just wait here like barmies?"

"Johns Dea!" called the captain. "Is thy weapon loaded?"

"Aye, Captain," shouted Dea, from the topmast.

"Will ye kindly begin shooting any Spaniards who are stretched out near the galleon's bulwarks without apparent wounds?"

"Aye, sir!" replied Dea. A shot rang out.

"That one was already dead," said Dea. "For he didn't so much as flinch. I do believe, however, that the man beside him moved a foot or so closer to the bulwark."

"Try another then!"

A shot rang out and there was a cry from the galleon.

"I thought so!" the captain nodded.

"What does it matter?" shouted Valley. "We have to board anyway!"

"So ye do," said the captain, "but now ye know what ye are up against."

"A cautious charge then," said Valley, who relayed the information to Payne. Payne then rose enormously in the stern and took a long slow slide over the gunwales of the two vessels, then landed with both feet on the deck of the pirate craft with his finger to his lips.

Meanwhile, Deas shot the supine Spaniards one by one, some crying out, others making no sound. Then, Payne made a signal to the cabin boys of *The Bleeding Gull*, who ran to the gunwales and tossed bucket loads of sand onto the deck of the Spanish ship so that our barefooted mates would be sure of foot and the booted Spaniards would be sure to slip.

That done, our boarders, fore and aft, crept over the bulwarks. Backed up by marksmen still hanging in the ratlines of the *Bleeding Gull*, they surrounded the galleon's hatches with drawn pistols and cutlasses.

"Go now!" Captain Jones shouted to me, ordering me from the quarterdeck and onto the galleon. "They'll not surrender to us, so don't be expecting it. Whatever they say will be a lie, and its goal will be to destroy us. Do not forget that about the Spanish!"

I stepped across to the galleon, the captain following shortly behind me. Then, I observed that everyone formerly of the *Bleeding Gull* was preparing to move over as well, though, for the moment, the fires aboard the *Bleeding Gull* seemed to be under control and the rate of its sinking greatly reduced.

"Captain of the *Spanish Lady*," shouted Captain Jones at the top of his voice, "I am prepared to offer ye and thy crew clemency and the use of our ship to return to thy port. How say ye?"

A little chill ran up and down my backbone.

Captain Jones was standing amidships in front of the captain's cabin, with all of our boarding crew no longer guarding hatches but lined up along the *Spanish Lady's* gunwales. It was a curious formation, I thought, especially so since the captain was not standing in front of the cabin door but a bit off center, as if he wanted to make a point of showing that he cared nothing for symmetry.

"Is that ye, Captain Jones?" called the Spanish captain in perfect English. He seemed in a daze from having suffered the most humiliating defeat of his life. "What a genius for warfare ye have shown! Throw away a ship to capture a better one! Sir, I salute ye!"

"Thanks ye for thy compliment, sir!" returned Captain Jones. "Now, if ye'll care to emerge from thy cabin and bring thy surviving crew from the hold, we'll send ye on ye way fully provisioned, sir."

"But, Captain," sang out the Spanish captain, almost cheerfully. "Did ye think thyself more capable of destroying thy own ship than I am of destroying mine?"

"Nay, sir!" roared Jones, "I had only hoped ye wouldn't think of it."

With that, he took a few running steps and dived face first to the deck.

An instant later, there was a great flash of fire and the Spanish captain's door and the wall of his cabin were blown into splinters that flew the length of the galleon. Then, smoke covered the charging Spanish soldiers who screamed like demons.

By the time we could see, I could guess that the Spanish captain had had a cannon installed in his cabin, and some sort of passageway had been devised to allow soldiers from the ship's hold to achieve access to the deck from the captain's cabin.

A breath later, they were upon us, in deafening numbers. They were popping up in hatches and rising from the dead to be killed again. In spite of all this—the fury, stench, blood, the confusion, the myriad of sights, and auditory images burnt forever on the brain—I cannot say I actually observed anything, not if the word implies an element of comprehension. I spent the time aghast, scarcely aware of myself or in touch with any element of the occasion.

I know that to save my life Mr. Starr raced about cutting many a throat and Deas kept his barrel hot. I remember Valley and Payne cutting a path through the screaming Spaniards before them, and the decapitation of Porter. The most pointless of the deaths were those of Fenwick and Lewis. Neither of the men should have fought below deck, for they were huge men whose fighting with swords was obstructed by low ceilings and bulkheads.

At long last, night came on and with it a much-diminished flow of Spaniards with their shields, swords, muskets, and curious lances. Then, finally, the light was gone, and there were none. I collapsed on deck, my arms heavy with weaponry, my head filled with the assumption we had won. Others of my kind were lolling about with me, receiving bowls of hot food from the cook and listening to whatever words the captain was speaking.

When I awoke, tiny fires in braziers dotted the decks, Mr. Musgrave was singing us one of the pleasant songs of the sea, and cups of rum were being passed about. We talked, we, comrades in arms, we, Brethren. It was then that the alarms of day gave way to one of the more intimate evenings of my maiden voyage.

"When I first killed a man, my conscience bit at me bitterly," said a mate, to whom I had never talked before. "Until, flipping through the Bible, I came upon a passage that stated the Spanish have no souls."

I did not recall such a passage but took him at his word.

"I put the ball through a man's forehead today and saw him lurch forward," said another, "but felt no part of it. My pistol and my hand and my finger that pulled the trigger seemed to be far away and I just a tiny thing engaged in a world removed from my own."

"Aye, mate!" I said. "I understand."

"And I was attacked at once by gaists," said another. "I loaded the grape shot in the cannon and saw from a few yards away how it tore through the bodies in the rigging. It blew their limbs and heads and entails against the sails…then… then I saw their ghaists crying and screaming like banshees and flying right for our port. Thank God for our sponger, Simmons, mates, for he waved a wet mop from the gun port and the ghaists veered off."

The speaker raised his arm and tried to hold it steady.

"Look here, mates. I haven't got back my nerve yet."

"And how did ye find thy first murderous action, young William?" said a mate, and all eyes turned toward me. It was not only my turn to speak, but also to help them determine whether I was one of their number or merely a cabin boy protected by the captain.

"I didn't know anyone saw my fight," I said.

"We saw," said the giant, Isiah Corn, leaning against the mast, blood soaking his shirt. "We saw ye running orders to the gunnery captains, safe as a child in its Ma's arms until the time of boarding. Then we saw ye leap across to the Spaniards, pistols blazing to no effect and then at last impale a Spaniard with a cutlass in an unusual fashion after missing with many a stroke."

"Aye, aye!" shouted the men.

"Aye! Ye are lucky to be alive!" shouted Fink, laughing. Then everyone laughed till my ears set to burning.

"But what we'd like to know," Isiah Corn said, looking deep into my eyes, "is, how did that first bloody poke feel, sir…made as it were through the body of a fellow traveler of the sea?"

Not allowing myself to be rushed, I sat upon a hatch cover and thought awhile upon my answer. The men were quite patient, for the captain had issued infinite rations of rum, and the men were sitting about the galleon in a peace broken only by the occasional taunting laugh. Glowing lanterns rocked slightly on the deck along with fires that comforted, and, hard pressed, one could find something cheery even about the burning *Bleeding Gull* lighting up the night sky in the distance as it sank. In competition with Mr. Musgrave, some of the men were singing soft sea ballads in the forecastle. The prisoners were locked in the hold, and now and then the surgeon's knife induced cries of pain below deck where the wounded were bunked.

Twelve of our men were dead and were being stretched out on deck and being sewn up into burlap for burial at sea in the morning.

"I felt nothing when I killed the Spaniard," I spoke finally. "Neither compassion or hatred, nor was I mindful of his ghaist."

"Did ye feel fear, at least, lad?" asked Corn.

"I felt fear before the battle started," I said. "After it started, I felt no fear."

"Do ye feel trembly now?" someone asked.

"Now? Why should I feel trembly? I feel rather good. It was a hard fight and we took the ship fairly. I feel a pleasant soreness. We'll sleep well tonight."

"Ye have no heart," said Prichard, a man of twenty, who, as captain of the first gun port, had seemed hostile to me before. "Come around to my station, mate, for it seems ye have a liking for battle, and if so it's a gunner's mate ye should be. I'll teach ye the fine points, I will."

"Gladly," I said, wondering for the first time about my immortal soul.

That night, however, in a hammock that was heaven to me, I did not sleep as well as predicted. Instead, I lived again and again the sights and sounds of the afternoon's battle, every beat of the heart. Rocking with the sea in a commodious galleon reeking of old spices, I saw again the riotous colors, heard the groans of the dying and felt the musket balls passing close to my ears, their turbulent airs as thunderous as hammers.

And every moment of it I loved, and would seemingly never have ceased calling it all up again before my eyes had the whole dream of it not given way to even more pleasant dreams.

From my first experience at combat I was inspired to construct an image of myself as a master of war and concluded first that my battle costume would not be the costume of the usual privateer. After giving the matter great thought, I rejected typical dress on the very good ground that its advantage in inspiring terror was quite overcome by its even greater ability to draw unfriendly attention.

I had not been blind during our attack of the galleon. Those of us who had frightened the Spaniards the most with wild screams and burning hair were naturally enough the first ones shot.

Accordingly, I decided that first night, always to go into battle in a simple white ruffled shirt with trousers and plain, inoffensive boots. Such a costume would inspire confidence rather than fear and do nothing to catch the eyes of former plowmen who long to shoot a dandy.

The color of the shirt itself, I concluded, was a very clever touch. Is not white the color of innocents of every description the world over? Who would not pause for a moment with an innocent in his sights? Satan himself might wait a beat too long.

As to arms, it was plain I would carry three pistols, two in thin belts like bandoleers over my shoulders and crossing my body, and one tucked in a sash at my waist. Upon first boarding an enemy ship, I would fire each of my pistols from point- blank range at the enemy and then slash my way with a cutlass to find a secure area in which to reload, even if in the rear.

If attacked trying to reload, I would fight with the cutlass in my right hand and kill with the knife drawn by my left hand from behind my back and, in general, fight with one more weapon than my opponent was employing. For instance, if one pistol were loaded, I would fight with a pistol and a cutlass at the same time. If I lost my cutlass and all three pistols, I would fight with the knife from behind my back and the knife in my boot. If at any time I had only one weapon, I would withdraw until another was obtained.

Considering the matter, I let the hours fly by without sleeping, in revelry of thought, each notion seeming less a notion than the discovery of a principle.

Not far down the string of my deductions, I realized I would have to learn to use both of my hands equally well. Therefore, the next quiet hour in my swaying hammock was spent in contemplation of how best to go about making myself as proficient in handling pistol, cutlass, and knife with my left hand as my uncles and Da had made me proficient in their handling with my right.

I vowed I would rise two hours before my watch each morning while the sun was still sitting raw in the sky. Then, when the men were a' bustle but Captain Jones not yet risen from his sleep, I would find enough bulwark along either side of the ship's waist to practice left-handed, seaward cutlass strokes to my heart's content. As for becoming ambidextrous with the knife, that would require more thought, for it seemed to me that a knife thrust into the wind would not do, no matter how often repeated, nor would it do to throw my knives overboard. I therefore resolved to take the matter up with the cook, who might provide me with a leaky barrel that would be sufficient for a target of my blade.

As for the practice required of my left hand, and even my right, for that matter, I stared open eyed at a bulkhead of the ship, in a quandary. Thinking, relentlessly, I was a lad in a trance.

Now, many another so long awake after a bloody hot battle may have puzzled less than I about such matters, for the stench of the hold was unbearable. There were filthy, sweat-drenched bodies, the odors of salves and ointment and wounds beginning to fester, and many a pants leg dripping with urine or untidy arse after the excitement of battle. But I was scarcely aware of the unthinkable air, except as a curiosity that distracted me momentarily.

How would I provide myself with powder and ball enough to practice sufficiently, that I might become the creature I envisioned—the master marksman, who fired unerringly with both hands? That was the focus of my attention, no matter the sobbing of my mates, who wept with their injuries, or the lamentations of Goode, who cried out all night for his friend, seaman Cecil.

Suddenly, the answer leapt for me. I would continue to cultivate gunnery captain Prichard, who had already offered to teach me the sweaty art, master his craft, and thereby gain access to his keys to the ship's stores of powder. As for the shot itself, well, the matter was simple. I would not use up shot but rather use shot over and over. This could be done by stuffing a target barrel with some substance that would retain fired shot after the barrel had been penetrated.

Thinking of all that, I smiled in the dark. Then I turned my thoughts to my own weak arms and hands and wondered how to make them strong, even as dangerous as the weapons were that I carried in my plans.

Finally, I slept, and imagined myself the equal of a Finman.

That is how I reacted to first killing a man.

Chapter Nine

One morning early, before my mates swinging in the forecastle had yet to climb from their sacks, a large hand lifted me by the scruff of my neck and set me to my feet.

"To the forecastle deck, now, William," said the voice of Lemuel Valley. Then Valley himself clattered up the hatchway and was gone, with me gone after him fully dressed, not twenty seconds behind. On the deck, in darkness, I stood at attention.

Valley stood beside me.

"Hush, lad," he said. "Say nothing at all. Look to the rail."

Looking to the rail, I saw a gaunt, starved figured looking out over the sea—a portrait of desolation. Even seen from the rear, the figure seemed beyond salvaging, but then it turned toward the stern of the ship and was caught in dreadful, crooked silhouette, with head thrust so far ahead of it shoulders that I could not guess what old man had been taken aboard our vessel.

"Top of the morning to ye, Platt!" called out Valley, and the figure exchanged a little salute with Valley, then went to his permanent quarters in the infirmary below.

"I killed him with that fight," said Valley.

I nodded my understanding.

"And must live with the shame. Don't think I feel no shame."

"I don't feel any such thing."

"Now, William," said Valley, "do ye or do ye not wish me to teach ye to deliver a death blow?"

"I do," I said, "for practical use."

"And ye will pay one half thy take of our first prize?" Valley said.

"With pleasure!" I said, not actually believing there were would ever really be a prize.

"Watch what I do exactly," said Valley.

Valley then stood across from me.

"Describe this!" he demanded.

"Ye are standing with thy legs apart."

"Nay!"

"Ye are standing with thy feet beneath thy shoulders and thy knees bent and thy body perfectly balanced."

"Aye!" said Valley. "This must feel like a natural position, even if it takes an hour or more a day to grow accustomed to it. Now describe my position in relation to the movement of each foot when it has moved from a previous position."

"Very well," I said, seeing his feet move. "The feet have moved simultaneously. The right foot has pivoted forty-five degrees, and the left foot has been lifted rapidly and brought in a large arc and placed parallel to the right foot. The two feet are once again under the two shoulders and the legs are still bent."

"What changes have been made?"

"The feet and legs are now oriented to the right, not center. What has been left with a center orientation is the head."

"This is position three," said Valley. "Can ye describe it?"

At this point I was beginning to see the point of Valley's game and was enjoying it thoroughly. "Ye have extended the left arm toward an opponent in the center for a reason that is unclear to me now and have flexed the biceps of thy right arm at an opponent who does not exist. Apparently, ye are about to strike with indirection."

"I am, William, I am," said Valley.

He then assumed an air of extreme concentration, as if he were listening to voices of his ancestors from the great fjords of Norway and not to the groans of our boards or the minor creaks of our hawsers. Then, slowly, he pulled back his left arm and foot to the original position, showing clearly how they provided a whipping action for his right hip and foot to spring forward.

At the same awful moment, his right elbow and shoulder raised and swung shut with the imagined impact of a slammed iron door.

"Do ye understand the principle?" he asked.

"Aye!" I said, appalled, in awe.

Valley then repeated the move for me at full speed at least ten times in succession. Each of the incredible strokes left me more open mouthed than before, more certain that nothing could survive the blow.

"Learned it in slaughter houses on bulls," laughed Valley. "Have ye a bull to practice on?"

"I'll have to get myself an Englishman," I said.

"Might do," said Valley, "but ye ain't finished practicing for the day until ye have practiced it a hundred times. That is, if ye want the good of it."

About an hour later, Valley was still going strong, but I had sunk to the deck in grief.

"Ye sure ye lordship is up to this, William?" gloated Valley. "Isn't it time to rise from this sweaty practice and spend a little time throwing thy knife and shooting thy pistols?"

"Aye, it is!" I said.

"And one thing more," said Valley, his voice taking on a sober note. "This I am bound to tell ye. Because I was able to master this little art I have shown ye, my family was caused such grief that not a man or woman of it has ever forgiven me!"

Again, that night, this time in the light of a bloody moon, I saw the Finman in his little boat, paddling behind us.

THE SPANISH SEA:
ANNE BONNY

Chapter Ten

Upon reaching the Spanish Main, we lowered anchor off the north-west sector of Hispanola to make repairs and take on pork and beef. Both were said to still be available in small pockets of the islands from descendants of the original *boucaniers.* These savage bands of French criminals and social castoffs, who had once hunted the feral pigs and cattle of Hispanola, had given their name, *buccaneers,* to all members of our brotherhood.

"Men," cried Valley, as we bent our back to row our dinghies to the sandy shore. "Now don't ye hesitate to smile with glad eyes at these beautiful *boucaniers,* for they will happily make wives of ye all, whether or not they already have wives or no."

"Enough," shouted Mr. Starr. "Do not play with these men, or ye will find thy throats cut in a second. It was such as these Frenchmen that helped Henry Morgan take Panama."

"They are a lower form of life even than the aristocracy," shouted Valley, "but, aye, they'll cut a throat. I'll give ye that."

Once on shore, the men spilled out of the three longboats and sat about on the driftwood of the wrack lines, polishing our cutlasses and sabers and axes and cleaning our muskets. Occasionally, Payne would fire a pistol at the sea to let the boucaniers in the forest know we were there, and Mr. Musgrave, who had brought his concertina, would favor us with one of his lively songs.

It was a blistering day, and what wind there us must have been blowing up on the east of Hispanola, for we knew not a breath of it.

The only man among us born a Frenchman and therefore conversant in that tongue, M. Tozier, strode nervously about, his long freakish legs covering surprising distances before doubling back and then striking out again, his primitive physiognomy of long, pronounced cheekbones and sloping forehead in various poses of pain.

"These primitives are Frenchmen in name only," muttered M. Tozier angrily. "Do not call them 'Frenchman.' I have a knife here in my boot for such as wishes to call these animals 'Frenchmen.'"

There was no sign of the boucaniers until twilight when our bonfires had the beach lit by balls of light, and shadows fell on the edges of our encampment. At first, there was a single man draped in black hair standing some forty feet away. Then, behind him, two men appeared, at first seeming frozen and indistinguishable from rocks, then ten rose up. Then, forty or more began moving about with twisted shadows, and a number of cooing women and smaller half naked shapes we took to be children formed, eerily waving their hands in the moonlight streaming through shadows, moving rhythmically behind them.

They were silent in the night for minutes and at last drew closer, smelling of blood and wild animals. In the firelight, their faces glistened with smeared-on fat. Their clothes were rude and crudely homespun, cut and saturated with the blood of slaughtered animals. About them hung not only the odor of unwashed bodies, but the stink of animal guts and grease. I recoiled from their silent presence, rose from my driftwood seat and backed away from the fire, as Tozier, doing his duty, approached them.

"Welcome," he said, in French.

"This is our beach," said a boucanier, with a snarl. "Ye will pay me or I will make ye dead."

"We will pay ye for meat," said Tozier. "Or kill ye all!"

All of the boucaniers laughed, shaking mightily in their ugly round hats, their boots and belts of untanned hog skin and cattle hide. Then, without another word, they lifted their weapons, their axes and forelock rifles, their cutlasses and sabers, and let them shine in the firelight.

A shot rang out and a ball of lead glanced harmless from an upraised axe, and every eye turned toward Valley, who stood in the firelight with a smoking rifle, booming with laughter.

To my utter astonishment, all of the boucaniers then laughed with him, some of them so fiercely that tears came to their eyes, and they hooted in the dark.

Soon, everyone was shooting, hitting no one, and everyone howling with joy. Then, abruptly, it all ended. Everyone had a quick cup of rum, courtesy of our quartermaster, and we all set off strolling down the beach, following our hosts to a break in the forest.

"Careful, mates!" sang out Valley. "Did I mention these Frenchies were cannibals?"

"Nay, man. Ye forgot it!" shouted Robb. "Ye might have informed us of it before we left the ship."

"It slipped me mind, lads. Aye, it did! So worrisome are me days!" shouted. Valley, "but anyway, lads. At the first sign of trouble, do not hesitate to shoot one of these Frenchie boys in the arse. For one thing, as ye saw earlier, it diverts them from their purposes, and can be done in safety, if done with a certain spirit."

"Say what ye will, Lemuel Valley, and paint as many eyes on thy eyelids as ye will," said Robb. "When ye fall asleep in thy hammock tonight, ye'll be paid a visit by the piss battalion."

"Maybe so, George Robb," said Valley, "but ye are a crazy man to tell me who'll be leading the party."

"Stop!" shouted Tozier, holding up a hand.

Tozier held up our group of beach strollers while he had a brief conversation with the one-eyed leader of the boucaniers on the fringe of the woods where a narrow path knifed into the dark interior of the island. Then Tozier turned back toward us.

"From here," he said, in English, "the problem is insects from which they are protected by the fat smeared on their bodies."

Then, we ran, it seemed, in total darkness, vines slapping at our faces, the cries of nearby animals propelling us forward. At last, we came to a clearing filled with human shapes and a large bonfire giving off a magnificent odor of roasting pork and the sound of popping animal fat.

Suddenly, the breeze shifted slightly and I was assailed by blinding smoke, causing me to rapidly shift my position in relation to the fire, and draw incomprehensible complaints from boucaniers lounging with their companions upon their animal hides.

I apologized profusely and a few minutes later was able to see well enough to get my bearings. For the most part, the boucaniers were lying upon the ground in groups of six to eight, as wild as hyenas, all laughing and drinking and many throwing dice, which seemed a favorite occupation.

Tozier was close to the fire, negotiating with the leader of the boucaniers, and my mates were being encouraged to help themselves to the pig that had been so superbly prepared for the palate by so grim a company.

"Have some food," said Mr. Pryor, coming to stand beside me, eating from a stick with a strip of hot meat impaled upon it. "It is excellent. Do not think these people to be bad cooks, no matter how lunatic they seem to be."

"And what is that contraption?" I said, pointing to the work of sticks that held the pig over the fire and the strips of pig flesh in the smoke of the fire."

"That is known by the Indian word, "boucan," said Mr. Pryor. The boucaniers devised it decades ago to broil pigs and cattle and to smoke strips of both in making jerky. They'll hunt and make jerky for a year or more before coming to the shore to trade with passing ships for spices or gun powder or shot or tobacco or beer."

A boucanier of some fifty years, it seemed, crawled up to me on all fours, shaking dice in his hands.

"No thank ye," I said. "I don't have anything to gamble."

In the firelight, I could see that the man had black teeth and blood all over him, as if he had spent days slaughtering animals without washing himself.

Mr. Pryor put his foot on the man's head and pushed him away. Undaunted, the man crawled back to his group, where the men, women, and children had stopping throwing dice and were rapturously sucking marrow from the bones of some freshly slaughtered animals.

"Have nothing to do with the men," said Mr. Pryor. "They are all gai men."

"But they have women."

"The buggering couples take a wife to share," said Mr. Pryor. "These people have peculiar ways. Don't gamble with them or palaver with them or roger their livestock or horny wives. They're as dangerous as priests. When the bloody hildago bastards drove the settlers from these savannas a century ago, the banished fathers of these ignorant killers came here to butcher feral pigs and cattle and roam like nomads. Since that time, no child on this island has learned to read a word or sing 'hallelujah.'

"The Spanish hired five hundred lancers to kill them, but the savannas defeated the lancers. Then, the Spanish hired hunters of their own to exterminate the livestock, which, in the end, helped weakened Spain."

At that, Mr. Pryor let loose a wild laugh and held his belly.

Knowing nothing of history but anxious to learn, I found his merriment irritating but had no choice but to let it run its course. In the meantime, I tried to concentrate on the drama being enacted fireside by Tozier, who was in some distress and gesticulating wildly, as if appalled at the shabbiness of the deal he was being offered.

It was a boring, expected spectacle, but I took special note of the leader of the boucaniers. Something about his good eye took on a peculiar madness, as if a mosquito had stung it.

"Without enough pigs and cattle to feed them," laughed Mr. Pryor. "The descendants of these monsters began attacking ships. They became the buccaneers and now their inheritors have laid the Spanish empire low."

"Mr. Pryor," I said. "Draw thy pistol, Sir."

"What?" said Mr. Pryor.

"Draw thy pistol!" I repeated. "It appears that that boucanier is about to shoot Tozier!"

In an instant, Mr. Pryor and I were standing with pistols in hand.

"Hold, sir!" both of us cried out as the boucanier's hand reached for the grip of the pistol in his belt.

But he did not hold.

Instead, the boucanier brought the pistol's barrel immediately to Dickie Tozier's forehead and pulled the trigger, sending the ball through Tozier's skull. Tozier's eyes opened wide with amazement. Then, he dropped suddenly to the ground and lay still.

My two pistols and Mr. Pryor's pistol blazed at the same time and the boucanier likewise dropped readily. He almost beat Tozier to the ground.

Everyone looked up at one another in shock, as if to ask what had happened. No one, it seemed, had been paying attention. Mr. Pryor, thinking quickly, put his pistol away and signaled for me to do likewise. I obeyed at once. Mr. Pryor then turned toward the stunned wild men and shrugged his shoulders, extending his open palms upward to either side. One of the boucaniers stepped forward to examine the bodies and I stepped forward too, looking down.

"Mort!"

"Aye, mort!" I said.

Then Mr. Musgrave came sadly forward, shaking his head and offering to continue the negotiations. He did not speak French nearly so well as Tozier, but he imagined he could make a quick enough deal to deliver us from there alive so began at once negotiating with the new leader of the boucaniers, who seemed quite happy to be taking over.

Within an hour, the deal was struck, exchanges were made, and the boucaniers were helping us carry our jerky and Tozier's body back to the boat so that the *Spanish Lady* could spend the night in mourning before setting sail with the coming of the sun.

Chapter Eleven

Leaving Hispanola, we caught sight of the island of Tortuga, so named because it bore the shape of a turtle, and those among us so inclined gave ourselves over to listening to the older members of the crew, who were kind enough to speak of pirate history.

Just as Hispanola had won a lasting place in pirate annals by providing the name buccaneers, Tortuga had won a lasting place in history by providing the great Henry Morgan with a staging ground from which to take Panama, perhaps the greatest feat of piracy in all time.

Captain Jones took off his hat and asked for a moment of silence as we passed the place.

From those hallowed waters we then sailed on a smiling sea to Nassau town on New Providence Island in the Bahamas, whose time had come as the principal stronghold in all of the Caribbean of the Brethren of the Coast.

New Providence, a place of wooded land and sandy beaches, lay near the shipping lanes to and from the old world and offered the best of defenses in the most beauteous setting on earth.

The pirates used relatively small ships that could safely navigate the area's treacherous currents, surfs, and shoals, whereas pursuing warships could not. The port of Nassau itself was further protected. Preventing the harbor of Nassau from invasion by any ships carrying a great weight of cannon was the presence of Hog Island, which rode the quiet water directly across the port from Nassau.

Rather than cruise by Nassau with all guns blazing, a ship of the Royal Navy bent on doing something serious about piracy in the Caribbean would find the channel and harbor between Hog Island and Nassau too shallow and tricky to negotiate. Therefore, a ship of size whose keel swam deep would end up moored at one end of Hog Island and its crew forced to attack Nassau by longboat.

So Nassau slept and gamed and drank and fought and thumbed its
nose.

When we arrived, the town was at its most defiant. No craft in the
harbor was other than rigged for piracy. All were sleek and fast, of
moderate size to fit their time and place. To my surprise, no ship in the
harbor was nearly as large as our galleon, and it was clear at once that we
would have to anchor off Hog Island rather than in the Harbor.

"God's blood!" said Boots. "We might have been better off to keep
the *Bleeding Gull*."

"Not at bit of it," said Mr. Courtney, standing behind him, making
notes in a ledger. "Ye might think of having trust in thy captain."

We waited to disembark in great excitement, for we longed for the
taverns of the town and less cramped quarters. After months at sea, it
did not matter to us as we waited in the harbor that Nassau appeared to
be a town without buildings of a respectable sort but rather a town of
improvised tents and palm leaf shelters as well as a few public shanties.

What mattered far more were the slabs of meat being roasted in the
lee of shelters, the great number of shelters under which seaman were
bunging kegs of ale and whores of every tone, tint, age, and feature, who
called out to us from across the harbor.

"Hurrah," screamed out the men, repeatedly, in great bursts of enthusiasm. "Hurrah!"

Jibes and invitations flew back and forth from our anchorage beside
Hog Island to the main streets of Nassau.

At last Captain Jones brought an end to it by coming from his cabin
with his officers and climbing the steps to the quarterdeck, where he had
the boson blow his shrill whistle to assemble the men. Reluctantly, they
gathered before him, grumbling and shuffling their impatient feet.

"Gentlemen," he said. "These are the regulations for shore leave,
during which ye will dress in full pirate garb and celebrate with the
locals, save in certain particulars. Ye will not engage in quarreling that
may endanger thy lives. If ye do so, Mr. Starr and Valley will take you
back to the ship. If ye drink to blindness or murder, ye will be taken back
to the ship and punished according to thy excess. Further, swiving with

whores in good health is held to be desirable, but swiving with those already likely taken by their deaths is not. If ye are unclear as to which world thy chosen whore likely belongs, consult with Valley or Mr. Starr, who have experienced eyes and the noses of hounds.

"Men, we have a clean ship, eat a proper diet, and maintain order, and therefore have had no unnecessary deaths at sea. I do not now intend to lose men to rum, the cutlass, or contamination. New Providence is not the Orkneys. If ye do not listen in this port, ye will drown in blood.

"I further remind ye that the regulations I have just stated are immediately revocable if ye so wish to leave our company. Boson! Release the men for shore leave."

At the whistle, we all tumbled into the long boats and rowed briskly across the harbor and at last to the a central pier, where in a few minutes time everyone but myself and the other cabin boys had a whore on each arm.

How everyone delighted in drinks of mixed fruits and mixed liquors and women of mixed races and thought himself in heaven! "Why die to go to paradise?" each of them thought. "Why die?"

There were boxes everywhere, sea chests and monkeys and parrots and gay pantaloons strewn about and nobody attached to anything much unless he was lying upon it, passed out in the sun. Looking about, I saw that I was quite swallowed up in a sea of rogues with no familiar face about and no good idea where anyone had gone.

Still, I learned that many of these Brethren of the Coast were men of vivid color and violence who had once been privateers and had now become pirates. I also noted among them a large contingent of traders, smugglers, and hangers on, all speaking of their crafts openly, which signaled to me there was no law upon the island but the force of arms.

How these villains wobbled when they stood and bumped together in their flamboyant silks and tricorn hats when they strode the muddy streets!

It appeared they all would drown in their pleasures, unless some captain of steel and blood-lusting spirit point a pistol at their heads and order them again to the holy work of terrorizing the Spanish Main. All of them but me had a laughing, cajoling whore with huge earrings draped upon his arm.

"Damn my soul!" I said, disappointed, in spite of the stunning natural beauty of the place, and walked off by myself, away from the others. After all that had occurred to me and the honors won from the likes of Captain Jones, I had lost track of the fact that in the eyes of a woman I might still be a lad.

So then a shame came upon me and I walked among the shielding trees, all the while bemoaning my lack of heavier muscles and wires upon my chin.

Behind me, in laughter, there echoed the voices of a hundred bejeweled and painted women or more, who, in relation to every guilty seaman of our ship, thought of themselves as whores, yet, in relation to me, thought of themselves as mothers or sisters or as righteous woman who would bid me return to the nursery.

Then, suddenly, how lonely I was, not for Da, whom I loved, but for my mother, who had died!

Wandering from tent to tent and listening to the bragging tongues, I sank to the bottom of a sea of my making.

Feeling the heat of the day, I stretched out beneath a palm tree and sought release in sleep.

"Swive ye, ye pirate bastards and ye whoresome bitches whose ragged quim ye may keep to thyselves, curse ye before god, ye damned bitches ye!" were my last words before drifting off.

When I awoke it was to softer words, the like of which I had never heard before, spoken by two women.

"What's this?" I asked myself, in shock, and did not move, as if moving would somehow break the divine connection between the heavenly words and my ears. Never had I heard anything like them. I lay very still, my eyes tightly shut. The words could not possibly be coming from this earth.

At last, I could stand looking no longer and opened my eyes. Then, I turned and saw in close proximity an area sheltered by palm fronds and occupied by a man seated upon the ground who appeared to be an Indian. His skin was baked almost black by the sun. He focused on two gesticulating women who walked about one another conversing in a language I could scarcely credit a single human on earth with being capable of speaking.

Neither woman was a sight familiar to me. One might have passed for a man, so boxy her shoulders and heavy her arms with muscles. Also, she wore her hair cut short like a man's, as well as a man's pantaloons and a man's blouse.

I might have taken her as a man had she consistently troubled to speak as a man, as occasionally she showed she was capable of doing. But the other, ah! No amount of playacting could have convinced anyone at all that she was ought but woman.

"Oh swear not by the moon, the constant moon…" she said, to the first woman, who, I was beginning to see, was merely playing that she was a man, perhaps in rehearsal for some kirk cycle play or pageant.

She paused for a moment, and my heart was much moved by the feminine tenderness of her voice.

"What shall I swear by?" replied her companion.

"Do not swear at all," said my love, most beautifully. "Or, if ye wilt, swear by thy gracious self, which is the god of my idolatry, and I'll believe ye."

"If my heart's dear love—" said the woman playing a man,

I held my breath then, so charged with pain became my love's true voice.

"Well, do not swear. Although I joy in ye, I have no joy of this contract tonight. It is too rash, too unadvised, too sudden, too like the lightning which doth cease to be, ere one can say, 'It lightens.' Sweet, good night. This bud of love, by summer's ripening breath, may prove a beauteous flower when next we meet. Good night, good night. As sweet repose and rest come to thy heart as that within my breast."

How struck, then, I was also by her appearance. For maid she seemed, though in no way did she dress as a maid. Even as she spoke the sweet words of love, she dressed in high boots, purple trousers, silk shirt with ballooning sleeves, and wore a red sash about her waist from which hung an axe, a knife, a cutlass, and a pistol. About her neck, she also wore a bandana, and I saw gleaming from her collar a long straight pin to puncture an unwary heart.

But it was not the pin that punctured my heart, finally. It was rather the beauty of her face, taken together with the glory and intelligence of her language and the novelty of her being that grabbed me at once. She was perhaps five years older than I, but within five minutes of having encountered her for the first time, I knew that there was no more perfect creature for me on all the earth than my magnificent Anne Bonny.

After another hour of entertainment, during which I ventured closer and sat with the Indian to watch the performance under the palm fronds, the curtain was apparently drawn, for the Indian and I clapped enthusiastically, and the two women came to sit with us on the grass.

The Indian offered us ale, and we all accepted gladly.

"My name is William Claddah," I said, "and I have sailed here with Captain Thomas Jones."

"We all know Captain Jones," said the Indian. "I am Joe Buck. I am Anne Bonny's slave."

Anne Bonny howled with laughter and then pointed to the blond woman, who like Anne was carrying an axe. "And this is Mary Read, who only lately has begun playing the part of a woman as well as that of a man."

"Shut thy yap, loathsome Anne," said Mary Read. "What if I should tell this murderous boy of thy stinking past? He'll no longer applaud thy puny efforts in regards to William Shakespeare. Now will he, bastard lass? Then who shall admire ye for other than thy axe and thy quim?"

"Aye, who?" laughed Anne. "Ye old bitch Mary. No need to rattle ye dairies. Be a good whore, bitch. And who taught ye Shakespeare if it weren't for Anne, who might also teach ye the axe?"

"Who is this Shakespeare?" I asked. "Is he the author of the words I just heard? I must know more. Please teach me more. I'll pay ye what I have."

"Teach me the axe!" screamed Mary, ignoring my pleas and leaping to her feet.

Then, all in one motion, she drew her axe from her belt and threw it forty feet, burying it deep into a palm tree, its handle quivering. "Good night, sweet prince," she said. "May a choir of angels sing ye to rest."

Then Anne rose behind her, and before I could think, a second axe flashed in the sunlight and buried in the same tree but deeper than Mary's.

"I have been ill," said Mary.

"Who is this boy?" said Anne.

"Let us torture him," said Mary.

"A good idea!" said Anne. "It's clear he has fallen in love with one of us and pretends his interest lies with Shakespeare. Actually, nothing can be clearer than that he's a daft seaman and drunk who'll run a line of bastards and end up swinging by the neck and good enough for him."

"I insist on a trial," piped up the Indian, Joe Buck, "or people will say we're no better than the authorities."

"Very well, Joe Buck," said Anne. "I'll play the prosecutor, Mary will be the judge, and ye will defend the miscreant to the death. Is the court ready?"

"I declare the trial begun," said Mary gravely.

"Well, well, William Claddah, if that is thy name. Who is it that ye love? Is it Mary Read or is it I? Come, come. Be quick about it."

"Why, it is ye I love, mum!" I said.

"Well, in that case," Anne said. "I am hereby dropping all charges and suggesting we all go for a horseback ride on the southern beach, away from this crowd of cutthroats and dullards."

"I agree with that decision, Barrister Anne," said Joe Buck, "but first every effort should be made to find Captain Jones, whom we've always held in highest regard, even when he served in the Welsh Navy."

"Let that be the ruling then," said Judge Mary Read. "Let us circulate our crew in hope of finding Captain Jones."

Chapter Twelve

Sitting on the white sand of the south beach with Captain Jones, Joe Buck, and Mr. Starr and now and then watching the howling naked forms of Anne Bonny and Mary Read roaring by on their white chargers, I though myself the luckiest creature of the Caribbean. Not only was the vision of my Anne altogether incomparable, it was admirably set off by the clear blue of ocean and sky and the drama of the wild Mary Read and the wild-eyed horses. How far I had come from the Orkneys, and how deeply I wished my Da were with me.

Captain Thomas Jones was, of course, a man of great fame, throughout all of the Northern and Western seas and Joe Buck, I learned, a hunter of distinction and teacher of Anne Bonny. Anne Bonny and Mary Read, I learned from Joe Buck and the captain, were the most famous female pirates of their time.

So, too, was Mr. Starr renowned—a runner celebrated throughout the British Isles.

I had high hopes that afternoon their qualities would find purchase in me.

Each time the horses passed, kicking sand behind them, Anne would be bent over the neck of her charger, screaming, "Freedom! Freedom!"

"I already be fifty year old when dat one be born," said Joe Buck. "She had an old cowl on her face I just had to reach down and pull off, and dere ain't been nothin' in dis world she let ta hold her back since.

"Her Da be a rich man but had to move to here from England when Nassau be called 'Charles Town' cause he took a mistress to live wid, and Annie be der bastard. She got everythin'. She got a teacher to teach her Shakespeare, and she got me to teach her hunting with an axe and everything else a man need to know. But that other one, Mary, she never had nuthin'."

"Mary's had to be what she is," added the captain, "no choice in the matter."

"Not a lick of choice," said Joe Buck. "Had to be a killer."

"Aye," said Mr. Starr, speaking for the first time that day.

The women were out of sight, having rounded a bend of shore to disappear into a cove. A flight of gulls rose suddenly to the southern sky. The captain and Joe Buck rose instantly to their feet.

"Mr. Starr," shouted Captain Jones. "Ye and young William, go!"

Without another word, Mr. Starr rushed off ahead of me, downwind, as if a gale were caught in his main and topsails, and breakers were throwing him forward. For his every three steps, I managed but two. He ran like a creature from a dream, a glory to watch, even in my agony and pain of heart. Before he quite reached the bend of the shore, he suddenly stopped, having appraised the situation. Then, we heard two shots, and I went chuffing up.

Two horsemen were chasing the naked Anne and Mary and attempting to bring down their horses with pistol shot.

"Draw thy pistols," ordered Mr. Starr. "Our aspects will do nothing to frighten them off. Such huge louts as these will think we are but children."

Mr. Starr had a point. He was no larger than I, and both of us must have appeared to the would-be marauders as dressed up children in fancy white-plumed hats, satin jackets, and knee boots fit for a party, the pistols in our hands merely toys.

The danger was that Anne and Mary, seeing us, might veer from us with the idea of protecting our lives. Luckily enough, Anne, leading Mary by several lengths, was having too fine a time to notice we were there at all until the last moment.

"Freedom!" she screamed at the top of her lungs, to celebrate their spunk.

Mr. Starr and I fired four shots simultaneously, and the two brigands dropped, as dead men drop.

The skirmish over, the captain and Joe Buck finally arrived at the scene and Anne and Mary dismounted, naked, from their horses.

"Who are these fellows?" asked Captain Jones, turning both over with his foot and noting not only their ugly faces but also the two wounds in each of their breasts.

Mr. Starr, Joe Buck, and the women shook their heads, neither of them knowing.

I failed to shake my head, for truth to tell, I was not looking at the men or their wounds but rather first at Anne's quim and then next at Mary's quim and then again at Anne's, and then again at Mary's.

"Have ye seen these men before," repeated the captain, irritated.

"Oh, no Sir," I said. Then I again looked at Anne's quim and pretty much settled on the notion that I did indeed prefer Anne's quim to Mary's though Mary's quim was beyond reproach. Still, I looked again at Mary's quim to confirm that I did indeed prefer Anne's.

Once again I found myself condemned by the captain's tone for having failed to respond to some question.

"For the love of heaven," said Anne, coming heatedly to my defense. "Isn't it as clear as the nose on ye face that young William is in love with me and therefore finds it impossible not to have an overwhelming interest in my quim? If such were not the principal of all life and reproduction of the species, why, there would be too little swiving, and humankind would disappear."

"Well, if it is true that young William cannot converse when ye are uncovered, then take my jacket," said the captain, offering Anne the ragged pirate coat he had thrown over his ripped burlap vest. When Anne was decently covered, it was thought to cover Mary as well. Joe Buck's outer garment was used, putting me in complete but regretful ease.

"Now study the faces of these men, young William," the captain said.

My first response was to dismiss the possibility I had seen them before. But then, at second glance, something about the slovenly manner in which they wore their hats struck me. I shook my head to clear it. Then, their faces, in spite of their disguised manner of dress, took on familiar aspects. It was not, however, until the wind picked up ever so slightly and drove the scent of the two rogues far up into my nostrils that I became certain of my judgment.

"Aye, I have it." I said. "They are French boucaniers!"

Our game was a short one.

"Our mistakes were those of greenhands," said Captain Jones, seated upon the sand and annoyingly grinding his teeth. "Not only did we sail from Hispanola to here on a leisurely tack, allowing the boucaniers to arrive here first by beating upwind in their tiny sloops, we also somehow gave them to understand that we had a rich ship worthy of taking."

"What a pity!" said sprightly Anne, not one to grieve over matters so trivial.

"And that isn't the worse!" said the captain. "We left our *Spanish Lady* barely guarded in the harbor, in the pirate capital of this hemisphere! That the boucaniers have already taken it and defiled it and are lying in waiting for us to return to its ravaged decks can hardly be in doubt."

"That does seem like a silly mistake on the surface of it," said Anne, "but nothing like this could have been predicted. It's a one-of-a-kind-piece of madness."

"And those smelly French bastards can't sail a real ship," piped up Mary Read, with a laugh. "They've probably sailed here with their log canoes and little sloops and are now waiting aboard the Spanish whore to jump thy carcasses and have ye sail them back to their sulfurous island."

"Loaded down with provisions we gather here," added the captain, with a laugh, running a bare thumb down the blade of his cutlass so that a trickle of blood was drawn.

"After picking up their boats from all these inlets and coves and stringing them behind the galleon," said Anne, the whole matter does indeed seem amusing.

"Tell the truth of it, Thomas!" said Mary Read, reaching over and gripping the bare blade of the captain's sword. "Have ye and each of thy crewmen already picked out a handsome husband back on Hispanola, or do any of ye gai lads have a hankering to be tossed directly into the pot?"

At Mary's witticism, Anne and I alone erupted with laughter. Then, seeing the captain and Mr. Starr settle down for a sober bit of thought, we adjusted our thoughts in spirit to theirs. Mary let go of the sword, and, still lost in thought, the captain slipped it back under his belt.

"Just let the *Spanish Lady* float where it floats, Thomas," said Mary, delivering up a good-natured slap upon his knee. "When the boucaniers run out of boiled beef and weevily bread and find ye have no plan to return to the ship with new provisions, they'll come to shore and come to grief one by one. They've no talent for living with civilized men, including the better class of pirate. Do nothing, Captain. There's nothing better to be none."

With nods of our heads, all of us agreed there was nothing better to be done.

"Alright!" agreed the captain.

So, as the sun settled over Nassau harbor, we turned our thoughts from the living boucaniers to the dead. Then, ceremoniously, we read a few passages from holy scripture and sang old hymns, before at last putting on our coats and giving our Brethren boucanier rapists to Fiddler's Green by carrying their bodies to the water's edge and launching them into eternity by swinging tosses.

"A silly mistake," I muttered to myself, quoting Anne.

The next few days were uneventful, so much so that our officers and crew, drinking and eating in open seaside establishments, took to getting up from their breakfasts of rank fowl and rum and idly rowing out across the harbor to Hog Island in longboats. There, they spent their time firing arcing pistol shots at the deck of the *Spanish Lady.*

The sport might have been more energizing had there been return fire or sight of a boucanier aboard the *Spanish Lady,* but there was neither. Nevertheless, there was often a laugh or cheer whenever a ball lobbed at the *Lady* was followed by a curse or yowl.

By late afternoon of the third day, it was not only the officer's and crewmen of the *Spanish Lady* who were amusing themselves by firing at her, but anyone at all who was inspired to do so by Valley.

"And do ye know why, lads, I am firing my best ivory handled weapons at that mess of boucaniers out there in the harbor in the *Spanish Lady?*" Valley would say, popping from one tent of pirates to the next. "I have no hatred of the French. It is because those boucaniers wish to sell that galleon back to the Spanish!"

"What? What?" The wide-eyed drunks would bellow, "How do ye know that?"

"From Morgan!" Lemuel Valley would say, somberly, flexing his powerful right bicep until it had swollen as large as a melon, as if daring anyone to contradict him. Then he would turn and fire a weapon toward the harbor, then run to the next tent, repeat his performance, then run to the next tent of recruits, who would thereafter refer to the whole affair as "Valley's War."

Soon, it was known, not merely in Nassau, but from one end of New Providence to the other, that there was sport to be had in the harbor at Nassau. Valley's War!

Hundreds of wine sellers and sellers of sweet meats and cakes established kiosks waterside under gay banners at both Nassau and Hog Island, not a few having hired musicians for their patrons' greater amusement. So, by daybreak, there was sporadic gunfire up and down the harbor, and by ten o'clock, the constant roaring of pistols and rifles underlying every burst of laughter, pitchman's call, or shriek of pleasure from the bobbing longboats.

Now and then there would be the impromptu hanging of a gambling cheat or a cutpurse, but after the hoarse shouts and the spectacle of some blackguard walking on air, the battle would resume. Soon, the sails of the *Spanish Lady,* reefed from jib to topgallants, hung from the yardarms in tatters and draped like torn clothing about the *Spanish Lady's* masts.

"We have spare sails in the hold," remarked Captain Jones.

"And the holes in the wood?" said Mr. Morris, who, with Mr. Courtney, were the two gentlemen of the *Spanish Lady* constitutionally unable to accept the ludicrous nature of the situation.

"She's a tough old girl," said the captain. "She'll turn most shot aside."

"And what if someone decides to use cannon?" fussed Mr. Morris, who felt a fool out of his officer's uniform and angrily tore at the lacy sleeves of the Malaccan shirt the captain had given him to wear.

"We'll see they don't!" said the captain.

Mr. Courtney got up from where he sat, his cheeks a ghostly white, and began a stiff-legged walk back to his temporary quarters.

"I think I'll go with him," said Mr. Morris. "For haven't I been trained to kill any man who takes arms against a ship in my charge?"

So saying, Mr. Morris followed Mr. Courtney, dejectedly, gunfire raining down about the soul of the *Spanish Lady* all the while.

By late afternoon, no one of our group seemed any longer attentive to Valley's War. Captain Jones and Mr. Starr napped on a grassy bank near the harbor and Joe Buck hunted the wilds of the island for edible fowl. Mary Read and Anne Bonny passed the time with their teasing.

"How perfect a little gentleman ye are, young William," Mary said, tugging at the lacy cuffs of my white silk shirt as she sat beside me on a knoll.

"Aye," I said, proud of the manner I had borrowed from Captain Jones as well as the dress of my own strategic devising.

Mary laughed at my presumption and ran a finger over the leather of my boots. "Cordovan leather!" she said with a cackle. "Obviously purchased by thy Hildago from the finest shop in Milan. And look here, Anne, a speck of the blood of the cow still on them."

My face heated a bit, but I pretended calm.

"Do not tease him, Mary," said Anne, "for he's my own lovely boy."

Then, as if to make up for her former remark that had set off Mary, Anne ran her wine sweetened fingers through the blond curls of my hair, and I closed my eyes at the heaven of her touch.

"Those are fine pistols, William," Mary said seriously, studying their ivory handles and iron filigree of barrel and housing. "However did ye learn to shoot them so well?"

"From my Da," I said.

"From thy Da," she said. "I, too, learned from my Da how to be a man."

"Did ye!" I said, struggling to take her meaning, for her words had been uttered with a touch of anger and a far-away look.

"Didn't I?" she said, her voice low but not with bitterness.

"If I have offended ye, I am sorry," I said. "I would never intend to do so."

"Aw, Mary," Anne said. "Do not be such a bitch to a boy who obviously loves ye as his own Aunt Mary. Let him know of thy life."

"He does not think of me as his own Aunt Mary!" Mary said, annoyed.

"But he does," said Anne. "Who does he have but ye and I that may be his aunt? Has it escaped ye that it is not I who may be his aunt, for he craves my quim? Who then, by deduction, must be his aunt, but ye?"

"Very well," said Mary. "The matter being so well reasoned, I yield to being the boy's aunt, under this condition—that he say to me this instant that he, in fact, does love me as his own Aunt Mary."

"Well?" said Anne Bonny, looking at me.

Startled, I saw that Mary was looking at me also.

"Understand," said Anne, "if ye admit ye love Mary as thy own dear aunt, ye will not only have her as thy own dear aunt, but ye must listen to her secrets as well."

"Then I shall hesitate no more," I said, "for I have been drawn to Mary Read from the first and were I not in love with Anne Bonny would be in quest of Mary Read. As is, I do love Mary Read as my own dear aunt and will protect her with my life."

When I finished speaking, a sob broke from Mary's throat.

"Then I am thy aunt," said Mary.

So saying, Aunt Mary stood up straight and tossed away the long skirt she was wearing so that she stood there in only a long seaman's shirt whose bottom reached barely below her privates. That done with emphasis, as if she were on the stage, she reached into a seaman's bag that seemed ever with her and extracted trousers and a tricorn cap.

After putting on the trousers, she added the axe and pistol she had been wearing with her female attire. A few moments later, she had tied back her hair, donned the cap, dropped her voice a register, and assumed a new walk and a remarkable new way of standing.

It was an astonishing change. While playing Romeo, she had seemed only a woman playing a man. Now playing this new creature, she seemed, of a sudden, the unmistakable embodiment of a man, one scarred and powerful, even dangerous.

"Matt Read at thy service!" she said with authority.

I shivered and then laughed, not quite able to believe it.

"Shhh, young William," said Anne Bonny. "Or ye shall never enjoy my quim. From the time of her birth until only now, Mary has been forced to play the role of a male to preserve her very life."

"Aye," said Mary. "It is true, Young William. There was the matter of an old bitch grand mamma pleased only by heirs of the mounting gender and then the need for earning my soup by my sword rather than by my back. But let's speak no more of such today."

"A capital idea," exclaimed my Anne.

"Let's return to tormenting our new friend, William."

"Tormenting?" said Anne. "Nay, educating."

"Aye," said Mary. "Do ye know where ye are, Master William?"

"Aye," I said, "I am in New Providence, in the township of Nassau, formerly known as Charles Town."

"And where is New Providence?"

"It is in the Bahamas."

"And in what empire is the Bahamas?"

"It is in the British Empire."

"And in what empire is Nassau in New Providence?"

"I don't know!" I said.

"It is in the Empire of the Brethren!" shouted Mary Read.

"Aye," I said. "I had not thought of it,

"And what are the Bahamas?" chimed in Anne Bonny.

"A Spanish graveyard!" I said, joining in the spirit of the occasion.

"Aye!" shouted both Aunt Mary and my Anne at once, clapping their hands with delight, for like every seaman, soldier, carpenter, or priest I had met from Hoy to the Caribbean, they hated the Spanish.

Anne had expected me to answer, I imagine, "Why the place I met my Anne Bonny!" but my answer pleased her well enough.

"And of whom in Nassau town must ye be most afraid?" Mary asked, her eyes grown most serious.

"I have heard that Edward Teach is here," I said, "and I'm told he is a man to fear."

"Aye, for most, but not for ye, for he is a friend of Anne's," said Mary. "Is that not so, Anne?"

"It is," said Anne, wiping the sweat from her lovely brow with the sleeve of her lacy blouse. "It tickled my father to invite the creature to our balls when Nassau was still called Charles Town. We spoke in Latin of animals rutting. T'was Blackbeard first informed me I was a bastard."

"A bastard!" I said.

"Aye," said Anne. "I'll someday force the acknowledgment of that truth from my father, the sorry cock! The bigamist devil! He forced my sweet mother to live in sin and never divorced his fat whore of a wife who would stand at her window exhibiting her quim to her English neighbors. So says Teach!"

"So says the pirate!" Mary said.

"And ye doubt it, Mary Read?" said Anne.

"Nay, I doubt it not!" said Mary. "Often I have thought to myself, there goes Anne Bonny, the bastard!"

"Pffff," said Anne. "Ye shall not distract me any longer this day, Mary. We must educate this boy as the captain instructs, so send for thy eunuch boy that he may fan us as we talk. Do ye not see how our clothes become drenched with sweat?"

Without a word, Mary motioned with her hand, and a nearby mate, whom I had not taken to be attached to our party but only an ugly pirate lolling on the knoll, jumped drunkenly to his feet and raced for the heart of town.

"Captain Benjamin Hornigold is in Nassau town," said Anne. "He is neither friend nor foe, but must be watched all the same. Though he mentored Blackbeard and gave him his first ship, not even Blackbeard may intercede in thy behalf if Hornigold is paid to murder ye.

"Hornigold is committed to nothing save money and would be privateer, pirate, merchantmen, pirate hunter, or whaler for a price."

"Aye," said Mary. "He is not of the Brethren. But his apprentice is Edward Teach, whom all call Blackbeard, is. Yet Blackbeard, by ye, is not to be feared. If ye wish to fear anyone, ye may fear the Great Pyrate Bartholomew Roberts, who would murder ye for sharing the air he breathes or Captain Vane, who enjoys whatever cruelties come his way, or Captain Bellamy, 'Black Bellamy' we call him. Most of all, ye might be wary of Calico Jack Rackham, who is the quartermaster of Captain Charles Vane."

"Nay! Jack is a fainting pussy cat," spoke up Anne Bonny, with a laugh.

"Calico Jack considers Anne Bonny to be his own woman," said Mary. "He would end thy young life on the faintest suspicion that ye are succeeding in a suit, which ye might well be doing, if I know my Anne."

Perhaps Mary meant to frighten me from my purpose, perhaps not. What she succeeded in doing, however, was cause my heart to leap with the most outlandish hopes.

"But tell me this, nephew William," said Mary, "if I might change the subject somewhat to thy own Captain? Why is it that Captain Jones has chosen to sail to the Bahamas in such a craft as a Spanish galleon? Does he think we are living in the time of Drake the Dragon or wish to challenge the ships of the Royal Navy?"

By this question, I was startled and supposed my face showed it.

"Come, William," said Mary. "Have ye not noticed that pirates today use light craft with shallow draft that are strong enough to hold great clouds of sail but have effective guns and maneuver like boucanier's sloops? Look to the harbor. "There's a cherbec galley, lateen-rigged by Barbary corsairs, and a one-masted sloop acquainted with speed, especially at night, they say, when she is two knots faster than she is by day. And look over there. There is a converted pink and there a brigantine and a snow. Do ye see a galleon in our harbor, nephew?"

"Nay, Aunt Mary, I do not!" I said.

"And perhaps ye can tell me what those two craft are and their purpose," she said, pointing to two boats in the harbor.

The first I would have scarcely referred to as a boat, but rather as some kind of primitive dugout canoe made of a huge tree trunk.

"That is a "piragua," said Mary. "It was first developed by South American Indians and has both stealth and speed for boarders. It is widely used as a principle means of piracy on the Spanish Main. And that boat, there, young William. Ye should know the name of it!'

"Of course," I said, "but I don't think of it as a pirate ship but rather as an ordinary sloop."

"As an ordinary sloop!" laughed Mary. "Well, yes, an ordinary sloop, a light, strong craft of great maneuverability and speed that has a shallow draught and may hide in many an inlet of the Caribbean islands."

Also a craft that may be added to!" remarked Anne.

"Aye, that too!" said Mary. "Six to ten guns are typical enhancements."

"As are a brace of swivel guns fore and aft," said Anne, "as well as ten to twenty pirates, each uglier than the next."

"I understand," I said, "but still I cannot answer thy question."

"Ye cannot?" said both women at once.

"I cannot," I said.

"I don't understand," said Mary. "Ye cannot tell us why Captain Jones chose to come here with the wrong kind of ship because ye are sworn not to reveal secrets, or ye cannot tell us why because ye don't know?"

"Because I don't know," I said.

"Because ye don't know!" said Mary, incredulous.

"Where is thy boy with the fan?" said Anne, mopping her brow.

"Oh, there he is," said Mary, "with that old blind man walking behind him. Now, what's that all about?"

"So ye have a man, Jack Rackham, whom I am likely to replace in thy affections," I said to Anne Bonny.

"I am in need of drink," she responded. "I suggest we repair to the King's Head Tavern."

Chapter Thirteen

I inched closer to my sweaty Anne, for though I sensed Aunt Mary would ever gentle me and harken to my pimply troubles, there sprang a fury in her eyes that set me a' tremble. I would have looked away, even into the smoky taproom of the King's Head Tavern, but seemed bound paralytic until a serving wench in a dirty blouse interposed herself between Mary and me in plopping down a tankard of ale that Mary ignored. Then, I glanced at Anne Bonny, who let a smile play about her lips even as she stared at maddened Mary and her deep black eyes.

"Say what ye will," said Mary to the blind old man. "If what ye have to say pleases me, I'll be thy patron for the night, if it does not, I'll cut away thy extremities, beginning with thy roger."

To this crudity of Mary's, the old man cocked an alert ear and loudly shouted to the serving wench to be supplied with the best of Nassau's sowbelly and rum. So loudly had he roused himself that the other great grandsons of sea dogs of the King's Head stirred from their drunken dozing, save one who was green at the gills and sitting slumped at a table with a blade stuck into his middle.

Then, perceiving his error, the blind man apologized for his volume and resumed his former mode of speaking,

"Forgive my tone," he said, tugging on a gold ring at his ear. "I become alarmed when the safety of my roger is in question."

The dew-lapped boy that Mary had brought with her to produce a breeze and keep flies from the table waved on with his fan of peacock feathers but slowed, if almost imperceptibly, when the blind man leaned forward to speak.

"Keep sawing at the air, my boy!" the blind man said.

The fanning renewed.

It was rumored about that the boy, who was dark-skinned and adorned by turban and silken pantaloons, had been taken by Mary from an Indian merchantman and was a gelding, but I was not the man to ask her, nor did I know of one who would.

"When I had sight as fine as any boy's, I was the barkeep of the Green Lantern Tavern of Plymouth, England," said the blind man, tugging at his frilly cuffs. His voice was gravelly in the shadows. The black bandage about his eyes smelled of an apothecary's sour ointment in the late afternoon's dizzying heat.

"Aye," said Mary.

There was something lurid in the blind man's voice yet a soupçon of milder spice as well.

"And I had the acquaintance of thy mother, Molly Read, who worked there as a common serving girl and fell in love with a married gentleman, whom I once thought to kill, but never harmed, though his sword alone might have fetched ten pieces of eight."

Mary Read appeared struck and smartly drew her pistol. "If ye have ever lain with my mother, I shall blow off thy head," said Mary.

The fanning stopped and the light streamed like hot daggers through the opened windows and door, so glinting off the Spanish gold plating on Mary's drawn flintlock that it was as if she held a sun to the blind man's temple. A fly buzzed and settled on my hand but I did not move. My breaths came shallow, and in the silence that settled over the oven of a place, I became aware of sweat sucking my shirt and trousers to my skin.

"If ye discharge thy weapon into my head," said the blind man, unfazed. "They will hang ye up, cut off thy teats and plunge jagged glass up ye bite. But that is not to the point. I tell ye, Mary Read, I was at the Green Lantern the hour of thy birth and know the tragedy of it. Would ye know it as well? Aye, or nay?"

Mary Read put away her pistol, back into her studded belt, plainly conflicted.

"Would ye know it, or no?" said the blind old man.

"Aye, I would," said Mary Read. "All I know at present is that my philandering father was a spy for the Spanish crown and was off to London, leaving my mother with a baby in her belly and an infant boy, all three to starve for a lack of regular wages."

"That is true only in part," said the blind man. "Ye are too hard on him. He left an address, but thy mother was too illiterate to read it and too proud to ask another to do it for her."

"Miguel Rivera will be dead if ever I find him."

To these words of Mary Read, the blind man did not respond, and I thought to myself that Mary was perhaps trying to trick him, that she only guessed the name of her father to be Miguel Rivera from some rumor or epistle and was attempting to draw from our guest some confirmation.

"My business is that snowy night of thy birth," said the blind men, taking a deep draught of his flagon and then settling his skeletal form back in the seven-rung chair.

"My patience grows short," said Mary, kicking over the chair of a drunken man with a bandage about his head that snoozed too close to our table. With a groan or two, the drunken man turned over on his back and lay in the blistering sunlight, not minding the thief who unbuckled his sword and made off with it through the door of the tavern.

Almost immediately, a pistol shot rang out in the cobblestone street. A few seconds later, a pirate with blocky shoulders who had been loitering outside strolled casually by the tavern door, running an appraising thumb down the edge of the drunken man's sword. The blade flashed with such light that I turned away.

I thought for an instant of the shining cross around the neck of the Padre on the Spanish galleon taken by Captain Jones and felt a twinge of shame which I drowned at once with a quick swallow of buttered rum. "Where am I?" I thought. "Who are these mates?" Then I looked all about me as if I had only new arrived from the island of Hoy and were seeing this very strange place for the first time. And then it came to me, roaring in with the sun. "Why, I am with the love of my life, my sweet Anne! And we are with Mary Read, in Nassau! I was having another of those little quirks of the mind that I had had before."

How much of the conversation I had missed I had no way of knowing, but as I rejoined the spectacle all around me, Mary and Anne were squabbling about something. Then, the squabbling ceased and both of them looked at the blind man.

The blind man interlocked his gnarled fingers and placed them over his stomach.

"On that night," he continued, directing his words at Mary and ignoring Anne and me, "the snow came roaring into the harbor at Plymouth. Thy elder brother, the infant Buttons, howled with fever, so yellow he was…and cold. We first put him in a basket by the fire, but then the lads complained, trudging in, leaving open the door to the snowy gusts, and Molly, big in the belly with ye, grew too tired to serve. So, we told her to take the baby upstairs and deliver, and we'd call the midwife to come. But the midwife wouldn't come, saying the lads in the Green Lantern were too drunk and the baby had the plague, and thy mother was a whore, so we called the apothecary, and waited.

"It was not long before thy mother groaned into labor, and her cries filled the Green Lantern.

"At these words, Mary screamed her rage and Anne, as quick as a fox, reached across the table and caught both of her hands and held them in her iron grip until she calmed down.

"My own wife attended," continued the blind man. "I stayed downstairs with the lads, lest they steal the place bare and deal out the rum. After a while, so many mates had come in to escape the snow that their laughing and swearing covered thy mother's screams, and though my eyes were in perfect trim at the time, I could soon see no longer. My head reeled with the snow gusting through the door, the heat of the bodies, and the thick clouds of sot-weed smoke.

"Finally, the apothecary arrived, and with a great sense of relief I sent him running upstairs to Molly Read, thy pitiful brother, and my exhausted wife, but not five minutes later he came running down the stairs again, swearing at me as he came.

"'That woman is from hell,'" he said. "'I prepared for her a fine purgative tea, and she has flung it in my face.'

"I paid him quickly and he left at once. My wife and I did not begrudge the money, for we loved thy mother. Otherwise, I would not be telling ye what I am telling ye now, no matter my need for ale.

"After the apothecary left, the barber arrived and attempted to bleed thy mother. So him, she bled. When he left the Green Lantern, he had lost a pint at least. There was blood running from the crown of his head down to the knees of his trousers.

"Still, I was not overly alarmed. My wife was not a midwife but she was a highly competent woman in the art of healing, somewhat practiced in assisting midwives, and an accomplished necromancer with a cool head and a loving heart. It was not until she raced down the stair and demanded that I take over her duties with thy mother while she took over mine at the bar that I began to fear for body and soul.

"I imagined thy mother lying abed in a horrid and breathless chamber above the ale room of the Green Lantern, a daunting prospect in itself, but also in labor and with an infant son locked in typhoid fever at the top of a long and narrow winding stair that was lit with neither candle, lamp, or window of moon or stars. I shuddered to think of the impending dark and narrow climb, hands scraping either wall, the moaning of snowy wind in the adjacent chimney, and the screaming of Molly, now growing more distinct with every step upward.

"So crowded was the stair, there could be no thought of carrying a lantern or, once started up, of turning back. So serpentine was the ascent that my body turned fully three times around before reaching the high chamber. How the walls themselves would weep. How the screams would corkscrew down the well as down the devil's shaft and trumpet down the stair! And I thought of Molly in her bed, the crying child bedside her, and the dark Lord behind the headboard, overlooking mother and child, spreading his cloak.

"Then somewhere in the distance, in the street perhaps, I heard the sound of cartwheels and horses and a somber voice crying out, 'Bring out thy dead, bring out thy dead!'

"Poor mad Molly, with only me to save her.

"My courage failed me with every creaking step. Before I was half way up the stair, I was half on my knees, forcing myself forward with tiny prayers and self-recriminations. Ever have I been a creature of such debilitating superstition. Then, at the top of the stair I pushed open the door a crack and peeked in, finding all of my horrors in the flesh at first sight.

"Molly and Buttons, he in her arms, screamed and cried, twisted and vomited across the dirty sheets, the light from a bedside candle rocking on its table like a light at sea. Shadows pitched and rolled through the chamber and I heard the banshee's cry.

"'Put the baby down,'" I shouted. Upon hearing me, Molly put the baby carefully on the floor, so as not to injure him with her thrashing. Then, she flopped back upon the bed with horrid screams, and I saw blood begin to flow from her.

"It was then I should have beaten back my fear and rushed into the room, but never had I seen such a thing before. I did not know whether the situation was of a medical nature or matter of the devil having crawled from the sea at Plymouth England and deciding to invade the upper chamber of the Green Lantern.

"Then, in the next few moments, events decided me, for thy mother began tearing at the bedclothes and shredding the mattress with teeth and fingernails, after which she stood upright on the corn shuck mattress, bouncing and screaming, blood shooting down her legs.

"I felt my face growing white, for, doubtless, she saw many a catastrophic vision on the swirling ceiling. Soon, she was pointing at the ceiling with both hands and yelling at the top of her voice such statements of horror as: 'The clods break away from the main!' and 'Port Royal be sunk!' and 'Comes now the fiery angels!

"Then fell the babe, Mary Read, shooting down the bloody legs of Molly Read, the mother, and piling into a squalling bundle. And I fell with ye, Mary Read, lapsing into unconsciousness at the place of thy birth. I do not know how long I slept, but when I awoke the sun was just rising into the Green Lantern's upper chamber onto a scene which I believe has contributed to this state of blindness that has plagued my life. Buttons had rolled over on the floor because he was lying with lifeless eyes beside an old sea chest in a corner of the room, having drowned in his own vomit, and his mother, Molly Read, was lying naked beside him, bloody bedclothes stuffed between her legs.

"And ye, Mary Read, were a shivering, squalid mess, with a bleeding cord ripped by a mother's teeth wrapped around thy throat and a white tissue draped over ye. Ye screamed a just rage in the middle of the tousled bed, as if screaming for a pistol in one hand and a sword in the other."

The blind man ceased talking. He fell silent and almost motionless, a specter in the shadows. For a few moments, there was no sound at all in the tavern or any sight to see, except the unmoving blind man and the shadows thrown by the fire across the blind man's face.

"But the worse part was the snow and the owl," the blind man continued abruptly. "The snow and the owl!"

"Then, before I could blink, Mary Read had a pistol drawn and cocked and was pointing it at the blind man's head. But the blind man only spat in his handkerchief and otherwise acted as if she'd done no more than take a straw to pick her teeth."

"While I slept," he continued, "the wind and snow had broken a window and the whole chamber was covered with white from bed to floor…and a thin film of snow clung to the ceiling and walls and lay like sheets over Molly Read and poor dead Buttons. But the snow upon ye, Mary Read, had a more chilling aspect, for an owl had flown into the window and was dressed all in white and camped upon the headboard of thy bed.

"Taken all in all, Mary, the snow-covered bed, the owl, and thy tiny form in the white room took on the look of a churchyard in snow, a mound of earth with ye buried beneath it, and a snowy owl as headstone."

"Cease thy comments," said Mary. "Ye are no seer or prophet."

The blind man laughed. "And so ye blame me for the message the devil sends ye?"

"Then what pray ye does thy message mean?" said Mary Read. "How should such a thing be important to me?"

"As a warning to prevent thy death, Mary Read," said the man, so careless of his life that I could not but be frightened by his words. "Have ye not read the Bible, and do ye not know the owl to be a harbinger of death? As ye were the death of thy mother Molly, thy child that shall seem to save ye shall bring about thy end!"

"Liar," screamed Mary at the top of her lungs, and jumping to her feet, she scattered all of the glasses on the table and violently pulled the trigger of her pistol. There was a blinding flash that blazed from the weapon to her eyes but the blind man's head neither slumped or exploded, there having issued no ball from the barrel.

"If ye take what I say to heart, Mary Read," said the blind man, unfazed. "Ye will be as great as Henry Morgan. If not, ye shall soon be joining thy mother, Molly."

"Goddamn ye to bloody hell, old man," shouted Mary, suddenly dizzy and throwing down her pistol before spinning on her heels, her hand before her eyes and her long blond hair wrapping around her head. Before she could fall to the splintery floor, Anne had her around the shoulders and the gelding about the waist. I, too, was doing my clumsy best to assist her.

The blind man was immobile, waiting for judgment.

"Let go of me!" Mary shouted at last, knocking away Anne and me with a wildly flung arm and regaining her footing, "I'll take my boy and we'll be going."

Then, Mary wrapped an arm about the now trembling lad and began marching him to the door, where pirates who had been peeking in to see the row quickly dispersed as Mary approached.

Suddenly, Mary stopped and pushed the boy on in front of her, and it was as if, all at once, the air rushed out of the place. Neither Anne nor I breathed, nor did the tavern keeper or serving wenches. Even Mary Read herself seemed made of stone as she turned toward the blind man and pulled the heavy purse from her belt.

In another instance, she had flung it at him and he was awash with gold coins.

"That ye might have everything and still see nothing, bastard from hell!" she cried out. "Ye have brought grief into my world. Now I bring it into thine."

Chapter Fourteen

After the blind man had gathered his gold pieces by kneeling to the floor and feeling them with his hands, Anne and I stayed on at the King's Head Tavern. Except for the dozing seaman in their gaudy gewgaws and the dead man in his bloody silks at the stinking table, we had the shadowy place to ourselves.

As if in response to Mary Read's leaving, the sky above Nassau opened up and poured a black rain, smelling of sulfur, mightily upon us. There were cracks of thunder and lightning bolts that ran horizontal to the still crowded streets no higher than needed to knock a gentleman's top hat from his head.

With each bolt of lightning, no matter how preternatural, my sweaty Anne shrieked with joy and clapped her hands together. She wore a black, laced-up vest over a blouse with lacy sleeves, and her long brown hair was tied up and flowing in a pigtail down her back. To my eye, she was the most comely bitch the Lord had ever conjured up from blood and bone. When she spoke, it was with dulcet tones.

"Ply my water with thy tiny prow if I don't believe that Molly Read foresaw some disaster befall the lately departed Port Royal of Jamaica!" said Anne. "What think ye, young William?"

"My prow is not so tiny as ye might hope, but I have put aside all beliefs of the occult," I said. "For I am from the Orkneys and know the grip of all manner of superstitious madness, such as selkies, ghaists, and resurrections and the like."

"Have ye put aside such hope for quim from thy Anne Bonny, young William, that ye should take on such a superior air?"

"Nay," I said, "I do regard quim from my sweaty Anne to be such a lofty prize that I would gladly believe whatever she instructs me to believe. I do apologize… in hopes of quim."

"It is too late for ye now, young William," said Anne, quaffing the last of her brew in one gulp and wiping her foaming mouth with her bare arm, "and such sad luck it is too. For this morning when I arose from my bed, I said to myself, 'Well, Anne, thy friend Captain Jones has entrusted the care of fourteen-year-old young William to me. Perhaps that means I should not only feed and clothe young William and further his education in the subject of piracy but also endeavor to teach him the art of swivery as well.'"

What horrors rushed into my mind! "What?" I cried out. "I am to lose thy quim because of my boyish foolishness? Say it is not so! It is too cruel a fate! Take my life instead, after granting me quim. Please, Anne Bonny, for I love ye! I cannot exist any longer without thy quim and will swear myself to any obedience if only ye torture me no longer!"

Tears were flowing down my face. The thunder pealed all about us. Anne Bonny's eyes were perfectly astonished at my humiliation.

"I was only teasing…" she said, but her words only brought new flooding.

"Teasing," I said. "What do ye mean *teasing*? When we talk about *teasing*, what are we talking about?"

We were both quiet for some time, both of us studying one another. At last Anne spoke.

"Well, it's true I'm a whore," she said.

"Aye, "I said, "and I've never been with a woman."

"And ye are only twelve or thirteen or fourteen," she said, "with no mother or lover?"

"Or grandmother either," I said, "And ye have no child!"

"And I love Calico Jack as a husband!" she said.

"I don't think so," I said.

"Nay, I guess not," she said.

"And ye can teach."

"So we should swive as teacher and pupil and mother and son and lovers and friends and any other ways ye can think of?" she said.

"Because someday ye may need me," I said.

"Why?"

"To kill Calico Jack."

"Let's go back to my place after another drink."

We ordered buttered rums and lit a fire to beat off the coldness of the storm that had started gusting into the doors, bringing with it cold men of the sea who came in stomping their boots and crowding up to the bar.

Anne and I moved to two rocking chairs on either side of the fire and watched each other drink and rock, our pistols resting on our laps.

"Well," I said, at last, "Does this mean that thy quim might well be mine this very evening?"

"Not if ye make the slightest mistake," said Anne, thinking it over. "I am not some doxy of the village. My father is landed gentry, as ye know, and I am a commanding beauty who can have any man she wishes."

"Aye," I said, "my heart is at thy feet, and I have my good points."

"Good points!" exclaimed Anne. "What I've heard is that ye can shoot people with both hands and have been taught to sail. What is that to me? Ye've a squirrel in thy pants."

"I've more than a squirrel!"

"Nonsense!" said Anne. "Ye are a lad, and ye have a squirrel! Yet must win me with perfect behavior, which is a commodity not owned by Calico Jack. More's the pity, for he has a mongoose in his pants."

"Let's go back to thy place now and I'll be good," I said, but Anne Bonny laughed and shook her head. Then, she quaffed another draft, her beautiful hair becoming splashed with beer and sticking to her face.

"I'm thinking," she said.

"What is there to think about?" I pleaded, careful not to do so in too whiny a voice, but rather with a devilish glint to my eye.

"If I take ye back to my tent," said Anne. "Do ye pledge to engage in all the proper preliminaries?"

"Be assured, I do!" I replied, my confidence growing, the heat from the rum warming my cheeks so that I glowed as a stove on a Christmas morning. And there sat my beauteous Anne, across from me, her flowing skirt all afire and her lacy blouse like a wrapping with bows.

"Very well," said Anne. "If ye agree not to mind how long the proper preliminaries may take ye."

"Lady," I cried. "I am thy own for as long as ye desire me."

"Come along, then," said Anne, rising from her chair and pushing aside several of the louts that stood thoughtlessly between her and the door. Following her, I was gratified that she reached back with her scented hand and took hold of mine to steer me through the crowd. Outside, it was night, and I saw that a thousand stars had bloomed above us.

"Tis lucky Calico Jack is currently at sea," said Anne. "Otherwise, I would not have this time for ye."

"He is a common pirate," I said, tiring of hearing his name.

"And what are ye?" Anne said. "Even less, perhaps. He is a quarter-master for Captain Vane."

I struggled for an answer.

"Never mind," said Anne. "I shall give ye ample opportunity to prove thyself. Are ye fit for the task and ready at heart?

"Aye, lady!"

"Thy Anne must be won. She shall not just be given away."

"Aye!" I said. "Let the preliminaries begin."

"They shall," replied Anne. "We have arrived at my home."

Anne's home was a tent of gaudy silks and sashes with flaps and nets for insects, carpets, and lanterns as well as a courtyard of stone and flowers, and an interior of polished furniture over which a corsair in a head wrap kept a silent watch with his scimitar.

"Do ye like it?" Anne said.

"Aye," I said, never having seen anything remotely like it.

Anne had a long laugh and led me inside. She bid me relax on a divan she said was stuffed with camel hair and sat before me at a long and low marble table supported by a wrought-iron elephant.

"And now for the preliminaries," said Anne.

So saying, she opened a cabinet on one side of the divan and extracted a document that had been folded numerous times and proceeded to unfold it so that it revealed its first pages. Then, she put the document on the table before me and sat beside me, close.

"*The Tragedy of Romeo and Juliet*," by William Shakespeare," she read.

"What is the meaning of this?" I said.

"When ye have learned to read this folio, ye shall have my quim," she said.

That first night of study I mastered half the alphabet and some two dozen words.

On the final day of Valley's War, two cannons, hauled to the water's edge, unaccountably misfired, killing men and causing a lessened interest in blowing the *Spanish Lady* from the water.

From one end of New Providence to the other, it was thought a pity that such a labor as hauling cannons and balls had come to nothing, and there settled over the place a palpable despondency.

This glowering cloud was made even heavier later in the day. Drunkards and others who had formerly enjoyed firing their pistols and muskets on the ship found themselves discouraged from pursuing the sport by a lack of howls from the galleon and a growing feeling that only those boucaniers who had stayed safely below deck were still alive.

Toward dusk, the only noises in port were the usual ones—of carousing and sleeping and gambling and arguing—and we were able to man our longboats and row out to the *Spanish Lady*, our pistols and cutlasses at the ready to take prisoners from the hold. Under the captain's direction, we tied to the *Spanish Lady* at four locations—the stern, the bow and larboard and starboard amidships—and climbed our boarding ladders simultaneously.

On deck, like my mates, I recoiled in surprise. Even the captain's face lost its usual control, and Mr. Starr's countenance, which customarily affected as studied a calm as ever cloaked the soul of a mortal man, let an eyelid half close. The boucaniers were dead, apparently all of them, or almost all of them, as if none of them had sought shelter in the hold. There were dozens of them stretched out in bloody lumps from the quarterdeck to the forecastle, some of them shot, as expected, but many of them dead by axe or knife or sword.

"What is the meaning of this?" stammered Mr. Morris.

"God's blood!" said Mr. Pryor. "Many of them have butchered the other."

"Why?" gaped Mr. Morris?

"Are there any explanations?" said the captain.

Everyone shook his head. We stood silently, unwilling to touch the butchered bodies and too sick in our stomachs to wash up the blood.

"We left provision below!" said Mr. Musgrave.

"So we did, Sir," said Mr. Morris.

"Well, think men," said Mr. Musgrave. "They couldn't have eaten all of what we had left in such a short time."

"Maybe they didn't like our preserved food," said Boots.

"Are ye saying they slaughtered each other for fresh food?" said Mr. Morris. "Absurd!"

"I don't know!" said Mr. Musgrave. "I'm saying some of them may have slaughtered some of the others for fresh food, or maybe some or them slaughtered some of the others in a fight to decide whom they were going to slaughter for fresh food."

"Or maybe they slaughtered each other for vengeance," Mr. Pryor said, "because of who was slaughtered for fresh meat. Or maybe there was a mutiny."

"Aye," cut in Valley, "or perhaps they slaughtered one another for the pure blessed fun of it, or because they blamed one another for the situation they found themselves in, or a Finman came aboard and made them all mad."

At mention of the Finman, I snapped to attention, but no one marked my sudden rigidity, and the conversation quickly moved on.

Billy Goode turned over a fly-ridden corpse so that its intestines spilled from its undersides.

"Don't do that," shouted Mr. Courtney, angrily, as if he himself would be handling the mopping and holystoning of the deck.

As if a great and horrible wonderment were upon them, the crewmen wandered across the deck, themselves in the dusk like eerie ghaists, half disappearing. After a time, a contingent of boarders sent below by the captain came back with the word that no boucanier's hid below.

"It's as if they thought the galleon haunted below deck," said Davis.

"Aye," said Mr. Musgrave. "It seems they feared something below deck more than the pistol and musket fire above it."

"And it's clear they went mad," pointed out Payne.

"And, surely, they dined upon one another," said Valley.

"Dear Captain," said Mr. Morris, adjusting his spectacles, "I had rather lose my sight than ever see such a scene as this one again. I should have retired in the Orkneys and let ye put me ashore."

"I'm sorry," said the captain.

From the look on his face, I divined the depth of his sorrow.

Too soon after beginning my indenture to my sainted Anne, the captain called the mates of the *Spanish Lady* together. To the "hurrahs" of most of us, he announced that we had put off for too long both a burial detail and a foray against the Spanish merchantman that had purportedly been seen in the waters of Jamaica.

By then, the thieves from Hispaniola had been sewn into their sacks and were stacked in the hold as far away from our noses as possible. So, with a minimum of fuss, we loaded ammunition and supplies and readied ourselves to sail.

We had found the various small boats of the boucaniers lying hidden in the coves and small islands around New Providence. Almost useless though they were, we had given them over to the care of Anne Bonny and Mary Read, who, in turn, had passed them on to Joe Buck for hunting.

"Take care of thy weasel, for, in truth, ye are a pretty boy," said Anne Bonny, a tear in her eye. Then, so moved was I that I stammered like a boy and seemed not a manly fourteen, which I had recently become, but a pathetic twelve and could not think of how to recover.

It was a most pitiful scene, especially so since all mates were loudly rogering their new Nassau brides in the forecastle below.

"And do not volunteer for battle," said Mary Read, who had taken a liking to me and whose horse's face was crisscrossed by scars.

Then Mary and Anne presented me with gifts for the voyage. Mary's gift was a burlap-covered poppet shaped of wood and rags by the hands of an Obeda man.

"Let no man know ye have this in thy sea bag," she whispered, covering the poppet's burnt face with a flap of clothe, or the needles I have bundled with it. But do not hesitate to use the doll, young William, if ye feel black magic near. There is no help for magic, but magic itself."

"I will use it in time of need, Aunt Mary," I said, for how was I to know I would not? In truth, I rather fancied using the poppet as an experiment, need it or not, and, like many another seaman who had spent more than a fortnight in the Caribbean, understood well enough how to use it. "I thank ye very much for the poppet."

Seeming very much moved, Mary stepped away and let me embrace my tearful Anne Bonny, who handed me a primer the moment we broke apart.

"And I have another very important thing to give ye, young William," she said. "It is a name: Henri Duplaissez. If misadventure should befall ye, ye are to use the name Henri Duplaissez and hope for deliverance. Here, young William, take this as a precaution."

Anne held out to me a medal and chain of no apparent worth, but on the medal were the words, "Reward. Deliver alive bearer, William Claddah, to Henri Duplaissez, Nassau."

"Wear this around thy neck, Master William," said Anne. "If ye do not swear to do so at once, there can be not more commerce between us."

"Of course, I swear!" I said. "Who is this Henri Duplaissez?

"A friend of mine but not a rival of ye," said Anne, "Henri is an artist of fame and wealth of Nassau who someday will be thy tutor. No need to speak further of him now. Just trust in his ability to help ye should the weather blow foul."

"Foul," I said, "foul? Why should the weather blow foul?"

"I don't know," said Anne, "I feel some foul weather coming on."

"As do I!" said Mary.

"But I do not," I lied. "I feel no threat from storms and expect to turn the waters surrounding Jamaica into a pirate's sea."

"Listen to ye," said Mary. "Thy headpiece is filled with sand, Young William. Ye might first content thyself with giving the sea back its buccaneers without provoking a maelstrom. Then, ye might perhaps think of taking the merchantman as a prize."

"It will be an armed merchantman," cut in Anne. "Such is the rumor. She'll have many guns."

I welcomed many guns, and the fight with the merchantman. What gave me trepidation was sending the boucaniers back to the gods of the sea in a state of putrefaction. I had always heard there was danger in so befouling the sea. Befouling the sea, I understood, was Poseidon's prerogative.

When the wind at last picked up and pulled us away from Nassau harbor, I stood at the quarterdeck rail, my mind in tatters as my dear Aunt Mary and my lovely Anne Bonny slipped into oblivion. And all the while I thought nothing of the looming combat with mortal men but only of the coming conflict with creatures of the hidden world.

"There's no help for it, mates," called out Captain Jones, bidding the boatswain whistle, and shortly the dozens of foul smelling bags of boucanier were dragged from the hold and up the ladder of the main hatch. We gagged and coughed and vomited and lost our grips on the bags, then picked the bags up again, our heads reeling with such horror that most of us could not help but laugh.

Finally, the boucaniers, in their bags (to be sure) were lined up on our deck and poor Mr. Morris was assigned the task of saying a few words over their bones before they were to be tossed over the side and there likely destroyed by guardians of the sea.

"May the Lord have mercy on these boucaniers," intoned Mr. Morris. There being no Bible present, Mr. Morris held a *holy stone*, a stone used for cleaning the deck that was called *holy* because it had the size and shape of a Bible. "Whereas it may be true that not one of them was a Christian or in any way practiced a religious virtue, it must be remembered that they had much to teach the world in regard to the preparation of beef and pork for the table. Therefore, O Father, we ask that ye deal not justly with these Brethren, but, mercifully, as ye would idiot children who have been raised in the wild by savage wolves and don't know any better. Also, Lord, I do remind ye that ye are somewhat complicit in their stupendous ignorance. Thank ye, Lord. Into thy hands, I commend their spirits."

Having spoken, Mr. Morris looked relieved and received Mr. Courtney's heartfelt handshake. Then Mr. Pryor ordered us to throw the bodies in the sea one by one, which we began, with great solemnity. Unfortunately, by the time the third body had hit the waves, bull and tiger sharks had sniffed out the proceedings and were tearing apart the corpses, a situation made worse by Valley.

Valley shot a bull shark in the head with a blunderbuss and the water turned red with blood, which drew other sharks. Soon, the sea was churning with fighting sharks, shark parts, and boucanier remains, and into this grisly fire the seamen were feeding boucanier bodies like logs and howling their pleasure.

Captain Jones wisely abandoned the quarterdeck for a nap in his cabin and Mr. Starr, Mr. Pryor, and Mr. Musgrave ignored the festivity in favor of keeping the *Spanish Lady* on course. Only Mr. Morris and Mr. Courtney, both of whom still struggled with their lack of authority as pirates, annoyed the men with their fruitless cries to cease.

Finally, Porter picked up Mr. Morris as if he were about to throw him to the sharks, and Mr. Morris screamed and turned deadly white.

"Jesus!" muttered Porter, later. "Ye would think the little fellow thought I was going to hurt him!"

In an hour it was over. All the rest of the day and for some time into the next I half expected a storm, in spite of the education the captain had been subjecting me to daily. We had thrown long dead corpses into the sea. We had pointlessly killed Poseidon's creatures. I did not breathe easy for two days, and then I had reason to wish my superstitious fears were still attendant upon me.

As those fears abated, my longing for Anne blew up into gale force.

I needed to find the merchantman. I needed the fight it could put up, the fear of it.

"I've heard twenty guns," said Payne, "and they say it might be carrying as many as eighty soldiers and have an escort as well. This could be tougher than going up against the galleon."

"A merchantman?" I said, incredulous.

"Don't think of a merchantman," said Payne. "Think ye of a treasure ship if ye wish to derive the greater fool's pleasure."

That night in October I woke from a fitful dream that disappeared from my mind the moment my eyes made out the row upon row of swinging hammocks of *The Spanish Lady*. Each bulged with the carcass of a comrade in arms, which brought me a feeling of security, as a man in gaol might feel protected by the company of his fellows.

But why should I wake in dread, the fighting yet to begin and the hold of our ship yearning to be stuffed with gold? I lay in the dark and listened for the cause of my trepidation, but heard only the chuckle of a quiet sea about our prow, the billowing of sail, and now and then the calling out of one seaman of the watch to the other.

I tried again to sleep and for a moment succeeded, but no sooner than I was asleep, I felt myself falling and again I woke sweaty, this time sitting up in my hammock and looking all about me. The forecastle was exactly as before, the hammocks swaying, the sense of security, even the sight of Peacock occasionally banging against a bulkhead as his hammock swung too freely to the larboard side.

I laughed a bit in the dark, but my laughter disturbed me, for no memory or antics of a person or a thing had provoked it.

I shivered and rose from my hammock, now unconvinced I was not in a dream, in spite of the familiar passageway, the hold, the barrels, and bundles of everything from salt beef to canvas.

On deck, I sought the blessed relief of the fresh night air, for always I had loved the night air at sea. I was sure that a night of stars in the West Indies would restore my wits just as any costly elixir and so it seemed at first.

There seemed a thousand stars over the *Spanish Lady*, each more beautiful and brilliant than the other, and the constellations so delineated that any child could pick out a hundred of the more prominent with no hesitation.

"Further," I thought, "the moon is...."

Before completing the thought, I looked for the moon through the rigging of the *Spanish Lady*, as if it were a beauty mark hiding behind a veil. I expected to find a moon so full and clear it could slough off any weather from a waterspout to a typhoon, but I saw no moon above the mast, where I expected to find it.

Then turning on my heels and looking high and low through the points of the sky around, I failed to find the moon there as well.

I shouted my grief, a great alarmed shout that should have brought men running.

When it did not, I ran from bowsprit to quarterdeck to alert the officers manning the wheel of the supernatural occurrence, but all I found there was the wheel itself, turning.

"I'm dreaming," I said to myself at last, satisfying myself about the matter, ever willing to stand by a bit and watch until at length I woke from the shadows, for well enough I could see that one by one the stars overhead were going out.

"There is nothing to fear," I said to myself, and, in truth, I feared nothing. The wind at last blew into a gale and only a few stars were left when a long dark figure crawled from the sea to the bowsprit of the ship.

The Finman had his hands in the bag of winds hanging by a cord from his neck. He seemed three yards high when he stepped forward on the storm-drenched deck, dressed in a cloak the color of night that shut out the last of starlight but harbored a residual flame of wind that flamed from a depth that no man knew.

When he pulled his hands from the bag he opened his long fingers toward me, and I was blown from the quarterdeck of the *Spanish Lady* into the deep, black sea.

Memory fails me, leaving only the barest imprint, the merest suggestion of flight and falling. There was the fantail of the *Spanish Lady*, myself arching above it into the night sky as if to the heavens, and a perilous descent backwards and dive into the warm Caribbean Sea. Then, I was swimming in darkness, my eyes wide open, my lungs filled with fire until I drove myself upward and broke the surface of the water that stretched out from me in all directions as smooth as a fine polished shell.

I was aware of no sound or temperature, only the lights of the *Spanish Lady* receding in the distance.

In an instant I was swimming, then bleeding, for a skin like sandpaper rubbed against my shoulder. I dove deeper, instinctively, and then felt the presence of a creature larger than me curled into a ball and then kicked off against its bulk with all of my strength and felt it give way. Surfacing, I touched my shoulder. Raw skin, but no blood.

I then struck out westward, guided by the stars, the nearest islands hundreds of miles away.

I swam for a night, then a day, then must have lost consciousness. When I awoke I could no longer feel my limbs or open my eyes but knew behind my eyelids the sun was burning and could sense, often as not, there were creatures swimming about me. Then, after an eternity in the sun, again, I felt the sun go down and felt a coolness slip over my skin.

The rain was falling, and I turned over on my back and drank deep and dove and when I surfaced the sea was in tumult, thrashing wildly about me. So, I dove again and again, my arms now moving of themselves, my legs kicking of their own volition until at last the sea threw me up on a bed of coral.

There I lay in the heavy rain, eyes tight shut, helplessly bleeding. In the morning, I pushed off into a placid sea, porpoises swimming beside me, fending off sharks. Sometime during that day, I again lost consciousness, then awoke in the evening to the sound of whales and caught hold of a section of hull planking, and then fell again into blackness and this time woke still swimming.

My clothing was gone. My pistols, my cutlass, my sgian dubh, my boots were all gone from me to the bottom of the sea.

How long the swim was is impossible for me to attest. Henri, who brought me back from the fishermen who picked me up sailing out of Nassau, made a rough estimate of its distance and called it the most remarkable swim in the annals of the Caribbean.

"Ah, William," he said. "Ze are truly a creature of the zea!"

Chapter Fifteen

How joyous it was that my beloved, for surely the last minute gift of Henri Duplaissez's name saved my life, had bound Anne to me like tar to a seam. Each day she visited, though I remember little but fantasies, such as she and I gamboling white as lambs in skies of blue. At night, it seemed, she rolled the sky around me and sang me to sleep.

How long I convalesced has receded from memory but there was a bit of pain and a step-by-step learning to walk again and then a time after that recovering my senses. Through it all, I steadily learned an appreciation and affection for the Frenchman, Henri Duplaissez.

"I do not pinch ze buttocks of any men who do not wish them pinched," he would say. "I myself am a rational man of much civilization and ze art…and ze humanity. Do ze see my house? Do I, Henri Duplaissez paint pictures of the crucifixion? Nay! Of human suffering? Nay! Look, Master William. Here is ze picture of a mother in love with her child. Es wonderful, non?"

"Why do ye live here?" I said, on one afternoon that stretched out before us through the balcony window like a glowing canvas.

Henry, reclined on the divan he had pulled into my sick room, opened a lazy eye. His long black hair and black mustache gave him a roguish appearance.

"I live here because it is beautiful here," said Henri. "And live here because I am rich enough to do so and because I am regarded as a great criminal in my own country."

"A criminal?" I said.

"Aye," Henri said, "I am a civilized man and have been influenced by the great French writers Descartes and Voltaire, which has led me to reject the concept referred to as the Divine Right of Kings. Do ye understand of what I'm talking?"

"Nay," I said, "but I would like to know."

"I do not believe zhat God determines who should be king and who should not and we should all accept a king on zhat basis," said Henri.

"Well, I don't believe that either, and I've never even read Descartes or Voltaire," I said.

Henri laughed quickly, a bark.

"Right ze are," he said.

"But I would like to know all those things," I said.

"Painting too?" said Henri, "and music? A curious thing, Master William. Most of ze world's pieces of knowledge just zeem to flow together. Astronomy and math, for instance, zeems to just naturally develop with ze biology, non?"

"And ye will teach me?" I asked.

"Of course!" said Henri. "Anne will teach ze English literature, and Mary will help ze practice with ze weapons, and ze shall study the sea, as the captain orders.

Henri's words had a dizzying effect on me. Beginning with my uncles and father and continuing through the crewmen of the Bleeding Gull and the captain and now the present threesome, it was clear that I had enjoyed an entirely improbable run of teachers and associates.

"We'll start in ze morning," Henri said.

The next morning, however, I started without Henri. Before he rose for the day, I pulled myself from bed. Using the polished stick that Mary Read had brought me, I took a walking tour of Henri's fine house. This time, I ignored the marble floors and antique furniture and concentrated on the art Henri had painted and chosen to hang in his home rather than sell.

In vibrant hues, many a child reached tenderly for its mother's face, and many a lover beneath a frosty moon listened to whispers in rapt adoration. But it was to Henri's paintings of the sea I was especially drawn. In them, white gulls swept upward in unexpected draughts that smelled of salt, and peaks of waves tossed square-masted ships with unchecked jollity.

Henri's krakens were laughing dragons swimming playfully amidst Spanish galleons filled with priests, his mermaids delightful creatures warning mariners of hidden rocks, his depictions of storms not at all depictions of nature's fury, but rather, uncannily, each a revelation of God's grandeur and glory. In front of a painting of a Portuguese carrack, I stopped, stunned, struck, and felt my legs go weak.

The wind behind it, the carrack was flying in a hurricane sea, its forecastle thrust far out onto its bow, as if riding the bowsprit, its ballooning sails so swollen with wind they filled the space of the picture and seemed on the verge of exploding.

"My god!" I cried. "My god!"

I felt myself unaccountably on the verge of tears, as if I had somehow been touched by something very deeply. But what was it? What was it? I stood before the painting for fifteen minutes or more, and again and again it elicited the same feeling. Someway or another, the picture had a power over me. It moved me. It could make me weep. It made me think of human greatness. Why? I did not know.

I did know, however, it had something to do with something I wanted from myself.

There was the ship. The terribly ornate, old-fashioned carrack with a forecastle pushed aft and huge billowing sails. There was the incredible wind, the billowing sails, my tears.

At length, I put the matter behind me and composed myself for my lessons of the day. Henri prided himself on being thorough, and therefore began with Greek philosophy, shipbuilding, playwriting, architecture, math, and art. By one o'clock in the afternoon I knew absolutely nothing.

"We begin again tomorrow, from ze beginning," said Henri, turning me over to the tender mercies of my bonny Anne, who had arrived to take me for a walk on the beach outside Henri's house."

"Ah, Anne," I said. "How fair are thy locks and thy een!"

"Ye are fair also, young William, with thy curly blond locks," said Anne. "But it is Calico Jack Rackham for me, pup, because of thy age, and because ye have not learned a page of Shakespeare."

"Not so, on both counts," I said. "I progress daily on Shakespeare, for I have mastered the art of working with the alphabet and its various sounds, which ye taught me. Soon, I shall show ye. Second, I have aged."

"Ye have aged?"

"Aye! I have aged!" I said. "Come stand by the mirror with me here, Anne. Look closely. Do ye not see in my face advancing age?"

"Aye! I do," said Anne Bonny. "Granted. Ye appear older. But it is because of thy recent ordeal. Not because of aging."

"Not so," I said. "There are private parts of my body, Anne Bonny, of which ye are not yet familiar, that have clearly aged—and I mean aged in such a way that a mere ordeal may not age a body. In fact, Anne, it would seem to me that I am no longer a mere thirteen, but rather fifteen, regardless of what may seem factual. Therefore, I am now only three years younger than ye, not five."

"Pshaw, Master William, let us go for thy walk before I tire of thy prattle and leave ye behind. Do ye feel ye can walk today?"

"Aye, and shoot!"

"Then bring along thy pistols, Master William. Thy time as an invalid draws to an end."

In some annoyance, I retreated to my night chamber to change from my nightshirt to my boots, trousers, and white shirt with sash. Then I strapped on two pistols and was surprised to feel how good they felt close to hand.

Anne and I walked out onto the beach and paused for a few moments looking out over the ocean. It was flat and blue as far as we could see but from where we stood to the coast of South America was the bloodiest stretch of water in the world.

For an hour we just walked and then returned to Henri's for weaponry and threw axes and knives until our arms grew sore, then slashed a bit with cutlasses. That done, we practiced shooting pistols, then various other firearms, these last with small groups of fisherman standing by, applauding our efforts.

Not all who watched, however, did so with entirely placid eyes, especially as the sun dipped below the horizon in the west, for it was thought among the more ignorant Indian fisherman of New Providence that I was not fully human.

"Zhey do no zing a human man could zwim zo far, especially wid ze shark." Henri would say, trembling with laughter, "and neither do I."

At nightfall, Anne and I built a small fire on the beach, for Henri had made an engagement in Nassau for the evening and left us his servants. They sat a table for us in the breath of the sea, then stocked it with wine in silver decanters and platters of scallops and lobster and crab.

"Do ye believe it wise to consort with the likes of Calico Jack Rackham, Anne? From what I hear, he's an immoral bounder of little breeding and no intellectual attainment."

"And what intellectual attainment do ye have, young William?" said Anne, "Did ye graduate from Orkney University?"

"How did ye come to meet Henri, Anne?"

"I lived for a time in the very room in which ye live now," said Anne, putting an lobster claw to her sweet lips. "Henri sympathized with a girl who was fleeing both a dominating father and a worthless husband. It was here I conceived the notion of becoming a pirate. Some friends and I outfitted a skiff and attacked a miserable little merchantman which surrendered its goods the moment we pulled out our pistols."

Anne laughed loudly.

"And do ye love the sea," I asked, cracking open a crab.

"Not as ye love it," said Anne. "I love the freedom of it, not the sea itself, for if it were the desert and as free of restraint, I would love it as well."

"And did ye study the Bible with other studies?" I said, for I did know something of the Bible because of my upbringing on Hoy and wanted to know if it was all on the level of krakens and selkies and mermaids and such or rather on the level of the history of Greece and Plato and Socrates that Henri had begun to tell me about.

"My father did not allow the study of the Bible," said Anne. "He condemned it for its condemnation of adultery, of which he approved."

"And do ye not love me, Anne?"

"Ye are a naughty boy, Master William," Anne said. "Here is the truth of it. None of us gives a fig for ye, except that we have been instructed to prepare ye for a fate unknown to us by Captain Thomas Jones."

"For a fate unknown?"

"Aye, quite unknown to us."

"Unknown, but important?"

"Aye, apparently so. But why such a cheeky lad as ye has been chosen we don't know. A nicer boy might have been better."

"But ye never would have been drawn to a nicer boy," I said, giving my Anne a long, sultry look that, in retrospect, I must guess to have been annoying.

"Perhaps not," said Anne, "but would it flatter ye as much to know that he would know of it at once if ye took on a daft look for a period of time."

"What say ye?" I said, astounded. "Does he think me daft?"

"Aye, sweet William," said Anne. "He fears the effects of this weather on your constitution."

"When have I shown a weakness of constitution?"

"I've had my fill of thy questions, William!" Sitting under a night sky on the dunes of New Providence, Anne turned her attention to the tide rolling in to the lemon trees. "Can ye not just enjoy the evening, as can I, without the company of Calico Jack, hopeless flirtations, or troublesome thoughts?"

"Nay, I cannot!" I said. "Just answer one thing more, or two!"

"S'death," she said. "Why did I take ye on as a pupil? I curse myself!"

"Tell me if ye have killed, and if ye have loved!" I said, hoping she would say "No!" to both, though I knew better.

"I'll not tell ye!" said Anne.

"Did ye love the pirate Bonny, whom ye married?" I asked.

"Pshaw!" Anne said, spitting into our fire. "He was ever a worthless pimp and a drunkard, and I never let him touch me. I used him to bring me here, for I had a proper life that needed escaping. But yes, I have loved, if ye must know to torture thyself."

"Not Jack!"

"Nay, of course not Jack! Cleanse thy mind!"

"Then who?"

"Why not ask whom I have killed?"

Annie's voice had become low and she was speaking so very softly that I was forced to lean closer to her.

"Well, first there was my father's maid, for whom I'm ashamed," said Anne. "Her name was Clara. My father had purchased her from a prison ship and brought her as a servant to our house in Charles Town, where I hated her evil disposition at first exposure. One day, she spilled hot soup in my lap, and when I called her a 'bloody bitch' she called me 'slut' and held high a carving knife."

Anne paused for a moment.

"And so I took a knife from the table and killed her with a quick stroke to the stomach."

"Then it was in self defense," I said.

"Nay," said Anne. "And Joe Buck spoke the truth of it. I was expert by then in the sword and the knife, as well as the pistol, and I could have disarmed Clara easily and with no danger to myself. Instead, I put her under the ground…and me, not yet thirteen years of age and a belle of Charles Town society."

To my surprise, Anne was crying.

"Joe Buck was so disappointed in me," she said, and then she looked away from me and at the sea for a long time. At last, she spoke again, this time without prompting.

"And now I'll tell ye a story of both killing and love and then ye will know so much more of thy sainted Anne," she said. "What say ye of that, young William?"

"Please tell me," I said. "Every word of ye is precious to me."

"When I first came to New Providence and shucked the weakling drunkard James Bonny, I chanced to meet my friend Henri, who had his many male amours and interest in me as friend."

"Aye, I have knowledge that Henri is one to squeeze firm buttocks if given the opportunity," I said.

"How I love Henri, and ye will too," said Anne, ignoring my comment. "I lived in his lavish home by the seaside for months and fell in love with a black man of his acquaintance, a simple fisherman— Tombay.

"Tombay's body flowed liked lava, so gorgeous the man, so smooth to the touch, so black and glistening in the sunlight as he drew his nets in to shore. Whereas the pirates in the taverns talked me to death in their cups, Tombay awed me with his silence. He was my unschooled Othello, without the boasts. He spoke with his tenderness, the quietness of his eyes.

"'But my beautiful Anne,' Henry would say, 'Calico Jack zis the man for ye. It zis he who ziz ze confidant and quartermaster of the great pirate Captain Vane. Diz Tombay ziz…'

"But I did not care whom Tombay was. We sailed past Little Island near New Providence to tiny Watlings Island, where his family lived with a dozen members of a village in one of the most beautiful tropical islands in the Caribbean. I tell ye, young William, it was a prison, but one of such beauty, decorated with red birds of all descriptions and swaying palms.

"On the southerly side of the island there was a small bay of a variety of fishes and close to the bay an inlet of clear blue water protected by cays. All day we made love, fished, sunned on rocks, and climbed to caves in high cliffs, where we slept exhausted until night drew close and it was time to return to the village.

"At night, we would sing and dance, and again make love, as sentinels would keep watch for ships that would send us into hiding."

"Pirate ships from New Providence?" I asked.

"Not all!" said Anne. "We kept a weather eye for the ships of Bartholomew Roberts and that of Charles Vane and Calico Jack, for both Roberts and Vane were not to be trusted with human life, but it was the Spanish and the English we feared above all."

I said nothing more.

"In such a circumstance, I gave birth to a child," continued Anne, remembering.

I turned away from her in pain. This information, I received with some shock, for nothing about her figure or manner had given notice she had ever had a child, and my heart had never imagined such. It beat upon my chest with such fierce jealousy that I put a hand to my chest.

"The child's name was Nditi," Anne said. "And still I dream of his light brown skin, his fair hair and blue eyes. Tombay and I covered him with kisses from morning till night, and slept with his body between us nursing at my breast. It was paradise, William."

"Not freedom!" I said.

"Nay, not freedom!" she said. "I can't explain it, sweet William. I had given up everything for freedom. My father, I loved and left for freedom. His estate, his fortune, I left for piracy and the open sea. And yet for Tombay and Ndita—who had nothing but skin and eyes and hair—I flew into a cage and slammed the door behind me."

"For love!" I said.

"Aye!" she said.

We were both quiet for a while.

"I know of thy mother's madness and death," she said. "Captain Jones has told me."

"Aye," I said.

"And of thy father's coming death!" she said.

"He is likely already dead," I said. "He didn't wish me to stay in Hoy and watch him die."

"I'm sorry, young William," said Anne.

"Aye," I said. "And did Tombay die?"

Gentle Anne bit her lip and I could see that there was a tear in the corner of her eye. After a wait, she gathered herself together and again began speaking low, as if she wanted no one but me to hear.

"One day I felt a great surge of energy and took my cutlass to weed a cabbage patch that lay half a mile from the village and hidden by dense foliage from the shoreline. I worked all morning under the hot sun, and, finally, exhausted, trudged back toward the village where several old women had been left to watch the children while the men fished the bay on the island's southern side."

"A quarter mile from the village I quickened my pace. I could smell fish and shellfish cooking over an open fire and was ravenously hungry. Emerging from a copse of bamboo shoots I came with a start upon a group of six seamen eating with their hands from bowls of fish and rice.

"'Where is everyone?' I asked, but received no answer, only friendly smiles and gestures from the men to join them.

"I watched them with my stomach turning, my despair deepening. If they had been pirates, even the beasts of Bartholomew Roberts, I might have had hope or bargained with them or demanded to see their captain, but they were unmistakably Spanish and richly garbed in heavy brocaded doublets.

"They were blowing me kisses, food easing from the corners of their mouths. The fattest of them patted the dirt beside him and gestured for me to sit. My lips forced a smile, and my hand gripped my cutlass as I slipped the blade under my sash.

""'Where are my captors?' I asked. 'Where are the beastly children?'

"The Spaniards shrugged their shoulders and looked around at one another as if they knew no English, or had seen no children. Neither was likely. My heart sank further.

"'Am I free?' I asked, still forcing a smile, blood rushing from my head, my legs shaking so hard I thought I would fall. I turned toward one of the huts with a feminine gesture: a lifting of both arms to shoulder height and a slight fluttering of my hands.

"Outside the closest hut there was blood on the ground. Blood! No noise came from the hut, no scolding from the women, and no chattering of the children. I felt I was staggering but forced a composed walk to the door of the hut and took a look inside."

"'Ndita!' I whispered.

"Then the horror of my life presented itself to my eyes. The decapitated bodies of two women and several children lay sprawled on the floor of the hut and in the middle sat Ndita's severed head, its blond hair soaked with blood.

"My soul's scream of terror and pain reached heaven itself, but my will drew shut my lips so that no sob escaped my throat. Never before had I acted with such discipline and purpose and art, nor yet performed with such cold malignancy. Employing my talent for the stage, I stifled the heart of the mother within me and took up the role of a rescued white captive and grateful whore.

"When I turned back toward them, the Spaniards looked at me with suspicious eyes, their hands close to the hilts of their swords.

"'I'm free!' I said, my smile broadening, my hands letting down my bound-up hair.

"'Si, Senorita,' said the fat Spaniard, again smiling. 'Ye are free. Come sit down beside me.'

"Then all the men laughed and looked at me up and down.

"'All free,' one of them said, and then they laughed again, and when I started forward, they all relaxed and went back to eating from their bowls. That is when I struck. My cutlass was free of my sash even before I had fully realized I had drawn it. To my great shock, a Spaniard's head was off its shoulders and had flown into the fire, where it threw sparks into all eyes, even my own.

"A great wail of fury rose from my being, and a second head went into the fire. Blackened branches scattered, spouting flame. My cutlass opened the stomach of a Spaniard who had jumped to his feet to rub his eyes. Again, my blade whirled about me uncontrollably and a hand went flying. Only then did my senses return to me, and what I found was two slaughtered villains, a third holding in his innards, a fourth gone white from the loss of a hand, a fifth quaking in fright, and a sixth soiled demon fleeing for his life.

"The paralyzed Spaniard, who stood trembling with the sword in his hand, I dispatched at once by a blow to the neck. Then, the frenzy upon me, I chased the fleeing man to the sea and there held him under the waves till he drowned. After that, I left the two other Spaniards to die in agony, the Spaniard with the stomach wound pleading for me to give him the killing blow, which I denied.

"I collapsed. I wept for an hour. I buried the pitiful children in the sand, neither feeling the sun on my head nor the heat of the sand on my hands. I left weeping to find the men of the village and my dear Tombay."

"And did ye find them?" I asked, slowly, in a whisper.

"Aye," Anne said. "I found them all. Everyone in the village had been killed, all for no reason. Tombay had been killed with several of the other men on the beach where they had been fishing."

Anne was weeping again. This time she turned from me and lay flat out on the sand and wept, her cutlass in her sash shinning in the moonlight, and I could imagine the fury with which she had wielded it against the slaughterers of her family. Yet, she had chosen such a life as she had led in this lawless region, and she would do so again if again she had to choose, and this I could see she knew.

"Is this the avenging cutlass, Anne?" I asked.

"Aye," she said, ceasing to sob.

"The moon plays a trick with it," I said. "There, it seems to have blood on it."

"I'll never part with it," said Anne. "Not until every Spanish and English ship of war has gone to its grave."

I sat upright in amazement, but said nothing, lest she think I was making up shared goals so as to please her.

"Ye were saying of Tombay," I said.

"So many of the men were mutilated," said Anne. "An old man, Cuffee, was beheaded, and his head was stuck on a point of a Spanish spear, and two others were gutted and stripped of their genitals. But Tombay was beautiful, still, in death. I pushed the small Spanish piracy boat to sea and let it break up on surf and rocks, and put Tombay's body in his sloop.

"How alive he seemed and how unwilling I was to let him go. I wrapped him in sailcloth and sailed to Little Island for the night. There, beneath the stars, I sat with his bloody body and wept all night, and then in the morning roamed the island for wild flowers. These, I brought back to the sloop and sprinkled on my beloved and then set sail again on a sunny morning, this time to Exuma Sound, on the way to New Providence.

"There, young William, I tied rocks to my love's feet and eased him into the sea, knowing he would seek out our son in heaven and take care of him there. Then, I cried my way to New Providence and took up my life again."

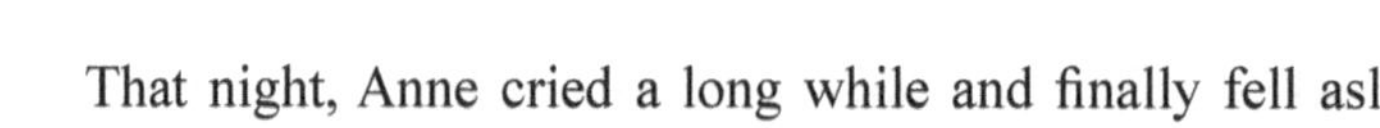

That night, Anne cried a long while and finally fell asleep on the beach. I lay awake at her side, looking at the stars, my arms around her, sometimes holding her closely, other times letting her go.

Once, she woke up and spoke to me softly.

"Tell me of Captain Jones," she said.

"Captain Jones?"

"Of course, I would ask ye of the captain. Did I not tell ye my tale?"

"I don't follow you, I swear!" I said.

"You've nothing to be jealous of," she said.

"Jealous?" I said. "Should I be jealous?"

"Come, come, William," she said, "There are things I want to know…"

"Why ever…?"

"For my own peace, William! Now, damn it! As you love me, will you talk to me about him, or do you want to leave me wretched?"

"I will," I said, "but explain yourself."

"I will do that," she said, "but speak to me frankly."

"Will there be quim?"

"At some point there might be quim."

"Very well," I said, "Captain Jones is a man of Wales, a Welshman, an heir to Francis Drake and Henry Morgan, and a senior to the Dread Pyrate Roberts."

"Let Black Bart Roberts hear ye talk of him so disrespectfully and he'll have thy head and pretty locks," said Anne.

"Well, Captain Jones is a killer too," I said. "He was raised to it by a military education and takes no joy in it, but kills when there is honor in it."

"I'm glad to hear what I know once again confirmed," said saucy Anne. "Yet, you withhold too much."

"Captain Jones likes to teach. I am witness to that and the chief bene-factor of what he teaches."

"And what does he teach?" asked Anne.

"He forever inveighs against superstition, and myth," I said, "and religion too when it borders on superstition and myth. 'Young William,' he says to me, over and over, as if has never said it to me before. 'Never lose thy base in the natural world, for that is the world that God has given ye to live in. It is especially important for a man who dares to go to sea.'"

"And what do ye say?"

"Aye, Aye, I say each time, as if I believe him."

"That's well and good," Anne said, impatiently, "but tell me of the man."

"Captain Jones is a difficult man to capture," I said. "There are no defining extremes."

"Explain that to me, William."

"Well," I said, "he always dresses well, but he's never the best dressed in any room. He drinks, but never to excess. He loves, but casually, and, it's said, without passion."

"I have heard that," said Anne. "How odd!"

"Nor is it ever said of him that he is too generous or desirous of gold, nor that he is too gay, nor too dour, nor that he is a coward, nor too reckless."

"He is like a ghaist," said Anne, shivering, "not human. Nor do ye seem human to me, sweet William, except in thy lust. But tell me. Have ye seen the captain in anger?"

"Nay," I said. "In no case that I know has he ever lost his temper or had cause to regret an action or fail to be polite or act in a obsequious manner. He is a pirate, yes, but no thief. I do not think of him as a thief."

"Nor do I," said Anne. "Then what do we think of him as?"

"I don't know," I said. "As a man of politics?"

"I know even less than ye," said Anne. "Why does he love ye?"

I sat up with a start. Never having had the courage or effrontery to have even dreamed the question before, I had no glib answer, or any answer for it now. Yet, was it possible to deny that the captain had some kind of inexplicable feeling for me?

A frantic letter from the captain had already been received by Anne inquiring of my whereabouts, and a second letter expressing relief and giving instructions as to my care was sent by the captain in response.

"What the captain loves best seems to be the sea," I said, "but one never finds him at the wheel in rapture."

"Ye and he are about a strange business," said Anne. "I am sure ye know little its nature, but also know that it is a strange. As Henri would say, n'est ce pas?"

"I do think it strange," I said, "and as you suspect, am but little aware of its nature."

"For instance," said Anne. "I assume his losing his ship to the boucaniers was deliberate."

"Ah," I said, marveling at Anne, for she forced to the top gallant of my brain the windy thought that all the captain's mistakes seemed staged, and all of his questions asked not for answers but to tease one's logic.

"And one question more about the captain," said Anne.

"Which is?" I asked, now anxious to learn the direction of her mind.

"What does the captain plan to hunt with such a huge ghost ship that must have come sailing toward him from a hundred years ago— the Royal Navy?"

"I do not know," I said, then moved to stand alone on the sandy beach, under a breaking moon.

"One thing more, William" Anne said, "I have noticed the quickness of thy hand and seen thee shoot, as well as heard of your long night swim."

"And what of it," I said.

"Other than the captain, are Henri, Mary and I the first to know that thou are not fully human?"

Chapter Sixteen

One morning, having noted both the shortcomings of the Greek trireme as a vessel of war and what he termed the "Seven Imbecilities of Marcus Aurelius," Henri tweaked his black mustaches in an emphatic fashion and strode impatiently to the balcony door.

"The sun ez shining, my friend, my friend!" he shouted out, "To thy clothes…thy clothes. Today, ze shall learn of the fine drinks of the Caribbean."

"But if Anne comes…" I protested.

"Not today, Mon aime!" said Henri. "Captain Charles Vane's *Condor* dropped anchor in ze harbor last night, which means zhat Anne Bonny will have her Calico Jack Rackham to deal with today."

"What!" I said. "I'll go to her."

"Let her alone," said Henri. "Or she will hate ze. Already, she begins to hate Calico Jack."

"Then why does she think of him as 'her' Jack?" I said angrily, my cheeks burning with sudden rage.

"Let her discover ze hatred for Jack and flail him from her bone," said Henri. "Do zee rival her with ze knife. Nay! However, for the moment, she might need her Jack, for he ez a wild one, and he makes her laugh…and, for now, she needs to laugh, n'est ce pas. Ye know the story of Tombay!"

To this, I had nothing to say. I dressed quietly in the fine clothing that Henri had provided for this special day of learning the fine fruit drinks of the Caribbean. On this occasion, he had decided to pass up the more raucous pirate shanties, such as the King's Head Tavern, and patronize instead the relatively genteel Admiral Skull Inn.

From what I gathered, the chief difference between the two establishments was the Admiral Skull Inn's policy of employing thugs to hurl abusive drunks into the muddy street before fights to the death spoiled everyone's drinking. A second, less important distinction, but one that weighted heavily with Henri, was the Admiral Skull Inn's use of matching glassware and tablecloths, both washed daily.

By the time we reached the inn, I was sore from walking and sat down heavily at a table near the rear of the establishment. There, I propped my cane against the chair to my left and consulted Henri. Seated to my right, Henri was perusing the rum drinks and wine list painted large upon a wall.

"Perhaps just a basic fine rum with a subtle blend of fruit juices added," Henri said. "When a bit of alcohol made from sugar cane was added to ze drinking water on ships, we had rum, a drink without ze impurities of water. Now, the making of rums has become an art form… Mon dieu!

"Mon dieu?"

"Certainement," whispered Henri, his mood completely altered. He leaned toward me ever so slightly, focusing entirely on the scrawled list of spirits as if it were his only concern.

"Do not look over thy shoulder or with obvious intent if ye do look," he said, under his breath. "Calico Jack has just come in with the pirate el Portuguese and they are taking seats at the long table by the hearth."

I let a few moments pass without looking. Then, at last, as Henri ordered our first drinks from the serving girl, I repositioned my chair so that I might observe the two men by a sidelong glance. The man I took to be el Portugues because of his long black braids and swarthy look was seated in profile, his nose long and jagged, his mouth a slash made downward towards his collar.

"Aye, Bartholomew el Portugues," said Jack Rackham, picking his teeth with a knife. "Ye seem out of sorts."

"El Diablo bites my arse," said el Portugues, swallowing the worm in the dregs of his bottle. "I recently captured a fine prize by pitting my thirty drunken buccaneers with four small guns against seventy Hildago bitches with seventy big guns. Then what does the devil send? Three war ships to reclaim 70,000 pieces of eight and throw me in irons!"

"But ye escaped," said Rackham. "Do be of good cheer."

"A hidden knife on my person provided for a fellow's ease," said el Portugues. "Then, I stuffed the mouths of some clay pots and floated on the pots to shore and from that shore made my way back to here."

"Where the world applauds," said Calico Jack Rackham.

"Where the world awaits news of the size of the bounty to be placed on my head," corrected el Portugues.

Calico Jack burst into a bout of such wild laughter that el Portugues followed his lead and the slash of his mouth turned upward toward his ear.

"Wine! Ten bottles!" shouted Jack at the serving girl, and in less than a minute the barkeep and the serving girl were filling the long table with glasses and Calico Jack was standing at the table pouring a first glass for el Portuguese and himself.

The sight of him filled me with anguish. When he stood, he seemed to be rising up forever, at least a foot closer to the ceiling than I when I stood, and his body was heavily muscled all over yet trim as a boxer's. Even more annoying was the perfect grandeur of his hair and well-trimmed mustache and elegant coat and trousers of calico.

Here, indeed, I thought, was a sophisticated man, a man with a weasel.

My spirits sank to the bottom of my glass of rum, indifferently brought to the table, and now tasteless to my tongue.

"Control ze emotions," whispered Henri. "There is perhaps something to be learned by remaining quiet and listening. It zeems we have stumbled upon a meeting of luminaries."

"Aye," I replied, and nodded, but all the while wished rather to test Calico Jack's pistols against my own. In another moment, there was a clatter at the door and a young Indian boy of ten or eleven came into the establishment and held open the swinging door behind him.

"Milord Stede Bonnet, Captain of the *La Ventura*," he intoned the best he could, and then along came a gangly creature reminiscent of a swan. Elegant white silks clung to his thin form, and upon his powdered wig rode a great white-plumed hat with a wide, silvery brim.

"At thy service," announced Bonnet, bowing from the waist. It is excellent to see ye, Jack. Will ye kindly introduce me to thy associate?"

El Portuguese turned toward Bonnet, his eyes aghast. "So ye are Stede Bonnet?" he said.

"And this is Bartholomew el Portuguese," said Rackham to Bonnet.

"Ah," said Bonnet, "A man of the lower classes, a Spaniard to boot. Ye'll bear some watching, I'll wager, Bartholomew."

El Portuguese's fingers tightened on his glass, so Rackham reached over and held his wrist for a moment, then whispered in his ear. Of a sudden, el Portuguese laughed, and then looked back at the ridiculous figure of Bonnet, now looming over the table.

"Do have a seat," said el Portuguese. "Thy exploits at sea have reached my ears and I am much impressed. Ye are very welcomed to join our counsel, since this new matter concerns us all."

Stede Bonnet then signaled for his Indian boy to take up a seat at the door and took a seat beside el Portuguese just as the door opened again and a man of some forty years and of unremarkable appearance entered and approached the table.

Introductions were made all around. The newcomer, who appeared to be a merchant or banker and wore the no-nonsense garb of the marketplace, was Captain Benjamin Hornigold, the mentor of Edward Teach.

"How many others are expected?" said Hornigold, making notes in a black ledger.

"Black Bart and Captain Vane," said Calico Jack, "And I expect Captain Vane to bring George Fetherstone, his boatswain. Then, I'm certain Bellamy will be here, as well as some members of the Flying Gang and other undesirables."

"Well, the Great Pyrate Roberts will be here!" said Captain Hornigold. "What an honor for us all."

"And why does Vane get to bring his quartermaster, ye, Jack, and his boson, George Fetherstone?" said Bonnet. "Ye'll have us outnumbered."

"Nay, Sir!" said Captain Hornigold. "The Great Pyrate Roberts will have us outnumbered just by showing up alone!"

There was a huge burst of laughter, and some of the riff-raff and leeches of the docks began to file in. Pirates mixed with the acrobats and hawkers and members of the Flying Gang began filling up the chairs all around the long table.

"Apparently," Henri said, "Everyone knows what ez going on but ze two of us."

Captain Bellamy, or "Black Bellamy," dressed all in black, walked in, cold as death himself, his long black hair combed straight down. He took his place at the table, saying nothing, acknowledging no one. When at last, the old man Charles Vane, scrawny and chicken-necked at forty five, made his way to the table with his boatswain, George Fetherstone, and young girl-friend, Nicole, it was with a dizzying array of squawked complaints.

Who were these uninvited onlookers? The room was too warm! Why wasn't there a better seat at the table for him? Why wasn't the meeting at the King's Head Tavern? Where was the Great Pyrate Roberts?

In five more minutes, it was decided not to wait any longer for Roberts, which suited me well enough. By this time, my jealousy of Calico Jack had been muted somewhat by my curiosity as to what was afoot, and the chance of my being discovered had been made to seem minuscule by the number of people crowding into the inn.

Calico Jack stood up again, called out loudly, fired a pistol at the ceiling, and pulled a scroll from his calico jacket.

"Gentlemen," said Jack. "For many a year it has been thought that Madagascar is the pirate capital of the world; yet there is new evidence that we of New Providence have now reached that illustrious height. This new evidence comes from no less than King George of England."

There were scattered hurrahs from around the room.

"On September 5, 1717," said Calico Jack. "King George issued at Hampton Court a proclamation for the suppression of piracy. In so doing he also promised certain awards of money for the capture of captains, masters, boatswains and officers of any pirate vessels."

"May the swine of hell fly up his royal arse!" remarked Captain Bellamy.

"But that's not all, my Brethren," said Calico Jack. If this were the entirety of the message there would be no meeting. So now I will read ye the part of the King's proclamation that most concerns us."

Calico Jack stood up straight and read in a rich baritone.

"We have thought fit, by and with the advice of our Privy Council to issue this, our Royal Proclamation, and we do hereby promise and declare that in case any of the said pyrates should on or before the 5th of September, in the year of our Lord 1718, surrender him or themselves to one of our principal Secretaries of State in Great Britain or Ireland or to any Governor or Deputy Governor of any of our plantations beyond the seas, such pyrates shall have our gracious pardon, of and for such pyracy or pyracies committed. Before the fifth of January next ensuing . . .”

“In short, my Brethren,” shouted Jack. “The crown offers us pardons if we give up our trade!”

By the end of the reading the inn was in uproar.

“Svive the king’s proclamation with thy ulcerous member!” was the unanimous response of all present. “Piss on’t till then!”

By popular demand, Calico Jack held the proclamation before the fireplace and one man after the other dropped his trousers and emptied his bladder on the document, after which Calico Jack flung the document into the fireplace.

Only the gentlemanly Stede Bonnet found the act of public urination too difficult to accomplish, so he expressed his defiance by firing at the ceiling instead and wishing the king ill health. Of all the pirates of the Caribbean, he was the most aristocratic by birth and the most dandified by taste. He had become a pirate late in life to escape his wife, and had purchased his vessel rather than stolen it, hired a crew rather than recruited it, and had befriended Captain Vane rather than fled him.

The pissing well done, Captain Bellamy uttered a version of a sentiment for which he had become so famous, that “he had as much right to make war on the whole world as any prince with a thousand ships of sail.”

“So the Brethren in cooperation with the British and the French and the Dutch destroy the power of Spain in the Caribbean,” said an angry Captain Vane. “And now the British wish to drive us from the Caribbean as well.”

“Anger?” said Hornigold, cleaning the mud from his boot with his knife. “Should there be anger, or should there be an appraisal of our position?”

“An appraisal!” cried Calico Jack, jumping so quickly to his feet that his shoulder bumped that of Nicole’s. With a little whelp, like a dog’s, she landed half in Vane's lap and was then shoved back into her chair, where she cursed at Jack through clenched teeth.

"Heretofore," said Hornigold. "We have never borne a sustained campaign by the British because of their interest in our destruction of the Spanish bastards, but could we hold them off if they attacked Nassau in small ships without let up? What if we were not together?"

George Fetherstone spat on the floor and idly banged his goblet on the table until the buzz of talk in the Admiral's Skull Inn ceased. Bending low over the table, he stared eye to eye with Hornigold and spoke in a nasty whisper.

"And why would we not be together, old man," he said. "It is not any of us whose loyalty is driven by the ledger."

Hornigold's cheeks turned a scarlet red, but he let the moment pass.

"Where is Henry Jennings? And Bart Roberts? And Edward Teach?" he said, pausing, letting the air grow heavy with the questions.

"Gentlemen," said Captain Bellamy. "Matters here grown sensitive, as I am sure ye all agree. I suggest that we now empty the room of common seamen and members of the Flying Gang and all cowardly beings who do not purchase their dinners by coins taken in piracy."

"A suggestion to my liking," said Vane, drawing both his pistols, prompting Calico Jack, George Fetherstone, and even Nicole to draw theirs. Immediately, there was a rush for the door, but then a jam in the doorway as Nassau's unqualified confidence men and criminals struggled to save their hides.

Henri and I too made a strong move toward the door but we were seated at a table far from it and when we attempted to make progress I was jostled from my feet and fell into a chair even closer to where Vane and his crew were holding pistols.

"Sit down, Henri!" Vane barked out. "We all know who ye are, whether or not ye know it."

At last, the only onlookers remaining in the room were Henri and I, the barkeep and serving girl, and Stede Bonnet's boy, who kept his station in a chair by the door.

"Who is that Indian boy?" said Captain Bellamy, pointing to the boy on his chair, who turned white with fright.

"He is my serving boy," spoke up Stede Bonnet, "and I will thank ye, Sir, for neither molesting him or speaking to him harshly. He is only ten years old."

That settled, there seemed only one matter of business remaining. As if time were up to illuminating the more awkward moments of my life, it first slowed down then painted the next fractions of a second a doubloon gold. As if members of a grisly jury, the pirates were first staring at Stede Bonnet's Indian boy. Then, with aching slowness, each face in unison filled with sunlight and turned toward me.

By then I had picked Captain Vane and Calico Jack for my first targets, then Captain Bellamy for my knife. Captains Hornigold and Benet seemed to me relatively harmless, but George Fetherstone seemed anything but. If I was to survive the morning, it would be necessary for me to take down Fetherstone with my cutlass before he had thought to properly draw his pistol. Captain Vane's mistress, Nicole, was an unknown factor. My hope was that she would grieve over Vane rather than immediately take arms.

"Who are ye, boy?" said Captain Vane, gazing at me intently.

"I am William Claddah." I said.

A great, explosive grunt of awareness burst from Captain Vane. He was suddenly filled with joy. All smiles, he turned toward Calico Jack, reached behind Nicole, who sat between them, and heavily pounded Calico Jack on the shoulder.

"Why Jack!" shouted Captain Vane. "Look who it is, Jack. It is thy rival. It is thy rival, Jack!"

With that, everyone in the room, even Henri, burst into laughter. Captain Bellamy laughed until tears came to his eyes, and Captain Hornigold fell against Stede Bonnet, laughing in his ear. George Fetherstone, instead of reaching for a pistol, chuckled, and Nicole murmured, "Jack, oh Jack, Jack, Jack."

"Damn ye boy to death!" shouted Calico Jack, leaping yet again to his feet, this time to draw his pistols and shoot me down like a dog.

Relief washed over me. My opponent was a fool and had learned nothing from experience. His shouting had cost him time, his leaping even more, and his flamboyant method of reaching for his weapon was a study in wasted motion. Long before he could raise his pistols, my own pistols were drawn and pointed at his breast.

The gentlemen assembled gasped, having mistaken my performance as an unnatural one from one so young, rather than the product of training.

Unfortunately for me, I had beaten Jack to such a degree that I was not entitled to pull the triggers.

"Ah, pup," Vane said. "I have heard of thy abilities as a marksman, as well as other of thy attributes. I had taken them as fantasies. Perhaps, I'll rethink my opinions."

"Aye!"

"Ye are a dead man, lad!" said Calico Jack.

"Nay, he is no dead man, Jack Rackham!" said a woman's voice from the doorway. "Not if ye value the affection of thy own Anne Bonny! If this lad comes to some bloody pass, ye will pay dearly for it, though ye are no way involved. My own dear sweet, I am now putting ye in charge of William Claddah and responsible, as others are, with his health and education."

"But Anne...." said Jack.

"Fight him no more, Jack," said Anne. "Either by my hand, or, more likely, his, ye shall be dead if ye do."

Captains Bellamy and Hornigold soon excused themselves until such time as another meeting of more principals could be arranged. Captain Vane, Jack Rackham, George Fetherstone, Stede Bonnet, Nicole, and Anne Bonny sat down to plan a further expedition against the Spanish.

"We can lie off the Caymans," said Vane, peeling back the tablecloth to carve a map on the table with his knife, much to the chagrin of the barkeep, who said nothing. "Our chances are good of catching a galleon bound for Havana."

As Captain Vane talked, Nicole moved ever closer to his side, as if she could not bear contact that did not impinge upon his private space. Except that he periodically pushed her away, she would have found herself constantly perched in his lap, his freedom of movement compromised. In compensation for this loss, she offered the sight of her white breast thrusting from her loosely laced bodice. The rope of her hair fell in a long braid down the middle of her back, and her person, from hair to boot, was decorated with weaponry.

At length, all but Stede Bonnet, Henri, and I agreed on the Spanish expedition.

"Captain Vane, it is good to see ye well," said Anne Bonny.

"Ever a pleasure, Mistress Bonny," said Vane, half rising to take Anne's hand and kissing it like a gentleman of the court. "How I envy my rascal, Calico Jack Rackham, to have the privilege of thy close acquaintance!"

"Thank ye, Sir."

"My compliments, also," said George Fetherstone.

"Come, talk with me," shouted Vane. He poured Anne, Henri and I flagons of rum punch and urged us to move closer to him at the longer table. "It is not often I have the honor of speaking with people of such learning," said Vane. "Too often I have to make do with the shadowy people of the world."

At these words, I noticed Henri glance at Nicole's face. It was as if Vane had struck her.

"I see that the famous painter Henri Duplaissez has taken a fancy to thy beauty, Nicole," said Captain Vane. "Perhaps ye two should withdraw to the studio."

Calico Jack ceased stuffing herbs into the bowl of his clay pipe and looked suddenly up at Captain Vane.

"I'll have her goddamned eyes," snarled Nicole, leaping to her feet.

Vane's leap was even faster than Nicole's. In spite of his years and wizened form, he was up in ample time to wrap his arms about Nicole's body, thus securing it and causing the two of them to pitch over backwards, Nicole screaming her rage but drawing no blood.

"Control thyself, damn ye!" shouted Vane, but he might with more profit have been shouting at a waterspout. Nicole squirmed with such fierceness that she tore an arm free and used a hand to tear away the captain's hat and pitiful wig. So bereft, he looked less the scourge of the sea than a chicken-necked old man concerned for his manhood.

"A thousand pardons?" he shouted to Anne. "She is prone to these jealous fits whenever she ferrets out my interest in a woman of real intelligence and loveliness. Please forgive her?"

"Forgive!" said Anne. "I am always one to forgive if one asks forgiveness. If one doesn't ask for it, however, I am not prone to give it. Therefore, Captain Vane, it would be well if ye were to hold on tightly to thy bitch, else I'll make a quick end of her."

"Hussy! Whore!" screamed Nicole, pulling a second arm free of the captain's grasp and unsheathing a knife with a cruel, curved blade.

With a desperate lunge, the captain dove for her ankle and held fast. Spewing curses, she kicked at his face to make him let go.

"Hold back, demon from hell," growled Anne. "I'll cut out thy heart!"

I could hardly move, so fascinating was the event unfolding before me. Henri shouted his warning to Anne because Nicole frightened him, and he thought there was some possibility Anne would die, but he was a painter, not a man of war. From the prospective of a man of war, it was clear from the start—from the first exchange of words—that Nicole was no match for Anne.

Anne had Mr. Starr's speed and economy of motion, as well as a beautiful coldness. She hissed with contempt, and waited, poised. Nicole finally pulled her foot free and spewed buckets of curses in her direction.

Anne said the word, "bitch," almost to herself and drew a rapier from her sash.

"Nay!" shouted Henri, as Nicole charged over the table, her knife slicing a great crescent of air as she dropped to the other side, her cutlass appearing from no where and slashing from the other side. Involuntary shouting rose from all sides. For a brief moment, a great noise arose in the inn as if we were in the midst of a storm at sea and all hands were going down.

Then there was blood everywhere. Blood in great clouds in the air and over the walls! Blood on the floor and on the faces and clothes of us all!

My darling Anne stepped back, and we could see the rapier blade stuck through the sacred space between Nicole's hips, and Nicole, turning white, was standing upright, staring down upon her wound in a stupor.

"And there ye are," said Anne. "May that be prick enough for ye!"

Chapter Seventeen

Since my time as a pirate, many a horror had I seen, not least the sight of cannon fire tear a good ship into long splinters half a foot thick that went hurling through the bodies of men. But nothing that I had yet seen had prepared me for the sight of Nicole stuck through her private parts, a dawning awareness of her certain death creeping into her eyes.

How long it took her to topple I do not know. I was not the first to force my attention from the gruesome sight. The blighter that held that distinction was George Fetherstone, who infamously used his lack of feeling to draw his pistols, so, at last, as Nicole, lay gurgling on the floor in her own blood, he laughed with pleasure.

Everyone turned toward him, as if he were mad.

"And ye are laughing," shouted Captain Vane. "Might I ask ye why?"

Fetherstone continued to smile, as if he had a great secret.

"Why?" he said. "Why? It's because I have the drop on that woman from hell, Anne Bonny, and that boy, William Claddah, Sir. Just say the word, Sir, and I'll send a ball into the brain of that murdering witch and do away with the boy as well."

"What?" screamed Calico Jack Rackham. "Ye'll shoot my quim? Do so, Sir, and ye shall die the death of a strangled fowl!"

"Nay!" shouted Captain Vane, picking up his wig and straightening it on his head. "Ye shall not die the death of a strangled fowl. Ye shall die the death of a scalded pig if ye touch a single hair on Mistress Bonny's head, for she is the most comely bitch in all of New Providence and will be mine at last when Calico Jack Rackham here contrives to swing by his neck."

"Swive ye, ye low mucking dog!"

"Swive ye both," said George Fetherstone. "Then, I'll just content myself with shooting the boy with both pistols. If that is alright with ye both."

"Ye may do as ye choose, George Fetherstone," said Calico Jack. "Ye are as free a man as I."

"Pshaw," said Anne Bonny. "Ye'll not be able to kill the boy. Are ye mad? You'll be a dead man, George Featherstone!"

"And how is that, Anne Bonny?" said George Fetherstone. "I am standing here with both pistols aimed at his heart and he has both of his pistols in his sash. How may ye say that he will kill me?"

"He is the best on earth," said Anne, matter of factly, looking at her nails.

"And what do ye think, Captain?" said Fetherstone.

"Anne exaggerates. But let him live," said Captain Vane. "I believe he is the devil come to earth. Look at that cold, fishy eye. Let's let him live that we might see what havoc he'll do."

By this time, I had become bored by the endless talk. It had been clear to me for some time that George Fetherstone would not succeed in shooting me, but only in entertaining Captain Vane. Henri cursed a bit in his foreign tongue and poured me another glass of wine. Sweat was thick on his brow, as if he had believed the appearances of things—the illusory danger presented by Nicole and George Fetherstone.

The afternoon was moving toward shadows and the serving girl lit lanterns and soon other customers began filling the inn, a few of the delicate ones noticing Nicole's body blocking their way.

"This lass is making my boots sticky with her bloody discharge," complained a codger named Yellow Dirk, but looking around, he found no one to accept responsibility for the circumstance and so passed by to sit in the back of the room.

"May ze blessed Jesus prezerve uz all," said Henri, making the sign of the cross, too frightened to get up and excuse himself from our company. As for me, I refused to leave my murderous Anne in the company of undependable pirates, for well I knew she repented of the boiling blood that had slain the whore. Once or twice I caught her eye and saw the same tender, repentant Anne that Joe Buck must have seen when he encountered the slayer of Clara, the maid.

Before long, Captain Vane, Henri, Anne, Calico Jack, George Fetherstone, and Captain Bonnet made a tight little group drinking purple wine in the golden lamplight at the long table, and still Stede Bonnet's Indian boy sat in his chair by the front door.

Suddenly, as if driven by the wind, the front doors of the inn were thrown open and six seamen stormed into the inn. Seeing us, the coarse lot, armed to their ears with cutlasses, bully clubs, daggers, various hooks, marlinespikes, and pistols marched toward our table with curious, high-kicking steps, then stopped and parted, allowing a tall gentlemen wrapped tightly in a black cloak to advance. He was an imposing figure, easily over six feet, and ramrod straight, his black hair peeking from the top of his cloak. He wore flashing jeweled rings on his long beautiful fingers and jangling silver spurs on his coal black boots.

"What?" he cried out. "Ye dared to have the meeting early!"

With those words, the Great Pyrate Roberts threw aside his cloak with a flourish and revealed as dashing a black-eyed creature as ever prowled the Spanish Main. The silver of his teeth matched the silver of his buttons, and both of these matched his earrings and jeweled pistols, which he wore in red sashes. His tricorn hat seemed a piece of the night.

"Aye, Bart!" said Captain Vane. "We took thy absence to mean ye had gone to sea for glory of God and our English King."

"Well," said Roberts. "Ye were quite right to suppose such a thing, Sir. As all men know, I have long been dedicated to righteous causes. The keeping of gold and silver in trust for God and the king is ever on my mind, second only to the moral instruction of lost young women."

"What a pity, then, ye were not here earlier," said Captain Vane, "As ye can see, Nicole here has died for want of moral instruction."

Bart Roberts shook his head, ruefully. "Long have I feared a dreadful end for Nicole. I'm right sorry, Captain Vane, but I suspect there is a bright side in this case. I will endeavor to find ye another woman who is not so painful to look at and is yet indifferent to beauty in the masculine form."

"I would appreciate it, Bart," said Captain Vane, shaking hands with him and sitting again at the table.

Captain Roberts removed his black cloak and I gasped, for he was dressed like a gentleman of Wales.

He wore a thick belt of leather bespangled with daggers and a lacy white shirt with a huge white medallion at his throat depicting the moon goddess, Diana. His kilt was exquisite, not of the Caribbean like Jack's pantaloons, but perfectly fitted Welsh wool and dyed to match his hat. So effortlessly made of Parisian and Moorish fashions were the foundations of his costume and then so accentuated by a woman's hand with Celtic badges and pins that the Dread Pyrate Roberts seemed a character drawn in bold outline and colored by sheerest fancy.

It was an impression greatly enhanced by his pack of cutthroats, who took up positions like hounds in every dark corner of the inn.

I would have applauded the cheekiness, but Bart Roberts was the worst of them that sailed from Newfoundland and now New Providence or so it was put about. Where another captain might take a prize, Roberts might take nine. Where another of the Brethren in a converted pink of ten guns or twelve might board an armed merchantman, Black Bart might lead his men in prayer and then attack a French flotilla. There was no buccaneer so daring or so careless of life.

In a single sloop manned by sixty men, he once sailed cloaked by winter's snow and attacked twenty-two ships sitting at anchor in a Newfoundland harbor, capturing a brigantine for use as a flagship.

But then, well I knew, he had an awesome tradition to live up to and, to some extent I'm sure, was driven to it. Preceding him from Wales there had been Drake the Dragon and his indestructible sea dogs, then Sir Henry Morgan, the conqueror of the Caribbean, and following soon after, Thomas Jones. Then, and I smiled to think of it, there entered my mind the wild thought that another factor might be impelling him onward.

Footsteps! Roberts lived each day as if some future buccaneer would surpass him, as I surely would, if possible.

"Captain Vane," said the Great Pyrate Roberts. "I will save ye, and Jack, Anne, Captain Bonnet, and George and even this cringing faggot Henri much discourse. I know all of thy business here today and have come to tell ye all to accept the King's pardon."

At this, there was shouting all about the room. George Fetherson, who was engaged in dragging Nicole's body out the back door, ceased his labor and seemed overcome with anger. He shook his fist at Black Bart.

"What a pity ye take my counsel for less than wise," said Black Bart. "Gentlemen, there are facts ye must consider. Now that ye have helped the British lay the Spanish low, the British Navy will be able to turn its full power against ye, and it will quickly develop a fleet of sloops and schooners and other smaller craft that can negotiate our waters. This, ye doubtless know.

"Now add to that the knowledge that Captain Hornigold and others will quickly accept pardons and revert to captaining merchant vessels. A goodly number will become pirate catchers. Some will retire and live off their riches or return to society in important positions. Increasingly pressed by the authorities and with fewer ports, captains will become more susceptible to mutinies, and each passing year will find more and more of ye gentlemen hung."

"Gentlemen, the golden age of piracy is over."

"Surely not," said Captain Vane, who was immediately backed up by loud protests from Calico Jack. George Fetherstone put on a look of disgust and dragged Nicole's body out the door.

When he came back in, I could see that a rainstorm was blowing up to the West of New Providence and would be upon us in minutes. Such changes of weather were not at all usual in New Providence. By the time the Great Pyrate Roberts had pulled up a chair for his usual cup of tea and a second lantern was brought for the table, there was a streak of lighting at the window and then the sound of distant thunder.

"What is needed now, if one is to continue in a life of piracy," said Bart Roberts, pausing, "is genius unclouded by alcohol."

He leaned back in his chair. The silver in his teeth, the silver daggers on his belt, and the silver spurs now resting on the table ran like a vein of precious medal through the entirety of his being. His eyes met mine momentarily, and then slid past to search the eyes of others.

"Let us be direct," said Bart Roberts. "Captain Vane, from all accounts, ye have many excellent qualities as a seaman, too many to bring up in a single meeting. Why, ye could teach many a course on navigation and seamanship in the King's university, but I know ye to be an aging man of waning strength and a wretched captain of faded nerve."

"Bastard!" cried Vane, reaching for his cutlass, but before he could so much as find the scabbard, Roberts' cutthroats had pistols aimed at him from the shadows of the inn. "Ye shall rue this day, schizzlewit!" he cried, his voice filled with reeds as a great blast of thunder shook the inn and rain hammered loudly on the roof.

"And ye, Calico Jack Rackham," said the Great Pyrate Roberts, "so ready for mayhem and strong drink and herbs for thy pipe. No body of men may be led by ye without being placed in immanent peril of their lives…so foolish thou art. Yet, ye are an amusing, pleasant man, and as quartermaster ye are perfectly placed upon any ship."

"Thank ye, mate, though I wish ye an additional orifice," said Jack, dreamy eyed. Only then did I notice what Bart Roberts must have noticed at some point earlier in his talk that the clay stem of Jack's pipe had been broken off bit by bit and the herbs of the bowl had been almost exhausted.

"And me, Bart," said George Fetherstone. "What slighting thing do ye have to say of me, and, having said it, what redeeming thing will ye say of me to bring me to thy side?"

"Ye are half way clever, George, and half-way brave and half-way a fighter and half-way loyal. I have nothing else to say except that I am offering ye a job on my ship."

"Nay!"

"More's the pity!"

"And what do ye think of my talents?" said Stede Bonnet, still the picture of an elegant gentlemen as he sat back from the table with his dainty cane before him, his softened hands and manicured nails resting on its crystal knob.

"My dear Sir," said Bart Roberts, all frivolity gone from his eyes. "I speak to ye honestly and as an educated man because I know that ye are an educated man. Ye are a buffoon, Sir, a poor, deluded soul who fancies himself a pirate and is rich enough to buy himself a boat and a crew and sets out to sea without knowing a bilge rat from a ratline."

"That is hardly fair, Sir. I have taken prizes!"

"Thy salaried crew has taken a few prizes," said Roberts. "Even so, ye would be dead were it not for Charles Vane, who champions ye because it amuses him."

"We are friends, Sir."

"Have it thy way, Captain," said Bart Roberts. "But, I tell ye frankly. The reaper is on his way for ye. I have no use for ye in my enterprise, and there is no use for ye in the enterprise of piracy. Ye must take the pardon and give up thy madness, or ye will die."

Captain Bonnet looked ashen, not because he feared death, I thought, but because the Great Pyrate Roberts had confirmed that he was absurd, which he was.

"My vision," continued Roberts, "is that only the greatest of pirate kings can survive in the new era coming, and that such a pirate king must be of necessity a sober man of the greatest genius and daring. He must command huge fleets of ships in coordinated raids, as well as hundreds if not thousands of smaller craft for hit-and-run warfare. Further, he must expand the notion of a 'base' to include a whole continent with multiple ports and defensible waterways.

"This is no idle speculation. The pirate king must found a pirate nation, or piracy will cease to exist. There are places to consider. Australia, New Zealand, both a bit removed. North America."

At last shadows fell all around the inn. Someone had lit a fire against the chill brought by the rain. To my great displeasure, Anne had taken a chair beside Calico Jack, and the two of them were dozing in one another's arms as I burned. Henri whispered in my ear, himself still terrified, but trying to calm me down. Stede Bonnet, in a sulk, was staring into the fire, and Captain Vane and George Fetherstone were negotiating for positions with the Great Pyrate Roberts' projected fleet as if they expected ones of their choice.

At last, Roberts rose and pulled his cloak over his shoulders, his two silver pistols gleaming in their sashes. Fetherstone and Captain Vane bid him goodnight, and he moved past Henri and me on his way to the front door, his cutthroats rising to their feet at the first sign of his movement.

The Great Pyrate Roberts paused above me.

"Ah, mate, I do not know ye," he said. "What is thy name?"

Behind him, I saw Anne, in Jack's arms, open her eyes.

"The boy is under the protection of Captain Thomas Jones," Anne said loudly.

"I but asked him his name," said Roberts.

"My name is William Claddah, Sir."

"Ah, is that so," said Roberts, "and where are ye from?"

"I am from the Island of Hoy in the Orkney Islands," I said.

"Ah!" said Roberts. "Well that is a very fine place to be from. I am happy to make thy acquaintance."

"And I thine," I said, noticing that Anne seemed to breath easier.

Captain Roberts was then joined by his band of thugs at the front door, but as they were leaving he spied Captain Stede Bonnet's Indian boy still seated on the chair by the door.

"And what is thy name?" I heard Captain Roberts say but didn't hear an answer. "My, my, ten years old. And where are ye from?"

There was an answer I missed, a smile from the boy, and then, suddenly, Captain Roberts drew both of his pistols. Putting them to the Indian boy's head without explanation, he pulled both triggers. The twin explosions tore the boy's head from his shoulders.

"Cod sucker, burn in hell," screamed Anne, with the full force of her being. Everyone snapped from the doldrums with screams and curses, even Captain Vane who roared like a gale. Anne broke from Jack's grip and threw her long-handled knife as Captain Roberts stepped out into the night and all six of Roberts' crew stayed behind with their bully clubs, knives, and cutlasses.

"Kill them, Jack," screamed Anne, her face a fury, as she pulled a pistol from her sash. "Kill every mother's dog of them."

But Jack was frozen, as was Fetherstone, Henri, and Vane.

Their degree of alarm seemed not in keeping with our circumstance. Fresh from the quays, Robert's hirelings stumbled about like oxen in the orange lantern light. Though one or two bore firearms, the rest knew but to threaten with axes, knives, and shouts. A slim pirate made a foolish, tentative step forward, his cutlass uplifted. Another cried out. Three were bleeding to death in seconds, two with my pistol shots in their breasts, the third a victim of a headshot by Anne.

Taking stock of their three dying comrades on the floor of the inn, the other three paused in their attack to apologize for the death of the child.

I heard the sorrowful lamenting of Stede Bonnet.

"One likes an explanation for these things," said Anne, still a wild beast, in her fury.

The lamentations and the anger took my soul on a wild ride beyond the Admiral's Skull and into a curious realm in which nothing about me seemed of substance but only of shadow, no matter the glow of the lantern light or smell of the rain.

"It's what the boy said to the captain," said one of the thugs named Duck, who welded a cutlass and lifted it toward Anne when he spoke.

"And what is that?" said Anne, reloading her pistols.

"Well, the captain asked the boy where he hailed from," said Duck, "as friendly as ye please."

"Ah," said Anne. "Then, perhaps, I have misjudged the captain."

"That is likely," continued Duck, now seeing the possibility of saving his life.

"And then?" said Anne.

"Then?" replied Duck.

"Then, what did the boy say?" asked Anne with such intensity that the three men shook in the lantern light, inviting derisive remarks from the many customers of the Admiral's Skull.

"Will ye piss ye pants, mates, at the threat of a woman and a boy!" shouted Yellow Dirk from his lair.

"Does Roberts pay for the laundering of ye clothes?" shouted another, a small man with a milky eye who was sitting at the bar.

"And the boy said what?" insisted Anne, lifting a pistol.

"The boy said that he was from Barbados," said Duck. "The captain hates the people of Barbados."

Anne's pistol barked, and Duck clutched his chest. Then, wide-eyed, he slid to the floor.

Anne turned to the second of Roberts' men.

"What can I tell ye, Mistress?" he pleaded. "Everyone knows that Captain Roberts hates both the people of Barbados and the people of Martinique and is sworn to kill them both whenever he finds them."

Anne cocked her pistol.

"Jack Rackham," she said. "I do ye the honor of allowing ye to dispatch this villain who helps the Great Pyrate Roberts dispatch children, which is an abomination before God. Get out thy cutlass or pistol or dagger or whatever ye wish, and make quick work of this one."

Calico Jack paled instantly and having already leaped to his feet now backed up a step, his pistols not drawn and his cutlass still in his scabbard.

"That is Captain Roberts' man!" said Jack.

"So it is!" said Anne.

"Then, I can do nothing!"

"Nothing!" seethed Anne. "Ye cowardly bastard, son of a dog! It sickens me that I have ever lain with ye and played thy whore. Ye are to visit justice on this murderer now and hang high the Great Pyrate Roberts on the morrow, or ye shall have me no more. Now think on that ye drunken, philandering dope, fiend, pimp, and murdering scum and tremble, mate. For its ye vengeful Anne that has kept and fed ye and will now desert ye!"

Against this attack of words, Calico Jack had no defense, so sat down at the table beside the weeping Captain Bonnet and stared at his flagon.

"We, all of us, have our eccentricities, brought out by the rigors of our trade," said Captain Vane. "Captain Roberts kills everyone he meets from Barbados and Martinique. Edward Teach talks to the devil. Thy friend Mary kills with an axe. I, myself, favor whippings with the cat o nine, and ye, Mistress Anne, as well as thy boy, William, are quick to shoot. If ye are to practice piracy, Anne, ye must accept the habits of thy fellows in the trade."

"Ye are too critical, Anne," said George Fetherstone. "How may we operate in partnership with ye?"

"He speaks the truth, Anne."

Tired of listening to the talk, I shot down the second thug where he stood. Then, with the whole company of revelers bearing witness, Anne and I procured the barkeep's rope and hung the last of Captain Roberts' thugs from the rafters of the Admiral's Skull Inn.

The Outer Banks,
North Carolina

Chapter Eighteen

My first view of Blackbeard is forever fixed in my mind, so striking was his figure, so notorious his reputation, so perfect the setting. I remember a blue sky filled with gulls, his two-masted sloop, *Adventure*, with a fore and aft sail in the stern, a dock at Nassau, a harbor of glassy water, the swaying trees of Hog Island, a keg, two men hauling cargo with a yoke and stacks of boxes on the landing.

In the foreground, Blackbeard's tall figure was dressed in all black, standing posing with a staff in his right hand tilted away from his body with an aristocratic flourish, his left arm and hand uplifted just so. Were it not for the sheer terrifying ugliness of the man, I would have conjured up some image of a prancing faggot at a ball, but the monster was there, the sarcasm, the brutality.

The waist of the demon was remarkably small, considering the broad expanse of hips and shoulders and swelling chest, and the arms and legs, though encompassed by coarse clothing and knee boots, were obviously heavily muscled, though exactly how the impression was conveyed is impossible to say.

As he leapt from his longboat toward Anne and me, it was also quite clear that the man was fleet of foot and a jumper, like a jungle animal, but, again, how he conveyed such an impression escaped me. Still, it was there: the height, the strength, the cruelty suggested by a twist of his lips. There was no doubt that the man was the physical superior of any man I had ever before seen, and that no one I had ever known, not Valley or Mr. Starr, would have had the slightest chance against him.

"Aye, Anne," he said, agreeably, a broad, frightening smile upon his face, "I have wondered when at last ye would come seeking sanctuary with thy old friend, Edward, and now here ye are."

"Aye, Edward," Anne said, sweetly, "Things have come to a pretty pass. If it's not Calico Jack hammering at my door with protestations of love, it's the Great Pyrate Roberts trying to put me beneath the earth. I tell ye, Edward, between the two, there's a worry in my mind. Even my friend Henri has battened his doors, and Joe Buck has yet to return from a hunting expedition."

"Well, then," said Blackbeard. "Ye have done right to come to me. Have I not been as an uncle to ye all of thy life?"

"Aye," nodded Anne. "Ye have. So, Uncle, allow me to introduce my young friend here, William Claddah, whose mentor is thy friend, Thomas Jones."

"Aye, I thought as much," said Blackbeard. "So this is thy killer boy chosen by Thomas Jones. It is good to have ye aboard, lad. It is said that ye can navigate like a star through the heavens, fight like a demon, and swim like a seal. Is there truth to any of it, lad, or are ye just some lucky boy from the Orkneys with brains enough about him to be looking for a Da?"

Teach's question cut into me like a knife and for a few seconds I was unable to speak.

"Perhaps ye will consent to be my Da," I said at last.

"Goddamn my soul!" Blackbeard bellowed, his bellow followed by a laugh, his laugh by a twisted sneer. "Well, swive my mother! May I burn in hell!"

I blanched at once and prepared to duck the lighting certain to come shooting through the frowning clouds.

All this I remember, and that is only a part of it. Anne and I talked to him at length that day and had many a cheery drink with him in the evening at the Green Parrot Inn. During all of that time my horror at his appearance abated not a whit but rather grew.

He had hair that inhabited his face. How else to describe it? Not simply possessed of a beard, as his name implied, he had facial hair that birthed in black, bushy eyebrows that ran in a thick line across his brow and then, like snakes, drooped in coils to his cheeks and thereafter spread from ear to ear and ran in thick braids a foot down his chest. How foul the smell!

"Does thy nose bother thee," he said, "oh smeller of fish and bishop fish!"

At his joke he howled with the fervor of a four-legged creature and poured me rum.

"Ye have greased thy hair," I remarked.

"Aye, lad," said Blackbeard, putting his elbows on the table and leaning across it toward me. "Do ye not divine that I have made other preparations as well?"

"Aye, Captain," I said, "I've noticed, but cannot guess thy purpose. I see ye have fuses of hemp cord tucked under thy hat and running down the sides of thy head, all of them smelling of salt, pepper, and lime."

"Aye true," said Blackbeard, absentmindedly lighting the fuses of hemp cord with his pipe as he talked. "Lad, have I yet told ye that no one living on earth knows my name? Nay, it is not Blackbeard, of course, but it is not Edward Teach either, for I have derived the name myself from Thatch, a name for the devil, rather than use my own. Nay, neither is it Drummond either, nor Tach, nor Tatch, nor anything the world may yet have conjectured, nor ever will."

On either side of his head, the slow-burning fuses were suffusing his black beard with whiffs of smoke and flashes of fire.

"Now isn't the captain a pretty boy," at last my gentle Anne spoke.

I would gladly have joined her in the making of sarcastic remarks, but Blackbeard still held me transfixed, and no words came to my tongue.

Blackbeard screamed with laughter.

"Pretty boy, pretty boy," said Anne.

Shortly after Blackbeard retired for the evening, we heard giggles from his cabin, and, then, later, as the evening progressed over a quiet sea, great gales of laughter. Anne and I planned to sleep on the poop deck, as unafraid as we were unwise, whereas the more knowledgeable of our mates who were not assigned specific duties atop hid below in their hammocks.

At last, his cabin door came bursting open and he himself rushed up, a book in one hand and a lantern illuminating the gruesome hilarity of his face in the other.

"William and Anne!" he bellowed, spotting us walking arm in arm in sudden anguish. "Come into the cabin at once!"

With that, he let loose such a belly laugh that both she and I assumed that we would shortly be the victims of some new bedevilment.

When Blackbeard laughed, how was one to know whether he shared a joke with God or the devil?

Say what ye will about the intelligence of Edward Teach, Blackbeard the pirate; of the scofflaws of his era, he was the greatest and most malicious explorer of the human mind. We were obliged to follow him into his cabin, which was, curiously, filled with books. There, we stood before his reading desk as he adjusted his spectacles.

"I have here a journal piece written about myself," he said, another great laugh ripping away from his belly, "and I must read it to ye before I shoot ye both dead."

"We're glad to hear it," I said. "It will sweeten our deaths."

"Charmed," said Anne.

"This is me speaking to the governor," howled Blackbeard. "Listen to the rhetoric."

Blackbeard laughed again, stomping his feet on the floor of his quarters, then read with great passion, dramatically sawing the air with a free arm.

"I will kill where I choose... when I choose. I slay when offended. I slay some times for pleasure and when I am not at all offended. Listen, damn ye! Two weeks since I took a Portuguese mulletta off the Virginia Capes. It had not offended me. Do ye know what I did to its captain? I sliced off his nose, both ears, both lips, and my cook fried them and I made him eat his own ears and nose and lips and then shot him in the bowels because I ordered him to smack his lips and he had none to smack."

At the conclusion of the reading, all three of us laughed together and Blackbeard was so moved by his lies and camaraderie that he decided not to kill us but, instead, to share with us a full bottle of Madeira, which we enjoyed in the throes of back slapping and boasting.

Of all the quarters of sea captains I have known, those of Blackbeard looked most like a library. It contained volumes stolen with great care from sea-lanes supplying the educated classes in Virginia.

"And I have read them all," boasted Blackbeard, observing my astonishment as I looked about the room. "Does that surprise ye, Sir?"

"Aye, Sir," I said. "Ye do not generally give out the impression that ye are a scholar."

"So now, young man, because I have read a few books ye think me a scholar?"

"He is but a virgin boy," broke in Anne, speaking of me. "It won't do to take after him so."

The next evening at the Green Parrot, Blackbeard laughed and his whole head seemed to go up in flames. He jumped from the table with every eye in the inn upon him and his burning hemp and swaggered about a bit, strutting from table to table amid the laughter of his seamen and pretending to comb his hair with his fingers.

"Pretty, pretty," he cried, and then bellowed again. "Pretty, Pretty!"

"Pretty, pretty!" cried his mates, causing Blackbeard to again roar with laughter, downing a glass of rum in a gulp, and then again stalking about in a happy drunken stupor that was terrifying in its levity.

At last, Blackbeard turned back toward Anne and me. In the broad belt around his waist were a full complement of pistols and knives and even a cutlass, and he wore a bandoleer across his chest with three pistols hanging in their holsters. These things were suddenly more important to me than other items of his costume. Was he immortal? That too was important to me, for once again no one had thought to take away my weapons.

"Ye are both very much welcome in my town," said Blackbeard, removing his hat and favoring us with a courtly bow. "I am very much in debt and in league with Captain Thomas Jones and accept ye both with the greatest enthusiasm. Ye are my Brethren of the sea, the Brethren of us all here. Am I right, mates?"

"Aye," they all cried out.

I relaxed a bit, and in an hour Anne found it necessary to find the outhouse behind the Green Parrot. Blackbeard caught my eye and winked, blessed man, and I winked back. An idea came to me and I leaned across the table and spoke low to him.

"She thinks I am too young for her," I said.

"What?" he said. "Absurd!"

"Aye," I said, "but she does. Could ye help me?"

"Well," said Blackbeard. "Ye are welcome to sleep with any of my wives. I have a number to choose from. What type do ye fancy?"

"Nay, not that, but I thank ye!" I said. "I was hoping that ye would help me with my Anne."

"I'm perfectly willing, lad," agreed Blackbeard. "How may I help?"

"Could ye tell Anne that ye have but one large hammock to give and that we'll have to share it?" I said.

"Done! But first we'll put to sea."

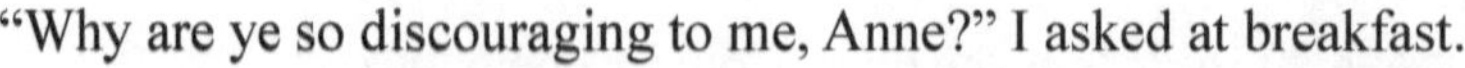

"Ah," said Anne. "Why, this is plenty room enough for the both of us!"

We were standing in a tucked away cubicle of the *Adventure*'s hold with moldy smells all about us, a single candle to light our domicile, and a shabby hammock our pre-nuptial bed, one as fine to my imagination as ever lay beneath a prince of the realm.

"Aye, there is room enough," I said, reaching for my beloved's uppermost button.

"I thank ye for thy sweet attention, my dearest William," said Anne. "Yet I would rather serve thy interest than be served. I beg ye lie down upon the hammock that I might comfortably arrange ye."

"Comfortably arrange me?" said I, not understanding the term, but then I reflected that Anne must know, regrettably, much more of these matters than I and so said nothing more to betray my ignorance.

"Go on, dear William," said Anne. "That's right. Lie upon thy back and spread wide thy arms and legs and shut thy eyes. There, ye have it."

In another moment, I had my Anne—all at once. For sure she leapt upon me, boots and weapons and all, and as if from a great height, and I heard the breath whoosh from me. Then I felt her naughty fist and elbows and various thrusts, and, at last, I was lying quietly beneath the hammock and she was in it, snoozing.

"Why are ye so discouraging to me, Anne?" I asked at breakfast.

"Pipe down!" she said.

"Why would ye pine for Calico Jack, the imbecile?"

"Stow it!"

"Do ye punish thyself because ye killed Clara?"

"Button it up!"

"Or because ye are a bastard?" I asked.

"Hush, little babe."

"Why would ye so defile thyself as to even bid good morning to such vile scum as Captain Vane or Calico Jack or George Fetherstone or any of the rotten buzzards that prey on their fellow man from the pit in hell called New Providence Island or, for that matter, the Royal Navy?"

"Shut up!" she said.

"And why are ye deaf to a higher calling?" I said.

"Why should I accept a calling?" said Anne. "Why should I embrace thy causes?

"Because they are noble."

"What are thy causes? Why am to believe they are worthy? And what have I seen of ye mostly, beyond a pretty face and curly blond hair? Well, I will tell ye. Unending mystery."

"What mystery?"

"Of thy swim, for one," Anne said, then got up from her breakfast and walked back to our quarters, where she was sitting on our hammock and waiting for me.

"And what noble causes have I seen ye about?" she said.

I had no answer for her.

"What do ye feel when ye kill a man?"

"When my pistols are drawn," I said, "I feel a higher calling."

"And killing makes ye feel that too?"

"Aye, I guess it does."

"And why is that?"

"I don't know. I'm guessing that killing is part of what I have to do."

Dear Anne grew silent for a bit, staring into my eyes. After a while, I could see that her eyes were moist, and it embarrassed me slightly to go on looking at her, so I ventured to sit beside her on the hammock. To my relief, she did not try to dump me off the backside or slap me with a backhand but rather cried quietly, pressing herself against me, her sweet face against my shoulder.

We stayed that way for an hour. When at last we climbed up the hatch to the light of day, we went about our business hardly thinking of one another.

Blackbeard loved standing at the wheel and often did so for hours, glorying in the gulls that flew above the mainmast and laughing with pleasure when some eccentric turn of the wheel caused us an unsettling dip into a trough and a rolling in the breakers. More than once, dozing seamen on the yardarms were pitched into the sea and hauled out again, as Blackbeard lay collapsed on deck with mirth.

Off the coast of North Carolina, he called me to the wheel and with great laughter bid me take over in a wind at near typhoon strength and him refusing to reef the sails. This I did proudly and with some amusement, for I was sure he would bare the masts at any moment.

Instead, he yowled with laughter at every burst of thunder or crest of wave that broke over the ship's gunwale or bow.

"I need help with the wheel," I cried out, finally exhausted, to some of the men close at hand. Then, receiving no relief, I assumed he had lost his senses.

"Captain!" I cried. "The sails must be shortened, or we shall turn over!"

To this obvious statement, Blackbeard said nothing, only busied himself soaping his long hair by the quarterdeck rail.

The winds picked up. Soon it was screaming like a thousand banshees all descending from the night sky at once, and the icy water followed, leaping onto the quarterdeck, tearing at my fingers on the wheel.

"Captain," I screamed, as calmly as I could, as if reason could prevail. "A ship is not just an assemblage of wood with masts upon it. It is a finely balanced marvel of design of sail, hull, and ballast, Sir, and it may not be trifled with, Sir! It may not be trifled with!"

Blackboard's black eyes fixed on me as if I was daft. Still, deep in my brain the knowledge was fixed that if the wind increased or if control of the wheel was lost, the weight of the ship's stores below deck would move.

Then, there would be a lurch to leeward of ballast and keel and the ship, like a shot bird, would plunge an injured wing into the howling surf.

Heeled over at forty-five degrees, the ship would then continue over, the tips of the yards would bury in the sea and then we would be over on our side, knocked down at sea. What then would happen to my treasured Anne, who was going about her business below in the mistaken belief that sanity ruled above?

In my horror, I imagined her tossed about, from bulkhead to bulkhead, unable to arrest her movement.

Imagine then my delight when Blackbeard ceased soaping his beard and came toward me with a laugh as if to help out with the wheel and to order the sails reefed, no doubt.

Then, before I could think to shove him aside, the captain flung himself madly upon the wheel. There was an immediate and mind-numbing shrieking of the wind in the rigging and an unimaginable creaking of stays and masts.

"Great God!" I cried and the ship rolled over and lay flat out on the sea. She was, as seamen say, "rolled over onto her beam ends."

On deck, men grabbed at anything to save themselves as the lee scuppers disappeared under thrashing water.

"Ye art one son of a bitch from hell!" shouted a drenched seaman at Blackbeard, who laughed at his own fate. I saw that the seaman was clinging to a hatch and that the clean-haired captain himself was hanging upside down on the deck, his foot caught in the rigging.

Everything moveable on deck either disappeared over the side or slid to port, and the foam of the sea covered all.

As for myself, I was comfortable enough. When the ship had knocked down, I had managed to grab the base of the wheel and now, though soaked, at least had the fortune to be straddling the base of the wheel from its starboard side as if sitting a horse.

"Well, Captain," I called out to Blackbeard. "Before I curse ye, how do matters stand?"

"Very well," shouted Blackbeard. "These knockdowns keep up the spirits of the men at sea."

"Do they?" I shouted back.

"Aye," thundered the captain. "For tedium is the worst enemy in this business. Day after day of endless nothingness... seeing nothing but water... doing nothing... the constant waiting... sometimes for months. Aye! The tedium will kill a man!"

"But the ship?"

"Aye, William, the ship. By and by a wave will come of enough ferocity to set us upright again. Then we will have something to talk and think about. What's more, we'll have repairs to make and ye to laugh about, for ye were at the wheel!"

"Don't listen to the bedlam boy, lad!" yelled the seaman, still clinging to the hatch. "Things are far worse than he is prepared to tell ye!"

"Go ahead, Royce, ye pansy arse!" shouted Blackbeard, in great good humor. "There are those that are girlish men and must tell everything they know."

"Son of a bastard heathen dog!" shouted Royce. "That woman I give ye, I now take back. I do not like these pranks of ye diseased brain, scoundrel bastard! Lad, well he knows that the lads below have been rained upon by cutlery, tables and chairs, the cook stoves, and every bit of gear below that has not been nailed down."

"A few bruises," shouted Blackbeard, waves splashing his face as still he hung by his foot, upside down.

"And he also knows that the ballast will not cause the ship to lift and twitch again to life if too much water flows in the hatches," said Royce. "And it could be worse. If the wind dies down and the ballast lifts the ship, there is a chance she will sail backwards with the sails pressed against her masts. If so, her masts will snap, and her stern will come apart."

This last remark set Blackbeard laughing with such renewed mirth that he could not otherwise respond to the statement.

"Beware this man, lad," warned Royce. "Though I admit he charms us all."

"Be aware of who I am!" said Blackbeard suddenly, sharply.

I needn't have been reminded. When Captain Blackbeard had thrown himself against the wheel, it had not been a jest or even a sign of madness, as Royce might have supposed. I saw very clearly, even then, that it was nothing less than a defiance of the forces of nature, and today, in hindsight, I understand even more profoundly.

Blackbeard was every inch the outlaw, more so than Kidd or Culliver or Jones or Roberts or even Morgan. He alone of all of them might have dared hold a pistol to the head of the sky and bid the sun cease to shine.

And on this occasion, he won out again. All hands, including Anne, were safe. After fifteen minutes on our side, we felt the wind back off a tad. The ship twitched again to life, lifted by virtue of its ballast, and then sailed backwards for only a few minutes before thrusting forward again.

Two days later, all repairs were completed, and Royce was put to work baiting Blackbeard's hooks as the captain fished off Ocracoke.

By the end of April, I had quite adjusted to sleeping below Anne's rolling hammock and, as luck would have it, studying Shakespeare whenever I was not trying to woo Anne, shooting at gulls, or conversing with Blackbeard about currents. My study of the bard was made possible by Blackbeard's library, which he threw open to me, either as a kindness to me or else to annoy Anne, who had taken to finding fault with me whenever she could.

"Ye are winning her, lad," said Blackbeard. "Ye shall soon be in the hammock and she shall be beneath thy jostling heft."

Now and then Blackbeard would come out on deck and set his hair on fire and call on the devil. Then he would jump about the boards, stomping his feet and firing his pistols while his crew ran for the hatches. One morning, with the froth still in his mouth and his eyes showing dead white, he ran to the poop deck like a demon and bellowed at the sea.

Not one of us moved.

"All hands on deck," he bellowed at the sky.

Still, we crouched in the hold, for we knew not what entity Satan had sent on this day to possess his spirit.

"Ye goddamned schizlewit idiots," he bellowed. "Get ye arses on deck. My fit is over, and a ship approaches."

Immediately, we rushed to the deck, all of us armed and all more willing to face a human enemy verses a supernatural one.

"I see nothing," said Anne.

"Nor I," said the first mate, Israel Hands.

"But ah, she's out there," assured Blackbeard, with something like joy crossing his features. At that moment, the fog cleared to larboard and the sloop he had spotted hove into view flying a skeleton with a sword.

"Why mates," said Blackbeard, "that is Captain Vane's ship, and yet that is not Captain Vane's flag. What do I make of all this?"

No one said a word, save Anne.

"Well I know readily enough, Captain, and I trust ye won't turn me over to him."

"Well, of course not, Anne," said Blackbeard. "It does surprise me though that Jack has worked up the courage to take over Vane's ship. I would have thought the drunken scoundrel likely to remain a quartermaster forever. What say ye, Hands? Has our good friend, the drug-addled Calico Jack actually killed his Captain Vane or merely set him loose on some island? Let five pounds rest upon it!"

Hands rubbed at once the long scar on each of his cheeks by touching one with his forefinger and the other with his thumb. He was the black-toothed, constant companion of Blackbeard and no man to let a wager by him.

"I'll take a wager, Captain," he said, "but first I'll be advised by Mistress Anne, for surely, knowing Jack, she'll supply me with a bettor's edge for the price of a pound."

"May ye both shove broken glass up ye arses," shrieked Anne, now wet to the skin from having leaned over the rail as a wild rogue wave rose up from nowhere and crashed into our larboard side. "What does it matter what Jack has done with that chicken-necked old captain? Perhaps he has made soup! The sole question, mates, is what are ye going to do with Jack, who has doubtless come for me?"

"Aye," said Blackbeard. "I guess he has, Anne. But who would have thought it? Thy worthless Jack has sailor enough in him to actually find us in this Atlantic sea and that after staging a mutiny and coming into his own, a captain of the seas."

A touch of tenderness came into his voice.

"I tell ye, Anne, and all of ye mates. It does my heart good to see a man make something of himself. Now here was a man, this Calico Jack, who was nothing but a whoring libertine either into drink or herbs, as common and cowardly a lout as ever shipped out of New Providence dressed like a clown. But now there he is yonder, the master of a fine pirate vessel, threatening us larboard, apparently with some scheme in mind to take his lady love from our sanctuary."

"Gentlemen," said Blackbeard, "I believe he deserves our finest gunnery."

There were hurrahs all about and a sigh from Anne.

"Let us save our response for his first communication," Blackbeard ordered. "For it appears that he wishes to talk before fighting."

Shortly after this remark, Jack's voice, amplified by the ship's horn, came blasting through the fog.

"Good morning to ye, Captain Teach. This is Captain Jack Rackham of the *Diamond.*"

"Why hello," called Blackbeard. "This is a surprise Jack. The last I heard, thy ship was captained by Vane. May I inquire as to what has occurred?"

"An unfortunate thing," said Jack. "By sheerest luck, Captain Vane turned up with the weather gauge against a French man-of-war but refused to attack her, in spite of my pleadings and those of the crew. So the crew rose up and elected me captain. I could not refuse."

"And Captain Vane," Blackbeard shouted. "What befell him? Did ye wring his chicken neck or set him ashore?"

"Neither," answered Jack. "We put him in a small sloop with a few who supported him, and that is the truth of it."

"Ah," said Blackbeard. "I hadn't thought of that. And now what will ye do, Jack? Will ye fight me for Anne?"

"Will ye give her over to me?" shouted Jack.

"Nay!" shouted Blackbeard. "Both she and the boy are under my protection. If ye threaten either, Jack, ye will die."

To this comment of Blackbeard's there was no response. Worse, the fog again closed and the *Diamond* disappeared, like a ghost ship. We watched for an hour from the quarterdeck and then gave it up. Neither Blackbeard nor Jack chose to make a sound, so matters stood as they left them.

That night, with Calico Jack Rackham sailing either to the north or the south of us or to starboard or larboard off Charleston, Blackbeard invited Israel Hands, me, and another seaman named Harley to drink a fine wine with him in his cabin.

Conversation soon turned to a time when Hands briefly captained the *Adventure* during a blockade of Charleston.

"I salute ye, my friend," said Blackbeard, shadows from candles flitting about his face as he held high his glass. Harley and I raised our glasses as well, and then drank them off rapidly with the captain. Then, the three of us together brought our glasses down on the table with a clatter.

Harley tottered with age, almost banging his chin on his glass, forcing a smile to my face, but then his expression changed, as if he were suddenly sober. He looked at Blackbeard, and then quickly looked away, coughed and excused himself. He rose and reached for his hat, which he had thrown to the floor of the cabin.

"Well, lads," he said, "it's late for me. I'll be off for my hammock now."

Blackbeard said nothing to stop him, and Hands, who was sitting beside me, gave a contented wave, as if there were no problem in the world.

But there was. The captain's hands were under the table.

When Harley exited, there was an explosion that rocked the cabin, and Hands pitched over backward in his chair, screaming in pain and holding his shattered knee.

Blackbeard pulled his pistols from under the table and laid them side-by-side.

"Notify the surgeon," he said to the first of the crew that came tumbling in, their jaws agape.

Hands' wound was so grievous that his screaming had already ceased and he lay in an ocean of blood that widened to the walls of the cabin and ran under the boots of Blackbeard and me, each of us in irons, figuratively, not a breath of air moving.

"Every now and then ye've got to remind them who ye are," Blackbeard said finally. "That is one of the things I am bound to teach ye."

In penance for his crime of making a cripple of his friend and first mate, Blackbeard sentenced himself to be hanged from the main mast yardarm until the devil bit his arse. Accordingly, he commanded drums to be sounded and himself to be tied up and hoisted by noose to the yardarm.

There he dangled kicking for a full fifteen minutes before he at last was cut down by the crew, half strangled and vomiting as well as befouled and laughing at the devil. Straightaway, he dove into the ocean and refused a rescue rope for such a long while that the crew at last lowered a longboat and was forced to subdue him with a bully club before getting him back to his cabin.

The next morning, he was awoken early by the creaking and flapping of Captain Stede Bonnet's craft, which had pulled near for a gam with the *Adventure*. Thinking himself to be in some sort of evil dream he stumbled from his cabin and into the sunlight, not remembering his trousers. Some of his crewmen were standing about on main deck and forecastle, plainly amused.

"Ye have time for jaking about, do ye?" he mumbled, wandering in circles.

"Aye," said Thomas Mapp, extending a thumb. "Look there, Captain!"

Upon first seeing Stede Bonnet, who was being ferried over in a longboat from his ten-gun sloop, Blackbeard rubbed his eyes as if he could scarcely credit the report they were making to his brain. Suddenly, he was fully awake, and calling out to the gods of the sea. "Why the dainty fellow's wearing a waistcoat and a periwig," roared Blackbeard, collapsing below the gunwale in laughter. "And he has a speaking trumpet in his hand."

An angry look came over Anne's face, for she was fond of Stede Bonnet and had always wished him well, having known him as a child. Bonnet was a retired Major in the King's Guard and had settled near Anne's father on a plantation in Barbados.

"And he was a sweet man, educated and cultured," Anne always said. "He still is, but quite mad now. Don't ye mock him, William. Who knows what will happen to thy own brain some day."

I, of course, had no intention or wish to mock Stede Bonnet and for the sake of Anne wished Blackbeard to desist, so approached him quietly.

"Sir," I said. "Major Bonnet or Captain Bonnet, if ye will, is mad, of course, but is beloved by thy niece, Anne, and she is much put off by thy mocking him."

"What?" said Blackbeard. "Oh Lord, why wasn't I told?"

All levity immediately drained from his features, and wrinkles of worry ran through his hairy face.

"Silence," he shouted, simultaneously firing his pistol, and every man-jack aboard ceased his laughter.

By this time, the longboat was within easy shouting distance of Blackbeard's *Queen Anne's Revenge*, but Captain Bonnet chose to use the speaking trumpet, nevertheless, it being perhaps his first opportunity to do so and perhaps his last, for all he knew.

"Captain of the *Queen Anne's Revenge*," Bonnet shouted into the trumpet. "I am Captain Stede Bonnet, lately a gentleman of good reputation on Barbados Island. Whom do I have the honor of addressing?"

For a moment it looked as if Blackbeard was going to collapse into mirth again, in spite of his best efforts, but, then, with a monumental struggle, he assembled himself and thrust above the gunwale a hairy, straight face.

"A Brethren of the coast. Come on topside, Captain."

Because of the fair weather and the odds against Stede Bonnet having anything worth keeping secret to report, a table was set up on deck, and all were allowed to overhear.

"Well, swive ye all," said Stede Bonnet. He had been at sea for some time now, and though navigation still came hard for him and atrocities even more so, he was making way with vulgar speech, if not with vulgar dress, which he could not abide.

"It's good to see ye, Captain Bonnet," said dainty Anne. "No need to ape the language of these ruffians."

"Certainly not!" said Blackbeard, putting on his trousers. "As I recently remarked to the queen, 'Mum,' says I, 'Trust not the scoundrel that says 'teet,' for it is well known the word 'bosom' is preferred by the proper lord.'"

"Aye, quite," said Stede Bonnet. "But I am here on pressing business, which I must communicate at once."

"Then do communicate it," Blackbeard said.

"In April," said Bonnet, "we learned that Great Britain was going to send a newly appointed governor to New Providence. What's more, our spies had it that the English are determined to pursue us and have built him enough shallow draught ships to enforce the pardon and drive us from the Bahamas."

"And who backed this intelligence?" said Blackbeard.

"Captains Bellamy and Jennings."

"And was the governor to be Woodes Rogers?"

"Aye. That was the name."

"Then, true it is," said Blackbeard. "There's no doubt of it."

"We gathered at the King's Head Inn to discuss the matter," continued Bonnet. "Captain Vane was there with Calico Jack. Captain Bellamy, Benjamin Hornigold, Thomas Burgess, Nicholas Brown, Oliver la Bouche, James Fife, Major Penner, John Martel, Richard Sample, and Christopher Winter were also attending. And Edward England was there as well. Captain Jennings presided, but nothing was accomplished."

"Nothing?" said Blackbeard. "Nothing?"

"No one did anything but scream at the other and threaten," said Bonnet. "It was as loud a dog fight as ever I heard, and no man there made a sensible argument or a single statement of solidarity."

"And how did it end?"

"It ended with Captain Jennings firing his pistol and every man fleeing into the night."

Blackbeard shook his head but laughed all the same.

"So the Bahamas are lost?"

"Oh my, yes," said Stede Bonnet. "They are irretrievably lost."

It was strange, somehow, hearing such news and believing it from such a man as Stede Bonnet. No man or woman aboard the *Adventure* had less credibility than he, yet for some reason not a single face I looked upon held a particle of doubt that what he said was true.

Even Blackbeard, in an instant, regarded the matter closed.

Some news seems so in accord with what we instinctively know that the most deluded prophet seems blessed with vision.

For Blackbeard, it was difficult to let such a savant go.

"Then North America is the next sanctuary?"

"Oh, I think so, aye," agreed Bonnet.

"And the pardon?" asked Blackbeard.

"Of course, take the pardon from the British," said Bonnet. "Ye have no choice, and ye can always break it. Is it not so?"

Blackbeard got up from the table and stalked from quarterdeck to forecastle, then to the gunwale on the larboard side, where he gazed westward toward the Americas.

"And are we likely to survive, regardless of what we do?"

"Oh, heavens no!" replied Bonnet. "Whatever are ye thinking of?"

At Bonnet's last answer, a smile again broke across Blackbeard's features. He turned at the gunwale and walked back to the table and there waved a hand in Bonnet's face. Bonnet neither blinked nor twitched. Blackbeard laughed out loud and sat back down at the table, where he called for rum.

"There ye have it, mates, the truth as the devil sends it," Blackbeard said. "Through the seized brain of some poor unfortunate. Let there be rum all around, boys, for we shall take the pardon, and it shall avail us of nothing. Let the joke be upon us."

Drinks were served all around.

"Let the joke be upon us!" shouted Jim Arthur, soaked with sweat, for the sun was coming up hot and red as a heated piece of gold.

"Let the joke be upon us!" shouted everyone. Then, when Stede Bonnet escaped at last from his trance, he and Blackbeard retired to the captain's cabin for further talks while the *Queen Anne's Revenge* rested at anchor, and Anne and I went for a refreshing plunge in our dirty clothes.

Now and then, as we swam, Jim Arthur took a shot at a passing shark. When we had finished our swim, we returned the favor, standing with drawn pistols by the gunwale on the main deck while he and his mate splashed in the waters below. From where we stood, it was impossible not to hear Blackbeard's roaring laughter from his cabin and most of his and Stede Bonnet's conversation.

"Ah, my good friend, Stede," said Blackbeard. "A pirate captain does not dress as a gentleman but as a parody of a gentleman."

"Good Lord!" said Bonnet. "Do ye mean to say that they do so intentionally? I thought I had been doing the pirate community a service by demonstrating the correct forms of dress for a gentleman!"

"Thy intentions were excellent!" said Blackbeard. "I can only admire them. But ye must modify ye dress or ye will be laughed at!"

"Good Lord!" said Bonnet. "By uneducated people!"

"And ye must stop mentioning how ye acquired thy ship," said Blackbeard.

"Why is that?" said Bonnet. "I purchased it for an honest price!"

"My dear Sir!" shouted Blackbeard. "A pirate doesn't purchase his ship. He steals it. And he doesn't hire a crew. He entices a crew to go along with him by promises of plunder."

"I have much to learn, regretfully."

"Sir, ye show great gaps of knowledge that must be addressed. For instance, ye don't know the difference between longitude and latitude and a few minutes ago expressed surprise that sailors travel roadways of winds around the earth. On the other hand, ye have a hint of strange powers that must be studied and applied to our trade."

"Ah, Captain. Then, I have a hint of powers to be thankful for and must seek your aid."

"Yes," said Blackbeard, "No one, as yet, has decided to remove your pants."

Luckily, Jim Arthur and his friends broke off their swim at this point and Anne, feeling free enough both with Blackbeard and Captain Bonnet, knocked upon the cabin door. Both men received our intrusion with good grace, and shortly we were a band of four, all enjoying fine wine and Blackbeard's finest chairs.

"This boy here, William, also has strange powers," remarked Blackbeard.

"He does, indeed," rejoined Bonnet. "For instance, he appears now to be sixteen years old or so, not the fourteen-year-old I knew him to be in Nassau."

"But ye are mistaken," Anne laughed shrilly. "The lad is but thirteen years old. He was thirteen years old in Nassau, and he is thirteen years old now."

"Now, Anne," said Blackbeard. "Ye are mistaken, for it is clear that he is but two years or so younger than thyself."

"Tis true," I said, to Anne's disconcertion. "Age is but a matter of determination."

Anne sputtered with annoyance while there were laughs all around. Even as he chuckled, however, Blackbeard went to his great, heavily polished bookcase and extracted a massive tome, which he then brought back to our circle and handed to Stede Bonnet.

"As pleasant as the subject might be," Blackbeard said, "this volume veers from fixing one's age by determination. It is a study of sea craft. Ye must become reasonably knowledgeable about ships and the seas, even to the point of understanding such language as 'The bilander disappeared beyond the storm-burnt tump.'"

"Good Lord!" shouted Bonnet.

"Crews have been known to mutiny against captains who don't know the difference between a spinnaker and a top gallant sail or those who have run out of water and run up on a lee shore."

"Mutiny?" said Bonnet, the idea apparently never having occurred to him before.

"Aye, mutiny," said the captain. "Think about it for a few moments. Have there been signs of mutiny about thy craft?"

"Why…" stared Bonnet.

"Nay, nay, nay!" shouted Blackbeard, red in the face. "Don't just blurt out the first answer that occurs to thy brain. Think the matter over. Consider what has been said to ye, whether or not conversation ceased when ye enter the room, whether or not thy crewmen bang their heads as if ye were a loon when ye announce the most obvious of strategies?"

"Are ye suggesting I take a minute to reflect…in spite of the company?" asked Bonnet, somewhat ruffled by the breach of etiquette involved.

"Oh, go on and do it!" said Blackbeard, turning to me in such a way that it was clear to Bonnet that he was dismissed for such time as it took him to ponder the nuances of his relationship with his crew. To make things easier for him socially, Blackbeard thoughtfully picked up the conversational slack with Anne and me.

"I say, Master William," Blackbeard said, his attention entirely shifted to me. "Have I yet taught ye that blessed are the dead that the rain rains upon?"

"Nay, Captain," I said, "but I believe it. Ye did teach me though that a blind man's wife needs no paint."

"A marvelous truth, Captain," said Anne. "Surely ye are among the finest pirate philosophers of the globe. Are ye not the author of the famous line, 'All that is grist that comes to the mill!' as well as the explosively perceptive 'Fine words butter no parsnips?'"

"Zounds, Captain," I said. "Little leaks sink the ship."

"And idle people have the least leisure," said Anne.

"Aye, yes, I have filled many a page with wise words," said Blackbeard. "Nine tailors make a man. Set a thief to catch a mouse. The mill cannot grind with water that has passed. None but the brave deserve the fair."

"Once a whore, always a whore!" said Anne.

"No river's so vile it's refused by the sea!" I said.

"In sum," said Blackbeard, "so many mists in March, so many frosts in May."

"Alright," interrupted Bonnet. "I have considered the matter."

Bonnet's voice, breaking through our revelry, had the unpleasant effect upon us of calling us back to the business at hand. Who was this peacock of a gentleman standing before us with a fussy mouth? Oh, yes, I remembered.

"There have been several threats on my life," said Bonnet, "but only when I attempted to give an order."

"Holy Christ!" said Blackbeard.

"But no conversations cease when I enter a space in which crew members seem to be conspiring," said Bonnet. "Someone usually just threatens to cut off my masculine member, and I go back to my room."

Blackbeard put a hand to his disbelieving forehead.

"If my crew actually hated me, my food would have been cut off, don't ye think? But, no. I'm allowed to eat with everyone else, pay wages, and participate in battles for prizes if I'm so inclined."

"And this is satisfactory with ye?" asked Blackbeard.

"I confess it is not," said Bonnet. "When I took up the piracy trade, I did so not just with the notion of escaping my wife and bringing zest to my days but also with the idea that I would be accorded the respect and dread reserved in the hearts of men for a pirate captain. Yet, to my chagrin, I find myself the least powerful person about my craft."

"And ye are disillusioned," said Blackbeard.

"Aye," said Bonnet, "and considering plans to murder the entirety of my crew, if ye long to know."

"Of course, ye are!" shouted Blackbeard, throwing his cup of wine to the floor. "And why shouldn't ye be? Here ye are, a good man of education and faith, who can bring to our trade both manners and wise counsel, which are sorely needed, and are ye valued? Nay, Sir! As I wrote many a year ago, 'Cast ye pearls before swine, and they shall turn and rend ye.'"

"Disgraceful!" chimed Anne. "Thy crewmen should be whipped or skinned alive. The wonder is, they let ye come here to tell this tale."

"They have no comprehension that anyone would ever take my part," said Bonnet, holding a handkerchief to his nose.

Had not Anne's quim been out of my reach forever had I laughed at the scene playing before me, I surely would have laughed, holding my sides at that and possibly rolling on the deck. No actor trained for the stage could have been more convincing than Blackbeard. He raged, he roared, he shook with anger. Tears came to his eyes and he swore by Poseidon to correct the matter.

"And thy recommendation, Sir?" said Bonnet, finally.

"I shall teach ye the art of command," Blackbeard said. "Ye shall be the equal of me, and no man shall dare cross ye!"

"Shall a woman cross him?" asked my spunky Anne.

"Nay," said Blackbeard. "Neither a man nor a woman shall cross him! Nor shall a beast of the field cross him! Nor shall a creature of the air or a denizen of the sea!"

"How will ye teach me?" said Bonnet, glancing briefly at Anne, who looked over to Blackbeard, indicating she had no knowledge of what he spoke.

"I'll have ye sail on my ship, the *Queen Anne's Revenge*," said Blackbeard. "Ye will sail with me and observe my every trick and bit of craft for a time and then ye'll return to thy own *Revenge*, a new-made pirate king."

"But what will happen to my ship while I sail with ye?" said Bonnet, alarmed.

"I have a wondrous second mate, Richardson. He will command thy ship, *Revenge*, when ye sail with me. We'll take pardons from the English and then prey on ships from all other nations in the waters from North Carolina to Florida. What say ye?"

"Good Lord!" said Stede Bonnet. "The trouble is, I hardly know ye!"

One morning early, the Finman came into my dream like a thunderclap. So furious it made me that I rolled from under Anne's hammock and rushed to the main deck from the forecastle hatches and from there to the fantail of the *Queen Anne's Revenge*. It was barely dawn, and the sun broke rosily over the placid green of the water and a distant shoal where gulls fed in the rolling surf.

There being no sign of him, I fairly ran up to ratlines of the mizzenmast and stood on the yardarm, one arm anchored to the mast, the hand of the other with a pistol drawn. No cardinal point of the compass rose turned up a Finman. All around the ship was unbroken water, except the small wake of the *Queen Anne's Revenge* and the gurgle of our prow.

My eyes grew misty with the frustration of it and I made my way down the ratlines wiping them with a sleeve, hopeless and unnoticed by the skeletal crew.

"And will ye tell me what that was all about," said my lovely Anne, all of a sudden perched directly in front of me, her sleeping bonnet still upon her head.

"Nothing!"

"Nothing?" pressed Anne. "As if I didn't witness from beginning to end all thy strange behavior."

I turned away from her and went to sit on the quarterdeck stair, she right behind me.

"Anne, I am given to strange dreams because of my place of origin," I said. "There, one is taught the existence of mermaids and selkies and sea trows and the like."

"I dream of human monsters," said Anne, sitting beside me and taking my hands in hers. "Those that go to parties dressed in all their finery while others starve. But what creature did ye dream of today?"

"The one I can't talk about…except…"

"Except what, William?"

"I am embarrassed to say, Anne"

"But ye must say it, William."

"But Anne, I'm afraid that ye will take it for some flippant joke or some foolish attempt by a boy to have his way, which I assure ye is not the case."

"Alright, William, ye may talk to me about this creature without fearing those things."

"Are ye sure ye want to know?"

"Aye, William, I am sure. So, ye may talk to me about this creature."

"If ye give me thy quim," I said, as seriously as possible.

To my disappointment, Anne then produced a curved knife with an ivory hand that appeared heavily laden with African scrimshaw.

"Have ye not yet learned respect for women, Master William? Might it take a poke in the arse for ye to learn?"

"How may I know anything of women?" I cried. "Ye are all I know of women, Anne, and all I care to know. If ye will agree to be with me and not this Calico Jack or some other ruffian I will be free to let ye know the shadows of my life. But if ye will not do so, I cannot burden ye! And should it not work the other way around also?"

Anne's voice immediately softened. She looked long into my eyes.

"Master William," she said at last. "We share an energy and a bravery and skills that make us brother and sister and of an indissoluble family, but every impulse of thy heart is toward duty, not one toward freedom. Though we were the same age, those impulses would forever prevent us from becoming man and wife."

"Do ye recall what the captain said when we were talking gibberish?" I asked. "He said, 'Only the brave deserve the fair.'"

"I recall it," said Anne.

"Well, I am brave," I said.

"And I love ye," said Anne. "Ye'll have to settle for just that."

Giving me back my hands, Anne got up from the stair and continued up to the quarterdeck where Blackbeard and Stede Bonnet were preparing for their first treasure hunt together on the open seas. Both had already decided on a last foray in Atlantic waters before returning to the town of Bath, North Carolina, to receive pardons from Governor Eden.

"In general," said Blackbeard, "it's a mistake to kill a soul. If ye kill a man, the man is not likely to take to the sea again to be robbed again or to generate capital to be lost at sea again to pirates. So, I am against all senseless killing and certainly will not allow it unless some obstinate fool absolutely insists on being killed over his trifling goods. In his case, I am saddened for his widow and children but hardly for him."

"Such fools should not be allowed upon the sea," Bonnet agreed.

"Captain Bonnet, thy job as a responsible pirate is to assume as fierce an aspect as possible, both to terrify thy crew into obedience and to hasten the surrender without loss of life of the crew or of any merchant man ye encounter on the high seas. I will show ye how to assume a hideous appearance, how to cause a maximum of smoke to pour from thy cannons with a minimum of shot, and how to compel an immediate surrender."

"What of atrocities, Sir?" I asked.

"Aye, atrocities," bellowed Blackbeard. "Always inflict atrocities for people to talk about, but remember a few atrocities become exaggerated and go a long way. Find a fat man who can't remove his ring and cut his finger off, a favorite atrocity that saves time, or pull a tooth that has a gold filling. As for making someone walk the plank, don't embarrass thyself. First, it leads to death, which is undesirable. Second, it's just not done, one of the fictions of piracy. Like hooks for hands and wooden pegs for legs."

"Good Lord!" said Stede Bonnet. "Are ye telling me that there are no hooks for hands and no pegs for legs?"

"There might be," said Blackbeard, "but I've never seen either. I've never seen a surgeon at sea amputate a hand, arm, or leg without killing the patient. I'd like to meet the man who can."

Stede Bonnet lapsed into a depressed silence, and, at last, we caught a wisp of the trade and were creaking away to our destination, me letting the wind wash my heart of Anne's rejection. For, as I told myself, it was not so bad a rejection as rejections go, since it had eventuated in the admission she loved me.

How my eyes followed her about the ship that day. She was dressed as she ever was, clad more in her pistols and knives than her clothes, but how the sun shone on her hair and kissed the places she walked. And whenever she went to the bowsprit and looked ahead of us to where Lieutenant Richards led the way in the *Revenge*, she leaned just so against the rail.

"Ye are swimming deep waters, lad," said Blackbeard. "Best ye think of piracy this trip out."

Not many days after reaching the Spanish sea off the coast of Honduras, we were lying in anchor to take on fresh water when a lookout climbed to the crow's nest of the *Revenge* and quickened our spirits with his cries.

We rushed to our positions. It was an awesome sight, this comparatively large but one-masted bird. It flew the high seas with feathered limb, sails fore and aft, and two flying jibs reaching out for an extended bowsprit that held itself proud and high. It was a ship to take, not burn, whose hold was made less to carry goods than plunder.

Upon spotting us, she lit out for harbor, but it was much too late. Long before she reached safety she came under the guns of Captain Richardson and the *Revenge* and so was forced to await the pleasure of Blackbeard and the *Queen Anne's Revenge*.

"Do ye see how a ship may be taken without firing a shot?" said Blackbeard. "Observe the position of Captain Richardson's ship and that of our own. The sloop had no tack but to give either the *Revenge* or the *Queen Anne's Revenge* the weather gauge. Now witness the result of our action."

Minutes later, the sloop struck its sails and swung to the stern of the *Queen Anne's Revenge*, where a rope ladder brought the *Adventure's* handsome Captain Harriot into the close proximity of Blackbeard, who was seated on a barrel and squinted upward toward him with milky white eyes.

"Burning tapers in thy hair?" said Captain Harriot. "And the smell of brimstone. Is the devil aboard?"

"Aye, he is!" said Blackbeard, then roared with laughter.

"Ye shall claim thy prize," said Captain Harriot, "but then I expect ye to place my crew and myself ashore."

"Nay," said the captain. "Thy vessel would be a greater prize if I took ye and thy crew with it. I would, of course, assign my crippled mate, Israel Hands, to captain thy vessel and disperse thy crewmen among my own. Also, there will be things to work out about percentages of booty to be taken by each of thy men. Have ye talents as a quartermaster, Captain Harriot? Do ye have heart enough to develop a smart head for figures?"

"Captain," said Captain Harriot, "these matters between the crew and me in relation to serving with ye have already been worked out in principle."

So fortified, our fleet of three ships, the *Queen Anne's Revenge,* the *Revenge,* and the *Adventure*, raised black flags and caught wind enough in our sails to sweep like marauders from bad dreams over a rising sea northward and into the Bay of Honduras.

Fishermen in their small boats sat silent, or eased toward the shore to make way with their paddles or subtle movements of their sails, some of them praying and crossing themselves, looking away from us. The day was a dark day, with saddened clouds. Anne and I, on the quarterdeck, watched the men and women on the docks gather up their gear, fish, and children and run for the forest beyond their shabby houses.

None of the ships in the harbor were yet prepared for battle. Four small sloops swayed at anchor with their sails tied to their yardarms and their crewmen leaping into the water. A fifth ship, the huge merchant ship, the *Protestant Caesar* of Boston, waited helplessly, its captain and crew all standing upon the deck in postures of surrender.

"Congratulations, Captain Bonnet!" said Blackbeard. "Here are five prizes for thy record as a buccaneer."

"My record," said Bonnet. "Why do ye say 'my record'?"

"What? Does thy modesty prevent ye from counting these as thy prizes, even when many of us last evening heard ye order an attack on the harbor in the Bay of Honduras?"

"Aye, I heard as much," I volunteered.

"As did I!" said Anne, putting an admiring hand on Stede Bonnet's arm.

"And I heard it too," said a cabin boy, who supplied Captain Bonnet with a speaking trumpet. He took the instrument from the boy but looked stupefied by his own action.

"And ye bear witness to it too?" muttered Bonnet, looking downward and giving his head a little shake of incomprehension.

"I heard it, I did!" said the boy.

"Ye heard it?" said Bonnet.

"S'death!" said the cabin boy, who had been brought to the scene by Blackbeard. "I heard it. The captain said to ye… he said, 'Captain Bonnet, should we attack the harbor in the Bay of Honduras?' and ye responded, 'Aye, Captain Teach, I'd sooner attack the harbor in Bay of Honduras than the gates of hell.' And ye then went to sleep, leaving the captain to convey the order to myself, who conveyed it to the helmsman."

"Aye," I said. "That is just how it happened."

"Well," said Bonnet, "I do remember the exchange now. Aye. I do."

There then came over Bonnet a glow that brightened the dark day. He stood on the quarterdeck growing taller, his chest swelling outward. In another moment, he seemed fit for business.

"Captain Bonnet," said Blackbeard, "might I suggest ye order a single cannon ball be shot over the *Protestant Caesar*'s bow to seal thy triumph?"

"Fire a shot?" said Bonnet, observing that the *Protestant Caesar*'s captain and crew were lined up on the deck to facilitate an orderly surrender. "But they have already capitulated and only have to be gathered in."

"Think of thy image, man!" Blackbeard shouted. "How will ye ever be thought of as the 'scourge of the seas' and have the very mention of thy name frighten little children from their sleep if ye continue thy policy of merely 'gathering' the defeated in, as if ye were some ministering angel? Fire the cannon! Then bellow furiously into thy trumpet so that the crewmen of the *Protestant Caesar* will spread far and wide the terror of encountering the mad Pyrate of Bermuda, Captain Stede Bonnet."

"Of course," said Bonnet. "I was thinking along the same lines myself."

In another minute, the quiet of the glowering day was broken by the sound of the cannon.

Blackbeard laughed uproariously.

Bonnet laughed too and then smiled a victor's smile as he took up the trumpet.

"Captain of the *Protestant Caesor*," he barked through the trumpet. "This is Captain Stede Bonnet of the *Queen Anne's Revenge*, and a gentleman pirate of Bermuda. We will pull alongside thy craft and board her, Sir, and then take possession in the name of...."

Bonnet blinked at that which was transpiring aboard the *Protestant Caesor*. There was no longer an orderly line of captained seaman waiting to surrender but rather a scurrying of rats to leave the ship. Some few were already swimming toward the shore and others were either clambering into longboats or shouting and shoving others out of them.

The captain of the *Protestant Caesor* had disappeared from view.

Bonnet cut loose with a little whoop of joy, and even Blackbeard himself was pounding him on the back for a job well done.

"Ye are the Gentleman Pyrate," said Blackbeard, "with a nosegay in one hand and a cutlass in the other."

By the end of the day, Captain Bonnet had robbed and seized the four sloops and ordered the burning of the *Protestant Caesor*, for the ship sailed out from Boston, where the authorities had hanged four pirates.

Leaving the Bay of Honduras with its dark water and cloud of smoke in the wake of our fleet, we pitched and rolled in a suddenly steep sea to the small island of Grand Cayman. There it stood, with the sun shining about it, even as its tall palms bent like penitents from the winds that had driven us. High above, we spotted an albatross soaring on long, broad wings about thirty leagues to the west of Jamaica

"Turtler, ho!" came the lookout's cry, for he had spotted a fish hooker that had been rigged as a ketch on the North European coast and Dogger shoal and had now been given over to the capture of the green sea turtle.

"Here's a case where a frightful face and a single shot across the bow will yield us food for a month," instructed Blackbeard.

And so it did, but it also drug up from the locker a grandfather of a troll in the dress of a seaman, who had so little time left on this watery orb, so tossed in fright, that he alone found no reason to fear for his life.

"Dingleberry! Foul ape!" he remarked to Blackbeard, even as his mates wrung their hands and cried out for him to be struck by St. Elmo's fire. "It is taking ye more time and energy to rob us than it would take to catch thy own turtles!"

"I enjoy taking thy turtles," replied Blackbeard, ordering the old man tied to the mast of the hooker.

"Thy silks and thy satins and earrings and stockings and such do not speak to me of what is proper to a man," said the relic of a seaman, the wind blowing long white hair into his eyes. "Nor does thy jewelry or braid of thy hair."

Blackbeard affected interest elsewhere, but the last of the giant turtles was being carried across the gunwale to the *Queen Anne's Revenge*, and, aside from me, there was no one else nearby to pester. In such a want of diversion, there was, finally, no choice but to focus on the old turtle man's words.

"And ye are saying exactly what?" said Blackbeard, moving his hairy face to within inches of the mariner's.

"Ye Sodomite buggerer and blazing faggot of hell!" shouted the old man into Blackbeard's mustache, his lips flapping like the edges of a luffing sail, "Ye pocked practitioner of the Turkish vice that ever plants, but will not reap. Ye girly man that pulls down his pantaloons to dribble. Ye gai, rogering blade and habitué of flesh pots from the pits of Cairo to the Southern Ocean. Oh ye bearer of Sodomitic whipstaffs that gush sulfuric flame. Beware thy man lust!"

Blackbeard staggered backward as if he were struck in the forehead by Mary Read's axe.

"Do I take ye to mean that ye take me to be a gai man?" said Blackbeard, recovering slightly and cocking his head to squint against the sun at the white haired fellow raving at the mainmast. The words were spoken softly, but, nevertheless, the old man's mates, a small group of Dutchman in their odd little hats, vomited over the gunwale as Blackbeard's interview with the prisoner continued.

"Aye," barked the old man, whose name, we learned, was Mick. "The matter is settled."

"Settled?" said Blackbeard. "Nay, old fellow, not even yet discussed. Know ye not that I am Edward Teach and have fifteen, nay, sixteen wives. What say ye to that, old rag?"

"What does it matter how many a skirt ye hide behind!" roared the prisoner, his skin taking on a firey glow. "Do ye not know that there is one eye that sees beyond all others in this matter?"

"Do not cite the Bible!" wailed Blackbeard. "I am currently amused to be talking to ye. If ye cite Biblical text, I will lose interest at once, for people are always citing Biblical references in my presence."

"The Bible!" spouted old Mick. "I do not quote the Bible or rely upon its authority. My malevolence toward thy kind is based instead on whimsy, the sort of stuff that make a man love one flower and hate another.

"Flowers?" said Blackbeard. "Were we speaking of flowers?"

"Sir, I admire the simple, single rose but can not abide large clusters of any purple flower or any flower of pink or suspect hue."

"Ye have then an aversion for the afflicted?" said Blackbeard,

"Aye, I do!" said Mick, his creaking jaw set. "Every man is entitled to be closed minded in at least one particular, Sir. I have chosen mine, and it's to be against ye gai mates that flit about the sea when the working man is hunting turtles."

"And what of this one eye that sees beyond all others in these matters?" said Blackbeard, as he absentmindedly discharged his pistol into the tarred deck of the hooker. "Who is the owner of that eye?"

Even as he spoke, Blackbeard looked all about him, but could find no hint of treachery in the tropical sun.

"That eye is within thyself," chuckled Mick, "and it knows what thy whipstaff requires far sooner than thy blood can imagine and so makes selections for ye. And what selections have these been, ye ask? Why, look about with the vision of that inner eye. Have ye not chosen a profession that requires close habitation with men in intimate quarters, all of them dress in the garments of women?

"And do ye not see that ye dance about with one another to sprightly tunes called *jigs* and *hornpipes* and *reels*, either aboard ship or on beaches before campfires? What's more, do the most of ye not sleep together in a hold, sharing thy various aromas, flailing about with thy whipstaffs in the dark?

"Do ye not strip off thy shirts at the first sign of sun and parade around the deck for one another, showing off the swelling of thy arms and chests or the latest parrots colored upon thy backs? Do ye not penetrate one another with blades?"

"Well, aye!" Blackbeard said, to my astonishment. "There might be grist here for the mill of philosophical examination." Then, pulling up a keg of turtle oil, Blackbeard seated himself before the wizened Mick and spoke in a most unguarded manner, his pistols ready to fire upon any of his watching mates who chanced to burst into laughter.

"There is a curious thing I have noticed about my own behavior," said Blackbeard, who noticed Israel Hands had come limping over the gunwale. "Immediately upon taking a new bride, I am more than pleased to share her with my mates, though many of my mates are scarcely worth the pots they attempt to piss in."

"Ah," said old Mick, at last calmed so that his white hair settled down reasonably over his aging skull. "Captain, I will tell ye, for I sense in ye one able to mend his ways with introspection. Ye share ye wives as a means of gaining a subtle egress to the bodies of ye crew."

"And my blood does not know?" wondered Blackbeard.

"It does not," said Mick. "It is a sub-rosa matter. Only the eye within knows, until now."

Blackbeard put his forefinger to his lips, as if cautioning him against waking a sleeping child and then slowly drew himself up.

"Israel Hands!" he bellowed. "Have all the turtles now been secured in the galley of the *Queen Anne's Revenge*?"

"Aye, Captain!" Hands yelled back, extending to Blackbeard a cheerful wave of his hand.

"Good man!" muttered Blackbeard, "Very well, Hands. Now have every blessed one of the beasts returned to this hooker with thanks, and while ye are about it, have this gentleman untied!"

Hands stood upon the deck with the expression of an ox just whammed by the slaughter's mallet or rather like Blackbeard had shot the second leg out from under him as wantonly as he had shot the first.

He reflectively reached for his remaining good leg and sighed in relief for finding it sound. Unlike the other leg, it was not heavily swathed in sailcloth and always on the point of festering. For Hands, life hung by a thread. If Blackbeard died or went mad or dismissed him from his post, he was doomed. Who else would employ him?

Come winter, his dead body would be found frozen beside his begging bowl in New York or Maryland.

"Poor Israel! Once first mate for Blackbeard the Pirate!" they'd say.

I watched his face, watched the sea turtles being moved back into the boat, watched his eyes follow Blackbeard, who had crippled him. Blackbeard, whom he had needed!

"Oh my fat arse," someone yelled. "We get the best eatin' on earth and now we are givin' it all back!"

"Do as ye are told!" shouted Blackbeard. "This is a plot against the English we are carrying out. The sense of it? Ye want to see the sense of it? I'll show ye! Ye want to conjure up a hell right here on earth? Well, then, step forward, I say!"

Chapter Nineteen

At night with Blackbeard, Anne, Israel, and Stede Bonnet, I rode the sea at the wheel in a wash of stars, only losing the mood when Bonnet complained of pains, of breeze, of his nag of a wife. As for Israel Hands, his wound grew less painful with applications of vinegar and brine, and Blackbeard sang on, combing his beard, sitting by the bulwark and lifting up his tuneful bellow to Israel's guitar.

Blackbeard loved navigation by the stars, figuring degrees by them, and was unsurpassed for his time in training men in their use and the handling of weapons and sails.

"Ye must drill thy crew, mates," he would say. "How will they sail ye home when ye are a wrecked ship, if ye haven't wrecked a ship and practiced it?"

"And that ye do?" asked Anne.

"Aye, it is so," said Blackbeard. "Have ye not lived through it?"

"Aye!" I said.

"Good Lord!" groaned Bonnet, putting a hand to his forehead.

Whenever Blackbeard's lectures wandered into worlds that seemed ever beyond him, Bonnet would despair of ever having come to the notion that he could survive upon the sea. One night when he detailed the practice hours and gauges of distance and a hundred other matters relating to the firing of the ship's cannons, Bonnet lay flat out on the quarterdeck in grief.

In spite of his recent victory in the harbor of the Bay of Honduras, Bonnet was not so mad as Don Quixote. In some respects, he was able to view his illusions quite plainly when dragged to the evidence, in this case, my aptitude for the adsorption of the secret of the craft in comparison to his own.

"Ah," I responded one evening to Blackbeard's questioning. "The kopf is a flat bottomed Dutch ship that employs sprint rigging but may carry a side sheet anchor if she chooses. To catch a kopf, ye must lie in wait in a hidden channel and linger with patience until it leaves shallow water. In the deep water, it is a slow ship and will wallow, so ye capture the weather gauge and easily bring down a sail."

"Ah, William, ye are a wonder!" Blackbeard chimed. "And ye, Captain Bonnet, can ye tell me the sailing ability of a French lugger rigged like a ketch with a fore and aft gaff sail in the stern?"

"I forsake this business!" Bonnet cried out. "Captain, beg ye to deliver my person to some Spanish or Portuguese port that I might retire in peace. Never, I tell ye, can I return to my plantation in Barbados. For never dare I look upon the face of an Englishman again."

"Stede Bonnet, my friend," said Blackbeard, his voice a perfectly steady, calm, and healing balm that floated reassuringly through the night. "We have taken many riches on this voyage and may fill the holds of both ships before we're through."

"When ye return to Barbados, ye will return laden with treasure and the envy of society, with a pardon in thy pocket, or ye may elect to further enrich thyself with continued education and further partnership."

"And that is how it will be?" asked Bonnet.

"Aye, Captain," assured Blackbeard with a bracing voice.

A few moments later Bonnet excused himself to crawl into the soft bed of the private cabin Blackbeard had outfitted for him in *Queen Anne's Revenge*.

Bound now and escorted by our fleet, we flew the black and white flags of both Blackbeard and Bonnet. Blackbeard's bore the skeletal image of a devil at full rant shaking a spear, and Bonnet's consisted of a single bone, a skull, and a heart.

At that time in the world of the Brethren there was much competition among pirates for the most striking flag. Jack Rackham's showed a skull with crossed swords beneath, which impressed me not at all, and Tomas Tew's consisted entirely of a muscular, severed arm lifting high, which did impress me, for it differed from the ordinary.

However, more strange yet were Edward Low's black skeleton on a black ground and Captain Kennedy's naked demon with a cutlass and hourglass as well as Captain Richard Worley's diminutive skull, in the distance a mere pinprick in a black flapping ground.

"And what fearsome design will ye someday have upon thy flag, dear Anne?" I said.

"I shall have an image of myself with my foot upon Jack Rackham's head! That miserable coward!"

I should have rejoiced at her word, but I couldn't, so unhappy she seemed. I knew she missed the gallant oaf for his jokes and games. Often she wandered about the deck with a gloom upon her features and often as not practiced with her pistols in a desultory fashion, missing entirely all manner of sea birds that flew close to *Queen Anne's Revenge*.

Forgiving Jack Rackham, however, seemed quite beyond her. Because of his cowardly refusal to avenge the child, she sniffled and cried and cursed to herself and bellowed at an imaginary Jack until even I was driven to the point I began to hope for Jack's redemption.

But no, not redemption! Not redemption so much, unless such also involved his death. In such a mood, I came at last to the hope that Jack Rackham and the Great Pyrate Roberts would cut each other down in the streets of Bath. Otherwise, I would be drawn to shoot both, without Anne knowing.

Jack would be lying in wait for Anne in the little town of Bath. Surely, he would guess that Blackbeard would sail there to seek a pardon from his friend, Governor Eden. The whole world knew, for Blackbeard had a home there and it was said that Blackbeard's house and Governor Eden's house were linked together by a tunnel.

"Sloops on the horizon, Sir!" shouted the lookout.

On the way toward Cuba, we rounded up sloops without firing superfluous shot, and then continued our bloodless rampage by searching the rocks of the Bahamas for recent storm-wrecked vessels. Upon spotting broken spars and planking, Blackbeard delighted in sending Captain Bonnet and contingents of longboats to the wreckage, where the crewmen scrambled over the rocks in search of valuables.

The captain allowed two days of such childish looting, for he was fond of laughing. When handed a ring or piece of jewelry, Captain Bonnet would first give out a great howl of joy and then launch into a little celebratory jig on a nearby promontory.

"Oh my bloody arse!" Blackbeard would bellow. Then, holding his side, he would double up with laughter and point a finger.

A day or two later, two more sloops were captured without a fight and then, as the sun went down, the lookout spotted in the distance a British brig. Blackbeard could scarcely contain his excitement, for on the morrow, as he wished it, there would finally be a fight to the death for a formidable prize.

Never before had I seen such a conflagration at sea, or otherwise. So brazen its imagery remains in my brain, I have never yet managed a chronological appreciation of it, recalling instead a continuing diapason of the cannon's roar and an unending stream of ragged half globes of fire that engulfed the sky and sea. Everywhere, it seemed, there were the screams of the dying, as if behind a drum line, and emerging from the smoke were an ocean of dark men burned in their longboats or plunged into the waves.

Sails toppled into the water, smoke exploded into great billowing clouds. Shards of yardarms and bows hurled from ship to ship like spears. Now and again, the great brig rose from the waves, its forty guns belching streaks of red and gold fire, its square-masted mainsail like a smoke-blackened miter, its fore and aft stern sail like the fluke of a whale.

Like so many whaleboats, our sloops went racing after her, their cannons and small arms firing, then ducking away to its bow or stern or else exploding when its hot cannons found them.

"Good Lord!" Bonnet cried, overcome by the sight, but frozen on the quarterdeck as small arms' fire whistled around him. Blackbeard laughed his way through the battle, instructing me at every turn, but what he saw I failed to see. Where he saw the *Adventure*, the *Revenge*, and the *Queen Anne's Revenge* providing artillery support for the organized strikes of our cadre of sloops, I saw only a confused hell that went beyond my imagining.

At last it was over, and the brig was seized.

"No need to be dazed, Master William," Blackbeard said to me on the quarterdeck, after sending the quartermaster of the *Queen Anne's Revenge* aboard the brig to take inventory of her stores. "No man sees a battle of many ships until he has seen many a battle, if ye take my meaning."

"I take it well," I said. "And I take ye to mean also that I might expect to see many a battle more."

"If ye are who I think ye are, ye will!" laughed Blackbeard. Then he would say nothing more about the matter.

We had dead to bury at sea and prisoners to abandon. Though our store of treasure grew, our number of ships had decreased and we had no room to take on the grateful impressed seaman we had freed of the English crew.

"It's sorry, I am, lads!" said Blackbeard to the Englishmen, setting them ashore on an island controlled by the French that had given its blessing for a few citizens more.

Then off we went into the Caribbean again, not this time for riches, for we had more in the hold than we knew how to spend, but rather to take on food and fresh water and spend some time in relaxation after the rigors of sea and war. With such in mind, we sailed again to the beaches of the balmy island of Turneffe, and spent some spring days and nights recovering from wounds and washing our bodies with fresh water running cool in the streams.

Even gentle Anne, by this time, had taken on the color of a rich mahogany, a condition caused by sweat, sun, and spray. Others of the crew were black as sin, and I, alone, unless Blackbeard was lily white beneath his hair, retained an unhealthy pallor.

"Ghaist boy!" my mates cried out in derision. But I, as I reminded them, was from the North Country and never browned.

The days were long, the beaches warm and balmy. Instead of boiled beef and hardtack with a little rum, which was customary, we hunted for game and fished, harvested shellfish, and ran down cattle and hogs in the wild. When there were islanders about, we tried their vegetables and exotic fruits of all types and spit them out.

There were island women who smiled and pressed old sails into service for private tents.

I raised a tent for Anne and me, but three days running she slept without, until a rainstorm brought her in, and then she slept as a fine young woman who was lately dead.

"Anne," I said, the two of us lying on a mattress of sweet smelling fronds. "Is not this the most pleasant place on the earth?"

Anne said nothing. The rain had stopped, bringing freshness from the island's flowers and just a touch of chill from the Caribbean Sea. The pirates on the beach had dragged dry wood into a pile and were singing melodic, heart wrenching songs before a warming fire.

"Anne," I said. "I smell buttered rum. It would take me but a moment to fetch ye a mug of buttered rum."

"Swive ye," she said, and then lay quiet.

For a long time, I dared say no more. Then, the smell of the roasting green turtle came inevitably to my nose.

"Anne," I said. "They are roasting a green turtle,"

"I can smell," said Anne.

"It seems to me they are roasting a green turtle with sherry wine," I added. To this indisputable fact, Anne said nothing, so I let her pretend to sleep for five minutes more.

"I would be happy to fetch ye some green turtle laced with sherry and a mug of fine buttered rum," I said.

Anne said nothing, but I knew I had won the day, at least in relation to roasted green turtle and a mug of buttered rum.

It was jovially known in the Caribbean that without the two confections there would be no inhabitants of the Caribbean, no island folk, explorers, adventurers, or pirates. But all that had come and stayed had done so, not for treasure or weather or boundless sky, but because of the succulent flesh of the green sea turtle, a repast without equal in the world, and the joys of rum.

Not even Anne in her truculence could long resist on so paradisiacal an evening, with the surf in her ears and the knowledge that wild flowers were blooming in the moonlight in the forest behind us.

"I'll have a little bit," she said, her voice having softened.

When I returned with her portion from the fire where a wag of a pirate was teaching a parrot to converse in the most loathsome of curses, Anne was seated on the sand beside the tent, her blanket drawn about her, her glorious cheeks reflecting the fire.

She ate quietly and drank, then put her head on my shoulder as I sat beside her.

"Have ye mastered the Shakespeare?" she asked.

"Aye!" I said. "For some time now."

"And ye have brought the folio with ye to prove it?"

"Nay!" I said. "I have not."

"Ye have not?"

"Nay," I said. "But what does it matter?"

"Then tell me what matters," said Anne.

"That we are together," I said, and that evening, thereafter, I said nothing else. Under the open sky, with the clear stars above us, we fell asleep, she and I, wrapped together. And I did not wake up until the night was almost over. Then, I woke in heaven, but sitting up, saw the shadow of Blackbeard standing down by the shore, gazing out over the sea.

"It is a lonely sound, is it not, Captain?" I said, catching an earful of the retreating surf as I moved up quietly in the dark.

"Aye, to be sure," said the captain, "But once it had the voice of the Brethren in it. The Dragon roared and all the Brethren sailed, and then came Morgan, the new lord of the Brethren and, hence, of the world. And then came thy Captain Jones and the Great Pyrate Roberts, the defeat of the Spanish and the betrayal of the Brethren by the English."

"What is out there now, Captain?" I asked, standing behind him.

"My death!" he said. "And the deaths of others like me."

"How do ye know?" I asked, for he spoke in a voice I had not heard before—a quiet voice that seemed eerily of the wind and the Southern Ocean. "Surely there are measures to be taken."

"Of course," he said, "but all of them lead to my kissing the king's royal arse! Shall a man lose his soul?"

"Ye are promised a pardon!"

"Aye," said Blackbeard, "but Master William, reflect. I have never promised to pardon the king nor has he deserved one any more than the Spanish lords we have driven from this sea."

"Then take his blood, Sir!"

"I have done most of what I can," he said. "Now my time runs out."

We fell into silence. For half an hour, we watched the sea roll in and out and listened to its interminable roar.

"I have heard that a Finman lives for one hundred and fifty years," said the captain, "but that is not the whole of it. From his majority, it's said, he sails the moments of his life in whatever order he chooses. What say ye?"

At the mention of the word "Finman," I felt my heart stop. "I am no believer in that particular bit of sorcery," I said. "I see no advantages to it."

"I see a thousand," said Blackbeard. "If a Finman may sail from one particular moment to another, bypassing all in between, then may not he sail from one port to the other in the blink of an eye."

"I have had that thought," I said, plainly lying.

"And may he not sail his ship backwards, so that neither time nor space has its usual meaning—not for a Finman."

"Aye," I said, following the captain easily but losing balance, as if the ship were suddenly caught in a whirlpool and spinning to the bottom.

Again, we stood in silence, looking out over the ocean, Blackbeard a reflective man, me an uncomfortable one.

"Tell me, lad," he said. "Ye are from the Orkneys. What images come to thy people when the Finman is spoken of?"

"Shipwrecks," I murmured, "harassment at sea, drowned men. The Finman comes in fog or rain or in snow storms or in dreams or in odd suspensions of thought, with storms of winds released from the black pouch at his neck."

"Aye, so it is the world over!" said Blackbeard, his eyes lit like St. Elmo's fire in the Caribbean night. "Such a creature could blow the English fleet to the end of the world, or transport the English king to some forgotten century. Is not that so?"

"How would I know?" I said.

"Ye know the heart of it," said Blackbeard, "I know that ye know."

Chapter Twenty

At last reaching the outer banks of North Carolina, Blackbeard ordered the entire fleet to sail into Topsail Inlet. Encrusted with barnacles that slowed the ship considerably, the hull of the *Queen Anne's Revenge* called for a thorough careening, which had to be done one side at a time. Unable to hoist it out of the water, we beached the ship on one side during low water and gave the other a thorough scraping. That done, we reversed the sides.

In the hands of a Blackbeard, such an operation could be done without thought, without care, while whistling. Yet Blackbeard missed the mark and the great ship groaned in its timbers, snapped a mast and twisted its spine beneath it.

"Holy Mary!" Blackbeard cried, steaming, red in the face. So florid he became with anger that I thought his heart would burst. "Hands, have the sloops throw their lines on her before she tears her guts out!"

Even as he spoke there was a great cracking of wood and Captain Bonnet ran to the gunwale, yelling. "She's giving way Captain. She's tearing up under us!"

Anne and I watched calmly, there being nothing we could do but leap for safety if the incoming waves broke up the ship completely.

"Hands, the line!" screamed the captain, not at all the same fellow who had once roared with laughter when he had deliberately knocked down his own ship in a storm. In another instant, the first of the lines from one of the other sloops was caught and secured on the bow, and then another caught off the stern. In fifteen minutes time, so expertly were the small sailing craft handled that three lines, including one handled by Hand's sloop, were engaged in pulling the *Queen Anne's Revenge* from the shoal.

"Something is wrong here!" I whispered to Anne.

"Right ye are!" Anne said, even as the captain continued to rage.

In a few minutes more, there was a snapping of the spine of the *Queen Anne's Revenge* as loud as a blast from a cannon. At the same time, Hands' sloop, drawn by its line, turned over in shallow water and buried deep in the shoal, its crew thrown skyward and lucky to escape.

With a final shout of anguish, Blackbeard took a look at his *Queen Anne's Revenge*, which had been rendered forever useless beneath him, and clapped his hands over his ears.

"If it worries ye, we'll get ye a new one with our share," called out my cheeky Anne.

Blackbeard looked up with little of his usual good humor and put a finger to his lips.

"Oh," said Anne, catching on to the fact that there was something to which she wasn't catching on.

Blackbeard then flopped himself down on a chair on the quarter-deck, despair again raining heavily upon him, so much so the crewmen were startled to see him in such a posture. As if one man, they bravely crept close to him before turning toward the gunwale to look down the damaged sides of the *Queen Anne's Revenge*. There, they shook their heads in disbelief to find the ship beyond repair.

"Aye," muttered one man, "and Israel Hands' sloop has found its death as well."

For an hour, there were only muted voices, the sounds of creaking rigging, dropping anchors, and all hands reefing sail. The only sloops left of any dimension or firepower were Stede Bonnet's *Revenge*, still under the command of Lieutenant Richardson, the ten gunned *Adventure* with its topsails and sprit sails, and several fishing craft rigged for maneuverability and speed.

All seemed, for a time, incapable of any action. Then, curiously, Captain Stede Bonnet, in the grip of some great anxiety, was able to fidget himself into life.

"Captain!" he cried, "There is business to attend to! There are pardons to be had in Bath from Governor Eden! There are fortunes to be divided filling the holds of all of these ships. I must have back my ship!"

"I grieve for my ship!" cried Blackbeard, his head in his hands.

"But we have no time to lose!" said Bonnet. "Who knows when the Royal Navy might sail by here and hang us all for pirates!"

"I am reconciled," said Blackbeard. "I grieve only for ye, my friend!"

"For me!" cried Stede Bonnet, wringing his hands. Then let me have back my ship!"

"But these two wrecked ships contain a disproportionate sum of the spoils!" objected Blackbeard. "I would not cheat ye, Sir. Ye must wait until the treasure is unloaded and properly divided. The riches aboard the *Revenge* now is less than thy just compensation!"

"Aye," said Bonnet, temporarily quieted. "That's true."

A moment later, however, a bleeding Israel Hands pulled himself up the rope ladder to the deck of the shattered *Queen Anne's Revenge.*

"Captain Teach," he cried, "these are dangerous waters. The militia plies these waters, as well as the navy. May I suggest, Sir, that ye take a fast sloop at once to receive thy pardon from Governor Eden in Bath and then return to receive thy treasure as salvage from the sea."

Blackbeard looked up at Israel Hands with admiration in his eye, but then dropped his head and shook it.

"Nay," he said. "I cannot do it. I cannot abandon my ship and crew, for what kind of captain would I be if I could?"

At Blackbeard's words, the men were much moved, and not a few of them huddled around him, urging him to go, not only for his safety and good fortune but for theirs as well. Anne and I hung back, as did Israel Hands and Lieutenant Richardson, who had recently climbed aboard with several of Blackbeard's mates who commanded other sloops.

Hands then approached Captain Bonnet, who had slunk back to amidships and was leaning on the mainmast, straightening his periwig in an agitated fashion until Hand's lips moved to Captain Bonnet's ear and Bonnet's face broke slowly into a smile.

Having worked his way through the crowd, Captain Bonnet then presented himself before Blackbeard once again, this time in less of a dither.

"Sir," said Captain Bonnet, the men falling quiet, "I propose taking a sloop to Bath myself and there obtaining myself a pardon from Governor Eden, as well as salvage rights. After that, I will return here, receive from ye my share of the booty and my ship and then be on my way, leaving ye all other sloops for thy disposal. That way, there shall be ample time for the division of goods and the minimum of time for making them legally thy own. It will also give ye opportunity to fight off the enemy if there is an intrusion. What say ye?"

Blackbeard rose from his chair as if struck by a revelation.

"Good Lord, Stede!" he cried. "I have taught ye ever so well! Thy plan has all the merriment of a plan brought to the firmament of the earth by the devil himself. By all the rogering nomads of the sea, I shall die proud of ye!"

Captain Bonnet's sloop sailed out of sight as Blackbeard supervised the appropriate division of treasure and setting of guards on each ship.

Then, as evening approached, the store of roasted meats and rum were pulled from the belly of *Queen Anne's Revenge*, and even as the great ship slowly collapsed into the shoal, a cry went out for feasting and entertainment to the crewmen of all the sloops. Blackbeard proved himself a jovial host.

How we drunk all night and ate and argued and fought and laughed! Parrots flew from shoulder to shoulder, and men sang songs like Sirens. Even the mates left to guard the gold coins and chests of fine silver of the various sloops were called to the joyous feast and, the flesh being weak, gave way to spirited cajolery.

I never knew at what hour it was that Israel Hands, Lieutenant Richardson, and those surviving members of Blackbeard's original crew crept from their cakes and frothy ale to shift the great bulk of the treasure from the creaking holds of the sloops to Blackbeard's *Adventure*.

By morning, there was a great pile of smelling seaman upon the collapsing deck of the *Queen Anne's Revenge* and no little clustering of other rutting lads still in the clinging arms of Indian girls in the white dunes and tall reeds of Ocracoke Island.

Anne and I and Blackbeard were awakened, quickly enough, and soon we had deserted our intemperate mates and were all gone away to Bath in the *Adventure* with most of the treasure in its hold.

"Captain," I balked, offended. "This is rank treachery."

"These are the rules," he shrugged.

"But ye have robbed thy friends."

"Ye are beyond thy place to say such a thing," he said, angry for a moment. "I did not make the world. This is how it is done."

Chapter Twenty-One

It was with some righteous hilarity that Blackbeard penetrated Ocracoke Inlet off North Carolina and then faultlessly sailed each treacherous wash and channel of Pamlico Sound to the Pamlico River, some fifty miles from the Atlantic, then called by some the *Northern Sea*. There, we discovered, as Blackbeard had hoped, Stede Bonnet had only lately left for his looted *Revenge* with a pardon in his pocket.

"I have likely saved my friend Stede's life," remarked Blackbeard, "for surely this blow will cause him to retire from the trade."

Anne's lips formed a grim line, but even she saw the captain's point.

"And if the disgruntled seamen attacked ye here?" I asked.

"Not here!" laughed Blackbeard. "For Bath is my town!"

Of this I was dubious until at last we had dropped anchor in the tiny harbor and had rowed ashore in our longboats and seen the people swarm from their dining rooms and parlors to greet us. Slaves came running from the barns, cooks from the kitchens, barefooted children with their hoops and fishing poles. In the "ordinaries" dockside, drunken mates stumbled into the sunshine, hailing us up and down the streets. Innkeepers threw open their doors.

"The secret of this," said Blackbeard, "is to avoid committing crimes by land and to arrive with money."

"Aye," I said, but I soon saw there was more.

No man or woman or child did Blackbeard meet upon the dock or streets without a hardy clasp or enthusiastic pleasantry, often followed with inquiries of health and kin and, in the case of misfortune, immediate offers of aid. Most often, however, there were cries for tales of new adventures, from adult and child alike, for who brought more accurate and interesting news than a man of the sea?

"Mark how they love the captain," said Israel Hands. "He is a prince in this country. He scatters riches among these people and wisdom as well as wit and wag. He connects them to the world. What's more, his force of arms protects them from the savages of these shores that the crown does nothing about, and his fearsome reputation causes other visiting pirates to mind their manners when they are ashore. Look there, Sir."

Looking about me, I saw there were a number of Moslem corsairs in their curious wraps lingering about the docks and not a few Frenchmen, all jabbering to Blackbeard too fast to be understood. In the harbor floated a French lugger with two masts and four fore and aft sails and an Arab dhow from the Red Sea, where it was said rich jewels lay on the beaches as plentiful as grains of sand.

"My good friends all," shouted Blackbeard, in his element, as fresh and vigorous as if he had only lately risen from his bed. "Let us go at once to the counting house and have rum all around!"

A cheer went up, and merchants rushed back to their ordinaries and taverns for kegs of rums and fruit juices. Blackbeard's crew, forming an armed but jovial guard, began hauling chests of goods to the dockside place of auction that the citizens of Bath had constructed in their wisdom.

It consisted of a long roof of planks to keep off the sun, a rudimentary floor of the same, and fifty or so crude benches for the more serious merchants of the town and bidders from other seaports. As often as not, casual onlookers, including women and children, found themselves standing around the edges of the shelter or having picnics in grassed area outside it.

The sound of singers' voices mixed with the sound of commerce.

"Now what will ye give me for this fine bolt of silk!" roared Blackbeard. "Think ye what a bold price it will bring in Boston or New York!"

"Aye," said a fisherman's wife to a neighbor. "I could get my Will to sell that bolt for a fancy profit in Baltimore."

"Aye," said another. "Do it then, Nancy. Why should these merchants take all the advantage, when it is plain to see that our husbands can find Philadelphia as well as they? And don't I wish to have a great family, as surely as another. Captain Teach, I bid another piece of eight for that bolt, and I offer ye dinner."

"And I accept ye offer of dinner, as well as ye bid, my lady," said Blackbeard, "and I offer ye and thy husband dinner at my home as well. Now what jeweler among ye wishes to pay a fine and fair price for this box of sapphires, which are the most lovely I have seen? Governor Eden, allow me to present one to thy engaged daughter, as a gift."

"Why thank ye, Teach. And let me invite ye to dinner as well."

"Accepted gladly, Sir!" Blackbeard said. "Now there are five sapphires left. Would ye like to buy the rest Governor, or should I sell them elsewhere?"

"I'll take them Teach," said the Governor.

"Now in the matter of crosses!" said Blackbeard, again addressing the crowd. "We have gold and silver crosses, fancy and plain. It does not matter if ye are Catholic or Protestant or Puritan or Quaker. We will sell ye a cross for thy holiness or, if ye wish an artifact of the sea instead. We have jeweled daggers, cutlasses, and skulls and cross-bone flags that have lately adorned masts."

That said, Blackbeard paused a moment and turned over the items he had just spoken of for others to sell. Then he turned back toward the crowd.

"Israel Hands," he called. "Leave off conversing with Master William and bring forth the flintlocks."

Hands excused himself and was replaced by a fascinated Anne Bonny, who stood agape at the spell Blackbeard had woven over townspeople and pirate alike. At his side, Hands reached into a black bag and extracted a mahogany case in which two heavily bejeweled and dazzling flintlocks were inlaid with gems like twin crowns.

"Such a prize as these cannot be bought, but must be won," shouted Blackbeard, holding the open case of flintlocks above his head, "and to win these two flintlocks worth a king's treasure ye must prove thyself a better shot than a child!

"Well, then!" shouted a rowdy in his cups, "bring on the child!"

"Why! The competition's tonight at the Golden Owl!' said Blackbeard. "The fee for entering a mere piece of eight, and if ye care to lay eyes upon the child that will best ye, why there he is now with the lovely Anne Bonny."

Blackbeard's finger pointed toward me, all eyes found me. Parrots screeched and murmurs arose from every quarter. Gentlewomen in their fine dress complained to see one so young in the company of a woman dressed so carelessly as Anne Bonny with trousers and loose blouse. Under their breaths, pirates praised savage gods to find such easy pickings.

I stood and doffed my hat, letting my blond hair fall down in ringlets.

"Disgusting!" said Anne, when I had at last tired of playing to the crowd and sat back down.

"Nonsense!" I said. "I'm just letting the old man know that his lessons aren't wasted on me!"

The afternoon moved outrageously on, our profits at sea becoming also the profits of the town, Blackbeard never tiring, but glorying in the role of salesman and provider as he had on the sea gloried in the role of black-hearted marauder. Anne wearied first, then I, and with Israel Hands in our charge, we succeeded in finding a doctor who reopened his shop and applied a poultice to the first mate's wound.

"Bones have been shattered in the knee," said the doctor. "The swelling and discoloration will give way, but ye should not expect improvement in thy walk."

"I thought as much," said Israel Hands to Anne Bonny, "but I shall be rich as a king, shall I not, Anne?"

"Aye, Israel!" said Anne, a touch of anger in her voice. "Ye have friends that will ensure that the captain deals honestly with ye."

Outside again, on the dock, we sat with Hands and watched the water go by. The counting house, with Blackbeard's voice still roaring away inside, sat half a town away. Governor Eden's mansion glistened in the sun directly across the harbor and not far from it, across a narrow river, sat Blackbeard's smaller mansion, thought by local seamen to be connected to both the river and the governor's mansion by tunnels.

"I don't think Blackbeard shot me on purpose," said Hands at last. "As ye know, when at sea, he likes to play the devil. I think he meant to miss and couldn't own up to it afterward."

When at last night came, the business was done and Blackbeard rowed us across the harbor to the river of fresh warm water that ran beside his house. There we bathed peacefully under lantern light, joined and assisted by eight or nine of his wives, beauteous creatures of various ages and figures who brought us glasses of wine and roasted shellfish from a fire.

Several of the wives lived in the big house and cared for the Blackbeard's goods and furnishings; others lived about the town. All lived where and how they chose by Blackbeard's largess, even with lovers of their own, all of whom he blessed.

"Every woman is a blessing, William!" Blackbeard said, treading water, a plump wife in either arm. "No balm of Gilead was ever so healing or tender to the spirit. No treasure of the earth is worth so much as the smile of a beloved. No whore so ill figured that in comparison to our wretched selves is less than a sainted lady."

"Aye," I said, agreeably, impressed that Blackbeard allowed no woman to pour him a glass of wine but rather insisted on pouring wine for each woman present instead.

After an hour of pleasure that may not be forgotten, I drifted to shore and lay in the shallow water, my head on the bank, my Anne asleep in my arms. For Blackbeard, however, there was no rest. No sooner had one of his wives swum from his embrace, another swam in, and those that weren't swimming in or out were busy plaiting his hair or pulling on his back or tickling his ribs and trying to make him laugh.

My eyes soon closed.

When I awoke, Blackbeard was being dressed on the bank by his wives, who had taken a fancy to gaudy breeches and a bright red waistcoats as well as heavy knee boots and sashes and innumerable ribbons for his beard.

"Let this be a lesson for ye!" said Anne Bonny, who was as awake as I, "To win the hearts of women ye needs but to be man enough to let them go."

"So, is that how it is?" I said, splashing her a bit with water.

"It is!" said she, splashing me back.

"Not for me!" I cried. "For surely my lady has promised me her favor if I can but accurately read from William Shakespeare's *Romeo and Julie.*"

"Oh!" said Anne, first in a diminutive voice, then "Oh!" again, as if she had seen the situation, suddenly, in another light. "Of course," she said, "a formal test of the text will be administered to ye on the morrow."

"On the morrow?" I said. "I was thinking of now!"

"Look there to the captain," remarked Anne. "Observe the physical ugliness of the man, yet how women flock to him in a passion. Do ye see him pleading with anyone for attention, or is it the other way around? As I understand it, not once has he proposed marriage to a woman. Each of his wives proposed marriage to him, and several he took to spare their feelings."

Anne's words were causing me to burn a bit. "Alright," I said. "I'm reconciled to being tested on the morrow. But think ye. Has ever a man succeeded in so difficult a chore for the sake of a woman?"

"Hasn't Henri taught ye of Paris and Helen of Troy?" retorted Anne.

"Going to war's less difficult than reading and writing," I said.

On the bank of the river we dressed in clean clothes brought to us by Blackbeard's servants and wives, both Anne and I choosing our typical garb and usual array of weaponry. It would have been most welcome to stay at Blackbeard's house, chatting away the gentle night on the veranda, but there was a public to serve. So, at length we bestirred ourselves and rowed back across the harbor to the Golden Owl.

A great hurrah arose in the black-flag-hung rafters of the Golden Owl when we entered with Blackbeard and his wives leading the way to a great long table. Then, sitting, we were lost in a sea of gibbering citizens and seamen pounding us on our backs and shouting wild oaths as a village boy drove a wild pony in one door and out the other.

The French pirate Oliver La Bouche sat across from us, still speaking too rapidly for me to follow, though I now had no trouble understanding Henri.

"He says there have been many hangings," said Anne. "This Englishman sent by the King, Woodes Rogers, is no ordinary commander but a devil and the equal of any pirate himself."

"What says he?" shouted Blackbeard, from the end of the table, having picked up a piece of our conversation with La Bouche.

The Owl Inn quieted down and Anne answered at once to a stony silence.

Blackbeard raised a hand and then called for a bowl of rum.

At once a girl, almost tripping in her eagerness, brought it from the barrel. Blackbeard placed it before him without a word, stared down a citizen who cleared his throat, and emptied his horn of gunpowder into the bowl so that it dissolved in the rum. That done, he lit the whole mass with his flint so that it flamed up like an erupting volcano.

"Gentlemen," he said, picking up the flaming bowl with both hands, "with this confection, I hereby toast the valiant deeds of the soon to be late Woodes Rodgers."

Blackbeard then drank down the fiery liquid with one gulp and remarked favorably on its flavor.

Again, hurrahs filled the Golden Owl, and soon enough a merchant arose to speak.

"My friends and neighbors," he shouted to be heard. "I have heard it asked if these colonies of this new world could survive without our friends who fight upon the sea, and I have an answer for ye this day. No, we could not. Without Captain Teach, where would we get the weaponry and ammunition to fight off the Indians, for surely no foreign power can be depended on to help us? And if our crops fail, who is on hand to do business with us and feed us?"

"Aye!" yelled one and all.

"And who provides the rum!" yelled another.

A second merchant arose, a short fat man, who wiped his bald head with a handkerchief as he spoke.

"I ship goods to Philadelphia, New York, Boston, Washington, and other cities to the north," he said, "and I tell ye frankly, when I walk the commercial districts of those cities, it is rare that I see any product that has not been stolen at sea. Gentlemen, the leading industry of this land is not tobacco, as many believe, but piracy. Without Captain Teach and Captain La Bouche and other fighters of the sea all would be lost."

"Aye," shouted a citizen.

"Hurrah!" shouted another.

There was a round of applause and then the shouting of bits of news.

"Captain Hornigold has turned pirate catcher," shouted one of La Bouche's crew.

"That fat old bastard!" said Blackbeard, his face turning dark with rage.

"Thomas Jones is in New York," shouted another.

"New York!" I thought to myself, my head starting to swim.

Blackbeard gave me a meaningful look. He and I had speculated many times as to where Thomas Jones could be, and now the answer had seemingly fallen to us. My impulse was to grab Anne and rush to the my nearest ship. It was an impulse I had to resist, however, as I did not have a ship.

The evening grew hotter and louder. Sweat wet my clothes and ran down into my boots. Sea captains sat about. Both pirate captains and captains of fishing craft smoked long clay pipes and filled the place with smoke as they told impossible stories of the sea to the boys of the town who sat at their feet drinking rum as quickly as the men.

Some cursed villain then remembered the flintlocks that could be won by besting Captain Teach's boy in a shooting contest. Accordingly, two apples were set up on a barrel at one end of the inn and my first challenger was sent with two pistols to the other side of the inn. He was a handsome fellow on the right side of his face, but a burnt devil with no eye on the left, and he hit neither apple nor so closely to an apple that we saw where the two shots struck.

I split both apples and new apples were set on the barrel.

Two misses again by another, then two hits by me.

The first nine contests went exactly the same.

"Schwizzlewit, bastard, white swiving cheat!" they yelled.

When at last a pirate taking lengthy aim hit one of the apples, the crowd burst into applause. Blackbeard laughed uproariously.

When I again split both apples at once, he almost fell from his chair.

And so it went, the splitting of apples by me, the collecting of wagers by Blackbeard, the cursing of me by the citizenry. By the end of the evening, it was necessary for Blackbeard and members of our crew to encircle me and walk me to the longboat. Then, as a precaution, they rowed across the lake with me, and, after, spent the night in my close proximity so that no one succeeded in cutting my throat.

"Fret not, Master William," said Blackbeard, a low rumble of laughter proceeding from his chest. "Though they hate ye tonight in their drunkenness, tomorrow ye shall walk among them as a legend from the sea."

"Have I done well enough to have accomplished the necessary preliminaries to receive thy quim?"

"Aye," admitted Anne on Blackbeard's shaded veranda, her head nodding slightly as she gazed down upon the folio spread open on the table before us. "Ye have missed neither word nor nuance in the reading. What manner of devil might ye be that ye have such an angelic center to thy soul?"

"And do ye give me thyself willingly, Anne?" I asked. "For I love ye, in spite of my years."

"Haugh!" said Anne. "Look at thyself in a mirror, lad. One moment ye seem still a child, the other a man. Will ye have me take my clothes off for ye, or will ye assist me?"

"I will assist ye, Anne!"

"And will it be here in the shade or shall we move to that wooded area by the harbor?"

"By the wooded area, I think."

"Very well," said Anne, leading the way down the veranda steps and across Blackbeard's dock on the way to the woods where hollyhock hung from every bush, and the air was sweetened by tiny blushing flowers. This morning, to my joy, she was armed as usual but dressed as a woman.

Her long dark braids were tied to her head by a rose bandana, and two golden hoops swung from her ears. Her skin was bronze, setting off the gold and topaz of her necklace, bracelets, and rings. No less striking were her vest and snow-white blouse rising from a brandy sash and a long skirt that swished over laced up boots. When she turned and faced me under a juniper tree, she smelled of the Spanish perfumes Blackbeard had given her, and I could not speak, so overcome was I by my own trembling limbs.

First, I removed the pistols from the sash and laid them carefully on the ground.

She closed her eyes in quiet surrender. "William," she said. Then I pulled the cutlass from her sash and laid it beside the pistols, then removed a knife from her boot, after which, my heart pounding, I ran my hand up her leg and removed the French knife she carried and laid it with the other weapons.

Taking her into my arms, I kissed her full on the lips and watched her eyes open and shut. Then I pulled the bandana from her head and threw it carelessly to the ground, so inflamed was my passion. I heard my Anne groan and felt her hands tugging at my shirt.

My hands began tugging back, and soon the tugging back and forth lost in organization what it gained in intensity, and the two of us began hurling bits of clothing about, inadvertently catching other bits of clothing on our limbs.

"Great God in heaven!" cried my dainty Anne. "This is no squirrel!"

"Whoa!" I cried, Anne clutching my member.

Then the two of us pitched over into the underbrush, so entangled we became.

"Halloo!" came a voice. "Halloo!"

My impulse was to continue reclining upon the brambles in the underbrush, without so much as a twitch of the eyes, in the hope that the "Halloo!" had not been intended for Anne and me, and, if we did not move, we might not be seen. But Anne's view prevailed. At once, it seemed, she was back in her clothes and popping up from the brush as if she been innocent of anything but going for a stroll.

Moments later, I heard her whoop joyfully.

Straightening myself out as quickly as I could, I too left the brush and went to the side of the harbor, and there, to my happiness and horror, saw the fourteen-gun sloop *Diamond* dropping anchor. I say "happiness" because Joe Buck and Mary Read were already preparing a longboat to row to where my dear Anne Bonny was waiting for them; I say "horror" because Calico Jack Rackham was watching from the quarterdeck.

That night at the Golden Owl, Joe Buck wept openly to be reunited with his protégé Anne Bonny, and Mary Read filled my face with a thousand kisses. To my utter surprise, Calico Jack kept his distance from Anne, Blackbeard, and myself and instead strutted for his own following at a distant corner of the inn. Now and then, he would stand and model his calico clothes and women would gather round him.

Like many another captain telling stories to boys at the inn, he smoked a long clay pipe, biting off the end until at last the pipe was used up.

"That's not tobacco in that pipe," said Mary. "It will be the death of him, but will he listen?"

"He is a cowardly man!" said Anne. "I cannot abide a cowardly man!"

"Aye, it is a fault," said Joe Buck. "But recent voyages showed Jack's courage on the mend. After we took the *La Santisima Trinidad*, Mary killed the captain and Vane and Jack hung all the officers from the yardarms. Is that not so, Mary?"

"Aye, it is!" said Mary. "Jack has progressed to atrocities. He and Vane captured the sloop *Diamond*, cut away the sails and masts, drank a toast to the damnation of the king, and executed the captain."

"I'm supposed to be impressed by his executing people?" asked Anne.

"Then, of course, there was the matter of his leading a mutiny against Captain Vane and attacking the brigantine."

"I know of that!" said Anne. "Ye may swive thyself."

"Has he yet challenged the Great Pyrate Roberts?" I remarked, helpfully.

"Do not speak to me like that!" said Anne. "Do not!"

Immediately, my ears were burning.

Blackbeard lumbered drunkenly across the floor of the Golden Owl and took a seat beside me, deciding once again to order a bowl of rum into which he could dump his gunpowder. Following him, as usual, were wives and those who wished to be wives. Tiring, he sat them in chairs backed with quaint tapestry rather than in his lap or on the rough planks beneath his feet.

"Who is that fellow?" said Blackbeard, sniffing at the aroma of roast duck in the air and pointing a crooked finger across the room to where Calico Jack sat.

"That's Calico Jack Rackham, as ye know!" said Mary Read, herself decked out in an island woman's trove of silver earrings and necklaces. "Black Joe Buck and I washed in with him on the pitch bucket, the *Diamond*."

"Aye. So it seems!" replied Blackbeard, thrusting himself to his feet. "Calico Jack Rackham, by my grisly arse, welcome to Bath, North Carolina!"

Having heard Blackbeard address him in such a fashion and seen the huge captain tower expectantly above his table, Calico Jack had little choice but to turn a chalky shade of white and dump two whores plump as quail from his lap to the splintery floor.

"Come forward, mate!" shouted Blackbeard, his eyes angrily noting the discomfort of the ladies. "It is rare enough I see ye and thy ornamental pantaloons. Besides, it is well I know ye would not be in Blackbeard's inn were ye not desirous of an audience. How may I serve ye?"

Calico Jack stepped forward slowly, the crowd of seamen, pirates, whores, and officials of the town all making way for his passage. He moved without fawning, I thought, but with the slightly apologetic air of one who was having second and third thoughts in regard to a position about which he had once seemed adamant.

"Why ye may give me leave to use Bath as a home port," said Jack, as bravely as he could, "and I will form an alliance with ye that will put gold in thy purse. What say ye to such an arrangement?"

"I say I don't charge my friends for the use of this port," said Blackbeard. "Why should I charge ye now?"

"I figured in my case ye might run me off if I did not pay dear," said Jack, "for there have been some ill feelings between us in the matter of thy niece, Anne Bonny."

"Aye, there has been, Jack Rackham," said Blackbeard, his left eye shutting and his head cocking to the right like a fighting bird's. "I have heard that ye have lifted thy hand to her and allowed her to pour ye wine as if she were a whore, though she is none. And I have heard that even now ye stay drunken all the day and smoke the Turkish weed at night and give no thought to winning her back.

"Worse yet, Jack Rackham, I have heard ye have failed to join in a fight to the death when it was her life that was imperiled. Are these infamies not true?"

"Aye, they are true," said Rackham, bowing his head. "And for all of those things I am heartily sorry."

"Liar." said Anne, turning in her chair so that she saw Rackham looking at the floor.

"I do not presume to ask ye for Anne, Sir, or to hope for her return," said Rackham. "I am reconciled to her loss, though it grieves me no end. What I ask for, Sir, is thy blessing on the right of my craft and crew to use the port of Bath for the trade of piracy. In return, I will pay gold and extend to any man or woman of Bath the privilege of shipping out with me."

"And do ye have a character witness, Jack?" asked Blackbeard.

"I may in part speak for him," said Mary Read, attracting everyone's attention by driving her axe into the table.

"Then speak," permitted Blackbeard.

"I have sailed now for some time with Captain Vane and Jack Rackham, so now I may tell ye all that both are bloody drunken bastards that God himself will doubtless swing by the rope unless King George catches them first. As to Jack's treatment of women, may he burn in hell with a brimstone poker up his arse! The man hath no known virtue, except the power to deceive imbeciles. If he says, for instance, that he is not here to carry away Anne, ye can be certain he has in mind carrying away Anne. If he says he will pay gold, it is only because he plans on stealing it."

"Aye," said Joe Buck, the hunter, in support of Mary's recommendation. "He is a man of near perfect perfidy and, therefore, both useful and amusing. We might, for instance, send him out against the Spanish or use him in chains to train the young or track him through the swamps or simply bury him up to his neck in the marsh or simply let him go. He'll cause havoc till he's dead."

"Aye," said Blackbeard. I thought as much. Then he may be of some little use to us. Very well, Jack, ye may use the port of Bath for a fee until we catch ye in acts of disloyalty. Then we will hang ye high. But tell me, mate. Have ye thought of the meaning of thy calico coat and pantaloons? Can it be that ye are a buggerer in thy willow if not in thy head?"

"What?" said Jack, a look of incomprehension coming over his face.

"And perhaps ye are drawn to the Great Pyrate Roberts," said Blackbeard, "whose dress, I understand, is as flamboyant as thy own?"

"Nay, my good Sir!" said Jack, missing the point and wrapping his cape about him with a grand flourish. "There has never been the day when the Great Pyrate Roberts has dressed with the fashion of Calico Jack Rackham."

"Never mind!" said Blackbeard. "It's clear ye have not the wit for this discussion. Let's proceed to something else."

"To something else?"

"Aye, to something else!" said Blackbeard, indicating me with a flip of a hand. "Do ye recognize this boy who has come to occupy a prominent place at my table?"

Jack looked at me stonily, debating with himself whether or not to acknowledge that he knew me, and then deciding on a middle road. "In New Providence, Anne took to carrying such a boy about with her as a pet, but this boy seems older."

"It is the same boy!" said Blackbeard. "Have ye not seen him fight?"

"Aye," said Jack, his stone eyes darkening. "If this is the same blond boy, as ye say, I saw him shoot his pistols into a body of men carrying only hand weapons and then hang a defenseless prisoner from the rafters of an inn."

"Well, well, as ye say!" said Blackbeard. "What would ye tell me of his marksmanship?"

"He is no marksman," said Jack "Mates cross the street at the sight of him, but he has no skill, only blood in the eye."

"Ye are the better marksman then?" said Blackbeard.

"Nay!" shouted Anne Bonny. "Do not set the two of them against the other. I forbid it."

"I do no such thing!" protested Blackbeard. "In this I am the physician, draining them both of bad blood. Otherwise, ye'll be following the coffin of one or the other before the moon's horns turn down to empty it of rain."

"I do hate the boy!" said Jack. "For he freely courts Anne, in spite of his age, and that impudence amazes me."

"And I despise Jack!" I said. "But rather than recite ye a long list of reasons, let me admit I despised him before I knew him or heard of his deeds. Indeed, I loathed him upon first hearing his name. Just as the Creator in his wisdom has given me Anne Bonny to love and elevate, He has given me Calico Jack Rackham to hate and desecrate."

At these words of mine, Jack Rackham became so infuriated that he leapt at me like a jungle animal, and I was forced to knock him instantly to the floor with the most perfectly executed shoulder thrust of my life. Lemuel Valley would have been proud of the footwork, the timing, the arc of the blow. Though Jack outweighed me by many stones, I actually felt him lift off the floor before crashing to it.

Such a sensation did Jack's flopping body cause in the Golden Owl that there was at first a silence and then a rising excitement. Then someone poured a pitcher of ale over Calico Jack's head and he rose groggily to his feet, his clothes not nearly so dashing as they had been before and his hair dripping ale.

"As I was remarking," said Blackbeard, as stunned as anyone else but pretending not to notice that Jack had already suffered an ignominious moment, "When two good lads are struck with a mutual enmity, I find matters may often be resolved by a healthy sporting event and then a good drink after. In this case, I recommend a shooting competition. Hands, may I trouble ye to provide a number of apples?"

"Nay, Captain," shouted Anne, reaching across the table for Blackbeard's arm. "Neither is to be trusted with pistols."

"Listen to Anne, Captain!" said Mary, taking him by an arm.

Blackbeard leaned close to Mary's ear. "Let go of my arm, Mary Read," he whispered fiercely. "Will it not amuse ye to see this boy put drunkard Jack in his grave?"

Mary Read removed her fingers from the Blackbeard's arm and took a step backward. Things were hard for Mary, I knew, for it was certain she loved me as her own nephew and knew Jack to be unworthy, but with Jack she had found a captain who let her pirate as Mary Read, not Matt Read, and, at times, command the crew.

Catching my eye, she mouthed words to me. "Let him live!"

The usual calmness came over me when danger was near. The movements of the serving girls and patrons of the Golden Owl slowed down. Israel Hands was returning with slow steps from the kitchen, two apples in his hands. Anne was returning tearfully from Calico Jack who had turned and was walking away from me for no apparent reason.

"Don't kill him!" cried Anne, throwing her arms around me. "Promise me ye won't kill him!"

Over Anne's shoulder I saw Calico Jack turn back toward me and start to draw his weapons, but how long it took! It seemed I waited a while and noted Blackbeard's alarmed expression and Israel Hands' shout, then entered a spyglass in which all noises and sights and smells of the inn slowly dissolved. There, I found Anne and threw her aside, despite her lamentations.

There, at the glass' end, stood Jack, his pistols rising as mine spat fire.

"Damn ye, I told ye, no!" cried Anne, leaping to her feet, her eyes blazing into mine.

Then I was quite abandoned, as Anne, Hands, Mary, and half the patrons of the Golden Owl rushed for the falling Calico Jack, as if they were all Obeda men with poultices of swamp grass.

"He is not grievously injured," I shouted. "I directed my fire on either side of the stomach. After a bit of bleeding, he'll feel no effect in organ or bone."

"Burn ye in hell!" screamed Anne, a poor sport in these matters.

"Aye! Burn ye in hell!" shouted one of Calico Jack's crewmen.

In a fit of whimsy, I fired yet a third pistol at Jack, striking him in the buttocks. This last shot had the effect of horrifying everyone, not just for the cold-blooded tone of the deed but for the amount of blood now spilled upon the floor of the inn. Old linens were brought from a back room and serving girls rushed over with mops, but for some time Jack outstripped with his bleeding all efforts to restore decorum.

"That last was a stroke of brilliance!" said Blackbeard, bending to my ear. "No one here will fail to embellish the story of it for the rest of his life. But I think it wise for ye to leave at once. Ye might try the security of my veranda."

"I must speak to Anne!" I said.

"I shall do that for ye!" said the Blackbeard. "She is upset now, but she will be more thoughtful when her hot blood cools and she is told that Jack went for his pistols first and may have gunned her down with ye, except for thy action. Second, ye did not kill him, though ye might easily have done so."

"Why must I flee?"

"Lad!" roared Blackbeard. "If ye stay, ye might have to shoot yet another. How would that be?"

"S'death!" I said, below my breath. "I shall never have my quim!"

"Heh!" said Blackbeard, putting a cupped hand to his ear. "Did I hear ye whine like a dog, or did ye speak like a pirate man willing to wait on my veranda for his love to come to him? What say ye?"

"I shall wait in the shadows of the moon on the veranda," I said, "and pray that there is more eloquence in thy tongue than mine."

"There is," said Blackbeard, deciding to light the tapers in his beard. "Ye shall have Anne. Go sit thy arse upon the veranda."

Then, having led me to the door of the Golden Owl, he hooted a couple of times pulling on his ears and lovingly kicked me into the street where I noticed at once Calico Jack's longboat pulled up to the dock. Bunging a floorboard with a marlinespike, I giggled like a girl in the moonlight and then rowed in one of Blackbeard's longboats across the harbor to his house.

There, I waited in the shadows. At first, I lurked in the shadows of the pines at the bank and then moved to the veranda itself, from where I watched the lantern light of the Golden Owl Inn wink over the water.

My senses grew acute. The air was fresh, as if there were a pinch of rain in it. A light breeze stirred the loblolly. The slight movement of the air, the honeysuckle blooming in the yard, and the night jars singing gave the evening a scented fragility, both beautiful and delicious as the rarest flower and so dependent on a balance of its elements.

What if she did not come? How the bloom would ruin, dropping petal after petal!

In an hour, I watched Calico Jack's crew carry Jack's complaining form to his longboat and begin the journey to the *Diamond*. For minutes it seemed there would be no mishaps, but then, to my satisfaction, I heard howls of disbelief and saw the longboat go under with a comic swiftness.

Then, there followed Calico Jack's curses until at last he was swum to the *Diamond* and pulled aboard the ship by means of flung lines.

In my heart, I celebrated that Anne was not with him. Still, the flower bloomed.

At last, a woman emerged from the Golden Owl and stepped with a large man into the shadows of the dock. I held my breath, for to my mind it seemed certain that Blackbeard and Anne were talking together and that I was their subject. How fiercely the longing for her came over me then! It gathered in my heart and roared like a tempest to my soul.

There seemed fragrance and dampness all around me, and everything whispered to me: the Spanish moss of the veranda, the reeds and duckweed of the harbor. In the whispers of the stars, I heard her holy name.

At last the woman's shadow parted from the man's shadow and I knew it to be Anne for certain. She climbed into Blackbeard's longboat in moonlight and I had the impression of the gentleness of her face and the soft whiteness of her hands as she rhythmically drew the oars toward her more smoothly than could any man. Half way across the harbor, she ceased rowing and listened for sounds that would reassure her— the voices of the owl, the katydid, the bullfrog in the marshland. Then, she came on, and, reaching the bank, turned up her lantern and walked toward the house.

I met her on the twisting path leading to the veranda. She pulled up short. I reached out for her, unable to speak.

"Thank ye for not killing him!" she said. "If he is to be killed, I will be the one to do it, for it is principally me he has offended."

"Aye," I said. "But ye must know by now that I am in partnership with ye."

"Aye! I know it!" said Anne. "The trouble is not that ye will not try to act in my interest, but that ye confuse thy interest for my own. Understand me, beloved wretch. It is in my interest to be free to mistakenly act against my interest. Otherwise, I am not Anne Bonny."

"Well said! On the one hand I understand it. On the other, I feel ye have a destiny just as rigid as my own."

"Haugh!" said Anne. "We shall see! However, I do thank ye for again saving my life. If what the captain says is true, ye threw me from ye to preserve me."

"Nay!" I said, "I threw ye from me before he had his pistols raised."

"It is all the same," said Anne. "I thank ye. But that is not why I have come."

Anne's eyes found mine in the way I suddenly imagined women's eyes had been finding men's eyes since the time of Adam and Eve in the garden. So intimate was the look I almost turned away from it but instead held my ground and bid my legs cease shaking.

"I have a debt to pay to ye," said Anne. "For well I remember that ye have mastered *Romeo and Juliet.*"

"O blessed, Anne!" I said, taking up her two hands in mine and covering them in kisses, "How I love ye."

"And I love ye too!" said Anne, taking my head in her arms. "But there is an understanding we must come to this night for our continued good."

"Anything, Anne."

"Well, I wish loving from ye," said Anne, "but I have not yet had my fill of pirating and long again to be at sea as soon as possible."

"Well," I said thoughtfully, "Blackbeard vows now to be a fisherman and it will be a wonder if Stede Bonnet returns, but there's many a captain that makes this his port. If I were to ship out with ye...."

"Nay, sweet William!" Anne said. "Ye have not understood my meaning. I wish to pirate without ye and with my friends Mary and Joe Buck. The three of us would find it convenient to ship out with Calico Jack Rackham, now that there is no entanglement between Jack Rackham and me."

I'll spare ye my emotions of that moment.

"Then ye'll share no bed with me, Anne," I heard myself saying, to my own disbelief. Then, leaving Anne on the path, I rowed across the harbor and took a room at an inn of the town.

From his lordly captain's chair, Blackbeard reeled in a striper that had swum from beneath the *Adventure's* keel. It was a murky dawn of moist skies and clouds like heavy sheep drifting in the sea-mirroring firmament. The winds drove the ship at trolling speed, which was pleasing to Blackbeard, who tipped his chair back on two legs and planted his boots on the *Adventure's* stern rail.

"Having vowed to seek my pleasures in a pardoned retirement," he said, "ye would think that a man of such plunder as I have secured would have few cares. Yet, I am careworn."

"How so?" I asked.

"I have learned that there is no time so dangerous as when one is led to believe that all is at peace!" said Blackbeard. "If I were to hazard a guess, I would say that at this very tide the militia is embarked on a surprise attack against me. What time would be better?"

"Wouldn't that be illegal?" I asked, having been the entire lovely morning worrying about the whereabouts of Anne, who might have left with Calico Jack or not, for all I knew.

"Of course!" said Blackbeard. "They'll have a good chance at me, if they play it just right. Young William, listen to what I tell ye."

"I am at thy service, Sir."

"Long have I taught my mates the use of the cutlass on the high seas because the weapon, when handled with brutality and skill, is unsurpassed in close quarters as both instrument of death and instrument of terror. It is the fearful sight of my wildly swinging pirates and their bloody cutlasses that has made my name the most feared on the seas."

"Granted," I said. "I have seen myself that many of thy prey lay down their weapons without a fight."

"Aye," said Blackbeard, scratching his face. "Yet, as a matter of sport, I have but few trained cutlass fighters with me this voyage."

"Good Lord!" I said, it pleasing me on occasion to imitate the late Captain Stede Bonnet, who had recently gone to the locker by the hands of a hangman.

"Also, I tell ye," continued Blackbeard, hooking a swordfish and watching his silver body break the filigreed crest of an oncoming wave. "I have allowed the worthless mates aboard to become so drunken now for three nights running that only the African negroes are still fit for combat."

To this news, I nodded in agreement. In those days of piracy, democracy led often to equality of the races, no man of the Brethren disparaging another's skin color or religion or nationality, unless he were Spanish, but rather judging a mate by his strengths, skills, and deeds.

Accordingly, Blackbeard then rose from his fishing and handed me his line to tire the swordfish while he handed out a few promotions to the most fit of the Africans. Then he set their drunken white brothers the precautionary tasks of racking cannon balls and grapeshot by the cannons.

Others soaked blankets on deck to smother fires and staggered about as they lay out knives and pistols.

All done needlessly, I thought, not yet understanding that the authorities, in the name of God and King, could be as treacherous as other men. Having taken care of business, Blackbeard again took his seat on the fantail and took back the line. The swordfish was now properly exhausted, so he was drawn to the *Adventure* by the line and gaffed by an African in a longboat and then hoisted to the quarterdeck.

"We come now to questions I would ask of ye," said Blackbeard.

"Aye, Captain," I said.

"Do ye know why the Finman appears to thy eye in particular?"

"I don't know him," I said, pushing back my surprise. "I tried to kill him in Hoy, but no words have ever passed between us."

"And what do ye make of his interest?" asked Blackbeard, letting the African take away the swordfish and studying me closely through his great face of hair.

"He is evil," I said. "Beyond that, I know nothing. There doesn't seem to be any cause for his behavior other than a general malice, unless I first provoked him with an act of piracy."

"Now that's unlikely, lad," Blackbeard said, shaking his head. "And his appearance?"

"Tall, dark, a thin face, dressed in dark fur, an unnatural coldness about him, long fingers and arms, a bag of winds around his neck. He paddles a small boat like a north man's kayak that rises into a point at each end and is covered in skin."

Blackbeard looked off to the Northern Sea, deep in thought.

"And the appearance of thy father?"

"Like my own. We are kin of Scotsmen, not Finns!" I said. "But how did ye know I had seen the Finman?"

"Some of the Brethren know," laughed Blackbeard, "Jones, Morgan, Bonny, Read, and Kidd. Vane knew, but Vane is probably dead. Hornigold knows, but he will be of no help to ye. Roberts knows, but let him be. What he can teach he has taught. Find Kidd, then Morgan. Ye must trust and love Jones, for he is the father to ye in all this."

"I am at a loss," I said.

"Have patience," said Blackbeard. "I perhaps know the Finman as well as ye do now, but it's clear to me thy blood is the blood of Drake, Morgan, and Jones, Roberts be damned. There is a bloodline that runs like a river from the Orkneys to Wales, like a path of the seal. One day, Master William, ye are fated to know all."

"S'death, Captain," I said. "I will think heavily on what ye have said. When I first saw the Finman in the tavern at Hoy I should have spoken to him, but no words came to me, only great anger. I blindly charged him, in a rage, with my sgian dubh, giving him no time to speak."

"With ye what?"

"With my little knife, which I tucked in a sock, but lost at sea."

"A sgian dubh?" repeated Blackbeard.

"Was of Scottish make," I said, "and had a stone handle and a three inch blade."

"I know all manner of Scottish blades," he said, scratching his beard thoughtfully, "and I tell ye, frankly, the sun has never shined on such a knife as that."

"Captain," I said, "I say to ye sincerely that I attacked the Finman in a tavern of Hoy."

"Aye," said the captain, "as did I when I first saw him in an inn in Bristol!"

"Good Lord!" I said, gazing out over a body of water off the tip of Ocracoke, called "Teaches' Hole" because of Blackbeard's love of the area as a fishing spot.

"Haven't I asked ye to stop imitating the speech of that ghaist?" Blackbeard said, "Alas, lad! His blood is on my hands. If I had but kept him with me, against his wishes, he would be living yet."

A cold shiver went down the back of my neck when I thought of Blackbeard's comment applying to Anne Bonny.

Both of us fell into deep thought. Nevertheless, we soon spotted a rowboat taking soundings in the waters of the sound with the obvious intent of finding a channel so that larger ships might avoid becoming grounded on the shoals.

"It's Maynard of the Virginia Militia, come to kill me in spite of the pardon," muttered Blackbeard, unable to keep the rising excitement from his voice.

"Maynard!" I said, incredulous as I stood.

Blackbeard bellowed to his crew, who were peacefully going about their duties. "Ye African heroes, my mates. Teach a lesson to those mates in the rowboat!"

With cries in a language beautiful to my ear, the Africans loosed their lines, marlinespikes, gaffs, and netting and grabbed up their flintlocks and rushed to the rail of the *Adventure*.

The soldiers in the rowboat were greeted by a descending cloud of shot that left several of them covered with blood and calling for their mothers and the rest in a frenzy of rowing. At last they moved out of sight and two militia sloops poked their bowsprits from the tip of Ocracoke Island.

In the morning light, still misty and cold, and with the sun only a red ball on the water, I could make out the name of the smaller sloop, the *Ranger*, said to be captained by a Mr. Hyde under the command of Lieutenant Maynard. The second vessel's name I could not make out, but I assumed it to be the flagship of Lieutenant Maynard himself, who was normally an officer of His Majesty's man-of-war *Pearl*, stationed in Virginia.

"Now, what say ye, mate?" said Blackbeard, speaking to me. "We have twenty-five men on board, many who do not handle the cutlass well and others who are but menials. They, on the other hand, doubtless have close to sixty fighting men on their two sloops. Should we then outrun our attackers and flee northward through channels known thoroughly by me and not by them, or should we stand and fight and again prove our mettle.”

“We should run today,” I said. “Then, we should gather our forces and destroy the British in Virginia.”

“Ah, nonsense,” said Blackbeard. “Ye’ve talked too much to Captain Jones. Ye may tell thy Finman that Edward Teach has no patience for politics. He’s here to teach ye the sport of things. We’ll attack, of course.”

Blackbeard then let out a laugh and took the wheel in hand, ordered the Africans to keep up a steady fire and headed out to meet the enemy. In response, Lieutenant Maynard hoisted the flags of both of his sloops and, he in the larger sloop and Hyde in the smaller, tacked directly into the path of the speeding *Adventure*.

Dozens of flashes and puffs of smoke threw lead around us, and Blackbeard took a shot, wounded in his rage. At once gripping his leg and laughing off the injury, he roared for more shot from our mates, and then turned the wheel subtlety, angling for the sandy shore of Ocracoke.

All the mates looked up from their firing, for it was madness itself to place the *Adventure* between the sloops and the shore.

“Captain Teach!” cried out our quartermaster, Thomas Miller, rushing to the helm and throwing a hasty hand on Blackbeard’s shoulder. “Do ye not see the land to larboard!” Bellowing unintelligibly, Blackbeard struck Miller so squarely in the face with his heavy fist that the quartermaster flew downward to the deck and rolled to the scuppers. Only after I had helped him climb to his feet and staunch the blood from his snout did he divine at last the genius that informed Blackbeard’s wild career.

In the brain of Blackbeard, there were thousands of bars and shoals, small inlets and channels, and perhaps millions of snags and tumps and shallows and bending trees, so many that ten lifetimes of the ordinary brain could not have acquired and catalogued all that was there so naturally.

Of the navigators I learned from in my life, only Captain William Kidd was greater than Blackbeard.

He knew there was an obscure but tiny channel between Ocracoke Island and a crescent strip of sand three feet under a sparkling wash. If his timing was right, he could cause the two sloops to ground themselves on the shoal. Soon, we were in the channel and close enough to see Lieutenant Maynard standing confidently beside the wheel of his sloop, a smile upon his features as the *Adventure* scraped the sand of Ocracoke Island and slowed with a groan.

To further distract the Lieutenant, Blackbeard took up the ship's trumpet.

"Damn ye for villains, who are ye?" he rudely bellowed across the water. "And from whence have ye come?"

"Ye may see by our colors we are soldiers and sailors of the King!" answered Maynard.

"Come aboard by thy longboat that we might examine thy arses for signs of buggery," shouted Blackbeard. "We are sworn to protect the children of our forest and shores from the deprecations of ye Nancy beasts from Virginia and England."

"I cannot row with my sword, but I will board ye soon enough by means of my sloops and grapples!" replied Maynard.

Blackbeard laughed, deeply, forgetting the blood running down his leg. "What say ye to my pardon?" he called out.

"Why argue about the law on thy last day on earth?" shouted Maynard, bursting into laughter himself, and continuing to laugh until both of his sloops hit the shoal at the same time and came to a crunching halt, throwing half the seaman in their rigging to their decks.

"Did ye say ye were to board my craft?" roared Blackbeard, our hands readying the cannons, even as Blackbeard took up a huge flagon of rum and prepared to direct a stream of it into his open mouth. "I drink to ye Maynard and Hyde and all ye servants of the king who are about to fall into the jaws of hell. Damnation seize my soul if I give ye quarter or take any from ye!"

Maynard shook his fist. "I expect no quarter from ye, nor shall I give any."

Knowing the rising tide would soon lift the sloops, Blackbeard ordered a broadside against the militia that there was no possibility of missing. Four of the *Adventure's* cannons sent a thunderous round of shot smacking into Maynard's sloop that caused devastation. Smoke and fire lifted into the sky with the screams of the twenty wounded and dying. Blood ran across the deck from gunwale to gunwale, and Maynard could be seen running about, screaming at his men, beating at them with his sword as they labored with the tide to free the ship from the bar.

Another round would finish them.

Hyde's *Ranger* was already through. The four-gun salvo from the *Adventure* had killed Hyde and either killed or wounded all of his officers, as well as rendered the ship useless for serious combat.

With a single broadside, we had reduced the numbers of the enemy by half. Another broadside would have destroyed them all.

But on the sea, the devil has his say.

Our cannons, which had done such damage to Maynard's crew, had also thrust us backwards and sideways with such force that we had become stuck on the sands of Ocracoke and were not then in position to administer a winning broadside. So, for a while, the contest between Blackbeard and Maynard became not one of arms but rather one of whom could free his ship first from the clutches of the land.

Here, Maynard, driven by fear of Blackbeard's cannons, proved himself the captain's superior. To lighten his ship, he had his water barrels staved and his ballast jettisoned. Finally, and probably with the aid of prayer, since he was aground, a breeze came up and his men, also in fear of their lives, managed to push their sloop free of the shoal and then move toward the *Adventure*.

We saw Maynard coming and prepared ourselves with swords and knives and grappling hooks. Even the drunks were sober and breaking open crates we carried to surprise attackers who should show us discourtesy on our fishing trips.

"Let us use the grenades, mates," said Blackbeard sourly, his swordfish all shot up in the stern and ruined for display.

"Aye, Aye, Captain!" everyone roared angrily, now fed up to see Maynard's ship heading toward us after all the heaving work we had done getting the *Adventure* out of the sand.

It was then that I knew we were headed for a bloody battle.

"Hands," I said. "Will there be survivors of this one?"

"Nay!" he said, sharpening his knife. "Those that survive the battle on our side will be hung. We'll kill them all if we can."

"Aye!" I said.

The crates open, everyone stuffed grenades in their belts, bandoliers, and sashes. The captain's grenades were of his own invention and consisted of bottles filled with powder, shards of iron, lead pieces and gunpowder. Fuses worked to the center of the bottle ignited them. When ignited, they resulted in a spray of glass, shards of matter of all sorts, including human digits, eyes and limbs.

In two minutes time, Maynard's sloop was drifting close and parallel to the *Adventure*.

"Now, mates!" shouted the captain, and the crewmen rose as one and pummeled the deck of the sloop with grenades.

The explosions resounded across the sound, echoing from island to island, and a great cloud of smoke rose on the water that enveloped Maynard's sloop and set Blackbeard and our crewmen howling. The sloop continued drifting toward us, but was no longer recognizable as a sloop, only as a black cloud with great splotches of red in it, for as the breeze blew gaps in the smoke, we could see the deck coated with blood and corpses from the first broadside.

Mistaking the carnage to be from the grenades as well as the broadside, Blackbeard lifted his cutlass in triumph.

"They are all knocked on the head but three or four," he yelled to his crew. "Blast ye! Board her and cut them to pieces!"

"Wait, Captain!" I cried, for suddenly I saw Maynard's trickery.

Blackbeard eyes met mine and I felt his mind, as if it were my own. Then, for an instant his shoulders sagged and he gestured to me, his palms turned upward. I knew that he saw Maynard's trickery as well.

"Bloody hell!" he shouted. "There's no help for it."

Maynard's sloop scraped the gunwale of the *Adventure* and there was a great, grinding lurch, then the sight of our grappling irons clanking across the bulwarks of Maynard's sloop. With the bellow of an animal leaping to his doom, Blackbeard leaped from the *Adventure's* gunwale onto the bloodied deck of the sloop, and then leveled his pistols on the forward hatch cover to await its opening.

Not so aware as he, the ten men who followed him leapt into the sloop, firing away at the bits of clothing of the corpses that fluttered in the breeze. Then, to their wide-eyed surprise, the mates discovered their hands without loaded pistols when the sloop's hatches sprung open, and the embittered mates of Maynard's crew came rushing up from the hold, pistols blazing.

I rushed to the sloop with my pistol, firing as rapidly as I could, continually slipping and falling in the blood of British seamen. Men stumbled over bodies of the dead. Everywhere in the air the silver of cutlasses flashed, all sending gouts of blood onto our faces and hands.

Never had there been so bloody a battle fought on the deck of so small a craft. The deck of the sloop itself was painted in blood, and so much flowed down the sloop's side and settled on the surface of the sea that it left a red water line.

No man had a moment to rest or think or nurture a wound or dare ask for quarter or seek mercy after a slip or attempt surrender. Rather, we fought on, to the shrieks of the wounded, in a cataclysmic rage, my own pistols and cutlass and knives claiming lives that fell about me like masts in a hurricane.

Blackbeard waded into the king's men, swinging his broad cutlass in a wild figure eight impossible to repel with a sword by the ordinary man, but I soon took a shot and blood filled my eye, so I lost sight of him. When I at last cleared the eye and killed the man before me, I saw the captain cut a man in half, but also receive a great wound in his neck inflicted from his rear.

Oblivious to shot wounds, which appearing to be popping up on his body like so many red flowers as I watched, Blackbeard drew pistols from his bandoliers and blew the head from the shoulders of a seaman who had thrown a knife deep into his chest. The knife sprouted there, quivering. I shouted in alarm for the captain but then a blade of some kind buried in my side and down again I went, firing into the crotch of the man who stepped over me.

On one elbow then, the blood again in my eye and no mate of mine in sight, I saw that Maynard's men, like yapping hounds, had surrounded Blackbeard on all sides. Their swords and knives, like teeth, were flashing in the light.

Then I saw the captain, his throat cut, clamber toward me, so frightful and bloody a figure that the soldier with pistols to my head leaped away from me to avoid his charge. Then, magically, I was in the captain's arms and, for a moment, held to the sun.

Shouts rang out. I found myself flung high in the air, where I felt, in my delirium, like a great bird, flying. Almost to the heavens I soared before, at last, I turned back toward the great earth and plunged into the sea.

Then down I went, as if a stone, and saw old Davy Jones himself, sitting on a prow of a sunken boat and smiling at me his gat-toothed, drunkard's smile, like the smile of Captain Vane's. Not for some time, then, did the cold, watery image revive me, but when at last it did, I, shuddering, tasted my own blood and with a flip of my feet powered upward.

Breaking the surface of the sound, I heard Maynard on the *Adventure* screaming black gum and thunder and shouting for two men to lower a longboat to pursue and destroy me. Then, Blackbeard slipped to the mast of the *Adventure* and was there held upright from behind by four of Maynard's men while another of Maynard's men took to sawing off his head with a crescent knife.

Then Maynard himself leaped in to grab off the captain's head by its hair and hold it up for all to see, which set off wave upon wave of lunatic baying.

In the midst of their celebration, the murderous crew threw Black-beard's body into the sea. Then, Maynard ordered his men to fix the captain's head to the bowsprit of the sloop. Still, I treaded water, watching. The longboat lowering to retrieve me had almost reached the water, two mates aboard wearing crucifixes, two Catholic boys, neither prepared for their fate. Soon, my nostrils would fill with militiaman blood.

By then, I was angry, and my head was clearing slightly, my wounds stinging in salt water in the act of cleansing. I swam a bit further away from the sloop and then went under to await the militiamen who rowed to their doom.

Maynard himself saw the longboat turn over and heard the screams of his men. I removed them from their wits in whorls of blood, my cloak flapping from the water like the fin of a shark. Then for the next few minutes, Maynard and his crew watched, mouths agape, as Blackbeard's headless body appeared to swim around and around his sloop until the powerful shoulders and arms, being thrust upward, sank forever.

After finishing his joke, the Finman blew me far out to the cold sea and let me go under to my misery. Then, in the giddy day, he reached down from his boat and lifted me up by my hair.

Captain Kid
and the Eastern Sea

Chapter Twenty-Two

In a white-walled room, I awoke in a world with no curtains or latches for shutters. Sitting up on matted straw that smelled of pigeons and fresh rain, I thought at first I was dreaming of a place that never was, for all around me were tall, oblong openings to the weather framed by bleached walls, and, in the center of my room, a polished bell as large as a man hung from a ceiling joist.

When at last it rang, I threw my hands to my ears and cursed, knowing myself then as a corporeal entity of flesh, blood, and salt that had spent the night in the bell tower of a kirk.

But in what country? I pulled on my clothes and tied on my stuffed purse, which had been left on the stone floor beside a wretched basin of cold water, and, finding my weapons accounted for as well, armed myself as usual, and took a moment to gaze at the town and harbor below me.

It was a dirty, busy village, larger than most and waking up for the day. At the harbor, three merchantmen were being unloaded directly into a marketplace of shops and stalls and clamoring women and men were already in their cups. In the harbor, an immense and lavishly rigged war ship with thirty-two guns was anchored, its unusual array of "sweeps," long oars, protruding below its gun ports, keeping shocking company with its endless scrolls of furled sail.

"So ye have gotten up, Sir!" said a voice behind me.

"Aye," I said, turning about.

A redheaded cleaning woman with a dead foot looked at me with little interest. "And will ye be leaving thy bedding for the day?"

"Aye." I said.

"And when will ye return?" she asked.

"Return?" I said.

"Aye! The gentleman who brought ye has paid thy rent for one week."

Having no knowledge that such a thing was other than the truth, I had no argument to make.

"And is board included in my rent?"

"As agreed!" she said. "The Reverend McNabb awaits thy presence in the dining room."

Shortly thereafter, I found myself to be in Trinity Kirk of New York town, a place of worship whose existence was owed in part to the generous contributions of Captain William Kidd. According to McNabb, the celebrated former pirate and privateer, who had long since retired from the trade, was now one of the richest men in New York.

"The captain is now of the verge of taking to the sea again as a pirate catcher of the vile criminals that ply the sea lanes from East Africa to Madagascar," said the Reverend McNabb.

Our breakfast was a delicious one of sliced bread and butter with veal and a dark, wholesome beer. McNabb was a ruddy Scotsman with a baldpate. He and I were alone in the refectory's smaller dining room but still we talked quietly, as if afraid of being overheard.

I ate as one famished, then asked for cheese and French wine, only then marveling that I could feel no wounds under my clothing, if there were any at all.

"What gentlemen brought me here?" I asked. "And with what explanation?"

"We did not know the gentlemen," said McNabb, "a dark, terrifying man."

"And what instructions did he give ye?"

"To board and feed ye for a week and send ye on to Captain Kidd as soon as possible."

"And ye agreed to do this for a stranger?" I puzzled.

"Nay!" said McNabb. "We agreed for the sake of Captain Kidd. The captain is a great friend of ours and, in his own way, a servant of the Lord. And those that serve the captain, we believe, also serve the Lord, no matter how rough they seem or evil their intentions."

"I had thought the captain to be a sinful man," I said.

"Aye! Many a sinner has been used by the Lord."

"And many a good man by the devil!" I said.

"I grant ye," said McNabb. "Yet I choose to believe that the Lord sails with Captain Kidd, and ye will come to believe it too if ye meet with the man."

"And what if I told ye I believe that the Lord has no power on the sea, but only on the land, that the sea is the devil's domain?"

"Then I tell ye that ye beliefs and opinions are too soon formed," said McNabb. "It is clear to me ye are not much over seventeen."

McNabb's comment had the effect of leaving me thunderstruck. Had my sense of discipline or decorum been one wit less, I would have bolted from the room in search of the nearest looking glass. But then, upon reflection, it came upon me that if I had greatly advanced in the matter of years, it would follow that my clothes would no longer fit. So, I relaxed about the matter.

But then, perhaps, my clothes had grown with me.

"I was sorry to hear of thy father," McNabb continued, "but how remarkable it was he lasted so long with the bleeding sickness."

"My father?" I said, puzzled.

"Aye!" said McNabb. "Thy father and I went pirating together in our day. What a bold lad he was and talented in every way as a seaman and man of arms! Our pirating as boys led me to the kirk and him to the life of a virtuous fisherman."

"Ye know him!" I cried out.

"Nay!" said McNabb. "I knew him."

"He's dead then," I said, slumping over the table, my hands over my head.

"These many years," he said. "I'm sorry, lad. I didn't know ye didn't know."

 I was in no condition to discuss the matter further.

"Where do I find this Kidd?" I said, tears in my eyes as I rose from the table.

"Stay with me, lad."

"Nay, Sir. I need to find Kidd!" I said, making my way to the heavy oaken doors of the refectory and, afterward, letting them swing shut behind me.

In the streets I slumped in many a doorway and found my way first to a bench and then to the harbor to stare into the refuse of New York town. By midday, I was quarreling in the taverns and tramping without purpose in the marketplace, without father or mother or my formerly beloved Anne or knowledge of the whereabouts of my mentor, Thomas Jones.

In such a situation, a young man seems best fit for a whorehouse. So after finding a poster on a shop window with Captain Kidd's office address upon it, I asked a man of the docks to tell me the name and location of the whorehouse that could justly boast of the finest whores in New York town.

"Aye, I know just the place," replied the seaman, standing upon a long plank that bridged a pool of slops dumped into the street, St. Martina's Whore Establishment for Gents is teeming with buxom whores."

"Not willing?" I said.

"Aye, not willing!" he said, "And for that pretense, ye must pay a few pence more!"

Soon, I arrived at the clapboard establishment of three stories and two gables, mud splattered on my coat, my boots coated by dung. Checking that my pistols were loaded, I listened on the porch for sounds of armed men awaiting my entrance on the other side of the stained-glass door. No shuffling of feet, no rattling of swords.

Having turned the door handle, I waited a full minute before venturing inside.

"Madame," I said, upon meeting the painted old doxy who greeted me in the parlor, "all my friends and beloved are slain by man or nature or myself. I need to restore my interest in life. Therefore, I am not asking for a mere animal experience, but an elevated one of such glory and magnitude and delight that the doldrums shall become a windy place and death shall at least for an hour lose its sting."

The Madame, a woman of some forty years with a horse's face, then brought forth some dirty-faced and recently beaten women who were addled by opium.

"No thank ye, Madame!" I said. "What sorrow shall I forget comforting these? Likely as not, I'll take their part and come gunning for ye."

The horse-faced old woman drew herself up haughtily and drove the sharpened handle of her comb deeply into my shoulder so that I laughed out loud with the pain of it, which sent her screeching into a further fury.

"Ye bastard son of hell!" she cried out. "Get ye out of my establishment or I shall call my wolf to open thy throat and feast on thy heart!"

At her words, all of the whores began screaming out their bloody guts and leaping upon the tables, which inspired me to wipe the blood from my shoulder and smear it in great streaks about my face and go hopping about the whorehouse nipping at ankles.

"Goddamn ye, young man!" shouted the outraged woman, and then she howled with such a howl of the wolf that I stopped my fooling and stood in astonishment. Suddenly, from the back door, there was a second howl and in bound a naked man who was painted blue and wore a wolf's pelt over his back and head.

"Good Lord!" I shouted, prompting another howl. The creature lifted his member and relieved his bladder on the floor, forgetting me for a moment. Then, he turned toward me again with the eyes of a maniac, his lips in a snarl, and the nails of his hands like claws.

A ripple of delight ran down my spine from my neck to my arse, and then to the bottoms of my feet, such was my merriment. I neglected to draw my pistols, but rather bent double and convulsed, leaving him an opening even Captain Bonnet might have taken advantage of. I awaited my doom, lost in laughter, at the end of my days.

"Strike, friend," I said, tears of laughter rolling down my cheeks.

In perfect truth, I was a bit more than surprised that he failed to rush forward to kill me at once, but rather stopped his charge in the middle of the room.

"What should I do now?" said the wolf, at last, to the chagrinned Madame.

"Ye can savage this young spawn from hell and then drink his blood after ye drag him to thy lair, ye buggering ass!" said the Madame.

"Nay, not I!" said the wolf. "Ye do not pay me to savage and drink blood, but only to frighten thy enemies."

"Then ye may swive thyself!" said the Madame.

"Very well," said the wolf. "I shall find other employment."

"Find it then," said the Madame. "I shall find another beast. Perhaps a python or a bear."

"That is well enough," said the wolf. "An ignorant python or bear may suit ye. As for this wolf, I have read for the law."

So forcefully and proudly was the assertion of legal training made that I believed it beyond question and, further, peered beneath the wolf's skin and human nakedness to catch a glimpse of heroic whimsy and intelligence rather than mere poverty of spirit.

"No need to seek other employment," I said on lucky impulse, adequately cheered for the moment. "I have the need of an industrious wolf. What is thy name, man?"

"Curiously, Sir," said the wolf, "while in the employ of frightening away with tooth and howl the unruly customers of this simple bitch ye see here, I have come to think of myself as *Wolf*."

"Well, Wolf," said I, "if ye have studied law and will be good enough to wash the paint from thy body and put on human dress, we'll be on our way."

"Certainly, Sir."

In a few minutes, Wolf had washed his body from a rain barrel behind the whore house, and then dressed, surprisingly, in a fine coat, albeit grown shabby, he accompanied me on a stroll down to the gull bespangled harbor. All the way, he tapped an ebony cane on the street before him, for some reason pretending to be a blind man, which amused me. I told him the bare minimum of myself, confessing my piracy, which bothered him not at all, and my nationality, of which he was most approving, for though he was British he hated the British and assumed that a pirate from the Orkneys did so as well.

He was a handsome, blond man, but at least ten years older than me, and in his soiled, well-cut clothes did indeed seem the impoverished country gentleman he claimed to have been born, as well as the debt-ridden student of law he had become at Oxford before his trouble with the Crown.

"Politics were my undoing," he said. "My letters to the London papers were taken amiss by those close to the king. One morning in May, I found myself loaded with hundreds of others into a prison ship in the Thames. There, I was kept in hunger and sickness for months before it was decided what was to be done with me and my fellow passengers."

"Aye!" I said. "I have heard of the penal colonies."

"For political enemies and the poor," he said. "It was our luck though to be sent to the penal colony in South Carolina rather than one of those in Australia. I was able to escape it and work my way up the coast, becoming at last 'Wolf,' which to ye I shall remain."

"Aye! That is wise!" I said. "What I don't know, I cannot tell."

"Truthfully, ye cannot," said Wolf.

"Wolf," I said, as a test of his wit, "I have an understanding in relation to my own evil, one reason being that I live upon the sea, but why is it that the English are evil both on the sea and off it, not only to other people but to their own as well? Every fool knows it is certain abuse and near certain death to sail the King's ships. Yet, the British press their poor to sail upon them and leave their families to live without shelter in the streets until they are dead or else ship them off on false charges to penal colonies in the wild lands of the globe."

"Having come from the aristocracy," said Wolf, "I am able to tell ye that the aristocracy never believe in the humanity of anyone other than their own. Now that the Spanish have fallen, blue England glories in the stink of its blood. Have ye studied ancient Rome, William?"

"Aye, I have!" I said.

"And the mad emperor, Caligula?"

"Aye!"

Wolf paused for thought and then spoke angrily. "One day in the coliseum," he said, "those meant to be slaughtered overcame their Roman guards and slew them, the rogues who had murdered so many. Caligula left the coliseum in tears and declared it to be the cruelest thing he had ever seen. His idea of the aristocracy, evidently, extended to his pets."

"Aye," I said, seeing the matter plainly enough.

"It is my ambition," said Wolf, "not to be a wolf in a whorehouse, but to be a wolf like ye. I would slaughter Caligula's pets, then Caligula himself."

I laughed to think of Wolf, naked in his wolf skin, roaring like an animal, and could not help but smile at his words.

He took it in good spirit.

"Listen!" he said. "Do not think because I refused the old bitch's order to fight ye that I am without the nerve to fight. There was simply no point in it on that occasion, for I hate that old woman and at once saw thy lack of fear as uncommon merit, as well as thy pistols."

"No matter," I said. "Why I took to ye, I don't know. But, I obey the prompting of my spirit and have found thy manner and dress a perfect expression of the world as I have found it up to now. Whose idea was the wolf skin and the howling?"

"Mine of course," said Wolf. "The toothless old bitch wanted a body guard. I gave her the wolf. Have ye killed many men?"

"Aye!" I said. "But I've not counted."

"And it doesn't bother ye?"

"I've no conscience," I said. "A gift from the devil."

"Have ye killed a Caligula?"

"Nay, Wolf!" I said. "I have killed only Caligula's pets, more's the pity."

"Perhaps ye should have kept ye mind more firmly on duty!" he said. "As a member of the aristocracy, I can tell ye that it is necessary to kill one of us now and then to keep us mindful of the ways of God. It's ye pirates that have saved the souls of Spaniards to come. Now ye must save English souls."

I laughed at Wolf's conversation, but his words brought me suddenly face to face with my probable relationship to the magnificent warship in the harbor, the *Adventurer Galley*, that lay stirring at anchor and then to the anchor lines plunging into the sea, as if there to take root and prevent the great bird from flying.

"Is that not Captain William Kidd's ship?" I asked, stopping to watch the dockhands of all races lifting bales and hurrying all around us in the midday sun.

"Aye, that she is," said Wolf, "and have ye ever seen a more handsome craft?"

"Nay, never!" I said, hungering suddenly to be aboard it. "I see the name on its bow, however, and it gives me shivers."

"*Adventurer Galley*!" said Wolf. "That doesn't seem a frightening name."

"Blackbeard's ship was called the *Adventure*," I said. "He was on it when he was killed."

"As were ye, I imagine!" said Wolf.

The *Adventurer Galley's* anchor cables were thicker than a woman's waist, its masts as large in girth as ancient oaks, as tall and straight as loblolly pines.

"We'll ship out on that one," I said. "Don't mind about the pay. Ye'll accept whatever the captain chooses to pay ye without complain and deal later with me. Tonight, ye'll bunk with me in my belfry and tomorrow we'll go see him."

"Aye, Sir!" said Wolf. "What have I better to do?"

"Do ye have skill with pistols or the sword or knife?" I asked.

"I was a schoolboy until the age of twenty-six and have expertise on the violin."

"Then ye have some rich boy's recreational knowledge of sailing?"

"I have knowledge of horses."

"Ye ride well then. That is a start."

"I have knowledge of the lineage of horses."

"Swive ye then!" I said. "Come, let's equip ye with pistols and teach ye to kill with them without mercy."

Awakening early, we had breakfast with Reverend MacNabb, who gave us his blessing.

"Gentlemen," he said, "I am delighted that ye have decided to ship out with good Captain Kidd, for after a life of crime he is now about the Lord's business."

"Aye," said Wolf. "It is our wish to do service, even this trifling one of ridding the world of pirates rather than of English lords."

"For his divine purpose, the captain is leaving his dear wife Sarah for a time," said McNabb. "Gentlemen, what a sacrifice! She's a young woman of great beauty and devotion and lately the richest widow in New York until the captain won her. It is touching to see them together, the toughened old pirate and the loving Madonna."

As McNabb continued speaking of the tenderness between the captain and his wife, a tear rolled to his cheek that he wiped away with a cuff.

After bidding him good morning, we headed off down the muddy New York streets to find the recruitment office of one Captain William Kidd, whom the posters said was taking on a crew to capture pirates in the vicinity of South Africa and Madagascar.

With Wolf as a guide, we became repeatedly lost before finally finding a sturdy little wooden building whose door was hanging open, letting in chickens, pigs, and flies. Asleep, sitting behind a counter, was a fat old man snoring heavily until we woke him from his slumbers. Then, waking, he fumbled for his glasses.

"Thy name?" he at last inquired in a beery voice, his ledger open.

"William Claddah!" I said, whereupon the fat fellow squinted into his ledger and ran a finger down a list of one and prepared to write my name on the second line.

"Wait, Sir," I said. "The first name on the list is also mine."

The man blinked twice, his jowls quivering. "So it is!" he said. "Why, Sir. Ye are already signed for the voyage. In fact, ye are the only one signed. Why would ye attempt to sign on twice when we intend to pay ye but once?"

"I have no explanation for why my name is already on thy list," I said. "Perhaps my man here and I had better straighten this matter out by paying a visit to Captain Kidd himself."

"Perhaps ye should, Sir," said the man. "It does occur to me that the captain might have said something to me about sending ye around to his house, where he'll be waiting for ye on his porch."

"And where does he live, Sir?"

"Well, walk to the harbor and then to larboard of the docks. Take the winding road to the north into the West Ward neighborhood, Sir. Continue up Pearl Street to the crescent of the hill, and there sits the mansion, Sir. Captain Kidd will be there among the willows, looking over his precious boat or, rather, ship, Sir."

"Thank ye," I said, cursing to myself. Then Wolf and I headed out to meet perhaps the most ill-famed pirate captain in the world.

"Sir, I tremble," said Wolf, as we trudged up the final hill.

"Wolf," I said, "when ye are nervous of meeting another man, just say to thyself, 'If all goes wrong, I'll just shoot the looney bastard and then get away.' If ye behave in such a manner, ye will be true to thyself and represent thy wishes exactly."

"Good advice," said Wolf.

From Pearl Street, Kidd looked a tiny man, even frail, rocking in an groaning old chair on his porch, but from a closer view, his hawkish nose and ropes of muscle in his pinched face suggested the opposite. He was dressed in sturdy dark clothes formal enough for a hanging but utterly without ornamentation and his straight black hair was cut off without flourish at his shoulders.

Even as he bade us up on the porch with a wave of his hand, he offered no salutation, nor any real greeting with eyes hard and black. We said nothing as well, but took up rocking chairs on either side and rocked as he did. Our gazes soon fell on the giant masts of the *Adventurer Galley* bobbing in the harbor. As he rocked, Kidd's face took on a number of unpleasant looks. At times, his eyes would recede in his sockets and grow smaller. At others, an agitation would center on his mouth, which would then pucker or tighten to one degree or another or discuss some disagreeable matter with itself under flared nostrils.

"I've had my ship outfitted with sweeps that the crew might row out of the doldrums," said Kidd, out loud, in a voice that reminded me of a rasp on an anvil. "With those sweeps and the great sail it carries, I think it may be the fastest craft to Madagascar in the world. What think ye?"

"Aye!" said Wolf.

"Nay!" I said. "It is a magnificent ship, but there are faster if their captains have luck in the doldrums."

"Swive ye, bastard boy of the Finman," said Kidd. "Who is this ye have brought with ye? I have had no discussions with Thomas Jones about taking aboard two of ye."

"Wolf is my man," I said. "Not the man of Thomas Jones."

"Not my business then," said Kidd. "I instruct ye, and ye do with him as ye wish. Not my concern."

"How was I brought here?" I said.

"How?" said Kidd. "I don't ask Thomas how. How is his business, as is why. Let this be the first lesson I teach ye, Master William. Mind ye what thy business is and do not mind what is not. Ye must bring thy full attention on thy part, lad, or hang or rot in some stinking gaol."

"Aye, Sir," I said, "I have learned from ye already."

At this point, a small girl child emerged from the house and crawled upon the captain's lap and placed her head upon his shoulder in a surprising display of affection. This affection the captain returned with a softening of his eyes and a stroking of the child's long hair.

"Dear Sarah," murmured the captain over and over, as if discovering an elixir. Then, he went on with even greater contentment when his wife, Sarah, the child's mother, also came from the house and added her kisses to the attentions he was enjoying. Wolf and I looked at one another with some bemusement, for the Reverend McNabb had been so perfectly accurate in his description of the captain's connubial enchantment.

Here was a case of pirate and Madonna, if ever there could be. When the elder Sarah had finished with her husband, she turned to Wolf and myself with flawless hospitality and returned into the house with the child to have the cook squeeze fresh lemonade.

I remember Sarah's soft white hand in mine, the slight tensing of her fingers.

"Why do ye weigh anchor at all, Captain," I asked, "such is thy comfort ashore?"

Captain Kidd's look resumed its sourness and he glanced behind him to be certain that his daughter and new wife were gone back into the house and would not hear his customary speech.

"And what have ye learned already?" said the captain, looking again at his ship in the harbor.

"Aye!" said I, feeling foolish. Wolf ventured a laugh.

"Lads," said Kidd, as if talking to himself, "after many a month in England procuring that wondrous ship, I have yet to sign aboard any but ye two, who have signed on in a highly irregular fashion with no thought to conditions for reasons beyond the apparent. Bloody imbeciles! Or saviors! I know not!"

"I am a master marksman!" declared Wolf, randomly.

"There are no calluses upon thy fingers or palms!" said the captain. "Say nothing else when I am speaking!"

"Aye!" said Wolf.

"Nothing!" said the captain. "I have not succeeded in signing crew because those king buggering, blue blood, fucks who hold title to the *Adventurer Galley* offer the mates of New York first a 'no prey, no pay' proposition, which is acceptable and pleasing to all, then insult with detail. That part of the profit to be divided by the crew is only one quarter, and from that quarter all expenses for food and medicine would be subtracted at the company's prices.

"Why a mate could risk life and limb on a long successful voyage and yet profit nothing while making the bastards rich. Such is the idea of just reward from our lords over the sea. Gentlemen, I have argued long and heatedly with them and swear to ye that these creatures believe in their hearts and minds that what they propose is more than adequate provision for ordinary seamen of no family name."

"Then the *Adventurer Galley* will rot in New York harbor for want of a crew?"

"Nay!" said Kidd. "It is my responsibility to bring what profit I can. Tomorrow, we'll offer the customary wages and set sail soon after in pursuit of pirate ships, as well as French ships and the ships of France's allies. We'll employ cutthroats."

"Cutthroats, Sir?"

"Aye," said Kidd. "It will do ye good to think of it that way. These men of New York are a cut below the Brethren of the Caribbean and I shall have to pick many I do not know. Is it true that ye are as excellent with those pistols as thy hands seem to say ye are?"

"Aye, that I am," I said.

"Then show me, lad," he said. "Don't fire them, of course. That will frighten my family. Just draw them from thy sash at thy leisure."

I did as he asked, then put the pistols away.

"Aye!" he said, plainly startled. "I'll teach ye as the others have and ye will watch my back."

"And my purpose?" asked Wolf.

"To do as Master William says," said Captain Kidd.

"I always do," remarked Wolf. "I have been indentured to Master William now since our East African explorations."

Captain Kidd glanced at Wolf, then looked away indifferently. Wolf fell silent.

The two Sarahs then came from the house with lemonade and Wolf and I received the refreshing beverage gratefully.

"Are ye enjoying thy stay in New York?" said Sarah the elder, sitting in a rocking chair and taking young Sarah in her lap.

"Aye, Madame," I said. "I understand that ye and Captain Kidd have greatly benefited Trinity Kirk."

Captain Kidd laughed suddenly, the first sign of mirth from him we had seen all day. When he laughed, his heavy eyebrows bounced comically up and down on his forehead.

Sarah laughed too. "There used to be only the Dutch Calvinist kirk in town," she said, "but we had to stop going to it. An olfactory problem."

"Those Dutch women in their long dresses," said the captain, no vestige of the dour iconoclast remaining. "Didn't they of a cold morning bring those tiny coal braziers with them to the unheated nave and there place them under their dresses for warmth, every now and then letting an odor seep out?"

The captain slipped into easy laughter and Sarah blushed. Then the two of them led Wolf and me on a pleasant tour of the exterior of their house and their extensive gardens. The captain's pleasure in showing off the mansion seemed as great as Sarah's. Though New York was already a heap of homes and buildings, one elbowing the other even in the better neighborhoods, the Kidd mansion sat in a huge square space of grass and trees and rose three stories high and was twice the width of the neighboring houses.

By new-world standards, its half-century of existence marked it as old and distinguished. Its six-foot rise to the front door and high-peaked gabled roof as well as its red and yellow pattern of Flanders glazed bricks, marked it as classically Dutch.

"Lads," said the captain, his arms about Sarah's waist. "There are no greater pleasures on earth than domestic pleasures."

"Aye," said both Wolf and I, as if we knew a whit of what he was talking about.

"I was once married to a South Seas Island girl!" proclaimed Wolf.

Ignoring Wolf altogether, the captain and Sarah, accompanied by little Sarah, led Wolf and me into their gardens.

At one point, I found myself alone with Sarah, the two of us admiring the hyacinths that blew lovely against a wooden fence.

"The captain loves the sea," she said. "He cannot resist a last voyage in that ship, for he has never before had command of such a wonderful thing—though he's long been deserving. Did not Drake and Morgan and many others receive fine commissions and honors from the king? Why has he not?"

"I have no answer for that," I said. "But I have pistols at his service."

"Then bring him home to me," she said.

Then, Captain Kidd and Wolf caught up to us and the conversation moved back to flowers.

And that is how we spent the afternoon, talking of hydrangeas and tea roses with the fiercest pirate in America and his family.

"Wolf," I said. "Ye must cease this business of lying to Captain Kidd. Ye must know by now that he knows ye lie to him every time ye open thy mouth."

"Aye! That is true!" said Wolf. "I can see that he knows!"

"What puzzles me," I said, "is that ye lie to no one else but him. How can this be? My experience with liars is that they lie to more than just one person, that they prevaricate generally or when it benefits them, but neither of these thing do ye do. Ye lie only to Captain Kidd and, invariably, without purpose."

Wolf wrung his hands together in a paroxysm of distress. "I don't know. I don't know!" he said. "This has never happened before!"

"The captain feels it some sort of mockery," I said. "Or some sort of madness."

"It's madness!" exclaimed Wolf. "Madness! I would never choose to mock the captain."

Wolf threw himself back on his hammock. We were two weeks at sea upon the *Adventurer Galley* and favored by the captain. We had been given a four-foot by six-foot cabin to share so as to avoid for a part of the voyage the vulgar company of the cutthroats and imbeciles Captain Kidd's haste and need for killers had bid him employ.

"Put on thy clothes and thy weapons," I said. "It is time to meet the captain by the helm."

Thus far, Wolf's training with pistols had proceeded better than expected. He was now capable of standing upright with pistols in his belt as if he were capable of using them. At night, in the privacy of our cabin, we were working on his drawing pistols from his sash in a convincing manner, which would be followed by instruction in firing them.

This morning promised to be a sunny one when the slight fog lifted. The sun was red on the horizon and spreading its rays across the water. A steady breeze pushed the rosy sun-lit sails. On such a morning, when the air was fresh and a patch of blue appeared now and then multiplied and enlarged to fill the whole sky, it was good to be a man of the sea, a pirate or pirate chaser or fisherman or whatever the case might be.

Just the knowledge that ahead waited Africa was enough to make my poor heart pound and my wild blood race. The rolling of the ship was somehow a part of all, as was the spray that found its way over the gunwales or flew at the bowsprit when we dived into a trough.

Where was Anne in this wide Atlantic sea? Whenever I thought of her I grew sick in spirit, but what was there to do about it but point my nose eastward and refuse the counsel of my soul?

At the wheel on the quarterdeck Captain Kidd, clothed in his finest waistcoat above rough pants and weathered boots, was arguing with his quartermaster, William Drummond, over matters of money.

Wolf and I took our usual places to the rear of the quarterdeck on either side, behind Kidd and his officers, a rough looking lot. Not one had had a jot of military training, but all had survived sailing out of New York with pirate captains.

"Now, Captain!" said quartermaster Drummond, "Ye must be a realist in this matter. If ye are successful, it's well and good to be privateer and sail under a letter from the British King to capture French and pirate ships. But if ye aren't successful in short order, ye must consider payment to the crew."

"Ye must be plainer in thy meaning, Sir!" said the captain.

"I mean this crew will demand ye take an English ship if ye can't find a legitimate prey," said the quartermaster. "It will expect ye to return to piracy."

"I am the captain and they will do as I command!"

"Captain," said the quartermaster, "Let me speak frankly on two matters. First, a captain of a privately owned ship is less powerful than a quartermaster in that a quartermaster represents the owners and determines all things financial. Secondly, even among pirates, the quartermaster represents the crew and determines the division of the spoils. Do not think the crew would accept thy authority over mine. Second, by recruiting in New York, ye have shown thyself to be a madman.

"New York is a pirate stronghold and no man that ye have hired would hesitate to mutiny or cut thy throat in thy sleep for a piece of eight. The one hundred and fifty criminals aboard wish to fill the hold of the *Adventurer Galley* as soon as possible. It is sheer hubris, Sir, for ye to think that ye have the ability to hold them in line or win their loyalty. Yestereen, they were strangling their mothers."

In another day's time, the following rules were written on parchment and nailed to the mizzenmast:

One:

That man that shall breed a Mutiny Riot on Board the ship or Prize taken shall lose his shares and receive such corporal punishment as the Capt. and major part of the Company shall deem fit.

Two:

If any man shall defraud the Capt. or Company of any Treasure, as Money, Goods, Ware, Merchandizes, or any other thing whatsoever to the value of one piece of eight shall lose his Share and be put on shore upon the first inhabited Island or other place that the said ship shall touch at.

Three:

That what money or Treasure shall be taken by the said ship and Company shall be put on board of the Man of War and there be shared immediately, and all Wares and Merchandizes when legally condemned to be legally divided amongst the ship's Company according to Articles.

Captain Kidd signed the document, with his signature featuring a large slashing *W* and a large capital *K*.

"See here, Wolf!" I said. "The theatrical grandeur of the captain's signature may be fairly seen as less egotistic than strategic."

"How so?" said Wolf, seeming to me slow of wit as he puzzled over the document.

"The captain foresees the need to shore up his authority," I said. "In these sea lanes, we may expect to see many a British merchantman and only awe of the captain will persuade this greedy lot of a crew to let them pass by unmolested."

"That and our pistols," said Wolf.

"Rather our pretense," I said.

"Aye!" said Wolf, the smile slipping from his features.

"After the shipping lanes, we will reach the horse latitudes," I continued, "where, had we horses aboard, they would be leaping into the sea to their deaths to avoid the heat. At that time, Sir, many crewmen who cannot hold an image of their captain before them like a splinter of the true cross will despair and die.

"Then, at the belt of the sun that catches the earth at its midriff, so thoughtless is that vast, flat sea known as the *doldrums* that men may die of impatience or starvation or thirst while waiting for the smallest breath of wind, or even blessed saints themselves are teased into madness by their own slack sails when not a mile off to larboard another ship might run off before a storm. Even worse for the spirit, with winds all around him, a captain might find an impossible hole in the winds of the doldrums and there wallow for hours, as if the devil himself were bargaining for his soul."

"Ye speak with the same flourish with which Captain Kidd writes," said Wolf, walking to a great coil of rope and sitting down upon it. "Yet, thus far on this voyage, other than the nastiness of the dispositions and persons of the crew, I have seen nothing remarkable."

"Then ye have not watched well enough," I said.

"Watched what?" said Wolf.

"The captain has not once corrected his course," I said. "From New York harbor, he picked up the Gulf Stream and sailed to the Azores. There, where latitude and longitude are known, he confirmed his dead reckoning. Then, he sailed to Madeira and Northern African, where he again confirmed reckonings rather than corrected them. Now, he is picking up the western trades to sweep the doldrums at the most advantageous place."

"Don't others know the route as well?" said Wolf.

"Nay, Wolf," I said. "Others know of the route and eventually find it, by trial and error. This man has sailed it flawlessly with inaccurate charts. Soon, he'll head into the doldrums where he wishes, and if there's no wind, he'll mount the sweeps in the gun ports and have the crew row the ship from breeze to breeze until we pass to the other side of the doldrums and pick up the trades again."

"Aye, William," said Wolfe. "He is a great sailor then?"

"It's said the captain has never been lost at sea," I said. "Nor has he ever wrecked a ship, nor ever damaged one severely, nor ever run aground. If all that is true, he is a greater sailor than any I have known."

"And do ye believe it all true, William?"

"Aye, I believe it all true," I said.

One night, in the creaking of the ship, Wolf came to my hammock and nudged me awake.

"William," he said. "I am troubled by dreams."

At first in the darkness, I could not see his face, but then the faint light of a candle left burning in the cabin next to ours made its way through passageways in the planking.

"Your dreams more than mine. Each night you speak of things… odd things…but things that are resident in my spirit…though I don't understand them."

"William," he said, "I remember the captain calling you the 'bastard boy' of the Finman."

"Aye," I said, "just words to denote that a Finman seems to follow me about."

"Maybe more," said Wolf. "For didn't ye say that the captain has never grounded a ship or lost his way and isn't that inexplicable for a purely mortal man? Could not his comment about thee being a Finman's boy have a sinister bent?"

"I cannot think of one."

"Perhaps ye are being watched by a supernatural creature of the sea."

At these words, coldness slipped into my blood.

"Listen, my friend," I said, "Ye have forced me to tell ye the truth of the Finman."

Several hours later, I had answered the last of Wolf's stunned questions. We lay together in the dark of our cabin, rocking in our hammocks.

"What think ye, finally?" I asked.

"I think there has never before been such a conspiracy to manage a life," said Wolf. "It is as if some dark prescience hand were guiding you to a specific destiny. But to what destiny, conceived by whom? Even I, to myself, seem a part of the conspiracy."

"Aye," I said, relieved, "but sleep easier, friend. Though I have but an inkling of the destiny you speak of, the chief conspirator is a friend, Captain Thomas Jones."

"And you know this for a certainty?"

"Aye," I said. "Once he took an antique Spanish Galleon that I might have a bulky old square-rigged vessel with which to better learn the art of maneuvering."

"I'm glad to hear of it," said Wolf, appearing doubtful. "But go back to sleep for now. I'll beat the truth out of you in the morning."

How I loved the downwind rush of the Southern Ocean and our vessel, sliding like a sleigh down High Hill of Hoy, the white spray all about our ears like thick flung snow. Having escaped the doldrums with the bare minimum of sweeping, we stowed the oars and broke out the mariner's age-old tradition to harass each and every member of the crew foolish enough to admit his first time penetration of milady, the equator.

"Whoa!" cried a number of such unwary rapists who were hoisted above their drunken mates and being delivered to a rude rite of passage only a bribe of money or hard liquor could disrupt.

Such a fate befell Wolf, who was caught up with twenty-one year-old heir Samuel Bradley, sailing for sport, and forty-six year-old Benjamin Franks, a Jew financier and friend of Captain Kidd's. All the men were dragged to the yardarm that was equipped with a rope of ominous function and a pulley.

"Ah," said Franks, pointing at the device. "The question is, gentlemen, do I fear that device more than I love my money?"

"I am relieved to have no choices to make in the matter!" said Wolf.

"I choose to accept the rope and pulley," said Bradley, which surprised no one, for he had chosen the hardships of the voyages for no apparent reason in the first place.

"And I would like to try it too," I said. "I have never yet been swung from a yardarm. It seems just the type of thing to do to put a fine edge to one's education."

At my comment, there rose an incredulous cheer, and after a few moments other seamen spoke up as well.

"S'death," muttered one. "When I first crossed the equator, our captain gave us no time for yardarm swinging, so I did without. I don't see why I might not have my go at it now. Why, I have rowed as hard as the next man."

"And I," shouted another. "All these years at sea and I have never been tortured. What will I have to tell the children when at last I settle down? Ye are a hard time, Captain William Kidd, if ye deny us this experience, which will cost ye little."

Captain Kidd scowled darkly in the sunshine, as if we had all had gone mad. "Know ye not that this is the voyage of a pirate catcher, ye bloody fools? I am in no way obligated to provide ye with toys or recreational devices."

"Captain!" said Hobbs, the crippled first mate. "We have already spied two merchantmen and a frigate we might well have taken. Had we done so, we would not now be so in need of gaming nor would we have an empty hold but a full one."

"Blast ye, Hobbs," said Kidd, his eyes flashing with anger. "They were ships of the British and Dutch, our allies for now. Cross me again and I'll murder ye!"

The captain's words hung in the air like a thunderclap. For a moment, none of us dared stir beneath the temper of them.

Realizing his mistake, but unable to undo it in good grace, the captain said weakly, "Alright, play thy games, goddamn it! Swing each other from the yardarm until one of ye kills the other." Then, he went back into his cabin.

Myself being dipped first into the ocean, I had the honor of being saluted by the firing of cannon.

It was an exhilarating trip, from the yardarm to the sea, then back to the ship, all hands pulling at the rope. So joyous it made me that I rushed again to end of the line for another turn, which led to other mates piling behind me. In another hour or so, what had once seemed a fearsome initiation now seemed a treasured amusement, and it took an infuriated Captain Kidd his most histrionic efforts to get us back to work.

"Mates," he shouted. "Do ye not know ships of the Royal Navy ply these waters to press British seamen?"

Such a warning was enough to make us heave to.

"Ye hear the captain," shouted the eloquent Hobbs. "Let me show you a reminder of the time I spent in service of the king."

There was a general murmur on the ship, for Hobbs had showed his mutilated finger many times before. Some crewmen turned away. Others cursed the British.

"For taking an extra weevily biscuit," said Hobbs, exhibiting an unrecognizable piece of flesh. "The captain ordered my finger stuck in a heavy wooden block. Then he ordered his man to drive in splintered wedges so that I could carry around the block for hours. What say ye? Gentlemen! Shall we linger in these waters?"

The sails were quickly dropped and soon Captain Kidd, on the way to the Cape of Good Hope, crossed paths with prize after prize but none of them French or pirate vessels. It was then I decided on an expanded role for Wolf on our voyage, one for which he was superbly suited.

"Wolf," I said, in Captain Kidd's cabin, the captain's terrible eyes boring holes in us both, "I have suggested to the captain that ye move thy gear to the forecastle on some pretext and take up the task of spying on the crew."

"Capital," said Wolf, to the captain. "I have both training and experience as a spy."

"Of course ye do," said the captain. "That is why ye have been chosen."

"Excellent," said Wolf. "Now, if ye'll excuse me, I'll tell the crew I'm tired of William's foul temper and thy refusal to attack British ships, so have decided to bunk with them in the forecastle."

"If there is suspicion, break it off," said the captain. "These men will split ye in two with marlinespikes if they discover the truth."

"I'm an excellent swordsman!" said Wolf.

"Of course ye are!" said Captain Kidd. "Now leave me with William."

Wolf having left and closed the door tightly behind him, Captain Kidd finally got around to the questions I knew were coming.

"How did ye get to New York?"

"Ye may ask the fishes. I was told a gentleman left me at the kirk. The last thing I remember before that was being with Blackbeard."

"And thy age?"

"It seems to me thirteen, but that makes no sense."

"Nay, it doesn't!"

"What does Thomas Jones demand I teach ye?"

"I don't know. Navigation, I suppose."

"Nonsense!" said Captain Kidd. "He says ye are my superior as a navigator and everyone's superior at a variety of other things."

"And what else does he say?"

"That ye know the Finman!"

"Do ye know the Finman?"

"Of course," said Captain Kidd. "Most of our circle do. It's just a question of how well one knows the Finman."

"I don't understand."

"I don't know him very well," said the captain. "I don't even know what he is, but I obey."

"Do ye fear?"

"Aye!" said Captain Kidd. "What madness not to fear such as dark ghaist as he?"

"Captain," I said. "Ye speak as if in all the world there is only one Finman."

"Well, that I don't know, though I may speak as if I do."

"Then there are more than he?"

I didn't say that either, Master William," said the captain, "but I know of only one, and have never heard that there is another."

"But how can that be?" I said.

"Now, I've given that very matter some thought," said Kidd, his face suddenly alive with interest, "And I deduct that Finmen must die in numbers before they are grown. I suppose so because it has been long thought by mariners almost impossible to kill a Finman after he's reached his majority."

"What is thy best guess as to why the young ones die?"

Captain Kidd leaned forward in his chair, a wiry little man sharing an opinion pulled from so deep within him that it seemed he was offering up a piece of his soul.

"I think they go mad in the exercise of their own powers," he said.

We sat silently for a few minutes.

"How do ye know there is something to teach me?" I said.

"Because Thomas Jones said there was," said the captain. "I don't know what it is, but teach it I may."

In a few days time, it appeared that what the captain had to teach me was steadfastness in refusal to give way to the foolishness of an impertinent and thoughtless crew. Each and every time sails appeared upon the horizon, all the villains took up the cry at once to sack the craft, no matter what flag she flew.

"I'll be goddamned if ye will!" Kidd would shout, at the top of his voice, standing on the quarterdeck like a fury, his rage holding the clamorous mates in check.

Finally, one morning, there was a roar from the men louder than ever I heard before. Topgallants rising from the underside of the world were followed by pennants and colors too far off to make out.

"Two prizes, Captain, huge ones," screamed the lookout. "There are riches for our taking."

"Burn ye in hell!" said the captain. "Have ye lost thy senses?"

Shortly, a third, fourth, fifth, sixth, and then a whole fleet of frigates and fully rigged war ships and merchantmen under escort appeared to every spyglass. Shouts of alarm then seemed to hurt from every orifice and peak of our vessel, from scuppers to topgallant masts, and the exultation of the fiercest of the mates turned to whitening fear.

"May the devil take us!" griped Kidd. "What chance is it that we should meet a whole squadron of the Royal Navy in this Southern Ocean, Hobbs?"

"The same as Jonah being swallowed by a whale," said Hobbs.

"Come now, gentlemen!" shouted Kidd to all the crew. "Do ye not feel a flutter of pride in thy breasts to encounter the Union Jack flapping over rows of guns itching for thy bums? And are ye not thrilled to have a chance at a whole fleet of such prizes, or would ye have been satisfied with a tiny pirate ship?"

"Ye may swive thyself, Captain!" shouted a mate.

"Ah! Ye might!" shouted another.

"Eh!" said Kidd, pretending surprise. "Then ye bid me attack the Britishers?"

"Nay!" cried the seamen, tasting the irony of Kidd's tongue.

"Captain," said Hobbs, "that squadron of escorts is making for us directly. That would not be true were it not set on pressing our men in its service."

"And are ye afraid of service, Sir?" said Kidd.

"Nay!"shouted Hobbs. "Only of being made a prisoner until death or of losing my whipstaff to the Sergeant's knife or of a thousand stripes upon my bleeding back or of purple gums while the arrogant officers feast on limes and beef. What say ye all, men?"

"Captain Kidd," said Melvin Blinker, stumbling forward, "I've a pretty wife and children I'll never see more if such as these filth takes us."

"Well, lads," said Kidd, "will ye continue to rise in near mutiny every time I elect to take or not take a prize, or will ye grant me sovereignty in such matters as befits a captain? Well, what's it to be, lads? Shall I give up the captaincy of this vessel now, allowing the British to catch us, or shall I remain unchallenged by ye forever?"

"Ye are the captain, Sir!" shouted Blinker, who was followed in the sentiment by Hobbs, then by every man aboard.

Hearing this, the captain allowed himself a tight smile. Then we lay sail upon every spar, gaff, and stay and run for out lives, ignoring all warning shots and the fleet's obvious intentions.

At last, in spite of the best sweaty efforts of myself, Captain Kidd, and all our frothy crew, we were unable to escape the much greater sail of the *HMS Tiger*, and its Captain John Richmond drew up alongside and ordered the fuming Captain Kidd to lay by.

A terrible groaning from the wretched mates went about the ship, for though most of them were English and not a one of them a foe of England, all counted themselves a foe of the Navy and would rather themselves boarded by cannibals than the officers of His Majesties' Ship. Still, no choice in the matter, Kidd ordered that the *Adventurer Galley's* sails be furled so that she would appear to be in happy obedience to protocol, which granted Commodore Thomas Warren of *HMS Winsor* the prerogative of inspecting Kidd's papers.

"We have to wait for the Commodore, lads" said Kidd, pointing to a distant sail. "There's no help for it. But they'll be minding their manners, ye lot. Wait and see."

Captain Kidd's words gave some of the men courage and they shouted out their curses for Warren, but most broke into small groups and mourned their probable fates if the Royal Navy conscripted them.

"Aye, it is death," said one fellow, "but it is also worse than death, for there is no honor in it. The African slave may at least be allowed to live and think himself a man, as well as a captive of another country but not so a conscript of the Royal Navy, who is expected to die without recompense, doomed to death by his countrymen because of his poverty."

There was the sound of spitting up and down the deck, as man after man spat and uttered the words: "And thus do I salute the Royal Navy!"

Finally, Commodore Thomas Warren's seventy gun *HMS Winsor* and an East India merchantman accompanied by four other British warships surrounded Captain Kidd's *Adventurer Galley* and all opened their gun ports, even as Captain Kidd stood on the quarterdeck, his eyes ablaze.

"Captain," said the mate. "They can reduce us to a pile of sinking kindling at the first volley."

"What's that, boy?" the captain said to me suddenly. "Did I hear someone speak?"

"Aye, Captain," I said, "but the words were garbled, and there was no sense to be made of them."

"Aye, so they were," said Captain Kidd, taking up the spyglass and looking to the quarterdeck of the *HMS Winsor.* "But look, there, lad. Isn't that a man who appears to be a commodore...in a spotless uniform of the Royal Navy...picking up a speaking trumpet?"

"Aye, Captain. That appears to be true," I said.

"Captain of the *Adventurer Galley*," roared Commodore Warren's voice through the trumpet. "I order ye to prepare thy papers and come aboard this ship."

"A distant voice," remarked Captain Kidd. "Perhaps the voice of some playful spirit, but not intelligible."

"Captain of the *Adventurer Galley*," again roared Commodore Warren. "Ye will prepare thy papers immediately, or we will open fire and put thy vessel on the bottom of the ocean."

Across our mates' faces came looks of pure terror.

Captain Kidd looked toward the *HMS Winsor* and put both his hands behind his ears and leaned forward as if he had not heard.

"Captain of the *Adventurer Galley*," again roared Commodore Warren, "I do not believe ye have twice failed to hear my order. Thy gesture is ridiculous, Sir. I command ye, Sir, to at once prepare thy papers and come aboard this ship."

Little titters of laughter began to run about the ship.

By the time Captain Kidd had taken to running about with his hands behind his ears there was open laughter.

"Kidd, Kidd, Kidd, Kidd!" the men were shouting.

Thus did I learn much of Captain Kidd in one fell swoop—of his courage, his loyalty, his recklessness, his cheek, and his hatred of authority. At one moment there had been only despair, at the next there was hope. Captain Kidd then looked at me intently and gave quick instruction.

"Now, ye go with me, lad, secretly armed to the teeth, for I have need of a bodyguard of talent and they'll not search ye, so much they credit their power."

Then, Captain Kidd he called to a tall man who emerged from his cabin and made his way quickly to the quarterdeck.

"And ye go with me too to their ship, Benjamin Franks, after negotiating my safe conduct with Commodore Warren and assuring him that I have thy firm's and the king's valid commission."

Benjamin Franks, the Jew, then took up the ship's trumpet and did Captain Kidd's bidding, assuring the Commodore that both his company of investors in Captain Kidd's voyage and the king would be seriously disturbed if the *Adventurer Galley* were interfered with or its Captain punished for failing to hear orders issued at inadequate volume.

At this point in the encounter, the Commodore suddenly doffed his hat and most graciously invited Captain Kidd aboard his vessel. A skiff was lowered and soon Captain Kidd and I, three officers of the *Adven-*

turer Galley, and Benjamin Franks in his rich burgundy frock coat were rowed to the *HMS Winsor.*

Once aboard, I discovered some few things at once that were not all together detestable. I would not have, for instance, hesitated to take my supper directly from the surface of the deck, so holy stoned with little Bibles of white rock they were, shining in the sun and all freshly tarred— both the result of hot and endlessly tedious work. Surely, the decks were as clean as any plate, just as sure as everything that could be properly tied down was properly tied down and everything that should be coiled was coiled and secured in its place. Even blood was washed out of the sails and the lines of seamen straight.

It was something I had never seen before during my whole life at sea—not even on the *Bleeding Gull* when she was making the transition from Welsh warship to privateer. At once, the thought occurred: when the crew is cleaning and primping this vessel, who is making it sail? Then I shuddered to think of what I already knew.

None of the seamen met my eyes as I passed, nor did any show a sign of living, but all saluted perfunctorily and looked with dull eyes out over the sea.

"Ah, here's another dead one," said Captain Kidd to the Commodore, both of whom were walking within my hearing. "Might as well slice the throat of this one and throw him to the fishes."

"Aye," said Commodore Warren, with a giggle, as if he were sharing a witticism with the captain.

"How like wraiths they are," remarked Captain Kidd, "with no morsels of grist upon their racks and without a watered look."

"The seamen have almost depleted their allotted rations of food and water," said the Commodore. "All that remains is the barest sufficiency. Yet, we have heard grumblings."

"Damn their eyes for the ungrateful wretches they are," said Captain Kidd, continuing to sport with Commodore Warren's stupidity.

"They are not the top rank of seaman," said the Commodore, stopping before a seaman with a sallow look. "Anderson, open thy mouth and be quick about it."

The seaman, Anderson, mechanically opened his mouth, revealing huge swollen gums and gaping holes where teeth had once been.

"This man has been whipped three times with the cat o' nines because of his compulsion to drink," said the captain. "He would drink our whole store of water if he could, such is his madness. Further, when his teeth fall from these sockets there is no pain. Now, look ye here."

So saying, the Commodore pulled up a trouser leg of the seaman Mr. Anderson and then bent over and pressed a thumb to his shinbone. The thumb easily made a half-inch indentation.

"Scurvy!" said Captain Kidd.

"Nonsense," sputtered Commodore Warren. "The cause of such an affliction, which has so plagued our fleet, is no natural disease, but a judgment of the Almighty against the English seaman, who must be captured like an animal and clapped in chains before he'll do his duty on His Majesty's Ship."

"Of course," said Captain Kidd, adopting a repentant tone. "I forget myself, Sir. But what is that spectacle on the forecastle deck?"

By shifting my position slightly I was able to see around the heavy forms of Captain Kidd and the Commodore to the forecastle deck, where a line of seamen stretched from starboard rail to port rail. Each of the seamen had his head bowed, not from humility, but rather from the weight of huge iron and wooden collars that had been placed about their necks.

"Those collars are fifty pound weights," said the Commodore. "In the matter of weeks, they take the pride and strength of a man and reduce him to a creature fit for moral instruction."

"And the crime of the men?" inquired the captain.

"Swearing," said the Commodore. "Sir, the English seaman, above all other creatures of the earth is a swearing creature. He is a 'G—damning' creature, committing blasphemy with every other spoken sentence. Do ye not know, Sir, that St. Joan, no less, named the English fighting man 'Les goddams,' A shameful circumstance, Sir. Shameful!"

"Aye, swearing," said Captain Kidd, shaking his head sadly. "Can there be a worse offense than swearing? Why, what is choking an innocent babe in his cradle to swearing, since the choking is an offense only indirectly to God, and in regard to swearing the offense is direct?"

"Why true," said the Commodore. "I hadn't thought about that. But to dinner, now, my good friend, Captain Kidd. It happens I'm famished."

Commodore Warren then led us all to dinner in his cabin. In our party were Captain Kidd, myself, Benjamin Franks, who bore all the papers, and the powerful men of Commodore Warren's fleet, captains of each of the three British warships, and the gaunt captain of the East India merchantman, Captain Clark, who was never for a moment duped by charm and peered at us only with the greatest enmity.

Once, catching Captain Clark's eyes and judging himself otherwise unobserved, Captain Kidd made a pistol of his leathery forefinger, hand, and thumb and silently fired the whole apparatus at the livid Captain Clark and laughed away merrily.

Captain Clark said nothing and took his seat when Commodore Warren had us arranged around his groaning table, bidding us sit, as gentlemen and friends. Around us there was rich, dark paneling, beautifully carved with depictions of mermaids and Poseidon and the familiar seal of the Royal Navy above a fireplace not used in the tropics but of a certain comfort in the cooler latitudes.

All of the officers were arrayed in spotless waistcoats, and the tablecloth was spotless as well and, as I noted, washed in fresh water, for if it had been washed in salt water it would have been stiff. Since it was not stiff, I knew, and Captain Kidd knew as well that Commodore Warren, his captains, and other officers had been using fresh water for laundry while common seamen had been howling and dying of thirst.

"What a fine setting for a meal!" said Captain Kidd, gazing with admiration at the cream-ware dinner service, the blue and white bowls, the crystal wine glasses, the lit candles in their silver candlesticks and tumblers. "Ye have brought civilization to these savage seas, Commodore."

"And yet ye ran from us and then defied the Commodore's order," cut in Captain Clark, grim veins jutting out from the cords of his neck.

"Now, now. None of that, Captain Clark," said Commodore Warren. "The captain was correct to be wary of any vessel that accosted him. We have now put all of that behind us. Let us have our wine and beef, gentlemen, and be of good cheer."

Serving boys then entered and filled every glass, which we drank straight off in a toast, then repeated four times before the boys brought in plates of fresh baked bread, a rarity on any ship, and great slabs of beef cooked in fine wine.

"This seems fresh meat!" Captain Kidd roared with gusto, rolling his eyes toward the ceiling. "Wherever did ye find fresh meat in these seas?"

"Find?" said the Commodore. "We took aboard a private officer's stock in Brazil, and we slaughter them as needed. We have twelve cattle left living in the hold."

"Consuming water? " said Captain Kidd, pretending confusion.

"Of course, consuming water, Captain," said Captain Clark icily. "Did ye think they drink beer?"

At this, with the exception of Captain Clark, every man jack present burst into hysterical laughter. Commodore Warren laughed so hard tears came to his eyes, and though he waved a new bottle of Madeira in his hand he made no move to open it. Finally, he managed to stammer that he could not see well enough to find the corkscrew. Captain Kidd then found it for him, took the bottle, and popped the cork.

"The trouble with water rations with the men," said Captain Clark, as if to challenge Captain Kidd, "is that we are obliged to continue giving water to dying men, which is an enormous waste of resources and causes the deaths of others."

"How lucky enlisted men are to serve under such an enlightened officer as thyself," said Captain Kidd. "One must sometimes be cruel to be kind, as the good book says. Sir, to those who say that our age is one of too much religion and too little charity, I may happily point to ye and Commodore Warren as evidence that the criticism is perhaps too general."

"Commodore Warren, Sir," said Benjamin Franks. "This is a most succulent beef. I've never tasted better."

"It is indeed succulent, Sir," said Captain Kidd, pausing a moment in the eating and wiping his mouth with the greasy sleeve of his jacket, "but I do have one suggestion that might aid ye in relation to health."

"In regard to health?" said the Commodore with surprise. "Is there some more healthful way to prepare this food. If so, I would know about it at once."

"Not prepare it, serve it!" said Captain Kidd, tugging on a mustache. "I suggest when ye serve such a meal the closing of all doors between this cabin and the crew's quarters in the forecastle. They are starving men, and the aromas from meals such as this one could lead them to mutiny."

Silence came over the table.

"Mutiny?" said the Commodore, who had obviously never thought of it before.

"Mutiny!" scoffed Captain Clark. "Ye talk rubbish, Sir."

"Things are not as they once were, gentlemen," said Captain Kidd. "There is a new liberality in the world that is much to be detested—owing to this fashion for piracy, no doubt."

"No doubt!" said one of the Commodore's red-faced captains. "Every man today thinks he has no better, no matter his lack of quality."

"Quite right," said Captain Kidd. "One of my own seamen so provoked me with his notions of 'equality' last month that I swung an intemperate hand at his mouth, and, lucklessly, felled him. Ye should have heard the Nancy boy braying of the crew. 'Hee haw, hee haw, hee haw.'"

"Hee haw, hee haw, hee haw," said Commodore Warren, this time uncorking a bottle by himself and pouring drinks all around. "I, too, have heard an endless round of complaints from the under-classes, though not without meeting them with a cat o' nines, to be sure."

"Quite right!" said Captain Kidd.

"Sir," said Warren. "Not seven months ago, our flotilla had the mission to act as convoy for one hundred merchant ships through the sea of French privateers that swarms the North Atlantic from the Bay of Biscay to the Iberian Peninsula. With our brave show of sail, we delivered fifty of the merchantmen to the West Indies without appropriate thanks and then continued with fifty ships southward, including three treasure ships groaning with thirty six chests of treasure. Then, misfortune struck.

"With no more means for calculating longitude than the Lord has seen fit to give his mariners, we sailed east of the Madeiras when we thought ourselves to be sailing west of them and then repeatedly gave the wrong coordinates for rendezvous' with our captains."

"Aye," said a sympathetic Captain Kidd. "Who hasn't done the same?"

"Precisely," said the Commodore. "And I have taken full responsibility for the loss of time and the deaths caused by lack of food and water. One would think the matter forgotten, but once beyond the equator all three of the treasure ships sneaked away to chance it alone on the open sea."

"And why would they do that?" said the captain.

"They felt the convoy was slow," said the Commodore, bristling with anger. "They complained of our frequent officers' meetings and dinners, which were necessary for morale, and informed us that the number of seamen dying each day—only two or three I believe—had become unacceptable."

"An outrage!" said Captain Kidd. "I should think that nine or even ten a day would have been acceptable, providing no officers were among them."

"So, I was ordered to St. Helena," said the Commodore. "Failing to find it, I was ordered to Brazil, where we arrived with three hundred dead. There we restocked many items and joined with Captain Clark, here, who, in common with the both of us, is bound for the Cape of Good Hope."

Captain Kidd wiped a tear from his eye. Deeply moved by Commodore Warren's tale, he stood at the table and offered up a toast for him.

"This is the greatest tale of the sea I have ever heard," roared Captain Kidd. "This is no simple swashbuckling tale for children but an adult tale of the Royal Navy and the all-pervading lack of gratitude that is shown to the greatest of Britain's public servants. Commodore Warren is a moral reformer and man of war who daily risks life, limb, health, and reputation as a navigator, all for the glory of his country, and I do pledge my loyalty to him as I am loyal to the crown."

"Here, here!" a captain shouted. Everyone drank to a wobbly Commodore Warren who was not sure he was pleased by everything he heard. Then Captain Kidd sat back down.

Now, I knew, would come the moment toward which the evening had been building. Others sensed it too, for again a silence settled over the cabin. Some of the braver captains present, such as Captain Clark, settled their gazes frankly on Captain Kidd, others on Commodore Warren, and others on their plates or on the men across from them.

Captain Kidd put down the long knife from which he had been eating his chunk of beef and calmly waited in a happy, drunken way for the Commodore to speak.

"Captain Kidd," said Commodore Warren, casting a wary eye on the captain, as if searching for sign of recalcitrance, "as ye know, we are disabled by the loss of some three hundred men, and as much as we hate to inconvenience ye, we must have some men from ye to replace some of them."

Upon hearing such unwelcome but fully anticipated news, Captain Kidd let a huge smile glide across his features.

"Oh, my dear Commodore," he fairly shouted. "I am most happy to serve ye in such a manner. I shall provide thirty men instanter. But, Sir, can ye provide me with a spare mainsail since I have given mine away to another ship in distress?"

"Nay, Sir," said Commodore Warren. "I cannot give ye a mainsail but I may offer ye plentiful dinners and wine."

"Well, excellent then," shouted Captain Kidd. "I shall get the mainsail elsewhere and gladly accept the dinners and wine. Let us pop the corks, gentlemen, and fill our bellies with rodomontade. Shall there be another dinner tomorrow night, Commodore?"

"Aye, of course," said the Commodore. "Perhaps the men shall be transferred by longboats then."

"Of course, of course," said Captain Kidd, swaying with drunkenness. "My happiness is complete. Oh my! I have had too much to drink! Come, young William, help me to the longboat."

At this point, I was disillusioned enough with the captain to wish to throw him into the water rather than help him into the longboat. Which sailors would we lose? What price would he pay for his betrayal? What burned me most, however, was not the look of shame on the Jew's face, a look I am sure mirrored my own, but rather the look of satisfaction of the face of Captain Clark, whom I hated.

"Careful, Captain," called down Captain Clark from the ship, as Captain Kidd drunkenly sang in the long boat. Then, we were being rowed back through the black night and the maze of Warren's ships to the *Adventurer Galley*, my disgust growing with each of Captain Kidd's songs until at last, we arrived at the ship and his singing ceased.

"Hurry aboard men!" he said angrily when at last we were fast. "We'll teach those bastards manners."

Captain Kidd then rapidly climbed the rope ladder with no sign of drunkenness, and the Jew and I followed, muttering to one another.

By the time we had reached the main deck, Captain Kidd had already ordered all hands on deck and the affixing of two lit lanterns to two longboats equipped with anchors. That done, the longboats were lowered into the water and their sea anchors set.

All lights on the *Adventurer Galley* were extinguished.

Shortly thereafter, we were sailing to the Cape of Good Hope, having left the longboats and the entirety of Commode's Warren sleepy fleet dozing behind us.

As for my reaction, aye, mates, I shall tell ye plain. Even after all these years I delight in my rocking chair imagining Commodore Warren rushing to his quarterdeck the morning after our departure and seeing our vanishing mainsail as only a black dot against the rising red sun.

Chapter Twenty-Three

Beyond the Cape of Good Hope, we gazed with dazzled eyes upon the eastern seas. In collusion with the hand-wringing and sneaking of Wolf between forecastle and Captain's Kidd's quarters, there hung in our imaginings of those enchanted climes such bejeweled gewgaws of the devil's whim that we gaped and shuddered. We howled at the moon to scoff off the weather.

Off the Nicobars, we dropped out jolly boats and rowed to the cluster of islands long deemed enchanted. On one of the islands, we found not only rocky ranges and fertile oases but also thousands of monkeys and parrots of all brazen colors and unnatural configurations and, to our great consternation, a race of primitive men with faces painted black and yellow, their tails wagging behind them.

We burst into nervous laughter and were showered with feces.

"S'death, ye bastards," screamed Hobbs, drawing his cutlass, which sent the naked men scurrying away on all fours. Their seven inch tails, either painted or fleshy white, went wagging behind them."

Then, there were the Andamen, the cannibals, who stripped men's flesh to the bone, and the new drink from the Middle East called "mocha" and as delicious as rum, but as addictive as opium. Also, we were drawn like tapers to the light of the African islands of Mohelia and Johanna that loomed ahead of us liked two green shards of paradise in a sea of blue.

Both islands were lush with oranges, bananas, lemons, and food-stuffs of every description, and their weather so indescribably beneficent that housing was effortless and warfare therefore pointless. In fact, all hostilities between the native people had become a matter of ceremonial stone throwing.

If anyone were hurt, combatants from both sides would instantly fly to his aid, their faces filled with tears. Yet, how fearsome they looked in their white robes, their coal black faces accentuated by red teeth and gums obtained by chewing betel nut!

"Aye," said Wolf. "This is the devil's sea."

Passing us, and challenged by Kidd, were many a strange craft, from Chinese junk a thousand years old in design to many a Moslem craft with lateen sail as well as Indian or Persian merchantman with scrimshaw of mysteriously beautiful swirls and curves upon its bow. Added to these were strange craft from the Islands of the South China sea and Japan, many inlaid with ivory and dripping with riches as well as Egyptian and other craft pouring south from the Red Sea, their seams bursting with the heft of heavy cargoes in their holds.

"Tis hell itself," remarked Hobbs, "to see this bounty and to suffer under the leadership of Captain Kidd, who will attack only the French or a pirate."

"Aye," said another. "It is hell we are visiting."

"Have ye no gratitude for the captain's saving us from the Royal Navy?" asked one.

"Aye," said another. "Were it not for that, I'd have mutinied already."

Time after time, Kidd ordered a fat India merchantman to take him aboard and then went aboard to examine its papers, and each time, the crew waited in anxiety, swearing, praying that the merchantman had French papers, not English. But, each time, Captain Kidd came back to the *Adventurer Galley* with a shake of his head and a crew near mutiny.

"Goddamnit! Captain!" cried Drummond, the quartermaster. "If we do not soon find a prize we will have a mutiny!"

"I know how the land lies!" said Captain Kidd, shutting the door of his cabin.

Putting in to port for a few days of shore leave did little to break the tension, for at such times the devil rose up on his hind legs and took a full step to the edge of the sea. In the eastern bazaars, the men saw the endless array of jeweled daggers and cutlasses and scabbards of all makes and belt buckles studded with gemstones. They were also able to stroll from kiosk to kiosk and stroke the fine silks, letting them slip between their fingers, and touching shining pistols, itching to fire them. Sniffing polished boots, they ached to pull the soft leathers onto their tired feet.

At the docks, they stood in awe and watched black men load tons of elephant tusks.

"We could take that merchantman easy," would say Mr. Hobbs.

"Were it not for the captain!" Drummond would add. "What say ye, Wolf."

"I say it is so," would say Wolf.

Then Wolf, at the opportune time, would carry the conversation back to the skeptical Captain Kidd, who always insisted on my presence.

"This young man of thine lies always to me," said the captain. "How may I believe he does not lie to me now?"

"It is the intimidation of thy visage, not the desire to deceive, that causes him to lie," I said. "The solution is to have him speak the truth directly to me and have ye receive his remarks indirectly."

"Very well, proceed," said the captain, scowling. "Ask him first of his family."

"Wolf," I said. "Of what place and society is thy family?"

"Of penniless country nobility of the environs of London," said Wolf.

"I though as much," said Kidd, breaking into a smile, for he loved the thought of a child of the nobility gone feral in the world and slapping his class in the face with an impossible appellation. "If that had not been at the back of my mind all along, never would I have allowed ye on this voyage. Here, lad, ye may have this glass of Madeira from a new bunged pipe."

The captain then poured the beaming Wolf a tall glass of Madeira.

We were in the captain's cabin late in the evening and seated at a plain oaken table nailed to the deck. In the lantern light, Wolf had a hearty, muscular look, as if the life at sea agreed with him, and I noted there was a new ease about him, though in his new role as spy he carried no weapons but hidden pins and knives.

"There is a developing danger we have not thought of," said Wolf to me, delivering a warning to the captain. "The men ashore brag to seamen of other ships that they will take India merchantmen as prizes. These hopeful boasts and musings are giving us the name of pirates."

I received this news with some shock, as did Kidd, whose jaw clenched in anger, but neither of us spoke.

"And that is not the end of it," said Wolf. "There is talk on the piers that Captain Clark of Commodore Warren's fleet has reported Captain Kidd for piracy in that he fled the Royal Navy. Further, the owners of the *Adventurer Galley* are calling Captain Kidd a pirate for promising members of our crew higher wages than agreed upon and then absconding with this vessel."

A long silence fell over the cabin. The only sounds to be heard came from the outside, where the hawsers creaked and seawater lapped against the hull. Miquel Gaspennio, on night watch, called out the midnight hour to the clanging of a bell. Through a portal, Wolf and I idly watched hen scratches wander the face of the moon.

"So we are susceptible to being branded pirates, as well as mutinied?" said Kidd.

"Aye, Sir."

"The solution to it all," said the captain, "is to take pirates and French prizes. If those two things are accomplished, all other problems will melt like snow."

Then began such an ill run of luck that one would think the Finman himself had been placed in charge of our voyage by the devil. No matter how promising the sails that loomed on the horizon, the ship once run down and surrendered to our mercy inevitably proved no pirate on Kidd's visit but rather a British or India merchantman or carrier of British Letters of Marque, which protected her from us.

To follow such a policy was especially hateful to the crew when the examined ship was from Madeira, for Madeira was aggressively Catholic, and Kidd's crew anti-papist. More grating, however, was the continued emptiness of the hold. By the time we had rounded the Cape of Good Hope and were fairly flying to Madagascar the mood of our lads had turned so dangerously dark that several of Captain Kidd's most loyal friends sought counsel with him. There, in my presence, they begged him to be set ashore at the first congenial place.

A hard look came into his eyes. The shake of his head was quick, "No!" Even today, I recall every nuance of the summary dismissal and the men filing from his cabin with their eyes looking at their feet.

"Young William, I tell ye," said a sorrowful Captain Kidd, when he saw that his cabin door was closed, "I could not let them go. Before this trip is over, we'll need every friend we have secured upon this ship, in chains or no."

At the time, however, I was not sure I agreed with him, but, surely, I spent alarming days convinced that my mates had fallen victim to some African disease that effected logical thought. To me, the captain's record was clear. Those ships it was not legitimate for us to take as prizes we had refrained from taking as prizes, those legitimate for us to take, the captain had shown much diligence to find. What's more, the captain had shown great skill as a navigator, great generosity as an employer, and great courage in defending his men from the Royal Navy.

To my mates, however, this same record was unclear. Since the captain was so excellent in every way and so estimable, why wasn't there treasure in the hold? They brooded about it and stewed about it and got steamed up about it.

"There was no reason to let that merchantman go," said Reagan. "If it claimed to be English, we could have simply looted it and sunk it to the bottom of the sea. Who could have said it was English then?"

"We could have taken one or two more as well," said Slocum, the fat man with one leg who had helped Captain Kidd assemble the crew in New York. "But the captain fails to realize that many of these ships carry any number of contrived papers to deceive old seamen such as he."

"Aye, true!" said Kipper Barnes. "I give him credit though for saving us from the navy."

"Aye. He's a hero!" cried Slocum.

"Aye! Aye!" cried all.

Captain Kidd came out of the cabin, as usual, dressed all in black, his greasy black hair pulled back in a bun under his tricorn black hat, his face as dried out and tough as whit leather, his eyes beady black darting all about him, as mad as a hawk's. He had fierce little leathery hands and a figure like a whip's.

No hair could have softened that face, for the skin was thick, perhaps too thick for even a bullet to get through.

"Am I to hear comments and criticisms again today, goddamn?" cried Kidd. "What sonuvabitch jackdaw has to say that we should be attacking British ships this morning?"

There was no comment now, though shortly before Captain Kidd had come on deck virtually every man aboard had been grousing about the captain being so careful about whom he attacked.

"What?" screamed Kidd, the rum on his breath causing me to turn my head. "Some genius who struggles with his letters aboard who would have me attack Henry Morgan himself and his fleet because the man has a swarthy, leathery look, like my own? What bastard, son of a one-legged whore is it that lately swore allegiance before me in the rooms of my home that now thinks we should give up the ranks of privateer to turn pirate?"

"For the love of Christ, Captain," said fat Slocum, pushing himself forward. "We signed on in good faith to capture pirates and divide the spoils, but now it seems there is no pirate sailing either the Atlantic or Indian oceans. Steps must be taken."

Under his black hat, Captain Kidd's thin face went livid with rage but he controlled his tongue. Walking quickly over to the fat cook, who backed up a step, he took his arm and walked him over to the back of the quarterdeck where only I was in a position to hear his poisonous, hissed words.

"Slocum!" said Kidd. "If there is a mutiny aboard this ship, I will see to it that ye are the first executed, whether or not ye appear to be among the mutineers. When ye enlisted men for this voyage, as I am now aware, ye signed up as many a cut-throat and robber of ye acquaintance as ye were able and all swore loyalty to ye.

"What? And ye will deny having me do so?"

"Of course I will," said Kidd. "It's against the law to hire known criminals for work on a privateer. Ye'll probably hang."

"I'd rather not hang," said the increasingly angry cook.

"The only alternative, of course, is for ye to control them. Give them the patience to wait for the fighting which is certain to come."

"That's a little for ye to say," the fat man said, breaking away from the captain's arm, but I have my life being threatened sunup to sunset by these ignorant mates and I've had my fill of it."

"Life threatened!" cried out Kidd. "Life threatened! Do ye mean to say that one of these miserable whore dogs from hell has had the temerity to threaten my cook and my agent over the matter of whom

I choose to attack or not? Is that what is meant to be said here on my own goddamn ship in my own goddamn sea on my own goddamn day of the lord?"

Captain Kidd seemed to explode inside with fury. An arm lashed out and plucked a bucket of dirty water from the deck.

"Some bastard son needs cleansing," he screamed, the leather of his face seeming to burn in the sun, his black teeth shining. "Is it ye Stephen Brooks, or ye Lankford Walker?"

"Look ye there for an opponent?" shouted the gunner, William Moore, who had tattoos of green parrots across his chest. "Ye buzzard prince, it is here I am! Ye are a sot and a fool and no man at all as well as ugly as the arse of a hound though never have ye smelled so sweet. When thy mother gave ye birth, she shrieked and tossed ye from the tree, where the leopard rejected ye."

With a single, fluid, whip-like motion, the drunken Captain Kidd used leg, torso, arm, and hand to create a great whirling blur of high velocity from which emerged a bucket of dirty wash water that traveled as a projectile to the forehead of the taunting gunner.

Not one month before, Moore had self medicated a genital rash with grain alcohol, a folly held to be by his shipmates the greatest ever committed upon the *Adventurer Galley*. After the landing of the bucket of dirty wash water, Moore's first folly was considered as nothing in comparison to his second—the taunting of Captain Kidd.

For the latter, he died.

That evening was a cold one, so I built a fire in Captain Kidd's cabin and served him a brandy. Then, knowing how much he loved the feeling of home, I took him a blanket as well, his spectacles, and a little light reading.

"Ye know why I can't be a pirate again, don't ye, Master William?" said the captain, not looking up at me.

"I absolutely do," I said.

"Why, lad," he said, "they would take everything from Sarah, and I would probably never see her again."

"Well, that won't happen, Sir."

"The fire is lovely, William."

"Ye are welcome, Sir."

"I appreciate it, Sir."

Chapter Twenty-Four

Ah, the failure, the supernatural, immense quality of it!

First, in the East, we had sailed off to Madagascar, the island of the lemur and zebu, preparing for bloody battle. Alas, there were no ships there, not one.

Then a storm picked us up from the water and threw us down with its windy fist just off the Comoros chain. It shook apart our seams so by week's end we manned the pumps the whole day round, even when the storm had gone.

Then, in the Johanna Road, the captain of a British merchantman took us for a pirate and refused Kidd's invitation to dinner. Captain Clark was among them and making false accusations.

"May the perjurer be damned!" shouted the captain, staying in the Comoros just long enough to prove to the British that he was not being bullied on his way, then weighing anchor to seek out a secure sandy shore on which to careen.

Finally, it was found. A beach of abundant fruits, perfect weather, subservient native peoples and unsurpassed beauty.

How grateful we were that the devil had at last stepped aside and let us recover our wits. But what did we know? Suddenly, misfortune fell upon us, not so casually as before, but as blow after blow of hammering wave.

When we sailed the *Adventurer Galley* up on the beach and let her flop to her side, we found no ordinary ship's bottom damaged by the creatures of the sea. Rather, we found hideously thick encrustations and two and one half inches of formerly hard plank turned porous by the thousand of holes made by worms of the Eastern Sea.

"Pray, this doesn't kill us all," said Drummond.

"Aye," said Hobbs. "If the work does not kill us, we'll sink soon after."

For many a day, in the blazing sun, we worked and sweated, stripping away the encrustations with hammers and irons and packing the seams with oakum. The task seemed endless, our strength near spent and our nights filled with the chewing of the narcotic betel nut to drive away pain.

One morning we began dying. One of the mates collapsed at work, developed dysentery, foamed at the mouth and shook all over. In a few hours he was dead. We went on with work after saying our prayers and continued until evening. In the morning, two of us lay dead on the beach and the captain called us all together so that the ship's surgeon could look at us for signs of illness.

No man had a fever or unusual complaint.

"There are strange diseases in these regions," said the captain. "At the first sign of complaint of any kind, sing out. If there is a malady stalking us, we must know it."

All claimed perfect health and worked as hard as before.

In early afternoon, the first man fell out and died in the grip of convulsions, his mouth full of blood. By the next day, the ship's surgeon, young Robert Bradingham of London had ten sick men stretched out beneath the shade of the trees and two more corpses. At his wit's end, the twenty-six year-old Bradingham tried laxatives, enemas, sweats, and bleedings.

Long before the number of us who were either dead or stricken ill had reached fifty, Bradingham could be found in drunken despair, exhausting his medical stores of alcohol in an attempt to pretend he was elsewhere. By the fourth day of his treatments, it was clear to him, honest drunkard that he was, that men recovered or not regardless of his doing. It was the breaking of the man, for he was too fragile for the sea and not rascal enough to take credit for the cures or make excuses for failing to lessen the number of the dead.

Before the illness had run its course, at least one hundred of us had been pointed at by death's threatening finger, and forty of us had been taken away.

Still, we sailed on, always after prizes, for Kidd was a stubborn man. Even freshly careened, our ship had to be pumped night and day, so badly damaged were its seams. The winds grew longer, harder. The scarcity of mates rubbed like a blister, making Kidd, chief navigator, captain, and often helmsman, and, possibly, saving his command.

As for Wolf and I, we took to meeting more often at night with the captain, in spite of the danger to Wolf. Two long years had gone by, or so I think, time's passing being a thing of which I have never been expert. I was led to think two years by Wolf and the captain, who often laughed at my attempts to put events of my own life in chronological order.

During our long conversations in his cabin, both Wolf and the captain would tell the stories of their lives, and, eventually, I began telling mine, leaving out nothing, not even my encounters with the Finman, whose mention always touched their eyes with fire.

"And still we do not know what ye are supposed to learn on this voyage," said the captain.

"Aye, I have no answer," I said.

"But what if ye have been considering the matter in the wrong light?" said Wolf. "What if ye were to learn something from me? Or the captain was to learn something from ye? Or from me? Or ye both were to teach me something?"

"Aye!" said the captain. "Perhaps we were all to learn something from one another or from everything that has happened?"

"Then, what have ye learned, Captain?" I asked.

The captain took a thoughtful puff of his pipe before answering.

"Something I've known before but forgotten too often," he said. "Between scoundrels and the general run of men there lies no differences but lack of hypocrisy."

"Ha," said Wolf, "a capital charge."

"And what have ye learned, Wolf?" I asked.

"I have learned that in the world there are mysterious forces," said Wolf. "They move like the tides or the winds. They are moving us now."

"Aye, they are," said Kidd, nodding, and I nodded too.

"And what have ye learned, William?" asked Wolf.

"Why, from this captain I have learned *character*," I said, "if I may put it in a word."

"And from other captains ye have known?" said Wolf.

"Such as?"

"Thomas Jones?"

"A father's care."

"Anne Bonny?"

"Freedom and love at constant war."

"Mary Read?"

"Unrelenting pain."

"Stede Bonnet?"

"Sadness."

"Charles Vane?"

"Unthinking cruelty."

"Calico Jack Rackham?"

"Ineradicable cheapness."

"The Great Pyrate Roberts?"

"The coupling of madness and genuine vision."

"Henry Morgan?"

"Strategy, vanity, and inhumanity."

"Blackbeard?"

"Tactics, vanity, and humanity."

"And which have taught ye the most in general, not just about the sea," asked Wolf.

"Why, those that knew the most," I said. "The intellectuals are Blackbeard and Jones and the connoisseur is Bonny. Kidd knows more about the sea and geography than the rest."

"I thank ye, Sir," said the captain, "but what faults have ye found in me?"

"A hasty temper," I said, "and a hatred of authority, though I am loathe to say the latter is a fault."

"And what have ye learned of thyself?" said the captain.

"What should I have learned?!" I said.

"That there is common death here even for one so wondrous as ye," said the Captain.

"Nay, perhaps not," said Wolf, quietly, so quietly that for a moment we broke off our discourse.

"Something occurs to me gentlemen," Wolf said breaking the silence he had created. "It rises like a fish to the surface of the sea. Why I have not understood it before it beyond me, for it has been there before me all the while beckoning."

"Speak plainly," demanded Kidd. "What do ye know?"

I said nothing, and waited, myself feeling the direction of Wolf's mind.

"By heaven I will," said Wolf, "but first, Master William, consider thy attributes?" said Wolf. "Have ye catalogued them?"

"Nay!" I said. "To what purpose?"

"To consider if ye are entirely human."

"I am not a seal or selkie," I said. "If I were, I would tell ye just to see thy jaw drop out of thy head."

"Yet ye naturally navigate with the best in the world," said the captain with a laugh, "and ye shoot unerringly with a pistol in each hand."

"And do seals shoot pistols?" I said.

"Nay," said the captain, "but if they did, they would be unerring marksmen."

"I imagine that selkies in man form would be fine shooters with pistols," said Wolf.

"I imagine wolves to be excellent swordsmen," I said, "and hunters who are guided less by their charts than noses."

"And there's the matter of swimming," said Wolf. "Actually, all three of us, I imagine, are excellent swimmers. Me, I swim the oceans of dreams."

"Aye, swimming!" I said. "And therein hides a mystery, for never have I practiced swimming a day in my life. If there is evidence of my being a seal, it is the swimming."

"Ye are of the Orkneys still, Master William," said Captain Kidd, returning the conversation back to deep water. Have ye not learned that about thyself in the course of thy life, if not in particular in the course of this voyage? Why, William, ye have us all believing in reasons for things and hidden destinies and purposes, do ye not? Look at Wolf here, an aristocratic lad lately given to running naked in a whorehouse, now a creature who considers himself gifted with the art of living by the stars."

"I take thy meaning," I said, "and see the same in ye Captain, who finds one Eden in a garden in New York and yet another in an ocean on the far side of the world."

"Aye, I confess it," the captain said.

"Aye, but there is one thing more, I ask ye, Captain," said Wolf, driving toward his point. "Imagine thy fate if ye were lost in these seas, not knowing south from north or in what direction thy Sarah waits or yea, even more, the day or year or season? What if there were snow and then a bright shining snow, then wind, then snow again, then craft paddled by savages giving way to those being driven by great clouds of sails. Worse, what if the stars themselves took a backward track and the rain rained upward and thy body grew long and short again…and the dead rose up and the living lay down. What then?"

"Why, I would go mad," said the captain, "without my bearings."

"And I as well," I said, "and probably die."

"Well, that is a part of the answer then," said Wolf, beaming with satisfaction.

"I miss thy meaning," I said.

"As do I," agreed Captain Kidd.

"Finmen go mad and die because they are alone and lose their bearings in regard to time and place," said Wolf, "his voice so low we could barely hear him for the creaking of the ship and the moaning of the wind.

"And how does this affect us?" said Captain Kidd, his eyes narrowing, darkening.

"A Finman follows us, Captain," said Wolf. "He's lonely, hostile, half mad, and feels that we are leading him to a particular destiny in the maelstrom of disappearing years and islands of shadow."

"Aye," said Kidd, "he follows us because we are most like him."

"Yet he brings death with him!" I said.

"First, he found ye company, Master William," as formerly he's found company with other Brethren of the sea touched by destiny, such as Drake and Morgan and Jones and Bonny and Hornigold, Read, even Vane and Roberts and Teach and me I'll wager, and now the three of us together."

"That is a wild conjecture," I said.

"But I have seen him, too," said Wolf, "most often in dreams or upon waking, when I am neither asleep nor awake. Once, I saw him standing hunched on the forecastle, his fingers on his bag of winds, the rains beating down all about him."

"And yet you said nothing?" I said.

"He may have been a product of my overheated brain," said Wolf, "I cannot swear he was there."

"Haugh!" said Captain Kidd. "There's nothing illusory about the Finman or the instructions he brings. I've seen him a thousand times in his little boat, following in my wake, opening his little pouch, filling my sails."

"Filling thy sail?" said Wolf.

"Aye," said the captain. "Ye are correct to link the Finman to our destinies, but too damned by pride to guess the primacy of his role. From where does the destiny of the Brethren of the sea come? Why, from his black pouch, gentlemen. Can you not hear the Finman's wind as it whistles of your glory or doom?"

Such words from the captain chilled me.

"Are you saying, Captain," I said, "that this sense of destiny we all feel derives not from ourselves but from him?"

"That he is not evil?" said Wolf.

"Aye, as to the first question," said the captain, "I have reason to believe that the affairs of the Brethren are driven by the Finman."

"That is unimaginable," said Wolf.

"As for the second question," said the captain, "that is far more difficult to answer."

Near dead but bickering with our cotton mouths and parched throats, we sailed from the coast of India with only news of Captain Clark's death in Marabar to freshen our sails. Then, at last, the devil used us as flail rather than chafe and we fell upon a vessel eight miles off the coast just north of Callicut at a place called *Sacrifice Rock*, where the pink of the rock had been made by the blood of those sacrificed upon it.

Just south of the rock, Hobbs spied a sail, and the captain gave sporting chase, hauling up French colors to gull a smallish merchant ketch, ostensibly a Dutchman but likely as not to be flying false colors, like ourselves.

"It's more than just a Dutchman we're chasing," said the captain, himself at the wheel for nine hours, and for part of that time giving instructions to a Monsieur LeRoy, who was a French pirate and dockside investor the captain had allowed on board back in Joanna Road. "But for whose benefit does the old sea dog sail for now? Drummond, will ye do me the great favor of having one of our gunners place a shot over the bow of that ship when we pull along side?"

"Aye, Sir!" replied Drummond, and a few minutes later, Captain Dekkar of the small Dutch ketch was receiving French Captain LeRoy and his aid, Monsieur Le Kidd, for lunch and a chat aboard his ship.

As the captain told the story of it later, LeRoy so brilliantly impersonated a French sea captain that Dekkar invited him to sit at the captain's table and handle all formalities, at which time LeRoy opined that it was his duty to examine the ship's papers.

"Certainly, Sir," said Dekkar, anxious to please, and then Captain Dekkar delivered up a stack of passes from various governments.

"Our being a French ship," said Captain LeRoy. "We are most interested that ye have a French pass."

"Oh, we do have one here somewhere," said Captain Dekkar, digging into the pile of papers. "Oh, yes. Here it is. This one will meet with thy complete satisfaction."

At that moment, much to Captain Dekkar's surprise, Captain's aid, Le Kidd, emerged from the background, shouldered Captain LeRoy aside and then studied the paper for a long five minutes before giving it over to the captain.

"By God, I've got ye!" Kidd finally exclaimed. "Ye are a free prize to England!"

Captain Dekkar scowled in defiance but to no purpose.

"With the French pass in my hands," Kidd whispered to me later, "I felt a mild exultation, altogether out of keeping with the meagerness of the prize, for the ship was a poor one. Yet the document was a handsome one in itself, ornately written in a florid hand. It bore the seal of the French East India Company and was emblazoned with the royal fleur-de-lis. It had the effect, in my own eyes, of validating my own captaincy."

I was shocked to hear him admit such a thing. Did I myself need such validation? If so, where was such a need hiding from me?

The crew, of course, was delighted, even delusional. While aware that the pickings had been small, the rogues gathered together in happy, superstitious talk.

"We have out-sailed the mermaid's curse," said Hobbs, an opinion seconded by Drummond, and the lookouts in the crow's nests kept fresh eyes fixed on the Indian Ocean.

Then, one January morning, seaman Abraham Guinn earned a reward of 100 pieces of eight about ten miles off Cochin by spotting the top gallants of the huge merchantman, the *Quedagh Merchant*, flying Armenian colors. We all ran to our posts.

"It's a fat one," said the captain.

"Aye," I observed, "riding the trades, low in the water."

"Not English!" said Drummond. "She's a Moorish ship and she'll be sailing under French papers, I believe, or I'll use my man root for a razor strop."

"This one will be the enriching of us," said the captain. "Let there be no doubt!"

After an easy and uneventful chase of four hours, the *Adventurer Galley* caught up with the four hundred ton *Quedagh Merchant*, carrying eighteen guns that remained wisely quiet.

On Captain Kidd's order, the French captain of the *Quedagh Merchant*, an old man who squinted in the sunlight, climbed shakily aboard the *Adventurer Galley*. Then, without making a sound, he stood and watched politely as Captain Kidd hoisted our British colors.

"What say ye now, Captain?" said Kidd.

The old French Captain looked up at the British flag with emotion, then reached into his jacket coat and produced a French pass.

"Here's good prize!" said the old captain, surrendering the pass and the *Quedagh Merchant* to Captain Kidd.

Kidd saw that the pass was authentic and ordered a fine table brought upon the deck of the *Adventurer Galley*, as well as our finest cheeses and wine. Then, with his best manners he bid the old captain eat and drink and engaged him in domestic conversation, inquiring after the health of his wife, his children, and grandchildren and genuinely replying in a pleased fashion when all was well and sympathizing when all was not.

For quite some time, the two talked of gardening. Only when the Armenians who actually owned the merchantman came up from their quarters below with their outraged faces and shook their fists at thirty-six cannons and our hundred edgy crewmen did the day grow tense. These seemed to be of two minds. Half were enraged that the *Quedagh Merchant* had not fought to the death to preserve its cargo; the other half angrily observed that an English privateer had no business attacking a merchantman of the East India company. One of the fattest of the Armenians turned apoplectic with screaming and fell to the deck, where he was quickly revived with dishwater thrown over his heated form.

Beyond that last kindness, Kidd paid no further attention to his guests other than to have them stored below. Then, he hallooed the first prize he had taken, the Dutch ketch now captained by his friend Captain LeRoy, to draw close to aid in the inspection of the *Quedagh Merchant*, which was a proper courtesy of the sea in regard to the sharing of spoils between fellow privateers.

The upshot of this was the frank astonishment of Kidd, LeRoy, Wolf, me, and many another from both ships of our expanded fleet, for what we found aboard the *Quedagh Merchant* amounted to the treasure pirates and privateers found in children's stories, not in real life upon the actual sea. So crowded with bales of silk, muslin, and opium was the forecastle, for instance, it was a wonder the crew was able to sleep at all, and probably did so only by making little pits between the bales and nestling in them.

The hold itself stored even bulkier treasures. Among the kegs of water, rum, and edibles and the usual beams and sails and tools and cables, there were crates of antique furniture and oriental rugs, rare pottery and paintings, silver plate, and ivory statuettes as well as elephant tusks and the hides of exotic animals.

But all of this in the hold was but prelude to the discovery in the captain's cabin, where Captain Kidd found a heavy mahogany chest wrapped with iron bands and secured with two thick padlocks.

"Shut the door and lock it, quickly lads," Kidd shouted to Wolf and I, and we leaped for the door, threw the latch, and turned the lock before anyone could enter.

"This is something we shall do alone," Kidd said, lovingly touching the top of the chest with his hands.

"Ye shall need a chisel and a hammer," said Wolf.

"Aye, Sir. I might," said Captain Kidd, gravely. "The trick, of course, will be to retrieve one without giving away our business."

"There is no difficulty, Captain," said Wolf, producing a hammer and a chisel from beneath his waistcoat. "It did occur to me earlier that it might prove a benefit if I brought these with me."

"Bless ye, Sir," chimed the captain. "It seems that I have underrated ye once again. And all because ye started thy relationship with me as a liar. Let that be a lesson to ye!"

"Aye, Sir!" said Wolf.

Using the hammer and chisel, Captain Kidd's wiry arms and hands crushed the locks from the chests in a matter of seconds.

"Ah!" he said, with great satisfaction. Then, he threw open the lid. "Why look at the little pouches! How they glitter! Red rubies, like blood, bleeding in my hand—do ye see? And the green ones— emeralds! And here, diamonds, hard enough to cut glass or a hole in the hardest heart! And here is gold! How many men have died for gold? Eh? Eh! That is nothing! How many men burn eternally in hell's fire for gold? Now here it is! So many gold nuggets that the three of us would be murdered twenty times over if men knew we had them! What say ye, Master William?

"Better not to have them then!"

"Aye!" said Wolf.

"That is so!" said Kidd. "Yet I have so allowed the natural way of things to turn about that only such a dangerous thing as gold can save me now. Without spoils, my crews will certainly cut my throat and thy throats too, gentlemen, in all probability. And so, too, will I need gold to satisfy the *Adventurer Galley's* owners, who, otherwise, may bring charges against me."

"Ye are not thinking clearly, Captain," I said. "There is not gold enough to appease either thy crew or thy owners. Ye must think of another way."

"I agree with William," said Wolf.

"Well, we can't kill them all!" the captain said.

"But we probably can!" I said.

"I won't hear of it," said the captain. "Look here, Master William. Have ye ever seen a thing so lovely? It reminds me of my Sarahs."

It seemed to me then the captain was going a bit dotty with love, but in no way could I blame him, for I had met the two Sarahs, and still I remembered the loveliness of both and the elegance of their garden. Captain Kidd held up a silver jewelry box for my inspection. It glittered in the sunlight streaming through a portal, and when the lid was lifted, the box's glitter increased four fold. Nestled inside were four lockets inlaid with diamonds and a diamond of monstrous luminosity blazing in a golden ring.

We gazed at the treasure, stupefied, for an hour. At length, the light coming from the portholes failed, and we lit oil lamps.

The captain sat back in a chair and bid Wolf continue the excavations from the trunk in his stead. There were silver rings and precious stones, each of which we examined one by one, guessing at the value of each. There was a bag of polished gems of some ten or twelve pounds, numerous agates and amethysts, a bag of silver and golden buttons, two full settings of crystal, carnelian rings, and a bezoars stone.

"And what do ye think the ship's worth to be?" said Wolf.

The captain leaned back in his chair and puffed out his cheeks, a sign he had lapsed into deep thought. At last, he spoke.

"The *Quedagh Merchant's* captain told me what it is worth."

"What is it worth?" I asked.

"50,000 in rupees!" the captain said.

"How much is that in pounds?" asked Wolf.

"I have no idea," said the captain.

Locking the cabin behind us, we swaggered to the quarterdeck where the crews of our two ships, the *Adventurer Galley* and the *Rouparelle/ November,* were still foolish with grog and spying out riches beneath every bucket and coiled line. On even footing with the princes of the earth in regard to earthly treasures and no doubt far less odious than they in the eyes of heaven, we were briefly fond of ourselves. Even struttin' old Kidd took on a balmy glow. Alas, the fall occurred in record time.

A sleepy Englishman raised from the bowels of the *Quedagh Merchant* came to identify himself by French ship's pass as "pilot Rette."

"My name is John Wright, and ye may listen well to this warning," he said, a maddening smile spreading across his face. "The taking of this ship will make a great noise in England. Do ye not know that an agent for the English East India Company is brokering the shipping?"

"S'death," replied Kidd, his heart now black as a pocket as he called the crew in around him from the ratlines, sail-room, forecastle, and boxes and barrels in the hold. The old man who had said he was the captain of the *Quedagh Merchant* and declared her a fair prize was then brought forward. With little prodding, he admitted he was only acting captain by unusual arrangement and he himself uncertain of whether or not the *Quedagh Merchant* could legally be taken by an English privateer.

At that moment, a black cloud blew suddenly over the sun and the *Quedagh Merchant's* reefed sails stirred, an indifferently secured topgallant breaking free and flapping in the momentary darkness as if heading off to a parade. For Kidd, the situation was desperate. In front of all the crew, he loudly called for the *Quedagh Merchant's* papers and poured over them, reading them again and again, calling for every literate man aboard to do the same.

Finally, after an exhaustive examination of the papers was done, the members of the crew shouting encouragement or curses all the while, Kidd conferred openly with all who had read the papers, including Wolf and me, and turned to the crew.

"There is no doubt in my mind that the *Quedagh Merchant* is sailing under a French letter of Marque, regardless of whom made arrangements with whom," he said. "Gentlemen, our taking this ship may cause some anger in London, but it seems to me that it is our legal prize and that it is our right to keep it!"

The loud hurrahs of our crews rang out at such length that two more shadows passed over the face of the sun.

"Are ye with me, men?" shouted Kidd. "Do ye vote to keep our prize?"

"Aye, Captain!"

"Is it unanimous, men?"

"Aye, Captain!

"We shall keep it then!" said the captain.

For a while, then, we were perfectly happy, the captain taking the time to send the *Quedagh Merchant's* crew ashore and man our two prizes, the *Quedagh Merchant* and the *Rouparelle/November*, for a return to Madagascar and eventually New York. So as not to antagonize the English, John Wright was allowed to remove the portion of the cargo that belonged to English merchants.

To convince them not to mutiny on the spot and take all three prizes and the treasure, Kidd paid his crew a portion of its wages and sailed to Kalliiquilon to peddle his goods and buy food and supplies for six months at sea. Over some week's time, we sold 132 chests of opium and 122 bales of silk, as well as plunder a Portuguese galliot, an act of sheer boyish duplicity. At the time of the robbery, its captain was having a friendly talk with Captain Kidd in the captain's cabin of the *Adventurer Galley*.

One morning, Wolf rose with the light and saw beyond the broad reach of the bay the sails of four large ships gusting toward him. His cries shortly brought everyone on deck, where we saw to our surprise four ships, studdingsails extended, not bent on inquiries, but on attacking at once. The captain and his officers rushed to the quarterdeck and, for a moment, stood there open mouthed.

"Bless my arse!" shouted the captain. "They are not only English and Dutch ships in full pursuit of our fleet, they know who we are without asking!"

"Our countrymen and allies." muttered Wolf.

"I'll not stay here to explain that to them," said the captain.

"Shall I order the anchors cut away?" asked the mate.

"Nay, ye blooming fool," replied the captain. "Do ye think I have anchor to throw away. We shall raise the anchors of each ship."

"But that will take an hour, Sir!"

"Then an hour it will take!"

"Aye, Sir."

Wolf and I went to the rail of the *Adventurer Galley*, there being a question in our minds as to the wisdom of the captain's frugality in this instance. At the capstan, the mates walked the groaning circle and looked to the sea fearfully. The anchor chain retreated down the hawser hole, the chain locker rattled, the cat's head trembled at the cat's grumbling pull. The capstan bars turned like the hands of a defective clock, and all the while the great ships drew closer. There were no larger merchantmen on the earth than those that plied the Indian Ocean on behalf of the English and Dutch. They were draped in sails like ladies of war and boasted well up to twenty-one well-tailored expressions of sail, such as spankers, flying jibs, top gallant, mizzenmasts, mizzen topmast staysails, and others in more or less common use.

Worse, for us, each of the merchantmen was more heavily armed than the entirety of our fleet and the odds were excellent we were outmanned to the same extent. Still, Kidd insisted on a proper weighing of the anchors.

"Heave-ho, gentlemen!" he said, his arms crossed over his chest.

To his designated captains of the *Quedagh Merchant* and the *Rouparelle/November*, Kidd gave the task of escaping the four pursuing merchantmen by splitting up, out-maneuvering them in the bay, and then losing them at sea. Further, he instructed, the three ships were then to meet at St. Mary's Island off Madagascar, at which time they would return to New York together and split all profits.

"To ensure they'll be there," Kidd whispered to me, later. "I made certain to move most of the treasure to the *Adventurer Galley.*

"But if they decide to settle for what treasure they have and for the gold they can make by selling their ships?"

"It will diminish my accomplishment," said Kidd, "but still we'll return with a fortune, and ye must watch, Master William. Sheer greed will get them to St. Mary's."

Captain Kidd was at last frustrated in his attempt to keep his anchors and had to order their cables cut. By that time, the two English ships of the East India Company were attempting to seal off the harbor and the Dutch ships had reached the mouth of the bay. Working in our favor was the lumbering nature of the four trying to trap us, which brought derisive laughs to Kidd's lips. Having lashed the *Quedagh Merchant* to the *Adventurer Galley*, Kidd was easily able to tow the Moor to open sea as well as free the *Adventurer Galley*, leaving the British and Dutch far behind him.

The *Rouparelle/November*, too, escaped but not so easily. Owing to the half-heartedness of the Dutch and a bit of luck, it was able to flee the harbor in a hail of English cannon balls.

"Ah, look ye there, Master William!" said the captain, with a nod toward the distant *Rouparelle/November*. "We'll have endless trouble with the crew of that ship if it survives. They are a bunch of ne'er do wells, and such as they always blame their troubles on others."

"Aye," I replied.

By early afternoon, the sun overhead was a bloody eye and all the sea flat and lifeless as if it were painted. We stood about in our sweaty clothes and waited for a tickle of wind to come and drive away the demons of heat. We were out of sight of land. No bird flew in the sky. No fish leaped from the water to show us a silver fin, and no ship appeared on either horizon. Not until dusk were we relieved by a summer rain that broke the heat and gave us breeze enough to make way in the reviving sea.

"Master William," said the captain. "Ye are to bring Wolf to my cabin instanter."

I found Wolf sleeping off the heat of the day in hammock. Across his chest were a few pages of paper with his handwriting upon them in ink.

"Have ye been writing, Wolf?"

"Aye, mate," he said, "a discourse on my hammock."

"On thy hammock!" I said.

"The nature of a hammock is that it swings and is therefore unstable," said Wolf.

"Aye," I said, "when the world around it is stable."

"How easily ye grasp my thought," said Wolf. "Yet, on a ship, which rocks and is therefore unstable, the hammock does not rock and is therefore stable."

"Ah," I said, "and the application?"

"I am working it out," said Wolf. "At any rate, that can wait until we come back from seeing the captain."

"How did ye know we are going to go see the captain?"

"Ye never summon me for any other reason."

"Of course."

Wolf slowly sat up in the hammock. To my eye, he had changed not a whit since we had first met in New York, except now he was stronger looking and better fed. No new blemishes or wrinkles marred his skin or signs of worry clouded his blue eyes. He might have shucked the wolf skin yesterday for all the ravages that time and hardship had brought him, he looked an aristocratic, blond, young man serving as best man at a wedding, not the spy or privateer or fellow still learning to shoot and kill with a knife.

The captain greeted us at the door of his cabin with unusual gravity, saying at first that he'd had a "realization, no, a revelation," then bidding us sit, closing the door behind us and then pouring us wine and himself taking a seat.

"Aye, aye!" he said. "I've had a revelation."

Both Wolf and I waited in silence.

"Wolf," said the captain. "What immediate problem do ye see that we have now in relation to our goals?"

"Well, Sir," said Wolf. "The first problem is the *Adventurer Galley* itself. The seams of the ship are tearing apart and the leaking is becoming untenable. Soon, we'll have to wind ropes around the whole ship just to keep her together, so it would be well to begin work with the marline-spikes, Sir, and plan on assigning men to the pumps night and day. Also, Sir, we should fly every yard of sail and catch every puff of air from here to Madagascar, else we will not arrive, except on the ocean's bottom."

"Well reasoned, Wolf," said the captain. "Now, it is thy turn, Master William. What difficulties will I find in Madagascar?"

"Terrible ones, Sir," I said. "That the India Company merchantmen attacked us means that it is widely known that we carry immense treasure from the *Quedagh Merchant*. We will therefore be attacked by pirates at St. Mary's and will have to forsake the *Adventurer Galley* because there won't be time to repair it. I agree that both our other ships will arrive at St. Mary's out of greed, but the *Rouparelle/November* will take the treasure or join other pirates at St. Mary's who will attack us. On arriving at St. Mary's, we should abandon the *Adventurer Galley*, move the treasure back to the *Quedagh Merchant,* and escape the pirates of *St. Mary's* and the crew of the *Rouparelle/November.*

"I agree with that assessment," said Wolf. "At St. Mary's we can salvage the *Quedagh Merchant* and most of the treasure. That is all."

Captain Kidd put his hand to his chin and lapsed into thought. Wolf and I looked at each other in some surprise. We were in agreement yet had never discussed the matter. Captain Kidd, however, seemed to be taking events in stride.

"Gentleman," Captain Kidd said. "The three of us have speculated in the past over our purpose in being together on this voyage, mentioning deity, fate, destiny, even the Finman, as I recall. Let us this evening mention the exalted Captain Thomas Jones, whom I believe to be mentor to ye both, though ye may not yet know it, Wolf, as well as friend and guide to me.

"Gentlemen, I have thought of Thomas Jones before and asked myself, 'Could it not be that Thomas Jones has sent me these two fine young gentlemen, by some manipulation of the stars, not only for purposes already discussed, but also to keep me alive?'

"So, I have now called ye forth in a new spirit and have asked ye questions upon which my life will surely hinge. Now, I must tell ye…

in all humility…the course of action ye propose is of such shinning brilliance that I am convinced that Thomas Jones has sent ye to me for this very meeting, this hour, and this conversation.

"Who knows the importance of this treasure we carry. Perhaps it will change the course of history. Perhaps somehow what we say next will advance the minds of men. Who knows, gentlemen? Let us continue this session."

"Aye, Captain," we said in unison.

"Reason with me then," said the captain. "What will be the result when we sail the Quedagh Merchant to a British port in the Caribbean and make ourselves known to a governor there?"

Both Wolf and I squirmed in our seats.

"We will be taken as pirates, Sir," I said. "There is no help for it. There is a high probability, nay, a near certainty that the owners of the *Adventurer Galley* reported ye as a pirate when ye sailed from New York promising the crew wages they did not approve. It would follow then that arrest orders for ye have long ago reached as far as the Caribbean. Further, the odds are high that Commodore Warren and Captain Clark both reported ye as a pirate two years ago, for Wolf has often heard rumors that such is true on the docks and in the taverns."

"Aye, that is true, Captain," said Wolf, "and it is certain that word of thy killing of thy mate with the bucket has also been passed on."

"What!" said Kidd. "I fear not such a report!"

"Any report, I fear, will do!" said Wolf.

"Eh!" said Captain Kidd, taken aback. "Explain thyself."

"Captain," said Wolf, "it is certain that ye have now powerful enemies who are beyond the law.

"It is because of the *Quedagh Merchant*, Captain," I said. "The taking of that ship will oblige the English to find ye guilty of piracy."

"Gentlemen, ye overreach thyselves," said Kidd haughtily. "What ye say lacks coherence. As ye both know, I have in my possession the French letters of Marque that prove the taking of the *Quedagh Merchant* a legal act."

"Those papers will be taken from ye at the moment of thy arrest," said Wolf, "and, unaccountably, on the day of trial, they will be lost by the prosecution. Apologies may or may not be made. In short, ye will hang, Sir, no doubt at the mouth of the Thames."

Many a man upon hearing such grave words from Wolf might have shuddered or flared into anger, but Kidd's natural toughness permitted him only a steely gaze and then a little wave of dismissal from a bony finger.

"Captain," I said, "the *Quedagh Merchant*, a Moor, sailed for the British East India Company under French papers, under the command of a Frenchman who claimed to be the captain but wasn't. Also, on that same ship, an Englishman who apparently had some shadowy status as captain was discovered below deck and warned us of a 'noise' that would be caused in England. Thirdly, a group of Armenian merchants who might not have been simply merchants screamed with rage when we took their goods and then behaved in every way as if we were violating an agreement with them."

"Aye, Captain!" said Wolf. "There seems to have been some international project afoot."

"Perhaps an accommodation involving two enemies, France and England, that was meant never to become known," I said.

"And a huge shipment of treasure from some criminal power now demanding the blood of the blue fly that bit it," said Wolf.

"An illegitimate power the British have determined to appease," I said.

"So ye say I'm to be a scapegoat for the British and French, who have bungled their sub-rosa business and now are expected to hang me to quiet the complaints of some Sultan or Chinese warlord engaged in illegal trade with Armenian officials."

"Aye!" said both Wolf and I at once.

"Now ye have it, Captain," said Wolf. "Nothing else fits the facts and rumors, or the circumstance of such a vast treasure on one Moorish merchantman."

"Therefore," I said, "it is probable that word is quickly on its way even now from here to England that ye has committed a new act of piracy in regard to the *Quedagh Merchant*. At the same time, the owner of the bulk of the treasure, an Armenian potentate, or the 'Sultan' or 'Warlord,' as ye put it, will doubtless send to England a letter demanding thy death and a return of the goods."

"In the Caribbean and North America," said Wolf, every post we reach will have a governor who has already an order from the king to detain us for interrogation and possible trial in the colonies. Such, in itself, will not be tragic. While we are detained, however, the King will doubtless receive the news of the *Quedagh Merchant* and send a new and more extreme order to all governors. This new order will not be merely to arrest us and send us to trial in the colonies where courts will acquit according to the merits of the case. The order will compel our immediate arrest and transport to England, where juries are obedient to the wishes of the king."

"Aye, Captain, it is so," I said. "What Wolf says is so. I see it bright as day, even in my dreams. I see rejection and betrayal even from the governors in the Caribbean who have professed to be thy friends. Even to escape them, we will have to abandon the *Quedagh Merchant* because it too outlandish in appearance and therefore recognizable."

"In thy view, is it possible to sail successfully to New York?" said the captain.

"Aye," I said. "If we acquire a new, smaller ship in the Caribbean that will attract no attention and if ye stay below deck."

"And will I be successful in New York?"

"Only if thy goal is to see thy Sarahs," I said.

"Aye," said Wolf. "Ye may even steal them away and take the treasure as well."

"May I clear my name?" said Captain Kidd, his voice low, almost a whisper.

"Nay, Captain!" Wolf said. "That will not be the way of it."

"And if I pay the investors in my voyage double their return," said Kidd.

"It will not matter at all, Sir," said Wolf. "Be clear on this point, I beg ye. Ye will not be hung because ye are a pirate or because of wages ye have paid the crew or because ye have killed a sassy mate or because ye are misunderstood. Ye will be hung by thy King to appease wild beasts that have slaughtered for the Crown."

"This is a case I need to set before my supporter, Governor Bellomont of New York," said Kidd.

"At thy peril," said Wolf.

"Have escape routes planned," I warned.

"Have the treasure hidden," said Wolf. "Ye may be able to buy thy freedom. Surely, Bellomont will betray ye like all the rest if ye fail to give him compelling reason not to. I have seen the gouty old bastard who has lost his humanity to the thousands of razors that inhabit his foot. He'll have ye in chains."

Captain Kidd sat slumped in his chair, pondering all that we had said. Minutes dragged by. An hour passed in silence, Captain Kidd not looking once up from the floor. At one point, he ordered Wolf to step out of the cabin and order an adjustment of our sails, for he had heard and gauged a change in the heaviness of the wind. Wolf came back in the cabin a bit amazed that the captain was able to pull off such a feat while entirely preoccupied with another matter.

I was less startled. In all my time with him, the captain had never stressed the use of any instrument or focused long on the northern star but rather sailed the urgings of his own knowing blood, finding tempests in his fingertips and distant shores by his throbbing bone. Often, at night, I had witnessed him rising from his bunk, having already divined by the length of the swells beneath him the arrival hour and intensity of a coming storm.

How then, was he ever so easily thrown against rocks by human ripples and waves? Wolf and I looked at one another. No word passed between us, but it was clear that the captain still felt that he could scuttle the pirating charge against him by paying the ship's investors double their investment, proving his thoughts in others matters as sluggish as hog piss in clogged scuppers.

Perhaps the captain was right. Perhaps Captain Jones had put Wolf and I aboard the ship to teach the captain, not the other way around. Or perhaps Captain Jones had put us aboard the ship to learn that even the greatest among us were flawed by nature in certain diverse particulars of muscle and shell and needed care.

"Wolf," said the captain. "It is unacceptable to me to live without my good name restored. Perhaps ye can offer me insight as to what might await me if I am taken to trial in England. For instance, will a solicitor be available, and will I be able to present my case?"

"It seems to me," I said, "that the captain is much in need of a solicitor."

"And so he is," said Wolf, "but it is rare for a solicitor to put up more than a token defense when it is known a conviction is desired by the king."

"Is justice not sought by an English court?"

"Not even in pretense," remarked Wolf. "An English court is the instrument of the king and a means of allowing the citizenry to become complicit in royal crimes. A judge may instruct the jury as to the verdict. If the wrong one is returned, the jury may be gaoled.

"In Europe, they still use torture to get confessions. In England, they don't need to. English prosecutors only have to awe the gallery with hidden trip wires the unschooled and undefended accused stumble over to their doom."

"How then is innocence ever established?" I asked.

"Innocence is seldom established," said Wolf, "and when it is, ignored. The court is a killing machine. England is a crowded nation with a rigid class structure and has embarked on a program of murdering those that aren't being used for pleasure and gain. It hangs to death even seven year-old children of the poor on the suspicion of offenses and condemns whole families to death by poverty by pressing young men into a service from which they might expect no delivery but burials at sea.

"Far worse, the entire peasantry of England lives in the most wretched of conditions, as engineered by the king and nobility, who deny them arms and all means of achieving adequate shelter and food. So, there is death by sickness and starvation throughout the country as well as constant imprisonments, executions, and transporting to penal colonies of the unneeded poor, who are branded criminals.

"Sir, when last in the stinking town of London, I took a walk toward the fabled Thames, my right hand on my purse as I walked. Every half block or so, some green corpse of a man, woman, or child was either being stripped or washed, left to rot on the cobblestones, or nailed up in a box. Several times, in broad daylight, I gave press gangs wide berths as they went about their business of knocking cold, unwary young men in their heads so as to drag them off to serve in the King's death ships.

"'Bring out ye dead!' yelled a cart man, patrolling the streets. "Bring out ye dead!'

"Now and then he would stop and someone would throw a body on the cart, and then the cart would move on through a contagion of venders hawking their rotting herring and crusty bread, loose weaves of cloth, and fruit unwashed because of the contagion in fresh water.

"For a long while, I sat on the foundation of an old tavern on the Thames that had been razed by fire. Save for the interminable racket of billows and anvil, it was a peaceful afternoon, filled with the stink of the city's stockyards and excrement, horse, human, chicken, and cattle. The night before, by torchlight, the fecal matter ground up by carriage wheels made an inverted orange bowl above the city, but now the air seemed almost fresh.

"The Thames was littered with hundreds of small craft from pleasure boats of the aristocracy to wretched longboats and skiffs turned over and half-buried in the sucking mud. Revenue cutters abounded beside brigs and brigantines and ships from Holland and Russia.

"There were bodies in the water. I saw them drift in with the tide. I saw their bloated, moonlit hands wash in as if reaching for the wrack-lines. This, Sir, is the legal system of England, the one that ye hope to speak rational words to and thereby clear thy name."

"Ye have given me cause for thought," said the captain.

"There's more!" said Wolf.

"Perhaps another day," said the captain.

"Captain," I said, butting in, "only ten men or so from the original crew shall return with us. The rest will surely desert ye for fear of being hung as pirates. Of those who return with ye, none shall stand with ye if ye are taken to England. Most will be persuaded to testify against ye, regardless of the facts, and those still determined to testify for ye will not be brought to testify or will be condemned with ye."

"Let me say one thing more, Captain," said Wolf.

"I will not stop ye," said Kidd.

"Sir," said Wolf, "if hauled back to England for trial, ye might expect a wait of two years or more in solitary confinement. That time will be spent without bathing or toiletries or a change of clothing or a decent bite to eat or benefit of apothecary. Ye shall also be without a means of keeping warm or cool, nor will ye enjoy a means of keeping the screams and stench of thy fellow prisoners from permeating thy cell and thy mind.

"Many die in their sorrows. Those reduced to lunatics are carted off to Bedlam. In Bedlam, their hair is farmed and sold to wigmakers. To be sent to England is to exchange the arms of thy Sarah for years of making thy bed in excrement and living with no hope that thy evidence of innocence will ever be brought to the court."

"I understand," said the captain. "Ye need say no more about it."

"It would be better if ye were to seek the protection of some foreign government," I said, "and then send for thy Sarah. I have not been to England, but have heard many stories, all in accord with what Wolf is telling ye now."

"Aye," said Wolf. "Make thy country elsewhere."

Again, Captain Kidd sat for a long time starring at the floor. Eight bells rang, signaling a dogwatch to which Wolf was assigned.

"I am assigned to this watch," said Wolf. "Would ye have me stay here with ye or go on duty?"

"Oh," said Captain Kidd, looking up, distracted. "Ye must go ahead, Wolf. Master William will stay with me here."

After Wolf's departure, the captain was uncommunicative until the daylight began to fail and I lit the lantern swinging from a rafter of the ceiling.

"I have about decided on a course of action," the captain said, looking up.

"Aye, Captain," I said.

"Let me tell ye first," said the captain, "that my difficulty is that Wolf has a history of lying to me."

"But, Captain…" I said.

"I know thy mind on this," said the captain. "Ye believe that he lied to me at first out of nervousness only, not darkness of heart, and has since recovered, and ye are probably correct, but consider this, Sir. Let us assume he has made up all of this business about me being reported as a pirate and that no such report has been made. Well, then, Sir, is it not true that taking the admittedly perfectly reasoned advice of ye both could lead me to the rope, not away from it?"

"Aye, Sir." I said. "I take thy point. If he has lied about ye having been accused of piracy, thy fleeing to another county with thy owner's treasure would indeed be an act of piracy."

"On the other hand," said the captain, "if, indeed, I have been reported for piracy, I think the analysis of ye both is indeed a godsend for which I shall be eternally grateful. Never have I seen human minds construct so convincing a view from bits and pieces!"

"Then what shall ye do, Captain?"

"I have decided to proceed as if I believed Wolf's reports that I am wanted for piracy," said the captain, "but not to the extent that I will flee my own country and actually become guilty of piracy."

"Which means…?" I asked.

"Which means I shall proceed homeward with utmost caution to see my Sarahs," said Kidd. "If I am wanted for piracy, I'll pay off some governor to arrange a dropping of charges or a pardon, if necessary, providing it doesn't involve my being send back to England."

"That is not likely to deliver ye," I said, at heart, despairing.

"I shall have the treasure hidden, escape routes planned," said Kidd. "Perhaps I'll deal with gouty old Governor Bellomont himself. At the very worse, I'll sail off with the treasure and my Sarahs, leaving my New York solicitor to handle our house"

"Ye are a hung man, Sir," I exclaimed, the truth exploding from me.

"Eh?" said Kidd. "What fault do ye find with my plan?"

"None at all, Sir," I said. "As a plan, it is a perfect one for an ordinary man. The fault lies in thy character."

"What then?"

"Ye are not capable of fleeing a gouty old man like Bellomont, Sir!"

A Trip in Time:
The Journey Home

Chapter Twenty-Five

"Ye are both being used by the Finman," said Sarah Kidd, rocking in her chair upon the porch of her house on Pearl Street. The scent of wisteria mixed with hydrangeas and morning glories and carried from the garden where the younger Sarah, now a young girl, picked roses for her mother. "The ultimate goal of ye lives is the destruction of the English empire by sea."

Wolf and I listened, not breathing, stunned by Sarah's knowledge and the iron of her voice.

"The captain and other seafarers of his generation had as their task the destruction of the Spanish," she said. "Now a new tyrant has emerged that shall swallow the world if left unchecked. Thus, we are together, sitting on this porch, talking frankly, one to the other."

"Aye," said Wolf, not knowing how to continue, nor did I know any better than he, for all my sympathy and wit.

Many a day of heavy thought had passed since Captain Kidd had rushed to Governor Bellomont's house in a fit of blind fury, where he was needlessly taken by the English. Already, it was rumored, he was afloat in chains, on his way to England to answer charges of piracy—in spite of Bellomont's initial politeness and seeming interest in championing his case.

"My husband's tarred carcass will be strung up at the mouth of the Thames," said Sarah. "There, it will inflame the hearts of poor mariners and turn them pirate against the British crown, thereby aiding thy cause."

"Bellomont tricked him," said Wolf, feebly.

"To Bellomont's grief," I hastened to add, "I'll let him live, for he suffers the tortures of the damned with his gout. In his pain, then, he'll watch the beginning of his country's fall."

"Aye," said Sarah, a grim smile playing about her lips, "I can see it all now as if I were a gypsy gazing into a crystal ball. There burn the sails and there the mast falls in its shrouds like a burnt tower sliding into the sea."

"Aye," said Wolf, "I see it as well."

"Here are the roses, mother," said the younger, fresh-cheeked Sarah, her eyes still shining from tears for her father. "Should I put them on the table?"

"Let me hold them," said Sarah, taking them in her arms and bidding her daughter sit in the rocking chair beside her.

"It is clear enough that Master William is to become the captain of a vessel or a fleet," said Wolf, at last, "but what is my role?"

"Why, that for which ye have been trained," said Sarah. "Ye must represent pirates in court, not in England but here, especially if they attack British ships. As for William, I am not sure of his role. I do not think the title 'Captain' encompasses it. Captain Jones does not tell me all."

Sarah looked deeply into my eyes then and handed me a letter.

"William," she said. "Captain Jones has been sent a letter to be delivered to ye. As ye can see, it has not been opened. Nevertheless, Captain Jones, I believe, has divined its contents and urges ye to act upon them at once."

"Where is the captain?" I said. "I must see him. I have questions that must be answered now."

"Read the letter now, William," said Sarah, her eyes suddenly as hard as her late husband's.

My curiosity piqued, I tore open the seal and extracted a number of thin pages upon which Anne Bonny had poured out the workings of my mind in a delicate hand.

My Dearest Master William,

How often have I cursed my bastard heart for its waywardness and my soul for its thirst for bloody freedom! The loss of ye, William, is as the loss of a swiving rose, bedamned my girlish heart. Sailing with Jack proved one bloody horror after the other. The murderous drunken pig took to raping and killing like old Vane himself and was a coward as usual to boot and secret faggot lover of Bart Roberts, I discovered. When news came of the great pyrate's death by sword off the coast of Africa, Jack cried for a week. Then we took to the sea to butcher whomever we could, over objections by Mary and me. It was after a typical session of murder and torture for no purpose that the authorities boarded us with drawn pistols and cutlasses swinging.

So drunk were Jack and his mates that only Mary and I were left standing to hold them off and we were, therefore, eventually overcome and hauled off to prison. Mary and I pleaded our bellies, Mary truthfully. So, we were spared trial for a while. At Jack's trial, I was called as a witness and said enough to hang him, and at his objection screamed at him that if he had been man enough to fight we wouldn't be in court at all.

Calico Jack Rackham died badly on the gallows, goddam his soul.

Then Mary, my Mary, as foretold, died of childbirth in prison. How I weep over that and longed to speak with thee, sweet William, to continue thy education.

Now, I write to ye wondering where in the world ye have gone. My father has interceded in my behalf with his fortune and, ostensibly, I am free, but the taste of this freedom, without ye to bother and barb and tease with my quim is ashes.

Now I have been forced to travel west by wagon as a condition of my pardon and instruct ye to come for me instanter at latitude on the western coast of North America. Do not object, saying no man could find me. Ye are not a man.

I send this letter by Captain Jones who is certain to deliver it.

I am ever thy saucy Anne,

Anne Bonny

Immediately upon reading Anne's letter, I struggled for words to say to Wolf and Sarah, but was not able to speak, so powerfully did my emotions, long stowed, flow even to my cheeks. Had there been just fired cannonry aboard, my heart might have shattered with the recoil. Both Sarah and Wolf reached out to steady me in my chair, and then Sarah picked up the letter from the porch where I had dropped it.

"There are no ships now in New York with plans for sailing to the great ocean," said Sarah after reading the letter, "but perhaps ye may book passage to the Caribbean and then find passage around Cape Horn from there!"

"Not likely," added Wolf, at a shout, or so it seemed to my excited senses, "but it's try we shall!"

For a week thereafter, Wolf and I strode the docks of New York seeking news of a ship bound for the Caribbean. Alas, the devil was against us in dreary, rainy weather at the end of the summer. Ye would have thought no sea captain of New York had ever thought of a voyage to the Caribbean either in pirate vessel, cargo ship, or small sloop for private hire.

"We are pirates, are we not?" said Wolf, at last. "What is to stop us from simply taking a ship of sail by gunpoint, thus settling the matter?"

"Aye," I said at once, "it has come to that."

"But no," said Sarah firmly, so firmly that we ended by apologizing to her that ever we carried such a thought in our brains.

"Ye are destined to pirate British vessels," said Sarah angrily, "not those of thy neighbors."

Slowly, with the waiting, came drink and with drink, despair. Each day Wolf and I would futile make the rounds of taverns where seaman brought tales of arrivals and departures but still no luck. For hours during the day, I took to sitting alone on a bench at the harbor and kept watch for sails.

How I came to such a low state of mind in such a short span, I can only ascribe to the madness of love. My dress became slovenly; my eating ceased no matter how succulent the roast put before me. My hours darkened, and, had Sarah not taken me into her house, my quarters would have become unclean, my linen saturated with sweat and tears in equal measure. Each morning, I woke to smells which were not present to any other being and often saw the hind quarters of a black dog leaving my room, as well as heard Anne's voice waking me from my slumbers.

"I fear ye are going mad," Wolf said to me one morning, but I turned away from him and would not listen further or speak. Doing so, I knew, would only confirm his fears.

Of all I did next I do not know. I can attest, however, that I was so struck by Anne's letter and now so deep in dislocation and grief that I wandered aimlessly for some time among the wretchedly poor and dying of New York's back streets. One day, at twilight, I at last found myself at the Hudson River, at a low place, where bodies floated, uncollected by the authorities.

There, I sat myself down for a while on a barrel, only to rise suddenly and put a shot in the throat of an attacker and then walk to the water's edge. There was laughter on the river and unidentifiable boats bearing torches some distance away toward the city proper, but straight ahead of me there was darkness and open sea and I heard myself praying.

"Finman," said I, "I am speaking to ye now for I know full well God's dominion ends with the sea, and I, William Claddah, a former enemy and pirate, am seeking a formal alliance in the rescue of Anne Bonny. Take me aboard, Sir. Take me to the Caribbean and be the star that guides me."

In truth, I expected little. If anything, I expected a long period of negotiation and the eventual loss of my soul. What I did not expect was the immediate arrival of black, gale force winds and the Finman's black boat gliding through the breakers.

Chapter Twenty-Six

It was a wet day in Port Royal, as if the sea were sloughing off its excess onto the sloped roofs of the houses and taverns and cobblestones of the streets. It was dark at noon. The sky was chicken scratched and the moon sat uncertainly in it as if likely to sink. When the carriages passed, their wheels kicked up the standing water and horse's manure of the gutter and splattered them on my boots.

I hurried, my head bent against the gusts and sudden sprays of rains, but only to get out of the weather. I had no love for Captain Morgan and was not excited to see him, though he was the most famous man in Port Royal and now a knight, Sir Henry Morgan, one of the most powerful men of the world.

He had numerous enemies.

Lately made a judge, he had sentenced many an old comrade to death with his sincere apologies.

"Which does not forgive it!" said many a Port Royal seaman, under his breath. "Nay! Not while he continues taking a portion of our earnings."

"Shut thy hatch, mate," said a pirate of some odor who had but one hand. "I have seen the captain's proceedings and tell ye that he finds the man who pleads innocence to be innocent if he is able. Haven't I seen the captain almost beg our stupid mates to plead innocent, and don't they refuse, as if they want to be hung?"

"They should be told more plainly!" I said.

"How may he tell them more plainly?" said the one-handed man. "His rivals are waiting to report his slightest scandal."

To these matters I had a forming opinion, in spite of my lack of formal education and experience in years. Unlike many a moralist of my time, I had had the misfortune to know many of the men that Morgan might well have hung, and as they swung above my head in my thoughts, kicking in air, I felt nothing about it except that justice had been at least half done.

Also, unlike the elitists, I understood that Holland and Great Britain had fed their poor to the new privileged class of industrialists. After starving, hanging, imprisoning, and beating the poor, these countries had succeeded in building criminals worthy of being shipped to places abroad so war could be made on Catholic Spain.

All that remained for justice to prevail was for their aristocracies to be hoisted up with the killers.

Turning a corner, I stepped into mire that sucked in my boots to such a depth that I paused to extricate myself. In this wet weather, Port Royal was not the shining, fabled emerald of the Caribbean but rather a shantytown to compare with Fleet Street in London, as I was soon told. The road itself was a soup of mud, human and animal waste, and vegetable and meat slops from the kitchen.

By that time, what I remembered of my journey with the Finman was next to nothing—only that I'd ridden behind him in his little boat, my face pressed against the black fur of his coat, my arms around him. There was the memory of salt spray in my nostrils and the splashing of cold water on my face.

At Captain Morgan's home, a black slave in livery met me with an umbrella at the iron gate and led me to the front porch, where I cleaned the mud from the sole of my boot on a dachshund boot scrape. I held my breath, for Morgan always frightened me. I followed the slave into the marble foyer, gave my cloak to a female slave, and took a seat before the foyer hearth to await Morgan's pleasure.

For a time, I dozed. Now and then, a doctor or a servant would ascend the sweeping staircase to my right and then come down flushed, more often than not muttering. The foyer clock ticked relentlessly. If it had not been Morgan I was waiting for, I would have climbed the stair and kicked the bedroom door open. But it was Morgan who lolled behind it, alas.

To my consternation, there was a bit of thunder outside and sleep deserted me, leaving me to envy Captain Morgan's stolen Indian carpets, sprawling from wall to wall, his chandeliers of Spanish gold, flecked with obsidian, rich oil paintings of his Welsh ancestors, for each of whom he claimed various titles and accomplishments though they were widely known to have been farmers.

I peered into the ash of the fire. If Thomas Jones were present he would doubtless ask me what value Captain Morgan's title of "Sir" carried with it, having been won as it had by the darkest means.

"What now?" he would say. "What now, young William, would ye say of the honors of the world?"

Suddenly, there was a clatter at the door that sent both the servants running and an explosion of words from without, or, perhaps, I say "words" too loosely.

What I heard were deeply intoned, guttural syllables from an inhuman tongue, each burst against the door like a thunderclap, until at last the door was flung wide open by the gaping servants.

What stood half naked and drenched at the door was a tiny black man not much more than four foot high and weighing far less than one hundred pounds, if one were to exclude the weight of his ponderous head.

The head, however, was enormous and may, by itself, have weighed fifty pounds.

So ponderous, it was ringed round by a leather band that was fastened to a cane shaft. The cane shaft was then secured vertically the length of the small man's spine so that the head could be held upright.

I half rose from my seat before the fire in pity, but the little man spoke again, and the syllables boomed like cannon fire down the long hall against my brain so that I quite collapsed again into my seat, convinced a voice of such depth and volume could not possibly issue from such a man by natural means.

The servants, on the other hand, became frantic with action. Shouting a thousand apologies, the male raced up the stairs, apparently to announce the new arrival's presence; the female produced a series of towels to attend to the strange man's comfort. First, she wiped dry the black stubble on his bulbous head, then carefully removed the enormous golden hoops hanging from his ears. Then, she dried the lobes. That done, she dried and creamed the beads of raised flesh that made swirls on his forehead before extending to the length of his nose.

I watched in astonishment, for he made no movement of any kind, requesting nothing, resisting nothing. She powdered his cheeks and neck, the former becoming an intricately carved bramble with a roseate hue and the latter an etched latticework of rich vermilion. Then, he released the fastenings at the shoulders of his wet, white tunic, which fell to the floor, and he stood naked before us, a figure no larger than a child but of glistening obsidian and crowded from heel to shoulder with geometrical figures of every design and combination.

The female servant fell to her knees with a great show of reverence and the male servant came bounding back down the stair with a dry robe for the little man who allowed it to be draped about him dispassionately. Then, with great ceremony, the male servant approached me. I rose to meet him.

"Judge Henry Morgan requests that ye join him now in the company of Dr. Stanley Walker."

"Of course," I said, assuming that Dr. Walker would shortly appear.

The little black man then stepped up and stood beside me, and the two of us followed the servant up the carpeted stair.

"It's good to meet ye," I said, noting the little man rocked from side to side as he walked.

"I eat ye up," said Dr. Walker, showing sharp little teeth as we reached the landing.

"I eat ye up, too!" I said. "Ye shizlewit little bastard."

"I am an Obeda man," he said. "I kill ye with a shout or with the tweet of a bird, or I make the air choke ye like hands at the throat, or, better, I eat ye alive."

"I'll carry ye about by stuffing thy little body up me own arse!" I said.

At this behavior of mine, the doctor exploded with a litany of such poorly formulated oaths that it threw the validity of his medical credentials into question and encouraged me to smite his nose. The blow was successful. It drove him back against a six-foot burial urn of the Ming dynasty stolen by Captain Morgan. From there, he hissed like a viper and called on his strange gods to eviscerate me like a goat.

At this, I was driven to laughter. Using my ten fingers to probe at the soft spots of the little man's head, I found the head seemingly filled with water and me intact. Still, I do not regard his call to his gods to be a failure. I am still alive, but there is plenty of time left for me to be eviscerated like a goat, yet the horned ones were not as quick about my evisceration as I think he may have wished. The only immediate response was from Captain Morgan's servants, who quickly rushed between Dr. Walker and myself and called to other servants for assistance.

After ten minutes of fisticuffs and the laying on of whips, Dr. Walker and I were thoroughly beaten and sufficiently composed to be admitted to Captain Morgan's sickroom. Instantly, upon being admitted to the chamber, I was very glad, for never before had I fully understood the opulence enjoyed by the upper classes.

Morgan himself lay yellow and bloated on satin sheets and circled rounded by physicians with their black bags who one and all seemed morticians, but that by itself failed to enthrall my eye. I knew a dead man when I saw one and recognized the smell of the fawning birds that circled the doomed one until the last with their lies and bleeding tubes and filthy potions. I had seen their sort steal the last sixpence from frightened seamen.

But what was new to me was the height of Morgan's bed—so high it required a ladder to mount and might have allowed a boy to run under it or a breeze to circulate, I imagined. Then Captain Morgan's family coat of arms shook me.

I had heard of such a thing as a coat of arms, and well did I know from my mentor, Thomas Jones, that Captain Morgan was a great one for family tradition and had good reason to be. Also, I knew he was now Sir Henry Morgan, acting governor of Jamaica, Vice Admiral, Commandant of the Port Royal Regiment, Judge of the Admiralty Court, and a Justice of the Peace, but nothing much about him had overwhelmed me until now.

Of a sudden, I realized that something in my brain fallaciously believed that only mythical people had coats of arms, people like King Arthur or Charlemagne, maybe even remote royalty but certainly not people I knew. It quite threw me over. Here, in bed. was a bloated old rogue I guessed to have lately drunk buttered rum in the bawdy houses of Port Royal, and, there, on either side of his bed, were coats of arms of two designs, both featuring the name *Morgan*, and one displaying a griffin looking left, the other a griffin looking right.

Then, most poignantly, I fixed my gaze on an old but meticulously polished cradle from the border region of Wales, a style known throughout the isles, even in the Orkneys.

Why did Morgan have it here? He had no children in Jamaica and he was in his forties. Had it been the cradle of a child whom had died? Had it been his cradle? Had he seen his own death coming and sent for it from England or stolen it like everything else he owned?

At last, the great man had been swathed in a urine plaster by the freakish Obeda man and was finished with everyone but myself. I was therefore called forward to his bedside both by a slight weary movement of his yellow finger and the more vigorous movement of one of his liveried slaves. I moved forward to the bedside and gazed down upon him. So heavy was the smell of urine upon him from the Obeda doctor's plasters that my eyes began to water. Still, I saw his feebleness, the bloat of his body doing nothing to hide the dissolution of muscle fiber and honest sinew.

Had I loved him, however, I would have been even more alarmed at the status of his soul, for its poverty was clearly stamped upon his face, not an inch of which looked ought but a burnt and cracked leather gone lifeless, even flaccid. So, too, was any steel that had been in the eyes far gone from them, leaving them a pitiable, uncertain yellow.

He trembled in his extremities, slightly but perceptibly, as if in a draught.

"William," he said, lifting a scrawny claw of a hand that had a ring with a bright jewel on each finger. "Bend closer down to me."

His voice was as weak as that of a newborn bird in a windstorm. I had no inclination to bend down closer to him and therefore did not.

"I know ye to be a buccaneer, William," he said, "and may hang ye for it."

At that, I laughed most cheerfully, and, weak as he was, he managed to laugh with me.

"Ah, William," he said, at last. "How much shot do ye have hidden about thy person? Is there enough to take my head off if I should order ye seized?"

"Aye!" I said, "and all thy toes and fingers and blade enough to carve up thy entire household staff as well."

Captain Morgan laughed a little at that, lightly, to himself. Then, he thought a bit, staring at me oddly with eyes that could scarcely see, tearing up from the thick smell of urine.

"Ye are a killer now. That is plain. I don't know if I am a killer or not, though I have killed many thousands more than ye."

"I understand ye, Sir." I said. "I do not think ye were ever a killer."

"I was a conqueror," Morgan said.

"Aye," I said.

"I did love the sea," Morgan said, "the touch of the wind and the cracking of the sail, and enjoyed the cannon, the chase, the grappling hooks being thrown, the shouting of the men and the boarding parties, pistols blazing, sweeping over the gunwales, but even during the most lively of fights, with blood all over me, I felt a stranger to myself. How can I describe it—like an actor in a play?"

"Ye put it very clearly," I said.

"Nor have I ever felt the pirate," said Morgan. "I imagine that ye do feel the pirate, William. Nay! I know that ye do."

"Aye!" I said. "Before ever I was a pirate, I aspired to the title and at the age of twelve, when I took my first ship or so fancied I did, was the finest night of my life. I was raised to the sea as a fisherman from Hoy, and what finer fish plies the sea than one with a gullet stuffed with treasure and fins of sail? Aye! I'm a killer too who enjoys a good fight, but after the battle is won, I would as soon the dead came alive, for I wish them no harm."

"And are there gaists?" said the captain, low, his eyes searching mine.

"Aye," I said, "for they are the wind that drives the sail."

"And shall I drive thy sail?" said the captain.

"Aye!" I said. "There shall be that day when Henry Morgan, the greatest buccaneer in the history of the world, shall be nothing but wind to drive a sail."

At these words of mine, Morgan laughed, just as I had previously laughed at words of his.

"I was never able to feel myself a pirate because of my bloodline," Morgan said. My ancestors were farmers, as I know ye'll put it about, and because of a sensibility and a vulnerably to love that the members of the Brethren know nothing about as well as a complexity of needs they do not share."

"Ye were once in love?" I said, plainly shocked.

"Aye," he said, "deeply, tragically. Long before the notion of becoming a buccaneer ever entered my head, I lived but for my love and the honor of my family. But my love was the daughter of an earl who would not hear of our marriage. That did not stop us, so in love we were. We took to meeting in the shadows, in a certain unfrequented rose garden where we reveled in our passions until almost dawn.

"One evening there was an informant, a Judas coin slipped into an unknown palm, and we were fallen upon in the roses. She was torn from me, and I was tied head and foot and shipped to Barbados until I won my freedom. So, ye see, young William, it was sweating in the cane fields of Barbados that the dreams that determined my life came upon me.

"They were dreams of power, William, engendered by love, made formidable by family pride."

I thought for a moment, considering how best to approach the matter and unable to drop it, for, at last, he had piqued my interest.

"And have ye not considered that even the most common pirate might have feelings of love and aspiration?" I asked.

"I have, of course, considered the matter," said the captain, "but I have reluctantly found such not to be the case."

"What?" I said. "Have ye not seen pirates grieve for their mates?"

"Aye," said Morgan, "but only reflexively, like monkeys howl when leopards carry off one of their own."

"And don't they love their wives?"

"If they did, why would they leave them so much of the time?"

"And don't they dream of captaining their own ships?"

"Only for simple motives," said Captain Morgan, "not for complex and powerful needs."

"Aye! So, ye believe thy sensibilities make ye one of a kind?"

"That is overstating the case, but that is the way of it."

"Then," I said, "that is explanation enough for thy sense of being alone, as well as thy sense of not really being a pirate but rather an actor in a play."

"And perhaps," said the captain, "it is, ironically, a cause of my great success, not being a pirate but rather a conqueror. From my very first captaincy, I treated my men with strict order and coldness, never confusing them with cajolery or friendship, as do Blackbeard and Kidd, who scarcely maintain command. Why, I didn't even let them know me or the full strength of my voice, and why should I have? I had a hangman. If I had thought them men like me, with lives of feeling and complexity, could I have led them to attack one of the most formidable places of the world? I am speaking of Panama."

The captain's eyes closed for a moment as if the sight of that golden city danced in his thoughts.

"Never did I feel at one with myself until I fixed upon taking Panama, known throughout the world as 'the cup of gold,' the most unconquerable of cities save the most mighty of Europe. There, the Spanish established the crossroads and fortress of the golden main and defended its limitless treasure with legions of foot soldiers, armadas of galleons, cavalry, and a thousand guns. And as if that did not suffice, it was protected by God himself, for such was its excess that each day ostentatious masses were held in its dozens of golden cathedrals."

"No one in the West Indies dreamt of attacking such a place, and if some mad man had, such a man would have been hurled into the street by his scurrilous comrades, nor did the Spaniards dream that any one would. How peacefully they slept in Madrid, in Panama, heaping up their riches, with no thought of Morgan."

"So, from south of Tortuga, I sent word to all men of the brotherhood to all points and isles and byways and havens of the Spanish Main and invited them to join me in an adventure that would bring one and all unprecedented spoils. And so come they did, as they would have for no other man—without requiring to know in advance where we were to attack, without questioning my representatives, who knew no more than they. came from several oceans, from the four corners of the West Indies, from the Red Sea and the Mediterranean, the Adriatic, and the Persian Gulf, from the South Sea islands with bones in their noses, from the coasts of Africa on flat-bottomed boats and naked but for sword belts and hats. There were Indians and Zeebooters, French Corsairs, English renegades in frigates and galleons, and innumerable unidentifiable mixed races of men in dinghies and hulks with rotten hulls, even junks and longboats with savage rowers.

"All these I blessed and accepted. At last, I had thousands of swordsmen and sailors and thirty-seven ships with a thousand guns."

"And it thrilled ye?" I asked.

"Aye," said the captain. "When the fleet was at last in place, I hiked to a high vantage place on Tortuga at midday and looked over what I had wrought."

"And what did ye see?"

"What I still see yet when I tightly close my eyes," he said pausing, "tall-masted ships of cannon in a quiet harbor—the most powerful force in the world—in my power. I cannot tell ye how fulfilling that moment was, how much I was of myself at that moment, how totally that moment recaptured for me the moment when I first had my love in a bed of roses.

"I shouted with triumph. I was the most powerful man in the world. The conqueror I had been driven to become, I had become. I could take my love back and take all Wales, or I could take Panama."

"Then why take Panama?"

"My love might not have wanted me to take her back," said Morgan. "I couldn't risk it."

Again the old murdering buzzard had drawn me into laughter. Still, I did not relax my guard. Captain Morgan was a man known for now and then establishing a sense of camaraderie, only to be embarrassed by it and quickly end it by delivering a sudden coup de grace. Putting my hand under my vest, I let him hear the click of my pistol.

"Ye are the killer," he said. "Not me."

"And what is a killer?" I asked.

"A killer is one who practices the art and trade of killing and then goes about it," said the captain.

"Then I am certainly the killer," I said, again drawn into laughter by the horrible old man, "and ye are certainly not, for thy method requires only a word to the hangman!"

"On Tortuga, I had the members of the brotherhood agree to follow me. Then, when I told them we were going to Panama, they didn't want to go, so I hired a professional to hang a few of them. Now, that was the act of a conqueror, was it not—worthy of Caesar?”

“Ye’ll be praised, Sir Henry, not for hiring a hangman, but as England’s greatest deluded fool of a strategist.”

At this, the old man’s eye’s lit for a moment, then receded in the next, and I thought of a sudden that the actual sunlight had dimmed in that place, but that was not the truth of it. Captain Morgan looked upward, defeated for a breath of time, for he was, after all, Henry Morgan and, in the end, incapable of any but the briefest delusions and utterly resentful of all.

"Alas,” said Morgan, his voice filled with bitterness and his hands shaking. “There was another who may have been greater than I.”

“The Dragon?” I said.

"Aye, the Dragon!” he said, shaking his head, “my countryman. For there have been three great Welshmen that have sailed the salt sea. There’s Thomas Jones, who loves ye, Drake the Dragon, and me.”

Both of us fell quiet. Upon hearing from Morgan’s lips that Thomas Jones loved me, my spirit soared, and I thought to cock both of my pistols and blow Morgan’s head off in bloody celebration. But, no. He was barely whispering then, and I had to bend down to hear him.

“Be not afraid of me,” he whispered with a breathless savagery. “Ye are no friend of mine and therefore have nothing to fear from my hand. It is also that I have need of ye now.”

I jerked backed suddenly as if to escape the bite of a viper, but he was quicker than I and, with a boney set of fingers, hooked my whole hand.

“Don’t move from me, boy, goddamn ye!” he hissed, then turned vigorously in his bed and bellowed at a servant. “Bring me the papers.”

Suddenly, there were papers stretched open on the bed. Captain Morgan was in a seated position, leaning against the high headboard, and a bearded solicitor who had slipped into the room was standing at the bed’s foot.

“Well,” said the captain. “What do ye make of all this?”

“I can read some of it,” I said. “It is thy will.”

"Good lad," said Captain Morgan. "There are some forty pages here deposing my earthly treasures—the last will and testament awaiting delivery to the hands of my executor in New York, Captain Thomas Jones, who is mentor to the trustworthy and uncommonly resourceful young killer I find before me."

"And what is it ye wish of me?"

"Do not be cheeky, lad," said Morgan. "Here in Port Royal, ye have yet to be born."

I shivered at that, but let the remark pass.

"Did ye hear me, lad?" said Morgan. "I have said that ye have yet to be born. And I tell ye further. Ye are invisible one moment, at the next ye appear but ten or twelve years old."

"I have heard that Port Royal was struck by a quake, Sir," I said, "and many years ago slid into the sea."

"If ye do not believe me, I shall bring forth a glass," said the captain, half sitting up in bed.

To that I said nothing.

"Ah, lad!" said Morgan. "It is not my wish to alarm ye. It is rather my wish as a dying man for ye to receive in advance from my estate certain goods and chattel that will endear me forever to Thomas Jones, my countrymen and Brethren of the sea. To legally acquire ownership of said gift, it is necessary for you to sign several papers."

"And what obligations do I incur by signing these papers?" I said.

"Ye might have guessed," said Morgan. "These papers include the map of a heathen shore on the mighty ocean where thy lady Anne Bonny waits in need of thy rescue. They require her rescue. Further, they require ye to harass English shipping. If no English ships are to be found, they require ye to harass those of the Moor, the French, the Spaniard, and the Dutch."

"Aye," I muttered, in lieu of fainting, for surely I foresaw the nature of the gift that was coming.

"Aye! Here's a sweetener for thy taste, William," said Captain Morgan. "The papers give ye sole ownership and therefore captaincy of one of my forty-gun galleons with enough powder and shot aboard to send ye half round the world in fulfillment of ye most black-hearted and grandiose calling."

"My black-hearted and grandiose calling!" I said, angered, in spite of my good fortune.

"Why as the future admiral of a pirate fleet, lad, as well as thy career as a Finman."

"I am no Finman, Sir."

"No Finman?" said Morgan, throwing up his hands. "Then I am no dead man, and Mary Read's mother saw no vision of Port Royal falling into the sea the day Mary Read was born, and you do not fade in and out of my vision like a spirit in sunlight. Where is thy sgian dubh? Ah. There it is, strapped to thy leg."

I felt of my leg, touched the little knife's handle of bone.

"Did ye think it lost, Sir?" said Morgan, smiling.

"Do I have the appearance of a Finman, Sir?" I said hotly.

"A Finman may appear as he chooses, as ye know," said Morgan.

"My father was no Finman. He was a Scotsman!" I said, my fist clenched tightly, blood running from my face.

"Aye, he was no Finman," said Morgan with a laugh, "but thy mother was a Finwoman. Ah, thy poor mother, who went mad as a child and thought herself a seal!"

Chapter Twenty-Seven

THE JOURNEY HOME

The good ship delivered up to me by the hands of Captain Thomas Jones and Captain Henry Morgan turned out to be a rugged brig of recent vintage, a fast, maneuverable, and forty cannon craft of two masts of square-rigged sail. What gift could be finer? Why only the gift of Anne herself. And what gift would be as fine? Why, only further means to win her!

Captain Morgan bid his first mate row me out to the *Man of Wales* and give me a ring of keys to allow entrance into every hatch, door, and larder. I, being a man of vanity like others, used first the key to the captain's cabin. There, my breath was drawn away by the mahogany furnishings and paneling, the displays of instruments and books all picked by the captain for himself, and now usable by me since I had learned to read and write with Anne's help.

But, beyond that, seated on my desk was a small wooden chest all tied up in a bow with a card upon it I knew on sight to bear my name. Fishing the proper key from the ring, I opened the chest and discovered at once how I would supply my ship with water and drink for a long ocean voyage and have at least enough left over to give a signing bonus to a crew.

Rushing to the deck, I tried to catch Morgan's mate to send thanks to the captain, but the mate was already gone. In his place were four crewmen, granted to me by Morgan. Beyond them, all I could see were the ancient, long forgotten streets of the old port teeming with strangers.

"No need for further goodbyes or thanks," said one of the crewmen. "Captain Morgan said to tell ye that. Now the four of us are to be the first to sign on with thy crew."

"Thank ye," I said to them, and felt a depth of gratitude with my whole heart.

"What does the sgian dubh prove?" I thought, "There are stranger things in the Northern Ocean."

If I were a Finman, why had I the need of a ship and a crew?

We left Port Royal, Jamaica, for the Straits of Magellan in two weeks time, pushed by favorable winds. So excited I was and so like a child in my desire for speed that upon encountering dark skies and a tempestuous sea, I cried out "sail on" to my newly recruited and startled crew. There was a growling all about, and the rascals might have mutinied on the spot had not the Morgan's men stood behind me with drawn pistols.

As it was, we rode the tempest gloriously, our main topgallant and studdingsails flying.

Having sailed the Greater Antilles in lively wind to the east, we bore north for the peninsula at Cabo Beato and there took our first prize, a Spanish merchantman. The captain and crew drew up a white flag and lay down all arms when we hoisted our skull and crossed bones and dropped a ball off the *Arabella's* stern. We pumped our arms and feasted half a day, for having taken a prize so soon. There were trinkets aboard of such splendor as to have the promise of making even my surly Anne happy.

Only the happy drunkenness of our crew spared the merchantman's passengers, for they were Spanish Hidalgos, and of the Spanish we hated Hidalgos the most.

"Let them go," I said, establishing myself as a merciful captain, but not as a Finman, for I wasn't mad enough to lose my crew. Only make very sure there is nothing left in their ship or on their persons."

So, for days thereafter, some us amused ourselves by dressing in the ridiculous high collared coats and sashes of Hidalgos.

East of Hispaniola then, we lost a squadron of pursuing Spanish warships by manipulating the weather gauge. From what decade the Spaniard sailed, I neither knew nor cared; so exhilarating it was to find the wind aft when I wished it aft or find us plunging down some windy trough of the ocean's road. In fine spirits then, we bore south to St. Lucia, where we raided a Spanish town and picked up light winds and a helpful storm at sea to drive us close to South America before braving the doldrums.

In the doldrums, we had our first hardship and might have had more had I not seemed to have been carrying wind upon my person, black bag or none, and, beside, hit upon the expedient of mixing our fresh water with salt water from the ocean, first as an experiment and then wholesale when it was noted that men fared very well on the mixture.

Fresh water nourishes and salt water prevents dehydration, lads. The whole trick of preventing death by thirst lies in mixing the two correctly. There is also a mean of preventing starvation at sea. Beating southerly off the Brazilian cape, Rio Deaneries, my hungry crew theorized that fish could not be caught from a ship as large as ours because its great bulk so disturbed the fish that they fled from it. To rectify the matter we thought first of sending out fishing parties in longboats but reckoned such a procedure would hold up the progress of the ship. Finally, an idea came to the mate, Joseph Hawk. Perhaps a craft with no gunwales would fish for itself.

I had the ship's carpenter construct a seaworthy raft of some four hundred feet square, which Hawk tied to our stern and let slide over the water as we sailed. Having launched it at night, we then all went to our hammocks, each man thinking Hawk mad, for none had thought of the flying fish that often knocked their heads on the gunwales of our longboat whenever we used them.

In the morning, thirty of our crew ate flying fish that had beached themselves on the raft. Taking the principle that a fish might not shy from an unobtrusive craft to its logical conclusion, Hawk then outfitted our raft during the day with fine fisherman who pulled in ocean fish until their arms grew sore. While many another crew before us had died for lack of rotted beef and biscuits hard as stone, we lordly tired of tuna, bonito, and dolphin.

Our fisherman, therefore, spend more and more of their time in developing the fine sport of sharking.

Having spotted a fifteen-foot monster, they would bait a hook with a huge chunk of fish and let it be taken without so much as a tug. Then, only after the shark had turned, they would contrive to pull him so that his back half would slide upon the raft, whereupon the men would grab the handle of his tail. Then, the shark would thrash in rage and bounce the rest of the way upon the raft where the mates would dance about with long knives and hoot like loons until the creature's life ran out.

For the greater part, though, the run for Cape Horn was a dicey business. I thought of Anne at every fall of star and my crew rising against me no matter how I ran the gales or fed them or kept them in water. The crew of a pirate vessel, beneath the trappings, is as like as not the crew of a whaler. All that matters in the end is what is stored in the hold, for at journey's end that is the stuff that will be divided and carried away in each man's purse.

Therefore, I blessed the stars and the Southern Cross that before we reached the Straits of Magellan, I was able to add more to our hold than the goods of a single Spanish merchantman and the meager takings of a poorly defended town. All night we had been barreling through choppy seas in our usual breakneck fashion when at dawn the lookout hailed two corsairs riding with shortened sails at varied distances before us.

It was a joke of the devil that we should be so wrong in our seaman-ship and yet to wake and find not one but two pirate treasure ships with the wind in my hands and neither with the ability to escape us. Taking to heart Captain Henry Morgan's teachings of years before, I angled off to starboard and caught the first corsair, bringing down a mast from a position where she could not return the shot. Then, I caught the second to starboard, where the wind had heeled her over and was pointing her helpless cannon into the water. She, I severely damaged and left barely floating.

Then I returned to the first corsair and assailed her with grape and chain until no mast stood and no sail flew. Only when there was no sign of life on either ship did we board. Even so, the Moslems met us with screaming corpses, swinging scimitars, rising from their blood with several limbs to blow us to hell with their pistols.

Before the day was won, we lost twenty-four men and sewed them in burlap to be dropped into the sea. We put forty more in the infirmary, where our doctors predicted the loss of twenty.

As for those who lost limbs, it is widely believed that such unlucky souls often lived, but I don't remember more than a handful of amputees having lived at sea, not during my whole time on it.

If God held sway on the sea, there might have been more mercy on it, yet, I do not repent of having killed so many corsairs that day, for I hated them and the French, if neither nearly so much as the Spanish. Each, in their time, was as evil as the Dutch, and it did no harm to destroy them when one had the need or the leisure.

What gifts for Anne! The crew was ecstatic at the unveiling treasures, as well as the ships themselves, a fleet and decorative adjunct of our new fleet, especially since the most damaged of the corsairs proved salvageable. New crewmen would be recruited from South American ports. The treasure lowered by some few inches the waterline of the *Man of Wales.*

All captains sought the Strait of Magellan rather than the dangers of the Horn, where ocean met ocean and changing water temperature brought about the greatest fury of wind and sea on earth. I reasoned that the Straits would provide us with rich opportunities for plunder.

But I speak now overlong of this trip to the mighty ocean to rescue my sainted Anne. What skills prevailed—those of the seaman trained to his craft or those born to a Finman? How often I have pondered that question and have come to no good answer, and how darkly it shadows my life!

In the Straits, I captured a good ship of the Royal Navy and took all her pressed seaman for my own crewmen. When the captain complained, I had him dragged across the keel until no patch of his skin remained, then called for my burliest seamen to cat o' nine the officers.

In the captain's safe, I confiscated the fortune he and the quartermaster had for twenty years been skimming from the allowance for the seamen's medicine, clothing and food. Then, thinking myself too agreeable, I called forth the bloody captain again and bid the crew toss him over the side.

For purely good luck, we tore the masts from the ship, stole the sails, cut away all anchors and hardware and set her adrift.

We celebrated with her brandy and laughed ourselves to sleep.

During our sojourn in the Straits, we dealt with in a similar fashion another English ship, a French ship, a Dutch Hoy, and a second French ship manned solely by Japanese raiders who had the effrontery to be armed chiefly with *quakers*, which were logs painted black to look like cannons.

Then, loaded down, but still flying in the wind, we turned north into the great ocean and saw no other ship on an ocean far more vast and terrifying in its immensity then any body of water any of us had seen before. No birds reached us; no grasses floated in our midst. Each day we rose to the sun, blue water, and sky, and nothing else.

At night we watched the stars and shadows. Sometimes, I saw the Finman paddling his tiny two-horned boat far ahead of us but only for the briefest moment, and after there would be nothing but the dark and the rolling sea.

Our fighting was over. We had done with it for a while. Our hold was filled and our needs for assuaging whatever wounds we bore were for now at rest. For most of the crew, the fixation changed from the winning of gold to extending out studding sails still further north to an unexplored place in the unending ocean.

There we found Anne Bonny waiting for us on a scimitar of sand on the coast of California.

Chapter Twenty-Eight

In truth, I exaggerate the ease with which it was done.

Off the coast of California, two hollowed out logs of Tonga Indians paddled out to meet our fleet of pirate vessels and engaged us in an hour of indecipherable sign language before a third log bearing more Indians and a Spanish drunk dressed like a friar pulled up at the ship.

"Diablo!" he cried, on first spying me, but a blow or two on his head rendered him an agreeable translator.

"Señors," he said, "the Tongva have a white goddess whom they will let ye see if ye will first make thyselves holy and then pay them."

"Es Anne Bonny!"

"Si, Señor!"

"Tell them, aye!"

My sense of relief was great, and my opinion of Henry Morgan greatly improved.

Following the Tongva inland, I expected every moment to encounter my love, and I grew almost feverish and delusional in anticipation of it. In every bower we approached and at the band of every shaded stream I saw her for a moment in the dappled air step toward me, her arms opened wide. At times, such tears of joy sprang into my eyes that I could scarcely divine the transparency of the images and rather reached out for them as if they were real, the scent of Anne in my nostrils.

Before traveling a quarter hour we reached a curious circular structure built of poles and grasses within what appeared to be the Tongva village.

"It appears these savages have a kirk!" remarked one of our seamen, which caused him to be thrashed across the fat of his back by a long willowy stick wielded by one of our new Indian friends.

"Ye would do well not to speak in this sacred place," remarked the friar, with a nod toward the three to four hundred Tongva warriors who surrounded the six of us from the ship.

"Aye," said the seaman, which won him a second thrashing.

The circular structure was then entered by thirty of the most flamboyantly attired of the Tongva and then by twelve women who sang in chorus. Next, we were escorted by warriors armed with spears to the center to the structure, where we found ourselves again surrounded.

Soon, an old Indian wearing only a loin cloth around his bony hips and a single eagle feather fastened in an unknown way to his shaved head came dancing forward, shaking a rattle made of a small skull and stones and mumbling in the language of the Tongva, which was interpreted for us by the friar.

To our amazed eyes the brittle old Indian turned out to be more priest than primitive medicine man, and his chief concern not magic or profit, but the salvation of our souls.

We were taught on that occasion that there was in fact a supreme being, regardless of what cynics say and that there was more to life than running around on the beaches making love to women and blowing our noses in the water. To this, we readily agreed, some of us even offering up the idea that fighting and rum drinking were also important, which brought down a couple of whacks upon our insolent shoulders.

"Blowing our noses in the water?" I thought.

We were also taught that the Supreme Being stopped the earth's wobble by first putting the planet on the shoulders of seven giants and only then making the animals and finally men and women. Curiously, according to the teacher, man was made in the northern country and the Great Chief himself had led his people to their present home in Southern California, all the while blowing his nose in the water.

At this point, the old man, whom we learned later was one hundred and fifty years old, broke off his dance and with the aid of the friar's skill as a translator, asked if we had any questions about our new religion we wanted answered. A couple of hands went up.

"Well, Captain," said one of our seaman, "I guess we've now got some evil spirits to worry about. What about that?"

"Nay!" said the medicine man, suddenly understanding English and controlling himself, with effort. "We believe in no evil spirits! What do ye take us for?"

"Well, how about hell, Mister?"

"Do ye think us to be children!" screamed the priest. "Do we look like the Spanish to ye?"

"Nay!" I admitted, "but what is this blowing of noses in the water matter?"

"The whale is the symbol of the Almighty!" said the old man. "He is neither to be mocked nor hunted. Nor may ye hunt or mock the owl or dolphin, but rather practice the art of healing and the virtue of bravery."

"Aye," I said. "We are all in agreement. Every man among us feels the holiness of the whale. As for the owl, we know him to be infinitely wise and a harbinger of death, and the dolphin we know to be a spirit of life and as intelligent as a man."

Having finished my little speech with the fierce looking Tongva all about me in their kirk, I glanced at the friar, whom I expected to translate my words. Instead of translating, however, he stood silent, staring at me as if I were a madman until I slapped him on the back of his head and words came rolling out.

The old man smiled, showing sharpened teeth.

"Be ye William Claddah," he said.

I was thunderstruck, and must have shown it.

"She said ye would be coming!" he said.

"And will ye let me have her, or must I declare war on all the continent," I said.

This sentiment seemingly being beyond the old man's capacity for understanding the English language, he looked to the friar for a translation and then laughed when he got it.

The old Indian explained that Anne Bonny had known I would come for her for some time because of messages sent her from someone far away. Again, he spoke slowly, finding his words in the words, seemingly, somewhere in the air, or in his memory, which was floating in the air. He said that I was a fortunate man in that Anne cried out for me at night, that she had become an object of worship among them, that they loved her, but that they would marry her to me and bless our union and weep when we left.

All the women and children would weep when we left.

The dogs in the streets would weep when we left.

"I thank ye," I said.

"But why was the Finman seen off our shore the day before thy boat arrived?" the old man said.

"The Finman seems to follow me through my life," I said.

"Does he hate or love ye?"

"I have thought different things at different times."

The old Indian thought this over for some time then bid me sit with him beneath the leafy branches of an ancient maple tree whose broad yellow leaves were detaching one by one and dipping to the ground. Pulling a long-stemmed pipe from his breeches, he expertly lit it with two flints and blew an aromatic tobacco first into brief flame and then into a smoldering mass whose smoke he took deeply into his lungs.

"When 1 was a young man I knew the Finman briefly," he said. "It was a time of death for my people, for the Spanish were killing them for sport, as if they were animals. So I prayed to the Finman, in my despair, and he came, saying nothing. I was standing by the sea in the moonlight when he came in his boat and held it still at the shoreline, saying nothing, just looking at me with his black eyes."

"I was so terrified 1 was unable to speak, but he heard me with his heart and withdrew a spear with a silver tip from his boat and held it over his head, as if to throw it ashore."

"I might have run, but I did not. The spear was in the air. It was headed toward my chest, but there was a calm settled over me, for I knew that the spear was intended not to impale me but to assist me. And so it was. Instead of impaling my chest it buried its head in the sand at my feet so that I had but to reach forward with my right hand to make it my own."

"And could ye use it," I asked.

"Not at first," said the old man, "but from that moment on it never left my hand, not even when I slept, except when I threw it, which I did, a thousand times a day, at every conceivable target, and from every possible hiding place in our forest. Then, a year to the day after the Finman's visit, six Spaniards from a galleon put to shore from a longboat.

Each died, with my spear through his breast. At news of my victory, my neighbors took heart and helped me kill the next twelve who came looking for the first six. After that, the galleon sailed away."

"And how old were ye at that time," I asked, astounded.

"I don't know," said the old man, "but I have shown the friar the armor and weapons and uniforms of the Spanish soldiers I covered with stones. He says I killed them a hundred years ago."

Soon, in the forest, the old man and I were join by a procession of forty warriors, each painted about his body in a variety of colors, their great plumes of hair tied straight above their heads and festooned with splays of eagle features. Behind them were row upon row of young women in light, summery dresses, their long black tresses of hair hung with flowers, followed singing.

"Thy wedding party," whispered the old man, nudging me in the ribs with an elbow.

"Thy bride, Anne Bonny, awaits ye in the village."

At these words, I assured myself I was dreaming. I had imagined a number of possible first meetings with Anne that ranged from romantic and tearful reconciliations to me abducting her in a wheat sack. But marching into an Indian village at the head of a wedding party of savages to claim her willing and regal hand had never crossed my mind. For part of the way to the village I felt faint, thought I was carefully fed to break my fast; and for another part I felt such elation that I fell into enthusiastic step with the drumbeats and singing of the young women.

Then, at the village, in the center of a group of dark-skinned maidens in flowing dresses, there stood my Anne in all of her sacred loveliness. Something seemed to break inside me and I heard myself sob, and in the bright sunlight I saw her running toward me and heard her sweet voice calling my name. In another instant, our arms were around each other and we were crying in the other's hair, kissing the other's face, then kissing the other's lips and exchanging promises when we unclenched.

She was dressed like a Tongva in white buckskin made soft by teething and sewn with precious stones, and her face and hair were powered vermillion. About her neck and wrists and ankles hung strings of pink and blue seashells of every shape, and tied to her waist were bone knives of the Tongva and a cutlass salvaged from her life years before.

"Anne!" I cried.

"My William," she said, "I hardly knew ye."

"But I am still thy own bouncing baby boy!" I objected.

"Are ye indeed, Sweet William!" said Anne, turning quickly to one of her ladies in waiting and procuring a large Spanish glass with an ornate handle.

"What do ye see here?" she said, holding the mirror before my face.

Considering the circumstances, it scarcely concerned me, but looking into the glass I was driven to admit that the man I gazed upon seemed every bit of thirty years old.

"Ye are now my senior by five years or more, Master William," said Anne. "What have ye to say to that?"

"I say that my advanced years entitle me to quim instanter," I said. "I have done without it for far too long a time! I suggest we hasten through the marriage ceremony so that the situation be rectified with all due speed else I arrive at the age of eighty before we achieve our fate."

"There is no need to wait until after a marital ceremony, William," said Anne. "Among the Tongva, the first night of swiving is the marital ceremony. There, Sir, is our lodge." Anne pointed to a little house of fresh grass erected at the edge of the village. "Are ye ready to retire?"

"I am ready!" 1 replied.

Trembling, arm in arm, we walked in twilight to the lodge, angelic voices singing to their loving god in the falling shadows behind us.

Chapter Twenty-Nine

We returned to New York harbor with our fleet of prizes behind us, their billowing sails seeming to fill up the whole southeastern sky. They were like ducklings behind our flagship, every schooner and sloop and brigantine and warship of England among them, so spruced out and obedient, their decks fresh holy-stoned, cream-white, their fittings, planking, spars, and shrouds immaculate. We were light on treasure, but sufficient in cannons, for that was our priority. The mates, nevertheless, were all handsomely paid and the majority happy enough. Having been only recently sprung by us from lifetimes of service and death in the Royal Navy, they leaped in high spirits from rigging to mast, waving high their hats to the stunned New Yorkers.

Ye would think those folk had never before seen nine pirate vessels with thirty or more guns each sail into their harbor at once. Still, there was no sign of rejection, only shrill high whistles from the soldiers at the earthen works who wished to sign on with us. With no trouble then, we suffered our cables to shudder out and cheered mightily as the last of our thirsty anchors dropped for a drink.

Shore leave began at once, and among those allowed to decamp were Anne Bonny and me, who were determined to find Captain Thomas Jones to show him our bounty and receive his pats on our heads, as well as fancied assignments. What I in particular wished to take up with him was my status as mythical being. Anne opined "Aye." I leaned that way myself. What would Captain Jones disclose? What further light would be shed?

What we found upon first stepping ashore, however, was a mud-splattering of my pants by Mr. Vanderspeigle's pigs. The pigs ran the muddy streets keeping them free of decaying matter with the exception of pig feces—considered desirable by Mr. Vanderspeigle, the aged sanitation man.

Then we found my old friend Wolf, practicing law in defense of every scoundrel who robbed his neighbors at sea. He was, of course, delighted to meet Anne and kissed her overmuch.

"I am astounded," said Wolf, "astounded, and yet I'm not."

He listened wide-eyed to my account of the meeting with Morgan, my ravaging of Spanish and English ships, our marriage.

"Thy mother died of madness, like many of the Finns, in a lonely maelstrom of shifting time and place" said Wolf, marveling at the astuteness of his own conjecture in regard to Finmen, but stupefied that he had never before linked my mother to the matter."

"How the need for thy mentoring clarifies now," he said, "No wonder of it that ye were taught to believe in only the most solid things of the world—geography, history, tactics, seamanship, navigation…and have been always placed close to hand to the Finman himself, or Valley or Mr. Starr or Bonny or Read or Joe Buck or Henri or Captains Teach or Jones or Morgan or Vane or Roberts or Kidd to boot."

"Aye, if Morgan is to be believed, which one may easily doubt."

"Ye have been an investment, lad!" said Wolf, "An investment from the first."

"An investment by whom?" I said, my anger rising.

"By the Brethren," said Wolf, "Having driven the Spanish from the Caribbean with the help of the British, the Brethren will be driven by the British to their deaths in the northern sea unless they build a new kingdom here, from South Carolina to New York, in every hospitable waterway."

"Aye," I said, "I've come to save all murdering scoundrels that seek shelter here."

"Ye shall be king of all this," Anne laughed.

"Aye," I replied, allowing myself to laugh and finding a half hidden brick walkway that led from the mud to a livery and an empty corral.

There we also found an old city hall building crumbling into its basement, and a few clap-trap office buildings and noisy stores, granaries, and small stockyards, as well as a few hundred shanties and dozing saloons and whore houses built over acres of muddy lanes. Everywhere there was dung and boards over dung. It was, by and large, a filthier place than Wolf and I had inhabited together several years before.

When we walked the fly-shrouded streets, we wrapped our mouths and noses in scarves to keep from breathing the noxious air.

Many of the townspeople were African slaves, and often, night or day, when the bell ringer clanged his raucous bell as if for vespers in hell, a gentleman and lady on the town, whose garb we affected, would be summoned to the whipping post down by the dock. There, they might watch at no cost the town whipper correct a slave. Then, if the whipping were satisfactory, the owner would tip both the ringer and whipper to the tune of eighteen pence each.

The strange practice of this ritual, Anne, Wolf, and I observed on the Sabbath, holding nosegays to our noses to prevent the stench of the virtuous from reaching our nostrils. Had we not been in clever disguise, as Anne remarked, we might have found it charming to scatter the crowd with shot.

As for myself, I had growth away from the kirk, but still had expected in what was supposed to be a Christian town a bit more attention paid to things that were holy. I did not expect in every doorway on Sunday morning the sight of some Dutch girl in a short dress and bare legs shucking corn, cleaning fish, or shelling peas. Nor did I expect them barefooted in their long morning gowns with no underwear beneath and going off with their laundry baskets to work the waters of some refreshing stream.

More than once Wolf strayed from us to follow them—for he loved to see where they would go, or if they would turn back toward him and let down their long flowing hair.

No matter the result, we were amused by it. If they failed to spot him on their trail, we looked at one another and laughed. If they spotted him and ran, we roared. If he were successful, we repaired to the nearest tavern and gave thanks to the Lord.

Often, we browsed the stores of New York Town for common household items and noted with some dismay that merely serviceable pots and pans and dishes were not to be had any price; rather, one was obliged to purchase the latest jewel encrusted goods from Italy, England, Spain, Portugal, India, and many other exotic ports of the world for pocket change and the most exotic silks for the price of coarse linen.

"I say, Wolf," asked Anne, "Is it possible in New York Town to purchase goods that have not been pirated."

"I don't believe so," said Wolf, "Unless one considers buying vegetables directly from farmers. Even so, it is difficult to tell a farmer from a pirate in disguise."

Virtually all or our time in New York was spent in search of Thomas Jones. We had expected to find him in a day, but even after a week we seemed no further along than we were the day we dropped anchor in New York harbor.

Then, finally, after diligent research and much talk with Sarah, who had greeted my every inquiry with the most madding and inexplicable vagueness, I arrived on Long Island, with Lady Anne Bonny Claddah on my arm. I stood as a gentleman in the little cemetery of the man I had loved like my own Da for the majority of my life and there I read on his cold gravestone this bit of doggerel scratched no doubt by some disillusioned seeker of his rumored treasure.

Beneath this Stone

Repose the bones

Of Pirate Jones

This briny well

Contains the shell

The rest's in hell

Ah, so lonely, lonely, lonely, is most of the world.

Wolfe, Anne, and I stood in silence then, the carriage waiting and horses stomping their hooves impatiently behind us. Oh, Lord, we were mice in the field and children of the wood and whatever death sang, we sang too. Then, inside of us, winter began and the white owl flew to the peeling birch. The snow dropped custard thick against the sail and over the shrouds and ratlines of my soul, the church bells rang out against the bitter cold.

The tombstone, the kirk, the horses and their carriage behind us seemed ten times their natural size.

Then the grief flowed in with the punches of a Lemuel Valley and I thought of my own dead father on his rough cot, his lungs filling with water, and my own dear mother as she dreamed of herself, not as a Finwoman who could send disagreeable starlight back upon itself or bring a new day forward, but rather as a seal on an ice flow bloodily flopping to the sea without her protective garment of skin. Tears came to my eyes and it was as if a great ribbed chest of accumulated weaknesses and sorrows that had been locked away and stowed now sprung open. Only with the help of Anne and Wolf was I able to stumble back through the muddy muck of the street and into the carriage. Then, the three of us rode back to the inn where we had taken rooms, unable to speak, our breaths driven from our bodies.

For the next few days we were scarcely able to sleep or eat and each of us found it impossible to turn his thoughts from Thomas Jones. From city records and newspaper morgues, such as they were at the time, as well as local gossip, we learned that Captain/Major Thomas Jones was referred to too often as, simply, *Pirate Jones.*

After his death, the brick mansion he built for his wife Freelove in Fort Neck, New York, called *Massapequa Meadows,* was likewise unfavorably dealt with in that it was called the "Pirate's" house. Shortly thereafter, when Freelove died, the house quickly became known as one of the most haunted houses in America, and everyone with an imagination from Bath, North Carolina to Portland, Maine, according to recent chatter, had made up a story about it.

How Captain Jones must have roared about it all in his grave! He, who became belligerent at the slightest superstition, to see ghost hunters and their fellows stalking witches even inside his formerly private rooms!

So ran a newspaper line of the day: "The Pirate's Grave belongs to the haunted house's builder, Major Thomas Jones and his loving wife, Freelove, the first Europeans to settle Massapequa."

Other notices must have been equally enraging to the dead Captain Thomas Jones.

The following line appeared in *Denton's History of New York*: "Massapequa Brick House is a dwelling on Fort Neck and has many strange and wonderful stories connected with it, and a lonely grave marked by an old tombstone some little distance from the house, on the banks of a small stream, a most solitary spot."

The New York Mirror put it thusly: "The venerable edifice is an object of awe to the people in the neighborhood."

And the most outrageous of all was written by the *Furman Antiquities of Long Island*, to whom I might have paid a visit had sweet Anne not stopped me. "Tradition says that at the time of Major Jones' death, a large black crow hovered over his bed, and when his life was extinct the crow made its exit through the west-end of the house. The hole through which the crow made its departure cannot be stopped, and, as soon as it is closed, it is again opened by some unknown means."

One day in June, Wolf, Anne, and I chanced to learn on the docks that Captain Kidd had been hung by an English court and his body placed on display at Tilburg on the Thames.

"Aye!" said the young captain who informed us. "Kidd tried not to struggle against the rope and kicked very little in air so as not to amuse the crowd. Then his slimy, wet body was immersed in preserving pitch and crammed into a fitted cage whose door was afterward hammered shut. Following that, I grieve to say, the whole apparatus was hoisted high by chains and hung on an oak gibbet where every seaman must see it that sails into London town."

"May the king and all his men in authority burn in hell," muttered Wolf, glumly, before launching a verbal attack on the fool and monster upon the throne of England. "I have sat in his courts and can smell them from here! Men from every civilized country in the world talk of their stench, which is overpowering to the degree that citizens faint while watching. First, there is the personal stench inflicted upon the prisoners to prejudice the jury, and then, more importantly, the stench of the justice rendered there, which is the justice of a tyrant and murderer."

"Ah, Wolf, calm down!" I said. "This fellow is but delivering the news."

"And sorry news it is," remarked Anne.

We all rushed to console Sarah, who still rocked on her porch on Pearl Street, but she brushed us away.

"I am satisfied," she said. "He is martyr to thy cause."

"Aye, he is," said Wolf, compassionately, his fierce eyes softening. "He was a great man and friend and genius at his craft," said Wolf, "And I do hope that some day the truth of his innocence and courage will make its way into the annals of history."

"I hope that people will come into knowledge of his softness and simple grace as well," said Sarah, "for therein was his measure."

"Aye," I said, agreeing with assessment of the William Kidd she knew. Of the William Kidd who had as an unmarried youth once delighted in pillaging the Mediterranean, I said nothing. Did she know of the degree to which she had reformed him?

"Ye gentled his spirit," I allowed. "He loved ye more, finally, than he loved the sea."

Sarah sat quietly, pondering my words, her eyes half closed. I observed the white comeliness of her hands, how one rested in the cup of the other– "like milk in milk, they were so white!" as was written later.

When will ye set thy fleet to burn the ships of the English?" Sarah said suddenly.

"But we are grieving the death of Captain Jones," said Anne, taken short by the abrupt change of tone.

"The death of Captain Jones!" cried Sarah. "Ye shizlewit numbskulls. To have a gravestone set with thy name on it is a common subterfuge. Get ye back to *Massapequa Meadows* and break into the place."

We leapt from our chairs.

At sunset, Wolf, Anne, and I drove our frightened horses neighing and snorting down the dusty road that carried us to the haunted mansion called *Massapequa Meadows*. There, in falling darkness, it raised itself from the cold ground, all six gables of it, and held true, its windowed bulwarks pitched on the fast ground of the wooded isthmus of a sandy spit shaped as a hook. Close on to its several teetering chimneys, the wind swept around in great swirling gusts, driving topgallants of clouds beyond the quarried shingles of its roof.

Branches of pine and dark maple struggled from their trunks and reached out for our horses as to grab their flying tails and grapple to their manes.

"Ye swiving rag of a horse," Anne said. "Ye buck me one time more I'll put a bullet in thy brain,"

"Are ye fearful, Mr. Wolf," I called out.

"Of the captain, no!" said Wolf. "Of what we ride to, aye. Who knows what is there?"

"It will be the captain there," said Anne. "Ah, don't ye see it. There is a light coming through the crack in that shuttered window."

In another moment, our horses were tethered at the hitching post and my hand was clutching the lion-headed knocker fixed to the oaken door. The knocking of the door gave rise to echoes and the chattering of birds, nothing more. Wolf stumbled over a boot scrape on the porch, cursing. The horses neighed and snorted at the post, their great bodies shifting.

"Open the door, Thomas Jones," shouted Anne. "Ye frigging wretch."

After many attempts, I ceased the dreadful banging.

"Sarah said to break in, so break in we will. Anne, my love, will ye do me the great favor of shooting the lock from the door?"

"As easy as holding thy whipstaff, my sainted William," she said, two explosions blowing the lock into useless hunks of iron.

Inside the mansion, there was no sign of life among the draped furnishings except the fire on the hearth, which emitted a faint light and threw long shadow across the room.

"Should I search the other rooms?" said Wolf.

"Aye," I said. "But first we search for what we seek is in this one."

"And that is what, Master William?" Anne said.

"I don't know," I said.

"Then we must begin immediately," said Wolf, pulling a sheet from an oil lamp which we promptly lit, filling the room with a golden glow, soon to be amplified by a small fire in the fireplace. In a matter of minutes then, with the day outside growing ever darker and the wind scratching at the window, the room had shed its winding sheets and had grown magnificent. No longer nondescript, gray masses of varying sizes became curio cabinets, drum and console tables, confidante and brocade fainting sofas, and a host of Italian mirrors, tin chandeliers, and vases made into lamps.

Chinese carpets lay three deep on the hard wood floor. Anne clapped her hands with enthusiasm.

"Aye," I observed, "A wonderful excess, eh Wolf."

"No difference save one from a mansion in England," said Wolf, flopping down in a decorative armchair, as if wearied by the task of making a fire."And will ye inform us of that difference," said Anne. "Or do we ask ye to search alone for a clue to the captain's whereabouts?"

"In England," said Wolf, "such treasures as these are gained by theft from the poor. In America, they are gained by theft from the king."

An hour later, all that had been found of the faintest promise was a rusted key left on the mantle.

"What is a key for?" asked Wolf, at last, collapsing in a chair still covered with a sheet.

"I am considering all the implications of a key at once," said Anne.

"Let us start with the simplest?" I suggested, "There is a door is be opened… does it open?"

"A door in the house!" said Anne, after which we spent a time finding and lighting candles from a pantry and then rushing up and down ornate stairways with polished banisters and in and out of rooms littered with mounds of sheeted furniture.

"This has been fruitless," said Wolf, sitting down on a sheet obscured bench in the foyer, "There is no locked door in the house, attic, or basement. All doors have been left unlocked, as far as I have discovered."

"An outbuilding then?" I said.

"There is no outbuilding near the house," said Wolf, "I saw that to be true from the widow's walk."

"I think I've found something!" shouted Anne from the dining room. "Aye, I have, I have!"

In another instance Anne was before Wolf and me, her left hand carrying a long tapered candle and her right hand displaying a crudely fashioned figure whittled from wood. It was wrapped in homespun. What appeared to be human hair was tarred to what could be taken for a head if the bulb rising from the homespun were examined uncritically."

"And what is the significance of that?" I said.

"Roger ye, mate. Ye are worse than Jack,' said Mary, "Do ye not remember thy Aunt Mary and the poppet she gave ye when ye where about to sail with Captain Jones?"

Then it was knocked I was, seven ways from Sunday. My lady Anne Bonny, in a fine blue frock of an afternoon and a fine frilly hat mounted by a single feather, had possession of the primitively fashioned poppet left on the Spanish Lady when the Finman had taken the liberty of blowing me into the sea.

"Is there a boathouse?" Anne asked.

"Of course," shouted Wolf, "There must be. Let us go to the river and find it! From that moment on, I glimpsed the truth of many new things.

Except for the light of a lantern and the clear, full moon and a heaven of stars, it was dark on the river, but before we had walked a quarter of a mile behind the mansion we saw the dark form of the boathouse looming over the water. How rapidly we approached it, our hearts beating like drums in our chests, our senses fairly reeling. There, to our tongues and ears and eyes were the taste of blood and cannon smoke, the cries of the wounded and dying yet to be born and the dread sights of ships of many nations bursting out in flame and sinking in the sky like so many falling stars.

"This is what we have lived for," I shouted to Wolf and Anne, both of whom shouted back.

At the door to the boathouse, the three of us pulled up short, as if a hand had reached out from the dark and pushed us back. The lantern swinging in Wolf's grip threw shadows against the heavy oaken door.

"What is it?" Anne cried out, her voice breaking.

"Is it a shadow of thy little knife?" asked Wolf.

"Aye," I said, "but well I know it is also strapped to my leg."

"Do not check thy leg," said Wolf, "It is there, also.

The shadow of my sgian dubh thrown upon the door. My…my own shaking hand. The lock gave way to the key.

What thoughts then flooded the minds of the three of us?

There, quiet in the water and visible only by moonlight leaking into the old shed, was the kayak of a Finman, and hooked on a horn affixed to a post, a Finman's bag of winds.

We stood, overwhelmed there in the dark, filled with both awe, and, inexplicably, tears.

"Mr. Wolf," I said at last. "Please rehearse for me a Finman's powers."

"Ye know them by now," he said, "but remember they include the ability to step back into human form at will, as well as the manipulation of time and wind and other familiar powers."

"I shan't forget," I said, and took Anne in my arms.

"I assume I shall be commander of a fleet," Anne said. "knowing ye to be ever in need of quim and desirous of only one woman, like all poor Finmen."

"Ye have my promise," I said, and climbed into the boat and hung the bag of winds around my neck.

When at last Wolf had drawn open the boathouse door to release the boat, I tried the merest dip of a paddle and found myself in the middle of the river and heading toward the sea. With the eyes of a creature now released into its maturity, I beheld the slow ticks of the largest movements of the sky and the smallest filigree of palpitations on the crests of quiet waves.

How even the evening seemed on fire with glorious light!

Up ahead the Finman and his boat were bobbing in the waves, awaiting my approach. With a stroke of my blade, I passed by islands and tumps, through little swashes and guts and over canebrakes and shallows and at last soared over breakers at the great rim of the sea.

"Finman," I said. "Captain Jones."

The captain turned toward me. His face and hair were dark now, but his features were as I had always known them.

"Was it ye I fought with at the Sea Trow Tavern in Hoy."

"Ye were a scrappy, lad," came the reply.

"And did ye, in truth, need a boy to guide ye through the Orkney Islands?"

"I confess I did not, lad."

"But ye recognized me as a Finn and desired my indenture."

"I see that many things are now known to ye, lad."

"Aye," I said, "But I would know more, if I might inquire?"

The Finman, with an effortless stroke, moved his kayak beside mine so that we moved as one boat through the chop of the salty waves, our passage utterly smooth as if we moved not through waves of this earth, but of another.

"My age?" I said.

"As ye would have it be at any within thy granted span of time," said the Finman, "Expect to live one hundred and fifty years and each day to those years in the order of thy choosing, at any age ye please, as ye have done."

"As I have done?"

"Aye, without knowing.

"Am I to have company?"

"Ye must have a fleet," said the captain, "Fight as man and Finman both. In your fight against the English, make these killers your lieutenants: Hancock, John; Jones, John Paul; Washington, George; Franklin, Benjamin. Enlist any pirate that will sail against the British, for they have the will to enslave the world. The Brethren must murder them."

"I thank ye!" I said.

"It is probable thy mother was my lost sister."

At these words, tears came into my eyes and I felt the Finman's spirit draw near.

"Aye."

"Of the mysterious things of the sea, believe only in Finmen, and that ye are one."

"And my father?" I said.

"He was a mortal man," said the Finman "Ye shall fight in his memory, for he was of the Brethren."

"And that is my purpose?"

"To replace me on watch, lad, for my time grows short."

I took a stroke with the paddle and saw the icy bergs of Greenland moving quickly toward me through the shining sea. The captain's effortless stroke kept his kayak gliding beside me.

"Do I have a choice in this?" I asked.

"Nay," said the captain, "No more than I did. Ye must lead the Brethren, even without their knowing. You must father a son soon, in spite of Anne's wishes. Ye are last of the blood."

Afterword

The American Revolution was won by colonists largely without benefit of victories by land, but 3,700 English ships were sunk during the course of the conflict. Such a loss crippled Britain economically and militarily and led to its fall as a world power, as well as its decision to withdraw from North America.

Such devastating losses at sea cannot be attributed to the American Navy, which in its infant state scarcely existed as a major factor. Rather, the losses were inflicted by pirates, or "privateers," many sailing as patriots, others sailing for gain, for revenge, or motives too diverse to enumerate.

History does not record that these pirates or privateers were recruited, trained, equipped, or organized in any way or by any one in particular or by any credo or force. Perhaps they weren't, or were. Ye may hold it luck that they were able to bring the British Empire to her knees, or that there was a conspiracy of tide and wind or some combination of the stars, or that a more sentient force, by hidden determination and intelligence, assembled and led the Brethren of the Sea.

As in all things, ye may believe as ye choose.

About the Author

Robert P. Arthur is becoming known as one of the more versatile writers in American letters. He has won awards for novels, short stories, poetry books, poetry, plays, poem/plays, feature stories, criticism, reviews, and journalism generally. He is a President Emeritus of the Poetry Society of Virginia, a former Writer in low Residence in poetry and playwriting in the graduate Creative Writing program at Wilkes University, and has twice been a runner-up for Poet Laureate of Virginia. His Collected works of poetry will be released in 2020, and many of his early plays will be re-released 2020-21.

Arthur became internationally known in 1993 with the publication and dramatization of his poem book. *Hymn to the Chesapeake*. Widely known as an important poet of the bay, which he calls his home, in *Master William* he exhibits his expertise in sea craft and in the oceans of the world, as well as, once again, his usual poetic gift for blowing aching beauty into language.

He lives with his wife, Gray, in Virginia Beach, about forty minutes from their bay-side cottage on the Eastern Shore peninsula.

ALSO BY ROBERT P. ARTHUR

BOOKS (POETRY, POEM/ PLAYS, FICTION)

New Gothic Restaurant

Quartet: Four Poets in Virginia

Hymn to the Chesapeake (a book-length poem)

Hymn to the Chesapeake (60 minute poem/play)

Expanaded Hymn to the Chesapeake (poems and photos)

The Libertine

A Chesapeake Celebration

Guests of the Nation

Passover

Phaedra (including *Apology*)

Winter Tales by Candlelight

Front Porch Trilogy

Strokes

Fut Gar and the Nature of Evil

Vija's War and Other Poems

Crazy Horse in Heaven

Black Gum Against Thunder

Music of leaves

Angel Band

Horse Hammock Point

Crazy Horses' Woman

Robert Arthur's Eastern Shore

Robert P. Arthur: Selected Works

River Country

Disclosures

Silver Beach Road

Hymn to the Chesapeake (full-length poem-play)

Floyd Collins and the White Angels of Sand Cave (to be published)

Shadows of Rain (to be published)

PRODUCED PLAYS:

The Libertine

Vija's War

Guests of the Nation

Jellies and Jam

King over the Water

Hymn to the Chesapeake (dance suite)

Floyd Collins and the White Angels of Sand Cave

Threshold to America

River Country

Phaedra

Under the Bed

Front Porch Trilogy

History of Love

Lonely in Onley

Ur

Matins of the Sook Snow

The Ghost of Marina

The Novelist

Fut Gar and the Nature of Evil

Roses so Red

Music of leaves

The Tackle

Horse Hammock Point

New York

Hymn to the Chesapeake (play)

Apology

A Chesapeake Celebration

Winter Tales by Candlelight

The Liar's Bench

The Liar's Ward

Snow

Love Story in Song

All Hallows Eve

www.ingramcontent.com/pod-product-compliance
Lightning Source LLC
Chambersburg PA
CBHW032157180726
48284CB00001B/76